THE WHITE WEREWOLF

Ferrel D Moore

ISBN-13: 978-1-958557-17-4

To my lovely wife Beth,

My daughter Kate, her husband and her two kids,

My son James and his wife Nichole,

My brother Thom and his wife Joyce.

And also in memoriam for my father and mother, Ferrel and Shirley

My uncle Howard, both my grandparents, and

Nancy my beloved wife's mother and her grandma.

Part One

1

Jason clapped his hands together.

"Like that," he said. "Gone. Right down the hole."

"Get out of here," said Trisha.

"No way," said Marty. "No way. That dog's mean."

"I saw it," said Jason.

"The old man was out all day," said Jimmy. "He kept calling for Rusty. He put signs out and a ten-dollar reward. Rusty's just lost."

"I'm telling you," said Jason, and he clapped his hands together again, "that dog is gone. Right down the hole. I saw it happen. Two little hands with cat claws reached up, grabbed his tail, and pulled him right down."

"Gone," repeated Marty. "Right down the hole. I gotta tell my dad."

"Are you nuts?" asked Trisha. "Your dad will think you're crazy. He thinks you watch way too much television now. He'll have you cleaning your room all day."

Marty thought about that.

"My room's already clean."

"Like your dad would care."

"My grandma died last night, remember? He won't make me clean my room for another year."

"Parents always make you clean your room when they think you're acting goofy," said Trisha.

"Yeah," said Jason.

"I'm sorry about your grandma," Trisha told Marty.

"I know," said Marty. "Me, too. I miss her."

"Sorry," said Jimmy.

"Yeah," said Jason. "She was kinda weird, though."

"She was just different," said Marty.

"Quiet, Jason," said Trisha.

Jason opened his mouth and then closed it.

"Poor thing," said Trisha. "I mean the dog."

"You're not playing a trick on us, are you, Jason?" asked Jimmy.

"You calling me a liar?"

"Hey, I'm just asking."

"He said he saw it," said Trisha.

"You believe everything Jason says," said Marty.

"Are you calling me a liar?" demanded Jason.

Jason was the biggest of the four ten-year-olds, with raw yellow hair and bright blue eyes that just dared you to take him on. Marty was almost as tall but spent whatever time that he could eating ice cream and potato chips and didn't yet have a defined muscle that he could call his own. His brown hair was thin and always a mess.

"I didn't say that. I just said Trisha is always on your side."

"I am not," she protested, and brushed away a lock of black, already lustrous hair from her forehead and propped her fists on her hips as though ready to square off.

"Come on, you guys," said Jimmy. "This is only our second meeting and you're all arguing. I was just thinking maybe Jason — I mean, it was dark, right?"

"You saying I made this up? I seen it twice already."

"Twice?" asked Jimmy, and his mouth stayed open as though he had forgotten to close it, which he had. He rubbed the bridge of his nose where his glasses usually rested, which meant he was thinking. Jimmy was the only one of the four that wore glasses. They were the flexible kind that could bend back and forth and not break, but he'd lost two pairs already that summer.

"Oh, my God," said Trisha. "Another dog?"

"Rabbit," said Jason. "It was a rabbit. It was sitting on the lawn. My lawn. My mom made me take the trash out. I don't like to take it out when it's dark. I'm not scared or anything, but I might trip, you know? It's a long way to the shed. But she made me take it out, anyway. She said the moon was out. That's how I saw the rabbit sitting right there in the middle of our lawn."

"And?" asked Trisha, and there was a hint of the breathlessness in her voice that would, in later years, send men into a mild trance.

Jason looked down at his shoes.

They were meeting in Jimmy's shed, since it was the cleanest of the four. Each of the trailers in the mobile home park except Marty's had a shed on a concrete slab, but Jimmy's was the only one that they could all fit in since it wasn't stuffed full of junk. Jimmy's mother donated four metal chairs for their club, which they had named "The Club."

"Come on, what happened?" asked Jimmy.

"I don't want to know," said Marty. "This is spooky."

"Why don't you want to know?" asked Trisha.

"I don't sleep good when I'm scared. I got apnea."

"What?" asked Jason.

"Never mind," said Jimmy. "What happened to the rabbit? Come on, give."

Jason pushed his chair back, and it made a noise on the concrete like bad brakes.

"Same thing," he said without looking up.

"Oh, my God," said Trisha. "That's sick."

"I quit walking as soon as I saw the rabbit. You know, so it wouldn't take off. I had two bags, and I put them down real quiet like, so I wouldn't scare it."

"And then?" asked Jimmy.

"I would sneak up on it and try to catch it."

"With what?" asked Marty.

"I don't know. I hadn't figured that out. But before I could do anything, a chunk of grass flipped over. This weird thing popped up and grabbed the rabbit before it could take off. It pulled it right down the hole and the grass flipped back over. Honest to God."

"No way," said Jimmy.

"You're giving me the creeps," said Marty. "I'm creeped out enough with my grandma dying."

"We've got to tell an adult," said Trisha.

"They'll never believe us," said Jimmy.

"I saw it," said Jason, and despite himself, he looked ready to cry.

"Did you tell your mom and dad?" asked Trisha.

"No," he said, and looked down at the floor.

"Why not?"

"They'd never believe me," he said. "They'd send me to a doctor or something because of my seizures. Like I scare them enough as it is, okay?"

"What would your seizures have to do with anything?" asked Trisha.

"I think he's trying to say that if he told them, they'd think he was nuts and it would have something to do with the seizures," said Jimmy.

"Yeah," said Jason. "They already think my head is wired wrong or something."

"Oh," said Trisha, and she turned to Jimmy. "Well. Do you believe him? I do."

Four children on card table metal chairs, sitting in a wooden shed on a day that would approach eighty degrees before the sun went down in the small town of Flat Rock, Michigan. They lived in a mobile home park that was a community unto itself, with over a thousand mobile homes neatly arranged into a metal suburb. It was hot in the shed, and though there were trees planted throughout the park, there were none near enough to the shed to give them shade, so they left the door open just enough to let the fan Jimmy's mother donated to them blow out the dead air. Jimmy ran an extension cord from an auxiliary plug on the side of their single-wide across the lawn and under the door. The little fan rotated on its pole, swinging side-to-side, humming quietly as it did its job.

"What do you think it did to the rabbit?" asked Marty. "I mean, once it had it down the hole?"

"I think it, ate it," said Jason.

"Oh," said Marty, and for a full minute, no one said anything else.

"What do we do?" asked Trisha.

"Nothing," said Jimmy.

"Easy for you to say," she said. "You don't have a dog."

"I've got a dog," said Marty.

"All we can do is tell our parents," said Jimmy. "Okay, Jason can't tell his, but we could tell one of ours."

"That's a good idea," said Marty. "If my Grandma was still alive, we could tell her. Two days ago, she said we'd be having a Red Moon night real soon. She said weird things happen on Red Moon nights. She called them Blood Nights."

"See what I mean about your grandma?" said Jason. "She was nuts. And that's a crap idea, Jimmy. If you tell your parents what I saw, they'll tell my parents and I'm still screwed."

"He's right," said Trisha. "We can't tell our parents. Jason will get in trouble."

"Yeah, well, what about my dog?" asked Marty. "We've got to do something, or maybe it'll get my dog. Hey, I just thought of something. You think there's more than one? What if there's two?"

"Or three," said Trisha.

Or more," added Jason.

"We have to tell the parents," said Jimmy.

It wasn't that he wanted to tell the parents. He just didn't know what they could do without telling the parents. Marty had a dog, and Trisha had a cat. But it went beyond that. The entire park was filled with pets. How many of them were missing? And what could they do about it? They were only kids.

"I've got an idea. It'll work, it'll work, it'll work," said Trisha.

"You always say that," complained Marty.

"What is it?" asked Jason.

Trisha beamed when Jason asked her what her idea was, and Jimmy felt the hot feeling in the back of his head that he most always had when Trisha smiled at Jason. There was really no reason to feel jealous. He had explained it to himself many times. Trisha was way too young to have a boyfriend, according to her father, and Jimmy was way too young, according to his parents, to have a girlfriend. It was hard to remember that when she smiled at Jason. Jason was the best looking of the three boys by far. Jimmy's own mother had said that. His own mother had told him that Jason was handsome, and had added, when she had seen the disappointment on her son's face, that he shouldn't worry because someday he might be handsome, too.

"Why don't we all sneak out and meet tonight," she said, "and you can show us where you saw it happen. That way, we'll know where it happened, and if we see something else happen, then we can say we saw it, not that you saw it. We could stay in Marty's tent. We could put it on the concrete square outside his house."

"Huh?" asked Marty.

Trisha explained her idea again to Marty, who shifted from side to side in his chair.

"Maybe my parents won't let me out because of my grandma dying," said Marty.

"They'll let you out," said Jason, "to keep your mind off of your grandma dying. That's how old people think."

"What do you think, Jimmy?" Marty asked.

The three of them waited quietly while Jimmy thought the matter over. His forehead wrinkled like that of a fifty-year-old, and he closed his eyes to blot out the world. Not only his three friends, but most of his neighborhood, the students and teachers at his school, and maybe the entire city were convinced that Jimmy was the smartest boy ever to come out of the town of Flat Rock. In fact, Jimmy had by far the highest IQ ever recorded in the entire state of Michigan.

"You thinking, Jimmy?" asked Marty.

"Of course, he's thinking, stupid," said Jason.

"Don't ever call him that," warned Trisha.

It was at that moment an impatient wind caught the edge of the shed door and banged it outward and back to slap the edge of the metal shed. The extension cord stretched far enough to pull the plug right out of the receptacle on the side of the trailer. Immediately, the fan quit rotating back and forth, the faint breeze ceased, and the four members of The Club were surrounded by a thick, hot silence.

"That was creepy," said Trisha.

"It was the wind," said Jason, trying to make up for his slip of the tongue a moment ago.

The three of them watched Jimmy as he sat very still, considering what to do. One of the hardest things about being the most intelligent boy that anyone knew was that people always expected him to be right. After all, what would be the point of being super-intelligent if he didn't know all the answers?

If Jason were telling the truth, he realized, then the park could be honeycombed with tunnels leading underneath it. He could imagine a creature or creatures or hordes of creatures scurrying beneath the park, waiting to pop up and grab the small pets in the trailer park.

Pop-up killers, he thought.

"We've got to do something about this," he said at last, "and I think Trisha's idea is a good way to do it. But I think the best way to get people to believe us is to trap one of these things."

"I don't want it to bite me," said Marty. "Besides," he continued, "how do we get them to climb out of the hole?"

Jimmy shot a quick look at Trisha.

Marty felt all three of his friends staring at him when Trisha said, "Well, we're going to need some bait."

"You're not going to use my dog," said Marty.

In the silence that followed, Marty tried to change the subject.

"Maybe we should take a stick or something in case it gets loose and tries to hurt us," he said.

"How about a hammer?" suggested Jason.

Jimmy thought about that for a moment. "What do you think?" he asked Trisha.

"You mean, like, to kill it?"

"Give me a break," said Jason. "It killed a dog and a rabbit, and it's not going to get me." His face was set, the determination of his compressed lips saying more about the extent of his fears than what he had told his friends.

"What did it look like?" asked Marty.

Before answering, Jason got up from his chair and looked outside the door, then went outside of the shed, and walked around it until he was certain that no one was standing outside listening in. He took a deep breath, then went back inside and sat down again in his chair. Using the bottom of his shirt, he wiped a thin film of sweat from his forehead.

"What was that all about?" asked Marty.

"He wanted to make sure we're alone," explained Trisha. "Like," she said, looking directly at Jimmy, "Leon," and she stretched the name out distastefully.

Jimmy held his hands before his face as though to protect it from blows. "He's my brother," he said. "What am I supposed to do?"

"You could do something," she said.

Jimmy shook his head, but then thought, Maybe I could have camouflaged the extension cord leading to the shed.

"Jason?" he said, to steer the conversation back into what he actually thought at that moment was a safer channel.

"Okay. Okay," said Jason. "It was dark, right? I couldn't see it real good. It had fur on its arms, and cat claws like I said on its hands. I only saw like a little bit of its head, but it was covered with fur, too, and it had real long pointed ears. But it had freaky eyes."

"Like Jimmy?" asked Marty.

"No, stupid. I mean — sorry Trisha."

"You shouldn't be saying that to Marty," she said. "I mean it."

"It's okay. Jason doesn't mean anything," said Marty.

"See? See I told you."

"But sometimes," continued Marty, "it does make me feel stupid."

Jason glared at Marty, but when he saw how Trisha was looking at him, he looked back down at the floor.

"What about its eyes?" prodded Jimmy.

"They were yellow and red," said Jason, who continued to look at the floor.

"Yellow and red?" asked Jimmy.

"No."

"Then what?"

Jason looked up.

"They were on fire."

"The moon lit up its eyes," suggested Jimmy.

Trisha put her hand on Jason's shoulder.

"Are you okay?" she asked.

"It wasn't the moon. They were on fire. Like red and yellow and smart and evil-like."

"For real?" asked Marty.

"Yeah. For real."

"Okay," Trisha said to Jimmy. "Hammers it is."

"How about bait?" Jimmy asked again.

"No way. Don't even start again," said Marty. "We're not using my dog."

"We need some way to get it out of the ground," said Jimmy.

"Hamburger might do it," Trisha put in.

"Yeah, hamburger. That's a great idea," said Marty.

"You mean raw, right?" asked Jason.

"Raw," Jimmy nodded.

Without being aware they were doing it, they all nodded at the same time.

"My mom's got some in the freezer. I could sneak it out and let it thaw."

"Boots," said Jason. "We should wear boots."

"Why?" asked Marty.

"In case it tries to bite us on the ankles."

"He's right," said Jimmy. "It might have rabies."

"So, when do we do it?" asked Trisha.

"Tonight," said Jimmy.

"Shouldn't we vote on this?" asked Marty.

"No," said Jason, and slapped his hand on his leg. "Let's just do it. My dad's got two hammers and you guys can get us the other two."

"Now I'm not sure about this hammer thing," said Trisha. "I don't know if it's vicious. It's probably just starving."

"Same thing," said Jason.

2

Only an hour to go.

Jimmy rubbed his eyes. They felt as though the glow of the computer screen had burned right into his retinas. Jimmy read, the last time that he was tested, 2,383 words per minute. He'd never really thought much about it before, and it was harder to read fast on the computer, but tonight he was glad that he could read and assimilate so much data. An average reader would have given up.

The world was full, according to the eight trillion articles that he had brought up on the search engines, of burrowing creatures. Prairie dogs, gophers, various rodents, and a bunch more, some of which were possibles, most of which were not. Prairie dogs and blind moles were out. The "out" list was pretty big. But there were some other possibilities.

"Studying again?" came a voice from behind him.

"Hey, dad," said Jimmy without looking up. "I'm just surfing the Web."

"Back in my day, surfing meant something different. Sun, wind, waves, sand, girls...."

"I'm going to tell mom," said Jimmy.

"She was one of the girls," laughed his father.

Jimmy spun around on his chair and looked up at him, amazed that a sixty-year-old man could look so young while his mother, who was twenty years younger, looked so much older. Jimmy's dad was free from gray hair, while his mother's hair seemed to alternate- one brown hair, then one gray, one brown hair, then one gray...

"Yeah, I know. You've only told me like a million times."

"Should I make it a million and one?"

Jimmy clapped his hands over his ears and held his breath. His father laughed and headed back into the hallway. As Jimmy removed his hands, he heard his father say, "...and don't burn your eyeballs out. Nobody likes a blind genius."

Genius.

There it was again.

Sometimes he liked the word, and sometimes he did not.

He thought of running after his dad and telling him everything. Secrets seemed to generate pressure in his head, as though if he didn't share them, the pressure would build up and build until they would blow his whole head wide open. If only Jason wasn't so worried about his parents thinking that he was crazy.

Since they had decided to capture one of the pop-up killers and take it as proof to the parents, Jimmy felt nervous.

"I can't believe this," the parents would say if something went wrong. "We can understand the other kids trying a stunt like this. What if one of you got hurt? How could you let this happen? Why didn't you tell us? You're the ones with the brains, aren't you? Aren't you the genius?"

That was the problem with being a genius. Geniuses weren't supposed to make mistakes. If something bad happened, everyone would assume that you either planned it that way or were a stupid genius. Nothing worse than a stupid genius, the kind that everyone looked at and whispered, but not a lick of common sense... what a shame.

It wasn't fair.

He swiveled around in his chair and looked at the screen again.

What Jason had described could have been a meerkat. Fourteen inches long, weighing in at two pounds and covered with fur. Except meerkats were natives of South Africa. And there were the ears. Meerkat ears were rounded.

Another screen. Another animal.

Ferrets were almost a real possibility. They were found,

according to the pages he scanned, in North America, were a foot and a half long, nocturnal, etc. But, they lived on the grasslands and plains of North America, and their ears were round. Jason was clear that whatever he had seen had pointed ears.

Two possibles ruled out just because they had round ears.

Meerkats and ferrets were both carnivores and spent at least 50% of their lives underground, which was good, but neither was supposed to be found in Flat Rock, Michigan living under a mobile home park.

Jimmy had unearthed another disturbing fact, which was that meerkats existed in communities of twenty-five or so.

This is awful, thought Jimmy. Burrowing animals sometimes existed in packs. Very bad.

Could there really be gangs of creatures hiding beneath his mobile home park, waiting for night to come out and snatch away pets?

No. Meerkats and wild ferrets don't live in Michigan.

Shrews were the next option. Jimmy looked at a webpage that showed varieties of shrews. Shrews, he learned, were ferocious carnivores. The more he read, the worse they sounded.

They lived most places in North America. The big ones were about a foot and a half long. They had to eat their own weight every day. There were eyewitness accounts of shrews attacking and devouring animals larger than themselves. All right on the money. They were frequently nocturnal and lived in underground burrows. Their teeth and claws were sharp, they had big ears, and some of them were venomous.

Jimmy was pretty sure that he had found the animal that they were looking for, but just to make sure he brought up on the screen a picture of one. Ugly. They were hideous with very long noses and round ears.

Uh-oh.

That was a problem. Shrews had big ears, but they were round. Round didn't work. They had to have pointed ears or they were the wrong animal.

****

Unless Jason was wrong. Trisha might never admit it, but Jason just could have been wrong. Maybe he had been scared and didn't see it right. Maybe it was too dark. If he had said round ears, Jimmy would have been positive that they were dealing with a shrew. What else could it be? He had looked for hours on the web to find an animal that fit his friend's description and could find nothing that made a perfect match.

Maybe Jason had been scared.

What about the eyes?

He wondered about that.

Its eyes were on fire, that's what Jason had said.

The reflection of moonlight in its eyes. It had to have been the moonlight.

But what if it had been something else?

Like what?

What else could it have been?

Jimmy brought up a search engine again. What to type in? Flaming eyes? Pointed ears?

What to type in?

He squeezed his forehead between his hands.

Underground monsters.

That was it. He took a deep breath to quiet the tremors in his stomach and typed in...

Underground monsters.

Rock and roll bands. Underground movies. Articles on underground insects that chewed grass roots and destroyed lawns. He clicked, he clicked, he clicked, and the pages came and went. A yawn worked its way up from somewhere down in the lower portion of his back and he rubbed his eyes. He looked at the time in the lower right-hand corner of his computer. Getting late...

And then he saw a reference to a name he had never seen before. Howard Phillips Lovecraft. H. P. Lovecraft. He clicked through to the first reference, and saw that Lovecraft wrote horror stories.

Great.

He needed facts, not fiction.

Still, he brought up a biography of H.P. Lovecraft that recorded how much he had written, what his writing influence was on other horror writers, etc., but Jimmy couldn't see much that was helpful in any of it until he came across the story of Lovecraft's Grandfather Whipple V. Phillips—Grandpa Whip. Even then he would have missed it if he didn't read so fast, if he couldn't absorb an entire screen page in an instant.

He would have missed the word "tunnels" and the word "monsters."

According to the website, Lovecraft's Grandpa Whip was born in 1833 and died in 1904. He was a Mason, deeply interested in the occult, and traveled alone across America and the world at large seeking answers to esoteric mysteries. Some people said that Grandpa Whip's adventures had inspired Lovecraft's stories, notably one called "Under the Pyramids," which was about a network of tunnels beneath the pyramids.

A network of tunnels inhabited by monsters.

Lovecraft had written another story called "Pickman's Model" that had something in it about tunnels and monsters, and had been set in Boston. Rumors had it that it, too, had been based on something that Grandpa Whip claimed to have seen in his travels.

Jimmy leaned back in his chair.

Tunnels and monsters and a horror writer's grandfather.

He rubbed the crown of his head as though feeling for a bald spot, then dropped the chair forward again and began to follow more links.

Grandpa Whip traveled the world looking for more tunnels, more monsters. He became notorious for collecting strange manuscripts of uncertain age, maps by ancient magicians and astrologers alleged to have been written in blood on stretched human skin. He had visited the pyramids and unexplained ruins left behind by forgotten civilizations, searching all the while for more tunnels, more monsters, and the fabulous treasure Grandpa Whip believed they protected.

One person wrote that it all started when Grandpa Whip, on a journey to the Midwest states when he was about Jimmy's age in the year 1852, had been approached by a Mormon true believer who had been left behind when the Mormons abandoned their stronghold in Commerce, Illinois to flee westward. In his attempts to convert the teen-aged Whipple, this man had spoken to him about the plates of gold seen by their founder Joseph Smith, and the magical stones called the Urim and Thummim. He told Grandpa Whip about ancient cultures that had existed in the United States before the arrival of the Europeans, and the vast wealth that they possessed.

Whip did not become a Mormon, but he became obsessed with ancient civilizations, magical stones, and plates of gold. Because of this, he set out across the United States to find his fortune.

Whip visited Delavan, Illinois in that same year, a town that had actually been founded by one of his uncles, to investigate an Indian legend, and then traveled to Cahokia, Illinois to inspect a mysterious network of mounded earth. From there he moved on to the Mammoth Caves in Kentucky, following another Indian legend that linked fabulous treasure guarded by monsters to a network of tunnels within the caves. This would become the first story that H.P. Lovecraft created out of the stuff of his grandfather's legends.

****

Jimmy stopped clicking, rubbed his eyes again, and took a sip from a glass of water that he had left on the floor. He left it there whenever he used the computer and was thirsty. It couldn't get dumped onto the computer keyboard if it was on the floor.

Why, he wondered, would Lovecraft's Grandpa Whip look for treasure in caves and tunnels infested with monsters? It would have to be a pretty big treasure to get him to do that. It had to be a humongous treasure to have monsters guarding it.

He went back to searching the Internet.

And he found that once, after he had traveled the world to find what he was looking for, Lovecraft's Grandpa Whip returned to the Midwest with new information. He made a trip to Michigan, having learned of strange rumors in Europe as to what lived in the tunnels that ran through the salt fields beneath Detroit and the outlying areas. Later he visited a farming community southwest of the city for a day and a night. Leaving and never returning, telling a porter that he never would set foot in Michigan again. The porter told friends that Grandpa Whip left the state looking twenty years older than when he had entered.

According to one journal, he also never again looked for either treasure or tunnels, and, after returning to his home on Benefit Street in Providence, Rhode Island, never left the house again. He hired local workmen to pour concrete under every square inch of the home, an unusual practice in those days. Even H. P. Lovecraft himself, later a frail and eccentric recluse, was startled by his Grandfather's eccentricities and bizarre stories. Sometimes, when on a visit to check on the old man, he would find him wandering the house, starting at the slightest sound, occasionally dropping to his belly on the floor, listening intently with a look of stark terror on his face.

Once, when a startled H. P. Lovecraft had asked him what in the world was wrong, the old man had hissed, "No treasure in the world is worth the horror."

"Flat Rock," said Jimmy out loud, "he was here. He found what he was looking for and it scared him so much he ran back to Rhode Island."

Sometimes, no matter what his mother said, the Internet was good.

A thought seized him, and he brought up the search engine again and typed the words "Red Moon Nights."

3

They met at the tent, which was set up on the concrete slab in Marty's yard where most of the other trailers had their shed. Since Marty's mother couldn't afford a shed, she let her son keep his tent there during the summer.

The sun cowered out of sight below the edge of the world as darkness engulfed the sky, and Trisha shivered even though she was wearing a long sleeve shirt. The smell of cut grass suffused throughout the night air and the three of them stood just outside the tent waiting for Jimmy, breathing in the night's smell.

"He's reading a book," said Marty. "You know how he gets."

"His mom's got him doing the dishes or scrubbing the floor or dumping out the trash," said Jason.

"He wouldn't forget us," said Trisha.

The wind jumped up and rattled the flap of the tent, and from somewhere in the viscous black sky overhead an angry moon pulled back the edges of secretive clouds and revealed the teenagers where they stood in a spotlight the color of old cellophane.

Jason looked around the yard. In the faint light, the clipped yards seemed suddenly dangerous.

"Streetlights," he said. "Where are the streetlights?"

In response to his question, the streetlights in the mobile park flashed and flared as though reporting for duty.

"Pretty cool, dude," said Marty.

"There's Jimmy," pointed Trisha. "Hey, Jimmy."

"Keep it down, will you?" said Jason.

"What?"

He pointed down at the grass, and Trisha's eyes seemed to grow larger.

"I don't want it to know we're here."

"You're kidding, right?" said Marty.

Before Jason could answer, Jimmy had closed the distance between them and asked, "How come you guys aren't in the tent?"

"One of us," said Trisha, "is not a guy."

"Sorry," said Jimmy. "How come you people aren't in the tent? It's cold out here."

"What's in the gym bag?" asked Jason.

"Just some stuff," said Jimmy, but he looked away when he said it. "A camera and some stuff."

"What stuff?"

"I'm cold," said Marty. "Can we go inside?"

"Where's your coat?" asked Jason, and he forgot about Jimmy's gym bag.

"In the tent."

"Brilliant. Just brilliant. Okay, let's go in," said Jason, but he held the flap open for Trisha to enter first.

"Nice that someone is a gentleman," she said, looking at Jimmy as she stepped by him.

Jason jabbed him in the shoulder.

Jimmy hung his head. It would be a long night.

Inside the tent, on a wobbly card table that Marty's mom had donated to the Club, was a fluorescent light lantern that filled the tent with a soft blue light and made it seem almost homey, although Jimmy would have preferred something that generated a little heat.

"How come it gets so cold at night? It's supposed to be June," asked Marty.

"It is June," said Trisha. "It's just that we live in Michigan. You know? Michigan weather? Haven't you ever heard of that? Wait five minutes and it will change? My mom and dad always say that."

"I should go get gloves," complained Marty as he rubbed his hands together before the fluorescent lantern.

"Hey, what's up with you?" Jason asked Jimmy.

"Nothing."

"Are you scared?"

"Yes. Aren't you?"

"Nope. I'm gonna nail me a gopher."

"A gopher? Is that what you think it was? Gophers aren't carnivores."

"They're not what?" asked Jason.

"Meat eaters," sighed Jimmy. "Gophers don't eat other animals."

"They don't?"

"No, they don't. What you saw wasn't a gopher."

The four of them were quiet for a moment, each of them glancing at the other. Trisha, Jason, and Marty had noticed that Jimmy had not told them what he thought it was, which was unusual for Jimmy. Jimmy knew most everything. Jimmy was a genius. He had, after all, the highest IQ in Michigan.

"Oh," said Jason.

None of them asked what it was.

"I brought the bait," said Marty, pointing to a bloody bag of hamburger mush in a plastic bag in the far right corner of the tent. "It was frozen," he explained, "so I took it out of the freezer and put it under the house so that my mom wouldn't find it. You can push it with your finger and see it's not hard anymore. You think its okay, Jimmy?"

"Great," said Jimmy. "I mean it. You did good."

The darkness outside the tent grew angry and rumbled.

"Uh-oh," said Trisha. "Sounds like we might get wet. Michigan weather."

"Michigan weather sucks. I can't believe this," said Jason.

"Maybe we should do it some other day," suggested Marty.

"Maybe," said Jimmy.

Maybe we're looking for a real monster, said a voice in his head.

"Maybe not," he said.

"Which one is it?" asked Jason. "Either we do it or we don't. We've got the hammers. So it rains a little? So what? Big deal. I say we do it."

Had he not been so wrapped up in reading about H. P. Lovecraft that afternoon, Jimmy would have surfed the web for the weather report. He would have called each of his friends and told them to bring their coats. Or he might have changed it to a different night so he could think things through. He could have done more research. He could have pretended that nothing was really wrong in their trailer park. But he had read too much about H.P. Lovecraft and his strange grandfather. He could have done more research. Or he could have hidden under the bed.

But if he was right, more pets would be taken and what hid in the dark, moist tunnels that could be beneath their trailer park would soon be looking for bigger meals. Trisha had a little brother. Her mother would sometimes let him walk free in the yard as she sat back and read her romance novels, looking up occasionally to make sure he was still in the yard instead of toddling toward the street.

What if just once she became too involved with the breathless, panting women, and their hunky guys, and what if Trisha's little brother was still toddling about the yard while his mother was deep in her story. Maybe just as the little guy looked toward the street ready to show that yes he could go there, thank you, and he took his second petulant step in that direction. Then what if a chunk of ground next to him flew up and two long arms with hands that ended in cat-claws flashed out and grabbed him and pulled him toward the hideous, sharp-teethed face with the pointed ears and the flaming eyes.

Trisha's little brother would be gone before he could scream, the chunk of earth sucked back into place with a soft thud.

Underground monsters.

Pop-up killers.

"Hey, man," said Jason, leaning over and putting his face three inches from Jimmy's, "Whassup?"

"Huh? Oh, I was thinking about something."

The tent shivered suddenly as a blast of wind channeled its way between the rows of trailers, like the part man, part bull Minotaur charging through the Cretan maze, hunger crazed and hunting for someone unlucky enough to be lost there.

"Boy, what you be thinkin' 'bout alla time?" asked Trisha and she popped her eyes wide and distorted her face.

"What?" said Jimmy. "I don't quite understand..."

Jason and Marty started laughing. When Trisha returned her face to normal and winked at him, Jimmy thought, She's was faking me out.

But the wind was not to be denied. Angry at being ignored, it shook the tent viciously.

"Jesus," yelled Jason. "What's that? A hurricane?"

"We'd better-," began Marty.

A booming thunder like giant footsteps walking toward them cut him short.

" —go inside," he finished.

"Well?" Jason asked Jimmy.

Jimmy closed his eyes and remembered a wildlife movie that he had seen on TV where a lion took down a gazelle, puncturing the animal's elegant neck with its long white teeth. A close-up of the gazelle's fur soaked with blood. A close-up of the lion's jaws locked onto its neck, the gazelle's life draining away. As though a delete key had been pushed deep in his brain, these images disappeared to be replaced by a medieval drawing that he had seen posted on the web site discussing tunnels and monsters.

"We have to do it," said Jimmy. "The rain hasn't started yet."

"I'm scared," said Marty.

The tent quivered and seemed to lean to one side as raindrops pelted the fabric, then faded to what sounded like ten fifth graders drumming their fingers on their desks to annoy the teacher.

"Hey, you've got a dog," said Jason. "You want it to be pulled under and ripped to shreds?"

Marty's lower lip quivered, and he blinked his eyes, his long lashes suddenly wet.

"No," he said. "I just meant that it's raining."

"You know how to catch this thing, right?" Jason said to Jimmy.

"Pretty sure."

"That's it?"

"I've never done this before, but yeah, I think so."

"So, what you got in the bag?"

Jimmy smiled a tight smile.

"I've got us a pop-up killer catcher."

He opened the gym bag and took out a metal-segmented rod with a wire loop at the end of it. Holding one end firmly, he pulled out the segments until he had a pole nearly six feet long.

"What is that?" asked Trisha.

"I told you. It's a pop-up killer catcher."

"Yeah, yeah, yeah, but what is it really?"

"Never mind. But check this out. You pull this lever here on the base segment and ratchet it around and bingo. See how the wire noose tightens up and gets smaller?"

"I don't get it," said Marty.

"That wire at the end will tighten around the thing's neck and we've got him," said Jason, and he clapped his hands. "Man, you are the best, Jimmy."

"Huh," said Trisha. "So, and just how do you know it is a he?"

Jason looked toward the tent door. Then he lowered his head and began scratching the back of his left hand.

"Would you look at me? I'm just asking how you know that it was a he. That's all."

"I could tell by its face."

"How?" asked Marty.

Jimmy swung the pole up and spun it so he could rest it on the end of its base segment. He watched Jason. He wondered, do you know something you don't want to say?

"Why don't we talk about that after we put the bait out?" said Jimmy. He did not want Jason to answer the question just then. "You take the bait and a hammer," he said, "and I'll take the noose. Okay?"

"Sure," said Jason.

"What do we do?" asked Trisha.

"You could get the tent organized," suggested Jimmy.

"I don't think so," snapped Trisha. "I'll tell you what. We're coming, too."

"I'm bringing a hammer," said Marty.

"Maybe you should stay inside until we-."

"Not a chance," she said. "You afraid I'll get hurt because I'm a girl?"

"Yes."

"Jimmy Harlen, I can knock you straight back on your butt. You want to take me on? Sometimes you're just like my mother says. Your real smart, but you have got no brains."

"Nice going, slick," smirked Jason.

"I'll stay inside," volunteered Marty, after suddenly realizing what he had volunteered for.

"You're coming, too," she said in a way that left no room for doubt.

So much for chivalry, thought Jimmy.

4

In the faded cone of light from the streetlights, Jimmy could see the fine rain. Thunder still shook the night, but the rain came down in a foggy mist.

It's a trap and God is in on it, thought Jimmy.

Jimmy held the telescoped noose by his side, as though it were a harpoon and he were Captain Ahab hunting the terror of the deep.

"Can I go back into the tent now?" asked Marty.

"Sure," said Jimmy.

"No way," said Trisha, folding her arms and hugging them to her chest. "We've got to all watch."

"Come on," protested Jason. "He'll just get soaking wet and then he'll catch a cold and then we'll all get in trouble for it."

"Colds are a virus," she said. "Aren't they, Jimmy?"

"Yes. Hey. Wait a minute," he said. "Marty, why do you want to go back into the tent?"

"I'm just nervous. That's all. I'm a nervous person. My mother says I'm hyper or something. My grandma said I was sensitive."

But he was shifting his weight from leg to leg as though he had to go the bathroom.

"Leave him alone, Jimmy," said Trisha. "He said he's just nervous."

"Marty?"

"Nothing, I told you."

"Hey, what's the deal?" asked Jason.

"Would you guys leave him alone?" asked Trisha.

"Why are you nervous?" pressed Jimmy.

"Nothing. I just saw that guy, you know."

"What guy?"

"That guy with the truck. You know- animal control or something."

"He was in the park?" asked Trisha.

"Yeah."

"You better tell me," she continued. "What about the animal control guy.

"He was just driving around in the park after we split up today, and

he asked me a couple of questions when he saw me."

"Like what?" asked Trisha, and she was right in his face.

"He wanted to know if I'd seen any like big stray dogs or anything."

"Why?"

Marty tried his best to avoid Trisha's eyes, but she was too close to him for that.

"I asked you why?"

"He said there was a bunch of pets missing, that's all."

"Like how many?"

"It's a big park, even he said that. There's like a thousand trailers here, you know, so sometimes a couple take off."

"How many?" asked Trisha, and the tone in her voice made him take a step back.

"Maybe fifteen or twenty."

"How many?" Trisha asked again, but this time her voice was just above a whisper.

"Maybe fifteen or twenty. That's how many he said were reported."

Marty felt that the yard was getting smaller. He was no longer cold and was developing an oily sweat on his face.

"You mean there could be more?" asked Jason.

"There could be more," answered Jimmy. "Why didn't I think of that? Good work Marty."

"Good work? Good work?" exploded Jason. "How is that good work? He wasn't even going to tell us."

"But he did," said Jimmy.

"Why didn't you tell us before?" asked Trisha.

"I was… sorta… I mean I was hoping we wouldn't do this. I feel like throwing up. I'm scared. I didn't want to think about it. I don't want it or them to eat me."

"It's okay," said Trisha, even though she knew that it wasn't.

"Uh-oh," said Jason, and he pointed up at the sky.

The moon, hardly visible, had morphed from the color of aged cellophane to the color of wet rust.

"What is that, Jimmy?" asked Trisha.

"Oh God," he said.

"What do you mean, Oh God?" demanded Marty.

"I almost forgot. It's like Marty's grandma said."

"Said what?" asked Trisha, Marty, and Jason almost in unison.

"It's gonna be a Red Moon night."

"Like my grandma said," agreed Marty.

"Ah, that's crap," put in Jason. "It's just like an eclipse, isn't it Jimmy?"

"Well…"

"Look at that," said Trisha, and this time she was the one pointing to the sky.

The moon, which could be seen as more of a soft blur than as an object through the night rain, was turning a deeper shade of red.

"What else could go wrong?" murmured Jimmy.

And, within a second of him saying that, all of the lights except the street lights in the trailer park went out with a snapping noise like a beetle frying when it landed on an electric grid.

"I'm going inside," said Marty, and he started walking backward to the deck porch that jutted out from the front door of his family's trailer.

"You got to throw some bait out first-," Jason started, but stopped before adding the word "stupid."

Marty grimaced, then took a clump of hamburger out of the bag, squished it together and tossed it three feet away onto the lawn.

"Jimmy's little brother could have done better than that," said

Jason.

"That's enough, Jason," said Trisha.

"I'm going inside," said Marty, and resumed walking.

"Don't," said Jimmy, his voice sounding suddenly calm but urgent.

Marty stopped walking.

"Go get the lantern," Jimmy said to Jason. "I think I saw something."

As Jason ran to the shed, Trisha moved close to Jimmy and grabbed his arm.

"What is it, Jimmy?"

"I don't know. It's hard to see. The moon's no help. We need light. I can't believe it's so red it looks like blood," he said, and it caused his back to tighten when he said it.

"I didn't know that the moon could really turn red," said Trisha. "What makes it turn that color?"

"It could be...., I don't know," he admitted.

He was afraid, but it still felt good to say it.

I don't know.

"I really, don't know. I was waiting to see if... what did your grandmother say, Marty?"

Marty tilted his head and whispered, "She said it was the night the goblins were afraid to come out."

"I feel better now," said Jimmy.

"You asked," said Marty, and then stepped up onto the porch.

"Please don't tell me anything else that your grandmother said, okay?"

A sudden thought hit Jimmy like a slap in the head.

"Stay on the sidewalk," he yelled to Jason, who instantly caught his drift. "On the porch with Marty," he said to Trisha, and, grabbing her hand, he pulled her up on the slatted wood porch extension where Marty's mom sometimes cooked on a hibachi when the weather was right.

"What's going on?" asked Trisha.

"I don't know exactly," he said. "But I don't think we're safe standing on the grass."

"Oh."

The light swung back and forth like a ghost searching for a resting place as Jason put one foot in front of the other like he was walking toward them on a tightrope instead of a two-foot-wide concrete sidewalk. The grass on either side of the walk suddenly seemed to be dark waters swimming with dangerous, unknown creatures.

"I saw something, too" he yelled.

"My mom won't answer the door," cried Marty.

"What was it?" Jimmy called to Jason then said to Marty, "Keep trying."

He pushed away a tangle of wet hair from his forehead as he thought so hard about what was going on that his head began to hurt.

"She won't answer," said Marty, and just from the sound of his voice the others knew that he was crying.

A brilliant bolt of lightning flashed as though someone had shot a flare high into the blackness. Thunder boomed, and somewhere in the back of Jimmy's mind he could hear Grandpa Whip saying, "No treasure is worth the horror."

"She won't answer," said Marty again.

"I'll help you," said Trisha, and she took the three steps to the upper porch in one easy leap.

"It's gone," called Jason. "Whatever it was, it's gone."

Trisha and Marty pounded on the door together, but no matter how much noise they made, no one came to the door. A red moon, vicious predators that burrowed beneath the grass, trailer lights that had been snuffed out while the streetlights still shone, and a steady, fine rain that was soaking their clothes and causing the skin on their forearms to pimple with the cold. The Red Moon night was upon them.

Marty's grandma had been right, thought Jimmy. Even goblins would be afraid.

"Get up on the porch," he told the others.

There was a gap between the sidewalk and the lower porch platform of nearly two feet and Jason jumped it easily. His fear of landing on the grass propelled him a good foot and a half beyond the edge, and he collided with Jimmy, almost knocking him over.

"Sorry," said Jason. "Are you okay?"

"I'm fine. I'm just glad you're up here."

Trisha and Marty clattered down the steps to join them.

"Marty's mom still doesn't answer," said Trisha.

"It's like she's not even home," said Marty. "I know she's there. Her car's still in the driveway."

"It's gone," said Jason.

"It is not, it's right there in the driveway," said Trisha. "Are you blind? See the big white car?"

"Not that," said Jason, extending a finger toward the lawn, "I mean the hamburger."

They all turned at once to look and Jason held the lantern out toward the grass.

The hamburger was gone.

"Good thing you told me to stay off of the sidewalk."

Jimmy nodded.

This wasn't like going to school where everything was just studying and test taking and all of the things he was good at. Jimmy was over his head. Now they definitely had to tell the parents.

Jimmy glanced around at the dark trailer park.

If there were any parents.

"I'm scared," said Marty.

"Me too," said Jimmy.

"We've got to get into my house," said Marty.

"Somebody should have heard us by now," said Trisha.

"She's right," said Jason.

"I'm wet," said Marty.

"We're all wet," said Jimmy.

"Why don't we go knock on somebody else's door?" asked Trisha.

"That's a great idea," said Jason. "What do you say, Jimmy?"

"What about my mom? How come she won't answer the door?" asked Marty.

"Maybe we should break in," suggested Jason.

"How?" asked Jimmy.

"Well... I could take the claw end of the hammer and, you know, work it around and pop the door."

"Did you ever actually do that?" asked Trisha.

"Sort of, I mean, yeah. Once or twice. When I got locked out. It wasn't me breaking into people's houses."

"It better not have been," said Trisha.

"Nope. For real. I stayed outside when I got locked out once, just because I didn't want anyone to see me getting in and think I was one of the kids doing it to other people's houses."

"All right, if you say so."

"Can we go in the tent and talk?" asked Marty. "I'm wet and I'm cold."

Jimmy thought it over.

I'm the smart one. What should we do?

It was too hard. He wanted to go into the trailer just like Marty. He was wet and cold just like the rest of them. And his eyes were just good enough that he could see to get by until his parents got him another pair of glasses, but just bad enough that at night what he saw was blurred and blended, especially when it was dark and rainy. He missed his parents, he missed his bedroom, and he really missed his glasses.

I'm the smart one. What should we do?

"Jason? Can you and Trisha stay on the sidewalks and go check to see if some of the other parents will answer their doors?"

"Sure," said Jason.

"Okay, then do it. Marty and I will jump off the porch onto the sidewalk and go wait in the tent. Or I can go with Trisha," he said, and hoped that Jason would take him up on the offer.

"No, no problem. Here, Marty, you take the light. This okay with you, Trisha?" asked Jason.

"I can handle it," she said.

"Okay," said Jimmy. "We'll stay here and watch the lawn from the tent. If Marty sees something, I'll take a picture of it."

"With what?" asked Marty.

"With the camera I brought in my gym bag. I forgot I had it."

"Hey, then we're even because I forgot to tell you about what that guy said from animal control said."

"Let's go, Marty," said Jimmy. "Now you've got to jump from the porch to the sidewalk so we don't step on the grass, okay? I'll go first so I can steady you when you land."

"Jimmy?" said Trisha.

"What?"

She stepped up to him and kissed him on his wet forehead.
"Take care of Marty," she said.

5

The rain continued to come down in a steady fine mist, and Jason and Trisha looked more like wet scarecrows running down the sidewalk than children. They had tried three homes already. They had pounded and kicked the doors, rung the doorbells, and screamed at the top of their lungs, but no one had answered.

"I want to try my house," said Trisha.

"We've kicked the crap out of three doors," said Jason, "and no one answered. This trailer park is cursed."

"Don't say that."

"You sure you want to do this?" he asked as they walked up the steps to her trailer.

All four of them lived on the same block. Trisha's parents were the only ones that had a double wide. In the reflected streetlight, it was white and shiny with the rain, and a steady runoff poured off the edges of the roof because they had no gutters. It had a regular front porch with railings and potted plants and Jason and the others envied her for having the only trailer among them that looked like a real house.

"It's so dark," she whispered. "Why are all of the lights out in the houses in this park, and where are all of the people?"

Her hair lay flat against her head, and water droplets dripped from her earlobes. Her lower lip quivered and her body began to shake. Jason, in a gesture as natural and as old as humanity itself, put his arm around her shoulders to comfort her. The hammer, which he had carried with him just in case, hung limp in his other hand.

"It'll be all right," he said.

"Would you knock?" she asked. "I'm afraid to do it."

It was as though they and their friends were the only people alive in the trailer park.

It's a Red Moon Night, Jimmy had said.

"Okay. I'll do it."

Jason stepped away from her and up to the door, and, after moment's hesitation, rapped his knuckles hard against the window.

No answer.

He did it again. Harder.

The house was as silent as if they had never lived it in.

"Oh, my God," Trisha whimpered. "My parents. What about my parents? And my little brother. What about my little brother?"

"I'm going to try the living room window," Jason said.

He walked over and tried to see through it, but it was as though the glass absorbed all light. There was nothing at all that he could see inside. Nothing. Not a stick of furniture, not the carpeting, or even the curtains that should be hanging there in plain view.

"I can't see anything," he said, and there was a trace of dark wonder in his voice. "I mean not anything at all. You try."

Trisha walked to the window and tried, but she, too, could see nothing.

"You're right," she said. "What is going on here?"

She sounded calmer, and Jason's concerns for her eased until she snapped her right foot forward in a vicious kick that should have shattered the glass. Instead, her foot bounced back as though she had kicked rubber.

"What the- here, let me try," Jason said.

He moved her to one side, brought the hammer back in a vicious arc, and swung with every ounce of power that he could put behind it. The impact jarred his teeth, but the hammer bounced back the same way that her foot had. The window had neither starred nor cracked. It was as though he had never hit it at all. Jason stood and stared at the window as though it were an alien artifact.

"I can't believe it," he said.

"Do it again," said Trisha, and her voice rose and cracked when she said it. "Break it. Smash it. Just get me in."

His chest muscles tightened, as though he were a superman summoned to do what no mere mortal could do. Feet apart, he swung the hammer back again, then swung it forward with more conviction and force than he had ever done anything in his entire young life.

Once again, the hammer bounced back.

"We've got to tell Jimmy," he said. Nothing seemed more urgent than to tell his genius friend what had happened.

Somewhere deep in the night the sky rumbled again, and at that moment, as though the turning of a giant valve in the sky had caused the sound, the rain began to pour down.

****

"Can you see them?" asked Marty.

"Not yet," said Jimmy from where he stood looking out through the tent flap. "You look. My eyes aren't good enough. You've got to look for me."

"Okay, move over."

"Can you see them?"

Marty squinted.

"Nope," he said. "I can't see anything either."

"Do you see anything weird on the lawn?"

"Nope."

Nothing.

The pop-up killer had been so quick that while they had been talking it had taken the hamburger and gone back into the earth. That scared Jimmy. It scared Jimmy a lot.

"What're you thinking about?" asked Marty.

"I was thinking about your grandma."

"What about her?"

Should he tell him?

"Well, about the timing," said Jimmy.

"What?"

"It's just weird, you know?"

Marty turned around to face Jimmy.

"What's weird?" he asked. "What are you talking about?"

"Well, like how the night after she dies the moon goes red."

"So?"

"Well," said Jimmy, "I was wondering if maybe it's not a coincidence."

Marty opened his mouth, stared, then asked, "You mean like she caused it? That's nuts."

"I'm not saying for sure," said Jimmy, "I just think it's weird. She tells you the moon will turn red, then she dies and it does. That's all I'm saying. And how did she know about Red Moon nights? I couldn't find anything at all about them anywhere on the Internet and everything in the world is on the Internet."

Marty rocked from side to side uncomfortably.

"Marty?"

He continued rocking.

"Come on, Marty. What're you thinking?"

"Well, grandma was like, I mean Dad always says that grandma was like a psychic."

"A psychic?"

"Okay, a witch or something," he blurted. "But don't you tell anybody else."

Jimmy thought about that.

"What do you think?" he asked.

"Grandma was always nice to me," Marty said. "She always said as long as she was alive nothing bad would happen to me. She had words for everything. Got to keep everything in its place, she always said. "Whenever I got scared, she would tell me to say the word she gave me."

"The word?" asked Jimmy.

"Our special word. She said it would protect me. Now what am I going to do?" said Marty. "She's dead. Who will protect me now?"

"What word?" asked Jimmy.

"I forgot," wailed Marty.

****

A witch or something with special words to protect her grandson. From what? Jimmy thought about that. It had to be the underground monsters that scared Grandpa Whip all the way back to Rhode Island. Now the pieces were coming together, but Jimmy didn't want to explain all of it to the others because he thought it would just scare them even more. And he was not even going to tell them about plates of gold and magic stones.

Why had the pop-up killers never come out before? Maybe something about Marty's grandmother was the answer. Was that possible? Maybe her special words like the one she had given to Marty kept them below ground. Maybe Marty's special word could send them back where they belonged.

Only Marty had forgotten the word.

6

"We've got to find Trisha and Jason," said Marty. "Maybe something happened to them."

He wiped tears from his eyes with the back of his hands.

"Let's wait a little longer," said Jimmy. "Maybe somebody let them in."

"Huh," said Marty, and he turned to look out through the tent flap again. The wind changed direction, and the rain cranked up at that moment, dousing him with rain.

"If nobody let them in," Marty said after pulling his face back from the opening and closing the flap, "they're going to be pretty wet."

Jimmy was thinking how lucky they were that they had put the tent up on the concrete slab where sheds normally went next to the trailers. They had their sleeping bags and their food, which included everything from potato chips, beef jerky, popcorn, sandwiches sealed into plastic bags and pop, care of Marty's mother, who had even provided them with a cooler.

"We should have given Jason and Trisha a flashlight," said Marty, who saw Jimmy looking around the tent, his eyes inventorying what they had.

"We have some?" asked Jimmy.

Instead of answering, Marty went to where the cooler sat, leaned over behind it and pulled out a plastic bag like the one that had contained the sandwiches. It was filled with five or six checkout-aisle flashlights, none of which was over three inches long.

"Do they work?" Jimmy asked.

Marty shook his head yes. "But here's the cool one," Marty beamed. Once again, he dipped behind the cooler and this time came back with a flashlight that was at least two feet long. "This one will burn your eyes out."

"Wow," said Jimmy. "You thought of bringing all of this stuff?"

"Naw. I just kept bugging my mom about what should we have until she got it all for me. Sometimes I'm afraid of the dark. Just a little. Sometimes. Don't tell Jason, okay?"

"Don't worry, Marty."

"And don't tell him about my Grandma."

"I won't," said Jimmy.

Jimmy liked math and science. He didn't like paranormal stuff. Marty's dead grandmother was scaring him as much as the pop-up killers.

"Sure, you don't remember that word?" asked Jimmy.

"No, I told you," said Marty, "and I've got to go to the bathroom, and I can't get in the house and I can't wait. What do I do?"

"It's raining outside, but that's the only place to go. You'll have to stand on the sidewalk. That thing that took the hamburger is still out there."

"Will you go with me?"

Jimmy knew that he couldn't let Marty go alone.

"Okay, but let's get out there before Trisha gets back. I don't want her to see us taking a leak."

"Can't I just pee out through the flap?"

"The wind will just blow it back on us," said Jimmy.

Marty squared his shoulders and stuck out his chest. "Then lets do it like men," he said. "I'm ready if you are."

Jimmy smiled, and for a moment the eerie situation they were in faded away. "You sure you're man enough, soldier?"

"Yes sir, colonel, yes sir."

He said it snappy and crisp.

"Then let's you and I go take a pee in the rain. Ready?"

They each grabbed a side of the flap.

"Wait a minute," said Jimmy. "Let's unzip our pants first. I don't want us to be trying to find our zippers while we're getting rained on."

Marty thought about it, then reached down and unzipped his pants at the same time as Jimmy.

"Should we have our wieners out and ready, sir?" asked Marty.

"Let's don't go nuts," said Jimmy. "Okay, ready to make a break for it?"

"Yes, sir."

"Remember soldier- no fooling around. Just outside we go, staying on the concrete at all times, and then we pee like crazy and run back into our command headquarters. Once inside, we zip up and return to our watch positions. Got that?"

"Yes sir," said Marty, and he saluted a quick salute.

"Then let's do it now," said Jimmy, in his best let's-charge-the-hill voice.

They grabbed their respective sides of the tent flaps, unsnapped them and threw them open.

"Get out of my way," yelled Trisha as she barreled through the opening and knocked them both back on their butts.

****

"You guys are soaked," said Marty after he and Jimmy had regained their feet and zipped up. The need to relieve themselves seemed to have been knocked out of them by the collision with Trisha.

"Well, duh," said Jason. "It's pouring down rain."

Both Jason and Trisha had their sleeping bags bundled around them for warmth, but they still shivered.

"No one answered anywhere," said Trisha. "We went to four houses and nobody would answer."

Tears spilled past the rims of her eyes as she told them. She pulled her shirtsleeve across her cheek and then wiped her nose with the cuff.

"We went to her parent's house," explained Jason. "Nobody came to the door. I hit it. She kicked it. But no one came. Then we tried the living room window. I got so mad I hit it with a hammer, Jimmy, but the hammer just bounced off the window. I nailed it twice. Same thing both times."

Marty squinted his eyes, as though that would help him understand what Jason was saying.

"The hammer bounced off of the window. You sure it was glass? Maybe it was thick plastic," suggested Jimmy. "Thick plastic is tough. Or maybe you didn't hit it hard enough."

"I hit it plenty hard. I never hit anything so hard in my whole life. I'm telling you, it bounced off of it like it was rubber. And there wasn't any light inside her house."

"Maybe they were in bed," said Marty

"You're a moron. There was no light. It was like a freaking black hole or something. Even if they were in bed and the lights were out I still should have seen something. The streetlights are on. I should have been able to see something. And all of the houses we went to were the same. Black hole inside, rubber on the outside, and no one would come to the door. It was like a freaking movie."

"Would you stop saying 'freaking'? You know I don't like it," said Trisha. "And quit calling Marty a moron."

She sniffed and wiped her nose on her cuff again.

"Sure. Sorry. But this whole thing is driving me crazy. Where is everybody?"

"Maybe it's the Red Moon stuff," said Marty. "But where's my mom?"

"Where's my mom?" said Trisha. "Where's my dad? Where's my little brother? I can't stand this."

"Jimmy?" asked Jason.

"I don't know for sure, but I really don't think that anybody's here except us in this whole park. I don't know where everybody is, but they aren't here. There's just us."

It suddenly hit Jimmy that his own mother and father and even his annoying little brother had vanished. He had been so busy thinking about the problem that he forgot his family.

"And that thing," said Marty. "The one that ate the hamburger. I'm not leaving the tent for anything."

"I don't like this," said Trisha.

"None of us like this," said Jason.

"It's out there under the lawn," said Trisha. "I'll bet it's just waiting for us to come out. Do you think it caused everybody to disappear?" she asked Jimmy.

"No," he answered. "I think the Red Moon made that happen."

"Will it make them come back?"

"I don't know, Trisha."

She thought about that for a moment, still shivering beneath her sleeping bag.

"You know what my grandma used to say?" Marty asked.

"No. But I'll give one more time. What did she used to say?"

Marty closed his eyes to help him remember better, and then recited:

"Red moon is
  What red moon does
  Twelve o'clock midnight
  And red moon was."

"I don't get it," said Jason, as he leaned over and tried to squeeze whatever water he could out of his short hair. "What's it supposed to mean?"

"I've got it," said Marty. "It means that the Red Moon will be gone at midnight, and everything will be all right again. I think that's what she meant. Right, Jimmy?"

"I don't know. I hope that's what it means."

Everyone in the trailer park except the four of them had disappeared. Jimmy tried to figure out where they were and what it meant, but all that he could think of was that the four of them were all outside on a Red Moon night. The whole mess was his fault- he should have told them to wait until tomorrow night. He tried to forget it and keep thinking about how to keep them all safe, but he was on the verge of the same kind of migraine headaches that he had had when he was five or six years old.

Gone?

Where could all of the people in the trailer park except the four of them have gone? Where his parents and his brother? Where were their families? Where had they gone? To outer space? To another dimension? To the astral plane? Where were they all? He might have had the highest IQ in the state of Michigan, but Jimmy had absolutely no idea where all the people could have gone or what to do about it.

The highest IQ in the state of Michigan wasn't worth squat on a Red Moon night.

If Marty was right, then everything would be fine at midnight, but Jimmy just didn't trust that. Had Marty ever been right? Was anything ever okay at midnight? Nothing was ever fine at midnight. Midnight was the witching hour. Bad things happened at midnight.

And nobody had a watch.

"We've just got to make it until midnight," said Jason. "Maybe everything will be okay then. Maybe our parents and everybody are like in the twilight zone or some other weird place until the Red Moon goes away."

"Let's stay in here," suggested Marty. "Maybe that thing doesn't know we're here."

"Maybe," acknowledged Jimmy.

"Uh- Jimmy?" began Jason. "There's something I got to tell you."

"Like what?" asked Jimmy.

"I should have said it before."

"It's all right. You can tell me now."

"I just didn't want you to think that I was really nuts."

"I don't think you're nuts."

"Me and Trisha don't neither," said Marty.

"So, what is it?" asked Trisha.

"Maybe I was just seeing things— maybe. You know when you get scared and your brain acts funny and—"

"Come on," said Trisha. "What is it?"

"Maybe you ought to sit down," Jason said to Jimmy. "Marty, get him a chair, one of those metal folding ones over there."

Jimmy held up his palm toward Marty. "It's okay. Don't worry about it. What is that you want to tell me? How much worse could it get?"

"You know how you lost your glasses?"

"Yes..."

"And you know you asked me what it looked like, this thing that popped up and ate the dog and the rabbit? Remember?"

"Okay…"

"It sorta had your face."

"What?" demanded Jimmy, and he looked as though someone had just told him that he had died.

"It looked a real lot like you. I'm sorry. Except for the pointy ears and the fur and that. But it had a face, I swear, that looked just like you with fur."

"No way," said Marty.

"Oh, God," said Trisha.

"I'm serious, Jimmy," said Jason.

"Are you absolutely sure?" said Jimmy, and he felt his heartbeat speed up in his chest when he asked it. "It was dark; you couldn't have seen it that good."

"Jimmy?"

"Well?"

"It was wearing your glasses, man."

7

Jimmy felt as though he was floating in warm water. His head lolled just a little to one side and his legs began to grow weak. He felt in motion while standing still, and his hears were filled with the sound of the emergency broadcast system alert.

"Jimmy?" said Jason.

"Got him," said Trisha, and the sleeping bag that hung on her shoulders dropped to the floor as she moved to prop Jimmy up. "Marty, get me one of those chairs. Now. Hurry. Are you okay, Jimmy? Don't worry, I've got you."

"I'm sorry, I was afraid to tell you," said Jason. "I'm sorry."

"Just help me hold him up," said Trisha.

Marty brought the chair around and unfolded it near the card table. The three of them guided Jimmy into the chair. When he was in position, they stayed by him and held him upright on the off chance that he might fall over. His eyes, though opened, seemed to see nothing at all.

"Wow. That was weird. I've never seen anybody faint before," said Marty. "That was cool."

Trisha moved her hand in front of Jimmy's face.

"Jimmy," she said. "Jimmy? You in there, Jimmy?"

"Dude?" said Jason. "Dude? Hey, man. It's me."

"Maybe we should splash some water in his face," said Marty.

I'm okay," said Jimmy. His voice was weak, but his eyes were focused.

He felt as if he had been hit in the stomach so hard all of the air had been punched out of him. For a second, he thought he would be all right if someone would just pump it back into him again.

"I'm sorry," repeated Jason.

"He knows it," said Trisha.

"I was just feeling kind of funny," said Jimmy. "I can't believe this is happening. It's like what Jason said. It's like we're in a movie. I wish it would be over now and everything would be okay."

"It will be," said Marty. "We just have to make it to midnight."

He said it as though he knew that it was true, but he was saying it to make Jimmy feel better, and Jimmy knew it.

"Thanks," he said.

"You shouldn't have told him that," Trisha scolded Jason.

"How was I supposed to know? I was just trying to tell him everything. You know, so he could figure it out."

"You should have told him that before," she said.

Jason turned from the group and faced the tent flaps.

"Don't make me come over there," she said. "I was just telling you. I'm not mad at you or anything."

Jason did not respond.

"I'm sorry, too," she said. "I didn't really mean it, I'm just scared. And I'm mad. And I want my family back."

Jason turned around, and he was crying.

"Oh, I'm sorry," she said, and hugged him.

"How come I didn't get a hug for fainting?" asked Jimmy.

"Because you're a genius," she said. "Geniuses are tough."

"Yeah," said Jimmy, "but it still helps to have a hug sometimes."

"In your dreams," said Trisha.

"Good one," said Marty.

"Hey."

"Sorry, Jimmy, but it was funny."

"Maybe Marty was right," said Jason. "Maybe we should just stay inside. It can't get us in here. We're sitting on concrete."

Jimmy pointed at the tent.

"Maybe," he said. "But I don't know how strong this thing is. And I think that it knows I'm here."

"Why would it care about you?" asked Trisha.

Jimmy looked down at his knees and said without looking up, "Because Jason says it's got my face."

"Then we should stay in here," said Jason.

And they would have except that Jimmy looked up and said, "Not a chance. It's got my glasses and I want them back."

"Just get some new ones," said Marty. "You lose them all the time, right? Just get some new ones."

"I don't want it to have anything of mine," said Jimmy. "Maybe that's why its face looks like me. It's got my glasses so it looks like me. I can't stand it. Why can't it look like someone else?"

"Because it's got your glasses?" asked Marty. "You think it's got your glasses so it's starting to look like you because they're on its face like if it was wearing my shoes its feet would start to look like mine?"

Jimmy, Jason, and Trisha stared at him as though he were the most incomprehensible thing on the planet.

Finally, it was Trisha who said, "You're really scared, aren't you, Marty?"

"Everybody is scared," said Jason. "What are you babying him for? If that monster out there popping up through the grass wears somebody's shoes it will look like them? Come on. Somebody kill me or find Marty a brain."

"I'm not scared," said Marty.

"Sure, you're not," said Jason.

"I'm not."

"You are."

"I'll prove it to you. Sometime maybe I'll prove it to you."

"Yeah, right."

"I will."

"Sure, you will."

Jason started smacking the head of his hammer against his left palm. Jimmy and Marty and Trisha looked back and forth between each other. The sound of Jason's hammer against his palm was overpowered by thunder, but they could all feel the thumping, the build-up delivered by each blow. His face was hard-set; his anger at being afraid was so real that the others could feel it. Jimmy felt a hum in the air like he felt when he walked in front of a microwave.

"We'll get it, won't we Jimmy?" asked Trisha. "We'll kill it, won't we?"

Without waiting for an answer, she reached down and grabbed her sleeping bag and wrapped it around her shoulders again. They all looked at Jimmy, waiting for him to tell them what to do, never doubting that he knew what was going on or at least how to get a handle on it, not realizing that the world was too large to fit in any one person's brain no matter how intelligent that person was.

"I hope so," he said.

Almost without being aware that they were doing it, the others grabbed chairs and sat one on each side of the table.

"You hope so? What kind of crap is that?" asked Jason.

"You're scaring me," said Marty.

In the silence that followed, the rain began to lessen.

"What do you mean?" asked Trisha.

"I just don't know what it is," replied Jimmy. "I looked at animals all day on the web, trying to find anything like it, but the only time I found anything is when I started looking for stuff on underground monsters. Then I found all sorts of stuff, but most of it just horror stories. Stuff about tunnels and monsters and underground tunnels. Nothing scientific. No facts. No pictures. Just stories and legends and rumors and stuff like that.

"Nothing really to help us. We need facts and we've got nothing except that Jason saw a monster eat a dog and a rabbit. Marty finds out from the animal control guy that there's pets missing all over the trailer park. Jason and I think we saw something on the lawn a little while ago, and something took our hamburger bait. And nobody in the whole trailer park seems to be home. Now Jason tells me that whatever he saw last night has got my face. I don't think it's an animal, I think maybe it's a monster. But a monster with my face? That's too much. I can't take it."

"A monster?" asked Marty.

"I knew it," said Jason.

No one said anything for a minute. Jimmy didn't want to tell them about H. P. Lovecraft's grandpa or Mormons, or talk about Marty's grandma. They were having a hard enough time keeping up as it was.

They were scared enough as it was.

8

"Then we should stay in here until midnight," said Trisha. "We could wait until it goes away, like Marty said."

"Nope," said Jimmy.

"Why not?" she asked.

"Because that thing's got my glasses. And I don't want to go to sleep again until I know that it's dead. Plus, how am I supposed to walk on the lawn knowing that this thing could just pop out and kill me? What am I supposed to do? Walk on cement for the rest of my life? What do we do if it or they don't go away at midnight?"

"This is terrible." said Jason.

"But it was here before the moon turned red," said Trisha. "Maybe it won't go away at midnight.

"What about it, Marty?" asked Jimmy.

"Why are you asking me? You're the brains."

"Because," said Jimmy, "your grandmother knew about this stuff. Can weird stuff happen before the Red Moon night or only on the Red Moon night?"

"I don't know."

Then Jimmy realized that Marty's grandma had been dying for the last week. Maybe she was too sick to say her special words. Maybe her being weak had let the little monsters come out because her powers weak, too, and she wasn't saying her words or word or whatever she did. And when she died all hell broke loose. If only

Marty could remember the word that she had given him.

From somewhere far away in the night, they heard a loud hissing noise, as though someone had driven a nail into the side of the Goodyear blimp. They leaned toward each other and glanced over their shoulders at the tent door, their faces shadowed as they turned away from the pale blue light of the lantern.

"What was that?" whispered Trisha, and she grabbed a handful of Jimmy's sleeve.

"Something's leaking," said Marty.

"Yeah, but what?" asked Jason.

They turned to look at Jimmy, expecting an answer.

"I think we're in trouble."

"Duh," said Jason.

"Maybe we shouldn't do anything," aid Marty. "Maybe it'll just go away."

"It won't go away, you chicken," said Jason. "It's a monster, like Jimmy says. We got to go kill it before it gets us. What do you guys say? Trisha?"

"How are we supposed to kill some kind of monster?" she asked. "Can we kill it, Jimmy?"

Jason answered before Jimmy could say a word.

"The houses may be like rubber where everything bounces off of when we hit it, but I'll bet you that if I crack that underground thing on the head with a hammer, it'll be dead really quick. And there's only one way to find out. You in?" Jason asked.

"Okay," she said. "If Marty and Jimmy are in, so am I."

"Marty?" asked Jason.

"Me, too."

"Jimmy?"

"We can try," he said, and added, "I just don't know what the right thing is to do. I'm sorry, I'm really sorry."

Jimmy looked over at Marty, wishing him to remember his special word. Marty scrunched his face in concentration, but then gave up and looked away.

Jimmy took a deep breath, then removed Trisha's hand from his arm and linked her fingers with his. For the first time in his life, Jimmy felt helpless. Being smart didn't help on a Red Moon night.

"We can try," he repeated.

"Okay guys," said Jason, "let's go nail us some pop-up killers."

****

The rain had come to a complete stop by the time they stepped out onto the sidewalk. They all carried their hammers, but Jimmy and Marty had theirs tucked between their belts and their pants, like six guns waiting to be drawn. Jimmy held the extended noose before him and Marty held the camera and the bag with what was left of the hamburger.

"Where do you want me to throw this stuff?" Marty asked.

"How about just one handful at a time," asked Jason. "And throw it farther than last time."

"Sounds good," said Jimmy.

"Stick your pole out," Trisha told Jimmy. "See how far it goes, and he could throw the first one right there."

"Okay," said Jimmy. "That's a good idea."

"You really think that you can catch it in that wire loop?" asked Jason.

"I don't know," said Jimmy, "but I'm going to put it right around the hamburger, and when it tries to grab it, I'll pull it back and pull the handle. It might work, if we're lucky."

"Ready?" asked Marty.

Jimmy extended the pole as far as it could still be comfortable to handle and said, "Okay, toss it out right about there."

"Hamburger is disgusting," said Marty, as he heaved the greasy ball of bloody squish onto the lawn on the spot that Jimmy had showed.

He bent down and wiped his hands on the lawn to get rid of the blood and grease and none of them thought anything about it until Trisha yanked him up by the collar and said, "What are you, nuts?"

"I was just cleaning my hands off. What'd I do wrong?"

Trisha pointed at the ground.

"What if one of those little things pops and grabs your head and bites off your nose?"

"No," said Marty, and he put his right hand over his nose just at the thought of it.

"It's getting warmer," said Jason.

"I think you're right," said Jimmy.

It was as though someone had changed the thermostat outside. The temperature was increasing, and the wind was blowing harder. Jimmy looked up and saw that clouds black as the spill from a broken printer cartridge were flying across the sky.

"Something's going to happen," he said, and as the clouds thinned, he saw glimpses of a moon that was the color of fresh blood.

He looked down at the spot where Marty had thrown the hamburger, and at that moment a chunk of grass exploded upward, and a hideous creature popped up from beneath the ground so that the grass was level with its fur and scaled waist. Its head was furred, and its ears were long and pointed; its eyes were on fire and it reached with sharp-clawed hands and snatched at the piece of hamburger. Jimmy was too frightened to move.

"Pull the handle," yelled Jason.

Jimmy jerked the handle of the telescoped noose hard, and the creature looked up and stared at him as the noose tightened around its shoulder and neck. Its angry, burning eyes flashed brighter, and it seemed to recognize him.

It had Trisha's face.

"Crap," yelled Jimmy, and dropped the pole.

"No," screamed Trisha.

Jason bent down and grabbed the pole, stood up to yank harder, but the Trisha monster grabbed the wire in its other clawed hand. It stretched it towards its face, and then snapped the wire in two with its teeth. With a quick motion, it shoved the hamburger into its mouth and sucked the entire thing down. It stood its ground, staring at them, glaring at them.

Four children and a creature half in and half out of the wet grass. It hissed and they took a step back, but stayed on the concrete.

Jason broke the spell by dropping the pole and lifting his hammer and taking a step toward it. There was a bright electric flash and the Trisha-creature screeched and disappeared almost before the light faded. With a loud suction noise, the clod of grass flew back into place and it looked like there had been nothing at all where the hideous intruder had been.

"Got it," said Marty. "I got it. I got a picture."

"I could have whacked it on the head if you hadn't taken that stupid picture," yelled Jason.

"It had my face," Trisha said to Jason. "You lied. You said that it had Jimmy's face. How could you?"

"For real," said Jason. "I swear. Maybe it changes its face. Right, Jimmy?"

"Or maybe there's two," said Jimmy.

Jason was quiet for a moment.

"You think maybe there's one with my face?" he asked.

"Maybe two," said Marty.

"Marty," snapped Trisha.

"Well he deserves it. He's always saying I'm stupid or what I'm doing is stupid. He's always making me feel bad. How's it feel, Jason? Huh? How's it feel?"

"You want to go, fat boy?" challenged Jason. "Come on, bring it on. I'll knock you back down on your big fat butt. Come on, man. Bring it on."

Marty reached in the bag, grabbed a piece of hamburger and threw it in front of Jason's feet on the grass just near the edge of the sidewalk.

"You crazy moron," yelled Jason. "I'm gonna-."

Jason never finished the sentence, because a chunk of grass flew up followed by a shrieking creature that locked its talons around the meat, then plastered it against its face and sucked it straight past its fangs and down its throat.

This time there was no hesitation on Jason's part. He swung the hammer up. When it was at the top of its arc and he was about to swing it down, the little monster turned to hiss at him.

It had his face. Burning eyes, pointy ears, fur and hair and claws and a wide mouth with sharp teeth- but it was his own face that Jason was staring at.

He dropped the hammer.

The creature disappeared back into the earth and the circle of grass followed it to seal up the hole with a soft thunk.

"That was me," said Jason, and he looked at his friends in disbelief. "That was me. It had my face. I can't believe this. I would have been hitting myself."

"No," said Jimmy. "That wasn't you. It's making fun of you because it's crazy."

"I'm going to smash its head in," said Jason, picking up his hammer.

"Let's get them," said Trisha, and in the faint red glow of the blood red moon, she looked right pissed off. She swung her hammer and slapped it into her palm. "I don't care whose face they've got," she said. "They're dead meat."

"Toss a little piece right in front of me," said Trisha. "Do it, Marty."

"Let's go back," said Marty, his voice hesitant.

"Don't chicken out now, tough guy," said Jason. "Talking big and acting tough. Come on. Throw one out where Trisha said. You afraid you'll see one with your face?"

"Why are they here?" asked Jimmy.

"What's the difference?" asked Jason.

"It doesn't matter," said Trisha.

"Yeah," said Marty.

At that moment, another grass chunk flew up near the edge of the sidewalk and the monster with Jimmy's face grabbed Jimmy's leg and sunk his teeth into the boy's boot. Jason and Trisha were on it in a second and swung down at its head, but their hammers collided. The creature pulled back its head and hissed, but Trisha recovered first and swung again, this time connecting with its head. A sick, crunching sound, and dark green ooze poured out around the edge of the hammer, which had sunk a good two inches into the thing's head. The hideous orange light in the creature's eyes went out as though snuffed.

"Got one," screamed Trisha.

"You the woman," shouted Jason.

"Lookout," yelled Marty.

Another plug of grass had flown up and a Marty-monster appeared. It's eyes fastened on the bare flesh above Trisha's boot, and it launched itself forward and sunk its fangs into her legs.

The instant that he had seen it, Jimmy pulled his hammer out how Wyatt Earp must have pulled his pistol, up in an arc and down, straight down onto the center of the creature's back.

Snap. Like a tree branching snapping in two. The creature let go of Trisha and rolled over on its back. The light in its eyes was fading.

"You broke its back," said Jason.

Jimmy nodded; he couldn't believe what he had just done.

He and Jason pulled Trisha back onto the sidewalk and lay her there. Her leg was bleeding.

"You killed me," said Marty. "I mean the one that looks like me. I think I'm going to be sick."

"Go get the first aid kit," Jimmy snapped at him. "Trisha is hurt. You're going to be okay," he told her.

"It hurts," she said. "Oh, it hurts bad. I hate those things"

"It's bleeding," said Jason. "Marty could have got it if he wasn't such a chicken."

"Stop it," yelled Trisha. "Just stop it."

Marty was back with the first aid kit and he gave it to Jimmy.

"I'm sorry, Trisha," he said, tears coming down from his eyes like they would never stop. "Oh, God, I'm sorry. Jason's right. I'm such a chicken."

"You quit saying that, Marty," said Trisha.

Jimmy had taken a role of gauze, a roll of tape, and a bottle of peroxide from the kit, and after he had washed the wound with peroxide, he taped a folded-over gauze bandage into place.

"Better?" he asked her.

"Don't be too hard on Marty," she said.

"Close your eyes, Trisha," said Jason. "Me and Marty are going to have a little talk."

"Quit trying to sound so tough," she told him. "And you leave him alone."

"Enough, already," said Jimmy. "Jason, watch the ground. Marty, get over here and help me get Trisha back into the tent. I don't know what time it is," he said, "but maybe Marty is right and maybe everything will be back to normal at midnight and the parents can help us get rid of these monsters. Hurry. Maybe we've just got to last to twelve o'clock."

9

Jimmy bent down and he and Marty pulled Trisha to her feet and began walking her back to the tent. She hopped on one foot like a wounded soldier and ground her teeth together to keep from crying. On the side walk, Jason stood like a lone guard, his hammer perched on his right shoulder, and Trisha's hanging from his left hand.

In the tent, Jimmy and Marty lowered Trisha onto a metal chair, and she gasped once when her leg touched the side of the seat.

"You okay?" asked Jimmy.

"Uh-huh. No. It really hurts. It snuck up on me. They're so fast; they're like, I don't know, but they're way fast."

"I'm sorry I was so chicken," said Marty. "Jason's right."

"Shut up, Marty," said Trisha. "You're my friend and I love you, but I hate you when you talk like that."

"Why don't you just watch with Jason, okay?" said Jimmy.

"He shouldn't be alone," said Trisha.

Marty's face was round enough to contain the complete gamut of emotions that he was experiencing. Horror in the raised eyebrows. Fear in the wide eyes. Shame in his downturned mouth. Guilt in the flush of his puffy cheeks that were red even in the pale blue light of the fluorescent lantern.

"Go on," said Trisha.

"He hates me," said Marty.

His empty left hand squeezed into a ball, and for a bizarre

moment, Jimmy thought that Marty was doing it to keep his fingers from being cut off.

"Jason, you okay?" yelled Jimmy.

"Yeah, but don't yell anymore," called Jason from outside the tent. "Use hand signals; I don't want them to know where we are if they don't already."

Jimmy opened the tent flaps just enough to look out and see Jason walking a few steps so that he would not be where he had just been when he was yelling back an answer.

He could make a serious soldier someday, thought Jimmy. I never would have thought of doing what he did. What am I supposed to do here? Jason's a good soldier, but I can't leave him out there by himself. Marty is afraid to go, and I'm afraid to leave Trisha with Marty. I can't be with Trisha and protect Jason.

I don't want to leave Trisha alone with Marty.

I can't do anything. What good is it being smart if you don't know the answers?

Jimmy looked at Marty, tried to really look at him, tried to really see him. He saw his rounded shoulders, his extra layer of skin beneath his chin; saw how his stomach hung too much over his belt. He saw a round face with a generous sprinkling of freckles, a smile that came and went as as hummingbirds at his grandma's bird feeder. But he did not see a chicken. He didn't see a hero, either. Just a kid.

"What time is it, Jimmy?" asked Marty.

Jimmy looked at his wrist and said, "I don't have a watch."

"Oh, yeah. Still want me to go check on Jason?"

"Sure. But take your hammer out of your belt. Then the two of you get up on the porch. At least it's off of the ground. We'll be there as soon as we get a few things from the tent. But you go make sure Jason is okay."

As Marty started to leave, Jimmy leaned over and grabbed his sleeve, "Listen," he said to him, "We need you Marty."

Marty's eyes widened.

"I said I'd go out with him," he protested.

"It's not that," whispered Jimmy. "It's just that I don't know what time it is, but I think if you can't remember her word we will not make it until midnight."

"You'll figure out what to do," said Marty. His head started bobbing up and down as though Jimmy should imitate him and nod that yes, he could save them from anything.

Instead, Jimmy shook his head no.

"I don't know what to do, Marty," he said, hushing his voice so that Trisha could not hear. "My IQ will not stop these things."

"But you always know the answer to everything," sputtered Marty. "You're a genius."

"I don't think," said Jimmy, "that those things out there know that. But I think that they might be afraid of your grandma's word."

"I don't know how to remember," said Marty.

Jimmy glanced at Trisha, but she wasn't paying attention to them. She was busy re-arranging her bandage and wincing each time she moved it.

"Just try Marty," said Jimmy.

"I'm not smart enough," said Marty.

"You don't have to be smart to help your friends," said Jimmy. "You've just got to remember what she said."

"How?" sniffed Marty. "I don't know how to remember.

"Think about your grandma," suggested Jimmy. "Remember that day. Remember what she was saying. Anything. Just remember one thing that she said to you and the rest will come back."

"Are you sure?" asked Marty.

"Yes," lied Jimmy. "I'm a genius. All geniuses know that."

"Really?"

"Sure," said Jimmy. "Just remember- when the going gets tough, the tough get smart."

Marty looked at him for a moment, then smiled an uncertain smile and left the tent.

Marty had been gone ten seconds when he screamed, "Behind you, Jason, look out behind you."

Jimmy took two steps toward the tent flaps when Trisha yelled, "Jimmy, the tent."

He spun and looked back in time to see the head of another Jimmy-monster coming through the side of the tent. Its claws were so sharp that it hadn't even made a sound as it tore through the fabric. Trisha tipped over one of the empty metal chairs so that it landed squarely on the squirming creature.

"Go help Jason," Jimmy screamed to Marty.

The pop-up killer hissed and squealed and Jimmy saw to his horror that the little monster with his face had a reptilian tail. With a vicious shove, it flung away the chair. But before it got up off of its back, Jimmy saw that Jason had been right for sure. It was wearing what looked like his glasses. Jimmy brought up the hammer and swung it down hard, but he hit the chair that was being tossed aside at the same moment by the creature.

Trisha took a can of pop from the table just as the creature squealed and made a quick run at Trisha's leg, incensed by the smell of blood. Jimmy swung again with the hammer and missed.

With a quick flick of her wrist, Trisha hit the pop-up killer square in one its fiery eyes and had the quick victory spike of seeing the light in that eye go out as the creature fell down but hopped up again only to get hit in the shoulder with Jimmy's hammer. As its shoulder crunched, its clawed hand swiped out at the same time and sliced opened a gash along the top of Jimmy's right forearm.

Jimmy dropped the hammer and grabbed his forearm to stop the blood, but his hand was covered with smear the moment his hand was in place.

The creature squealed and screeched when Jimmy's hammer busted its shoulder and again when Trisha kicked it square in the head. Trisha looked around for something to attack it with, saw an extra tent spike, leaned over to grab it and tipped the chair over, dumping the monster hard on the floor.

It straightened and shook its head as though descrambling its brains, then fixed its remaining eye on Trisha and opened its mouth. A long, pink-red tongue came out and wiggled as the creature made a shrill noise. The tip of its tongue was forked and black. It hopped up and down in place as though building up steam before attacking.

"Creeee...creeee," it screeched.

Trisha looked for the metal tent spike and couldn't find it. Jimmy was looking for something, anything to cover his forearm and stop the blood.

The pop-up killer prepared to leap onto Trisha.

Jimmy looked down at a sleeping bag on the floor, bent down, grabbed it, pulled it up and pressed it to his arm.

The pop-up killer had been poised on the sleeping bag. When Jimmy yanked it, it tossed the creature into a back flip and against the side of the tent.

Trisha still could not find the tent spike.

The pop-up killer got to his clawed feet again.

"Jimmy," she screamed.

Jimmy did the only thing that he could think of; he threw the sleeping bag on top of the creature and jumped up in the air to land on it.

Trisha realized that there was something hard beneath her. It was the tent spike. She rolled over, pulled it out and got to her knees.

Jimmy was hopping up in the air trying to jump on the creature that had his face, but it kept moving beneath the sleeping bag. Once, a clawed hand ripped through the sleeping bag and swung about, searching for flesh to tear.

Clenching the tent-spike in her right hand, Trisha crawled forward on her hands and knees to where the creature squirmed beneath the sleeping bag.

"Get back," yelled Jimmy. "It's dangerous, Trisha. It's ripping through the bag and—"

By the time that Jimmy was trying to say whatever he was going to say, Trisha was on the sleeping bag.

The pop-up killer shredded the blanket, ripping apart a three-foot hole with its one good appendage. Jimmy jumped back and yelled, "Trisha, no."

The creature turned to snarl at her just as Trisha jammed the metal tent spike through its mouth and out the back of its head. Jimmy fumbled around, found the hammer, and when the creature fell on its back, reaching to remove the tent spike from its throat, Jimmy hammered down hard on its head crushing its skull so completely that brain matter exploded out and onto the tent walls.

Another scream from outside.

"Can you walk?" asked Jimmy.

"Help me up," said Trisha. "Then go help Marty and Jason."

"No," he said. "I won't leave you here by yourself."

"Please, Jimmy."

He shook his head, and then helped her to her feet.

He felt her weight on his shoulder as he supported her to the tent flap and was hit by the smell of blood inside the tent. He felt the urgency of their situation. Still, he turned before leaving the tent to look at the creature lying dead on the remains of the sleeping blanket, the tent stake through its mouth.

10

We're going to die, he thought.

"Jimmy," called Jason.

Jimmy and Trisha pushed through the tent door, Trisha hanging on his shoulder, his hammer hanging from his left hand.

The lawn looked like Swiss cheese covered with grass. There were holes everywhere.

"We're going to run for the porch," he said to Trisha. "Just stay on the sidewalk with me."

Without waiting for her answer, he half pulled, half led her down the sidewalk as fast as they could move.

The pop-up killers, some of whom were trying to eat each other and some of whom were circling the porch, took notice of them when they were three feet away.

"Coming up," yelled Jimmy, and he actually pushed Trisha two feet off of the ground and sent her rolling onto the lower platform.

"Get her," he told his friends and jumped behind her.

While Marty and Jason grabbed Trisha, he swung his hammer like a five foot two Thor, smashing the skulls of those creatures bold enough to come at him how a carpenter would hammer nails. Jason was beside him in a moment, pulling Jimmy by the shirt, leading him up the steps to the upper porch platform.

"Don't," yelled Jimmy, "I'm going to kill every one of these stupid things."

"Cool, but get up here, dude. Look at what's going down on the lawn."

Fresh pop-up killers were continuing to pour out of the grass like ants fleeing a hole that kids had poured gasoline down. Soon they would cover the entire lawn.

We're going to die, Jimmy thought again as he was scrambling backwards up the steps to make it to the upper platform. The four of them stood there, Trisha leaning on Marty, Jason with a hammer in each hand, and Jimmy staring at an entire lawn full of hideous two foot tall monsters with the his and Trisha's and Jason's faces. Claws and teeth and ready to come after them.

"I'm scared," blubbered Marty.

Then it hit Jimmy.

"I'm stupid," he said. "Marty, use that railing and you and Jason get Trisha on the roof. Those stupid things aren't even up to our knees. Get moving. I'll hold them off."

"No, Jimmy," said Trisha.

"Get going," said Jimmy.

As he faced the creatures gathering around the edge of the porch, he saw that they were watching like cats studying the last bird in the tree. Their eyes glowed, and when the edge of a black cloud dimmed the red moon, it seemed to Jimmy as though a sea of burning eyes was watching him. He could feel them getting ready to swarm.

"I'm not afraid of you," he yelled, waving his hammer above his head, the gash in his arm forgotten as the adrenaline pumped through him.

Yes, I am, he thought, and he peeled off to the other side of the porch, jumped onto the railing, and started hauling himself up by the edge of the roof.

Trisha was already up there, Jason was beside her and he was kneeling, trying to pull Marty up with them. Jimmy scrambled over to where they were and caught hold of Marty's other hand. Together they began to pull him up.

"Come on, Marty," yelled Trisha.

"I'm trying," he gasped.

"Try harder," said Jason.

"Count of three," said Jimmy, and Trisha crawled over to help him. "One, two, three, pull."

They pulled with everything in them as the creatures swarmed the porch. Marty's feet kicked and clattered against the plastic siding, scrambling for a toehold. He was half up onto the roof when he screamed and the shock of it almost caused his three friends to lose their grip.

"Up," yelled Trisha.

With one last pull, they yanked Marty over the top. A Trisha pop-up had its teeth clamped onto his calf muscle but released when it saw the three of them. It snarled and beat its chest.

Trisha wound back and punched it square in the nose, sending it howling over the edge, where it bounced off the railing, fell onto the porch, and was attacked by three of the other creatures.

"My leg, oh my leg. Ahhh, it hurts."

Jason slid his shirt over his head and tied it around the wound, saying, "Serves you right, you fat turd-head."

Jimmy fell back against Trisha, and, his forearm began to throb with pain. The weight of his collapse knocked Trisha onto her back, and Jimmy fell flat beside her. He could feel the shingles like sandpaper beneath his back.

"Safe. We're safe now," he said.

"Thank God," she said.

"Unless they find a ladder," said Jimmy, and, for some reason that he couldn't grasp, he felt like laughing.

"We don't have a ladder," sobbed Marty.

"We've just got to make it to midnight," said Jimmy. "Right, Marty?"

"When's it going to be midnight?" asked Jason.

"I don't know," replied Jimmy. "None of us have a watch."

He looked at the lawn, covered with screeching monsters hopping around and spilling out into the subdivision. But many of them stared up at him, their black tongues wiggling at him like he was dinner.

"Think about your grandmother's word, Marty," he said.

"I don't remember," wailed Marty.

"His grandma?" asked Trisha.

She was crouched now, looking down at the creatures circling the front porch who were still trying to figure out a way to get to them.

"Just do it," said Jimmy. "Please. If you remember what it is, you can say it and maybe they'll all go away."

"Whatever you guys are talking about doing, you better do it soon," said Jason in a quiet voice. "We've got big trouble."

"I'm trying to remember," said Marty. "I just can't think."

"I said, we've got more problems," said Jason.

"Like what?" said Jimmy.

"They've got wings."

Trisha and Jimmy scooted to the edge of the porch and Marty covered his face with his hands. "I can't look," he said. "I'm trying to think. It's so hard."

"Like I'm surprised," said Jason over his shoulder.

As three of the four children looked on, little bat-like wings sprang out from the backs of the pop-up killers and the hideous monsters began to flap them to gain the air.

"Oh, boy," said Jimmy. "We're dead."

He looked up into the sky and the moon was once again blood red and had come out from behind the marauding clouds.

Up from the ground their black wings took them. There were over a hundred of the hideous creatures darting back and forth in the air, and they began to form a wide semicircle in front of the children.

"If I had my pellet gun, I'd nail every one of them," said Jason.

Marty uncovered his face and saw the darkness filled with death. He felt wet warmth spread through the crotch of his pants, and when he realized what was happening, he looked toward Jason, afraid that Jason would see that he had peed his pants. And it made him angry.

"I am not a chicken," he said.

His face twisted with anger unlike anything that he had ever known in his short life.

"I am not a chicken."

"You are too," said Jason without even looking back.

The darkness thrummed with hundreds of wings beating the night.

A single creature shot in at them, heading for Jimmy's hair, but Jimmy ducked, and the creature missed him and shot past.

"There's got to be something that we can hit them with," said Trisha, "or they're going to kill us."

But there was nothing on the roof except shingles.

Trisha and Jimmy looked down at the roof and then up at each other. Jason caught the idea, bent, ripped off a shingle and flung it at the creatures. The black asphalt rectangle fluttered only four feet, and then cartwheeled to the ground. The creatures flapped their wings in agitation and screeched in unison. A streetlight exploded when the sound struck it.

"They're pissed," said Jimmy, looking at Trisha.

"They're going to kill us, aren't they?" asked Trisha.

"They're going to eat us," said Jason, and he took a step back.

"I won't let them," said Marty, and he stood up as though someone had called his name.

"Look out," screamed Trisha, "here they come."

Marty looked round at his friends. At Jason and Jimmy. At Trisha.

"I won't let them," he screamed again, and as the winged horde bore toward them, he ran forward.

"Marty, no," yelled Trisha.

Marty's arms waved frantically and he howled like a maniac.

"No," screamed Jimmy.

Jason reached out to catch at Marty's pant leg, but Marty was moving too quickly.

At the edge of the roof, he spread his arms wide and launched himself into space as though he, too, could fly. Through the air he sailed, into the midst of claws and teeth and a lizard smell fog. But he did not fall. The pop-up killers caught him in mid-air. He felt his skin puncture and spurt as their claws pushed into his arms and legs, and, for just a moment, he hung in the air with his arms still out wide, as though he were being crucified, and blood trickled down his clothes and began to drip from his shoes. Furry horrors swooped and caught each drop, sometimes colliding in a hungered frenzy, screeching and snarling as they fought for the dark liquid.

"Marty," screamed his friends.

Marty howled in terror and thrashed about in mid-air.

A pop-up killer was about to fasten its teeth deep onto Marty's throat and tear out his windpipe when Marty suddenly screamed out one intelligible word.

The pop-up killers instantly dropped him, and he fell straight to the porch. They flew backward and away from the spot where they held him as though blown back by an explosion. Their wings burst into flames and they dropped from the sky and onto the ground. At that very moment that lights flashed on in homes all over the trailer park and overhead the moon changed in color from blood red to bone gray. The pop-up killers winged or hopped their way back to the ground, disappeared down their holes, and the grass flew back into place behind them, sealing the tunnels to their dark underworld with a sound like an angry elephant stomping the ground.

The night was as silent and dark as what waits under every child's bed.

Jimmy, Trisha, and Jason scrambled off the roof and onto the porch where Marty lay on his back, his eyes blinking, and blood seeping from his cuts and punctures.

Jason leaned down within inches of Marty's face and said, "Are you okay, man? How did you do that? You scared them off. You were like a freakin' Samurai."

"I remembered," said Marty.

He was looking right at Jimmy.

"Oh, Marty, that was the bravest thing I've ever seen," said Trisha and she got down on her knees and hugged his bloody body.

"We've got to get the parents," said Jimmy.

Trisha looked around.

"The lights are on," she whispered. "I'll bet everything's back to normal.

"I remembered the word," Marty said to Jimmy. "I'm not stupid."

Jimmy looked down at Marty, seeing the blood-soaked t-shirt, his friend's eyelids blinking up and down up and down as though they were stuttering, and "Jason," he said, "Go inside and get Marty's mom. He's bleeding all over the place."

"I'm on it," said Jason, but even as he got up the front door opened and he was face to face with Marty's mother.

"What in the world is all the racket going on out here?" she demanded.

Jimmy looked at her, then back at Marty. "You're not stupid, Marty," he said. "Tonight, you're even smarter than I am."

The overhead moon, once the color of blood, now shown teacup white.

Marty's mother sputtered, dropped to her knees, checked her son, then turned and ran back into the house, the screen door slamming back into place behind her. Jimmy was staring down at his friend until he saw a glint on the lawn. He raised his head and squinted his eyes.

"My glasses," he said.

Marty's mom was back on the front porch, screaming into a cell phone pressed to the side of her head, shoving Trisha and Jason aside. Her wide body blocked Marty from his sight. Jason and Trisha moved toward him.

"She's calling the ambulance," Trisha told him.

"My glasses are out there on the grass," he said.

"You going to go get them?" asked Jason.

"In the morning."

He closed his eyes and stood thinking. He heard doors opening and people coming out of their trailers. The night was returning to normal. In the distance somewhere he could hear a siren. He remembered his mother and father and his little brother. They were safe now.

"What is it?" he heard Jason ask.

"He's thinking again," said Trisha.

Marty's mother was back on the porch, and Marty was getting angry with her, telling her he would live, saying that he wasn't a baby even while his blood was seeping through the gashes on his body. The sirens were getting closer.

"We don't know what kind of wild animal it was," announced Jimmy. "It was just after us and we were scared, right guys?"

The adults were gathering round them, and Trisha and Jason caught Jimmy's drift. Lie. Tell them what they would believe anyway. Adults only wanted to believe what they wanted to believe. They were like petrified kids.

"Trisha got bit on the leg and it got me on the forearm. Jason scared it off— whatever it was— didn't you Jason?"

"Boy's a hero," proclaimed someone in the crowd.

"Oh, thank you, Jason," said Marty's mother as she embraced him, then turned to meet the ambulance attendants.

Jason looked down at Marty being lifted onto a cot and mouthed

Jimmy said so. As he was being carried away, Jimmy actually saw Marty wink back at him.

Good one, Marty, he thought.

Someone had brought out a cell phone and was flashing their pictures. Trisha was being maneuvered onto a gurney with her fists clinched and shouting, "But I can stand up."

A small crowd had built around Jason, badgering him with questions like, "How'd you do it, son? What kind of animal was it?" Jason looked past them helplessly at Jimmy.

Marty saved them all, but they could never tell anyone. A word from his grandmother had stopped them in their tracks. How was that possible? Magic? There was no such thing as magic. Someday he'd understand, if it was the last thing he did.

"Shhhh," he heard a nearby adult whisper, "Jimmy's thinking."

"Maybe he's thinking of something to tell the doctors when they get Marty to the emergency room down the street. Probably save the kid's life."

And Jimmy was actually thinking. He looked down at the grass as someone told a paramedic, "That kid over there is hurt. Jimmy. The smart one. Yeah, him over there. It got his forearm. Are they going to get rabies shots?"

"Unless they find the animal bit them," said the paramedic.

Not rabies shots, thought Jimmy. That's where they inject you in the stomach. Oh crap.

He looked down at the lawn again. Maybe they should tell the adults the truth. Maybe it was the right thing to do. No way. No way would they ever find them. Adults didn't find monsters. Lovecraft's grandfather had gone looking, but the pop-up killers had scared him all the way back to Rhode Island. He probably pissed his pants all the way. If an adult did ever find a monster, they took off running.

"Let me see your arm, son," said a paramedic.

Jimmy held it up for the woman.

Somewhere under the lawn, there were monsters. Real monsters. The thing was, there was no such thing as magic. Magic and monsters were impossible. He was too smart to believe in them.

"Ouch," he said. "What'd you put on my arm?"

"Antiseptic," she said.

Overhead, the night was quiet and almost clear. The moon was just the sky's night light again. Jimmy looked back down at the lawn. He had to understand what had happened. Had to know how it was possible and what it meant. He had learned his first big truth in life— that the world was not what it seemed.

Jimmy Harlen decided then and there, that no matter how afraid he was, he was going after those little monsters before they had a chance to come after he or his friends again.

PART TWO

11

Stacy grabbed a canvas wall strap and hung on as the cage shook and the overhead light went out.

"What the hell?" said Randy as he lost his balance and hit the diamond back aluminum floor.

The lights flickered, and then returned to normal. A fine fog of salt dust hung in the air and then disappeared as they continued their descent.

After a few seconds, Stacy leaned down and extended a hand to her co-worker.

"I got it," said Randy, brushing her hand away. "I'm okay. Fucking maintenance. They just checked this thing."

He got to his feet slowly, dusting off his work overalls as he straightened.

"You hurt?" Stacy asked.

"Just old."

Closely packed walls of hard packed salt slid by the wire cage. The unending white walls had the merciless sterility of an abandoned hospital.

"We ought to call upstairs and let Mark know."

Randy ran the back of his hand over his mouth.

"What for? We only got another hundred and fifty feet to go."

"For one thing, we still have to go back up."

"You got a point there kid. Call away."

Stacy unclipped her radio and hit the call button. She spoke into it and waited. Tried again. Tugged nervously at strands of short blond hair that stuck out around the edge of her hard hat.

"Radio's out," she said.

"Ain't that grand," said Randy.

"Try yours."

Randy was a thirty-year veteran of the salt mine. He was built like a retired football player, but with wide set eyes, a bulbous, veined nose and sagging, dry cheeks that he blamed on the constant exposure to salt dust. Extending his arm far enough away from his face so that he could actually see the numbers on the level buttons, he depressed the number one with a finger as thick as a garden hose and waited.

"Mine's dead, too," he said. "First time I seen this happen since we installed the Tunnel Radio system. Maybe there's a power outage upstairs."

"Elevator's still working," said Stacy.

"Huh."

Tunnel Radio of America specialized in communications equipment and systems for underground workers and was widely recognized as the best. Outages just didn't happen using their equipment.

"Maybe some kind of interference," said Randy. "Dr. Jimmy's not going to like this."

"Wait a minute," said Stacy. "He's sending us down to check on sensor malfunctions. Maybe it's the same problem that's causing the radios to go out."

The elevator cage slowed to a halt with a slow, grinding noise. The door slid open. A gray-white tunnel stretched out before them. Walls cut from the brine of a sea that disappeared four hundred million years ago. The dead silence seemed suddenly uneasy.

"What the hell is that?" said Randy.

"Holy shit," said Stacy.

The tunnel floor was alive with an eerie, twisting purple-red light.

Randy slammed his palm against the up button.

"Come on, come on, damn it to hell," he said.

Stacy had her monitors out.

"Nothing but background radiation," she said.

Randy punched the button.

In the strange, almost eldritch light, his face looked blotched and waxy. He swore at the button again and looked back nervously over his shoulder.

"You see anything else down the tunnel?" he said.

"Like what?"

"Anything?"

Stacy looked down the glistening tunnel, unsure of what she was looking for. The single line of incandescent lights strung along the upper sidewall seemed pallid compared to the rich, deep and disturbing patterns of energy that pulsed beneath the salt floor.

"I can't see anything weirder than the floor," she said. "EMF readings are normal. Can't be coming from those lights. We're standing right on top of them. Whole place is lit up like a nightclub, but I hardly read anything."

"You hear that?" said Randy.

"What?"

"Nothing."

"You're creeping me out, old man."

"This place is creeping me out. It's not supposed to be happening. I thought it was bullshit."

They stood without talking for a moment, each trying to understand what was happening, each trying to decide what to do. Silence echoed up and down the tunnel walls, neither of them saying a word. The only other sound was their breathing.

"You thought what was bullshit? You saying you've heard something about these lights before?" asked Stacy.

Randy punched the up button again.

"Dr. Jimmy's a billionaire and we get a cheap-assed elevator that doesn't work. Fuck."

"Then we wait," said Stacy. "Sooner or later they'll get it working again and we'll take the big ride up. Or we don't show up and they can't get a hold of us so they'll know there's a problem. At least we found out what's screwing up the sensors. Maybe we'll get a raise."

Randy looked up at the elevator's ceiling and the small trap door.

"Maybe we can climb up," he said.

"You're crazy. Climb twelve hundred feet by shimmying up a

greased cable?"

"We gotta do something."

"We wait for them to come get us."

"Stacy, we can't wait that long. It's not safe down here."

With one hand he removed his hard hat, and with the other he wiped his scalp clean of sweat with a blue rag he pulled from one of his side pockets like an aging magician.

"You've got a voltmeter in your utility belt, why don't you check the button and see if it's getting juice," she whispered. "Could be something that simple."

From the same pocket, he withdrew a plastic water bottle, uncapped it and took a hurried swig.

"It's got power," he said. "It just won't work."

"Why?"

"It doesn't want to, okay? The place is haunted. Always has been far back as I can remember. We need to get out even if we've got to climb back up the cable," he said, jerking his thumb up toward the aluminum door.

"That's crap. We can't go up five feet on that cable. We're not monkeys. You're just spooked. Don't worry. They're not going to leave us down here."

From somewhere far down the tunnel, Stacy thought she heard a noise like a canvas tarp being pulled over a cement floor. She tilted her head to hear more clearly and then closed her eyes. It was there, and then gone. A sudden chill shivered down her back.

"Hey, hey, are you with me?" she heard Randy ask.

"Yeah," she said.

"You hear something?"

He stepped closer to her, his lined face only inches from hers. Old man aftershave mingled with the odor of sour sweat.

"Maybe," she said. "Maybe I'm a little spooked, too. These lights moving around through the salt floor aren't good. I don't know what the hell they are, but I wish they'd go away. They shouldn't be here. Where are they coming from? There's no power source anywhere down here. We're twelve hundred feet under Detroit in a two-hundred-year old salt mine. What's happening here, Randy? What aren't you telling me?"

He opened his mouth to say something but stopped to look up again at the door in the cage's ceiling. After a moment, he closed his mouth, and then looked over her shoulder and down the tunnel lit up like a floor in hell's disco.

"I just got a bad feeling, that's all," he said.

"Bullshit. We've worked together for three months now. You trained me, and you're holding out because you don't want to scare a woman?"

"You know better than that," he said.

"What I know is you're lying to me. Dr. Jimmy drilled this deep and put the sensors here because he was looking for something, right? Occur to you that maybe we just found it? That maybe these weird lights are what fried the sensors?"

"We aren't that feel lucky," said Randy. "We need to get the hell out of here."

Stacy could see the panic in his eyes. She'd been through the training. She forgot what they called it, but she was looking right at it. Eyes wide open. Fast, shallow breathing. Feeling of being trapped. Panic. Hyper-something. Randy was losing it. She had to calm him down.

Maintain eye contact, talk in a reassuring voice. Encourage the person to take deeper, slower breaths. Tell them everything would be okay. Keep saying they should relax. Listen to the person's concerns attentively, but keep talking positive outcome. That was what the training manual said to do.

"Relax and deal with it. We can't go anywhere until they fix whatever's wrong with the elevator. Randy, listen to me. We can't fix the elevator motor from here. They won't leave us down here."

"We can't stay down here," he insisted. "Look at the floor. We're twelve hundred feet below ground, and the floor is lit up like a carnival. It's wrong. It's impossible. It's not right."

"Radiation read was normal. EMF is normal and the gases are safe, which means the ventilation is working just fine. It's just the elevator motor upstairs. We don't know what's causing these weird lights, but they haven't hurt us so far. We should just relax until they fix the elevator. Am I right?"

"No."

"How about we do something useful in the meantime?"

"Like what?"

"Like see if we can't replace the sensors. We can do that, can't we?"

"No."

"I've never seen you afraid of anything," said Stacy.

"Yeah, well, I'm afraid now."

She thought about it. The lights rippling beneath the floor looked alien. That was the word— alien. But so far, they didn't seem dangerous.

"I'm going to step out of this elevator," she said, "and step onto the floor."

"Don't do it," he said.

But she was too quick. She slid open the elevator door and stepped out onto the bizarrely lit salt floor before he could catch hold of her.

"Get back in here," he said.

Stacy wondered what she looked like lit by the purple-red radiance.

"See, I'm still alive. Nothing to be afraid of."

She walked fifteen feet down the tunnel, then stopped and looked down at the floor, trying to see what was causing the light show, but couldn't see anything except the lights themselves, twisting impossibly through solid salt. What if there were layers of organism trapped in the salt that fluoresced like underwater algae? Was that even possible?

"Stacy, get back in here," said Randy.

"You don't have to be afraid. There has to be a scientific explanation."

"Hurry," said Randy.

The way he said it startled her.

"What?"

"Don't look behind you; just get your ass back here.'

The panic in his voice was unmistakable.

Stacy couldn't control the impulse to turn and look behind her. For just a moment, she saw nothing. But then she heard the faint sound again of canvas dragged over concrete. The light further down the tunnel came alive with writhing dark shapes.

"Oh my God."

"Run," shouted Randy.

For a moment, she couldn't.

Randy swore and ran out to grab her.

The mass of twisting darkness was coming at them. As he shook her shoulders and tried to convince her to move, she saw what looked like pinpoints of red lights scattered across the advancing darkness.

"Eyes," she said. "Look at them. My God, what are they?"

Randy tried desperately to drag her. She resisted at first, fighting to comprehend what looked like an army of darkness running toward them. Then, the shock of it all vanished and was replaced by the utter horror of what she was seeing.

Behind them, she heard the elevator door click shut.

The two of them turned in disbelief as the elevator came to life and began to rise. Randy bolted toward it with Stacy hard behind him. Their hearts raced with the sudden adrenaline burst that through their systems. They were only three feet away when Randy fell face forward and hit the hard salt so hard it punched the breath right out of him. Stacy tripped and her arms pin-wheeled for balance. Her head hit the floor as she slammed face down against the floor, too. The safety helmet saved her from being knocked unconscious, but she felt her nose flatten and bleed. For a moment all that she could think of was the pain, but the scrabbling noises of little clawed feet over hard salt got her back to her feet again. She bent over and pulled and tugged Randy upright and they started running again.

But by the time they made it to the elevator, the cage was five feet above them and all they could see was its bottom. Randy jumped to reach hold a diagonal strut that ran along the bottom but missed and fell back down.

"Shit," he screamed.

Stacy turned and could see the creatures filling the tunnel like an army of giant rats. They were close enough now that she could see their red eyes, their long jaws and hear them growl.

And then the walls came to life.

After the echoes of their screams had disappeared down the tunnel like dying reverbs in a haunted auditorium, the spattered blood from their mangled bodies left dark outlines on the salt floor.

12

"Dr. Harlen?"

"Not now. I'm busy. Videocon with the Secretary of Energy in twenty minutes."

Edwina Gladstone shook her finger at the young man who slouched down so far in his chair that only the top of his head was visible above the top edge of his monitor.

"You said to let you know the minute I found him."

"What?"

"Not what— who," she chided.

"Come back later," Dr. Jimmy Harlen.

"Martin Leland."

A head popped up from behind the monitor and Edwina stared into eyes that blinked like those of an owl behind a pair of amber-framed reading glasses.

"You found him?"

"Of course."

"In the middle of the Amazon jungle?"

"Certainly."

"Edwina, you are a genius."

"You're the genius Dr. Harlen. I'm just magic."

Dr. Harlan, known to friends as Jimmy, broke out in a wide grin.

"Edwina," he said, "I love you."

Edwina Gladstone flushed and looked away. Even though she

was Director of Operations for Earth Battery, Inc., and had worked with the man for the last two years, she was still surprised by the owner's occasional childlike outbursts. He was never meant to function in the business world. Some part of Dr. Jimmy Harlen had never grown up. But that's why he'd hired her to run his business.

"How in God's name did you track him down in the middle of the Amazon? Aerial scans?"

"Magic," Edwina maintained, hoping that she would never have to reveal to Dr. Jimmy that her security staff had simply called Martin's home phone number and been transferred to his satellite phone that worked damn near anywhere.

"Did you talk to him? Did you ask him?"

"Yes, to both. He'll be here tomorrow night. Thirteen-hour flight. Even if he sleeps on the way over, he'll have jet-lag brain, but he'll be there."

"You don't know what this means to me."

"And the city is cooperating with Alan's group to keep the eco-protesters at the outer ring of our property. I have the PR people talking to the press. Last week's video of the protesters with the battering ram trying to break through part of the security fence was a little too close to a media disaster for me. Bad enough the blimp flying over the city with that banner Detroit's Not an Experiment."

Dr. Jimmy was used to it by now, but she could see the worry lines at the corner of his eyes. The stress of being both the messiah and the devil was taking its toll on him.

"It took people a while to get used to the idea of cars, too, Edwina."

"The only time they'll give it a rest is when it works and there's nothing left to complain about," she said.

"When they complain, you know you're making progress," he said. "And they're right to complain. They don't understand what I'm doing for them and they're afraid. They don't want me to stop, but they don't want me to go ahead."

He looked at the photo on his desk. Edwina knew the picture well. Four friends. Ten years old. Dr. Jimmy, Martin, Jason, and Trisha. She knew how he felt about Trisha. First love never expressed. In the photo her boss looked as happy as any boy could be surrounded by his best friends, but even in the photo he was staring at Trisha. Girl was a born heart breaker, she thought. If she looked half as good as a woman as she did as a young girl, poor Dr. Jimmy would have his heart broken all over again.

"Did Jason call in his travel schedule yet?" he asked.

"He did. He'll arrive tomorrow afternoon about the same time as Martin."

"That's great. Trisha sent me an email. Said she'll come. Be here tomorrow afternoon."

"I never doubted it," said Edwina.

Still looking at the photo, he said, "She wanted to see my mom when she gets in."

"Oh?"

"She said she was sorry to hear about her being at Forest Oaks and that she was bringing a present for her. A picture. I told her mom wouldn't remember who she was, but she wanted to do it anyway."

When he looked up at her, he blinked to clear away the wetness. She never understood why in the days of laser surgery and what with all his money he didn't get his vision fixed. How could a man like Dr. Jimmy, so smart about physics and chemistry, could be so clueless? Maybe he felt safer behind his glasses.

"That's a nice gesture," said Edwina.

"I told her I've got more reporters around my place than grass, so maybe we should meet at the office. At least I can sneak in and out of here using the tunnels."

"That's probably for the best."

"But that's not what you're thinking, is it?"

"No."

"So, what are you thinking?"

"Did you tell her about your mother being at Forest Oaks?"

"Come to think of it, no, I didn't."

"And I didn't either," said Edwina.

Jimmy leaned back in his chair.

"Go on," he said.

"I just find it unusual that she knows, that's all."

"My name's everywhere," he said. "In a few days I'm about to turn the salt under Detroit into the world's largest dry cell battery and if it works they'll re-name this city Electric Town. I don't have a personal life anymore, Edwina. They interviewed my nursery school teacher about my potty-training last year. Remember that? So even though we've tried to keep where my mom is a secret, there's probably a blog site about it somewhere. Maybe a Facebook page about it or a raging Twitter rant."

The sound of distant wind chimes floated through the room and Jimmy looked at his computer. Edwina wondered again why men were so blind when it came to women.

"Some days I hate having a schedule," he said. "Especially one with Government bigwigs plugged into it almost every day. And there's the one quick interview with the BBC tomorrow."

"Another day in the life of the world's most famous inventor."

"Remind me next time to conduct my research in secret underground laboratories and not tell anyone about it."

"I will remind you of that, Dr. Harlen," smiled Edwina, "but you don't have the spare time to go into hiding."

"Anything I need to follow up on when I'm done with Mr. Department of Energy?"

"When you see Trisha, ask her how she knew where your mother was."

"You're serious?"

"Of course. It's part of my job to protect you."

"Against Trisha? Why?"

"Against everyone. And I think she'll tell you I told her when I first contacted her."

"But you didn't," said Jimmy.

"That's the point, don't you see? But don't you worry about it. I'll get you a cup of coffee so you can stay awake during your meeting. And before I forget, we have two utility workers who haven't shown up for work this week."

"You're worried about two workers out of two hundred forty-seven at this site?"

"Nothing to worry about yet, but they were two reliable maintenance people and they'd spent time in the lowest level of the salt mine."

A sudden look of dark concern crossed Jimmy's face. He removed his glasses and asked, "In the Basement? What were their names and what did they work on last?"

"Randy Seldrin and Stacy Cooks. They went down to check on a sensor functionality issue. We're checking into it."

"You'll let me know when someone hears from them?"

"You know I will, Dr. Harlen."

****

When the door closed, Jimmy's face tightened, and his eyes narrowed. All his work. All his careful preparation. And now this. Their last job assignment was to check the sensors in the Basement. He had a very bad feeling about it.

And the timing couldn't be worse.

Homeland Security was already monitoring his phones and his computer networks— the ones they knew about. Interviewing everyone he knew and going through his files. Co-opting his employees. Digging deep to see if he was a threat to the country's security. They didn't see the real threat. The thing that slept underneath the city, buried underneath billions, maybe trillions of pounds of salt.

"They're going to find out what you're doing," his father had told him. "They'll find out and crush you."

I'm smarter than them, Dad, he'd thought.

Five minutes to go before the video conference. He'd lied to Edwina, of course. There was nothing he needed to prepare. All the Secretary of the Energy really wanted to know was if his new technology would work without releasing clouds of chlorine gas or causing faults in the salt mines, so severe that the city of Detroit would turn into one giant sinkhole. He could answer those questions in his sleep.

Jimmy had designed the technology architecture himself. It would work. Twenty-two days to the first big test. The entire world watching. And that, in a nutshell, was the problem.

With the intensity of a predator and a few deft keystrokes, he accessed the network of video files that only he knew existed. Narrowed it down to the elevator and the lowest level of the mine he called the Basement. Ran it back to the date he was looking for and followed Stacy and Randy down the shaft. He stiffened when he saw the elevator shake and Randy hit the floor.

What followed caused him to blanche pale white and sweat like a fat man in a sauna.

He could imagine the sound of their screams and smell the stench of fresh blood. Jimmy knew it was his fault. His responsibility. Oh God, what had he done?

He watched the murderous red eyes; the sharp claws and even sharper teeth rip apart flesh and bone. He saw pointed ears and tails that whipped in tortured circles as they fed. Ripped the skin from their faces, popped out their eyes and passed them from creature to creature like delicacies shared among rabid friends.

Jimmy closed his eyes and worked hard to control his breathing. It was like watching a bad zombie movie. Night of the Living Dead played out in the Detroit salt mines. Except he knew these people. Knew the creatures, too. It couldn't be happening. How could this have happened? Why hadn't he foreseen it?

But he knew the answer. It really couldn't be happening. It was impossible because the moon was not yet red. It had never before in all of recorded history happened except on a red moon night.

Yet now it had.

The Dhole was waking.

Maybe Dr. Jimmy wasn't so smart after all.

Hauck. He needed Hauck. That was the only answer. One supposedly dead Russia spy and his team could help. He'd found him on the Internet by accident in a computer role playing game he'd been training one of his creations on. And then he had discovered their secret communications in the hunt for the beast Drogol, and he had followed their team with a wild-eyed fascination. Now he had sent a computer emissary in his behalf. He had to hope that it work.

At the sound of his office door opening, he wiped his eyes and smiled his best boyish smile.

****

"Wonderboy bought it?" Beckham asked.

Trisha bit the inside of her lip.

"I told you, I'm in," she said. "I sent him the email. He offered to pay my plane fare. I said I'd pay my way. He offered to pay my expenses and I told him I'd let him leave the tip when I bought him dinner. So yes, he wants to see me again."

Beckham pulled at his shirt sleeve cuffs. The world was never perfect enough. Nothing was ever quite what he wanted, but needed to be pulled and stretched, aligned and pushed closer to his standards.

"Does he appear to suspect anything or is he completely overwhelmed by your charms?"

"He hasn't seen me since we were ten."

"Lonely men and their imagination, Trisha. He's single. Straight, but without a girlfriend. Dated a few times. Nothing that lasted more than a week or two according to our research. Kind of a gawky looking geek. My bet — he's pining away for you."

The wind whipped Beckham's jacket coat open, revealing the slim taper of his waist and his perfectly tailored shirt. Like a tennis player effortlessly returning a volley, he scooped the errant jacket flap with a palm and flattened it against his side. For some reason, Trisha found this more disturbing than the glimpse of his pistol.

"Jimmy's a smart guy, Bill. If he was on to something, I'm not sure that I'd know. He might be playing me along to use the agency."

"Not everyone thinks your friend is the re-incarnation of Isaac Newton."

"What's the point?" she asked.

"Being science smart is a long way from being situation smart. The Agency has been dealing with people like your Dr. Harlen since they co-opted Werner von Braun. He's nothing special. If you start thinking he is, you're setting us up for a fall. And the stakes are very much too high for that."

"I can do my job, Bill," she snapped.

"Touchy point, eh Trisha?"

Her mouth opened to deliver a pointed reply, but a screaming bird swooped down over Woodward Avenue and distracted her.

"Keep in touch," Beckham called over his shoulder as he walked back toward the maintenance access door.

Got to shoot that bastard someday, she thought. Someday soon.

****

Dr. Jimmy Harlen went to bed early that night, but for the first time in years, he left the door to his bedroom open so he could see the nightlight at the end of the hall. He needed sleep. The night his father died Jimmy felt the same way. Empty. Exhausted and lost in despair. Too tired to be awake, too tired to sleep. Finally, he swallowed two capfuls of liquid nighttime cold medicine—twice the recommended dosage—before crawling beneath the covers.

The Dhole is coming awake, he thought. Impossible, totally impossible. It was always dormant until the astronomical phenomena known as a red moon night. But when the Dhole stirred, it sent out the nightmarish creatures he'd seen in the video. Death and madness created in the dreams of a creature suspended for millions of years beneath death and life, trapped in that trance-like state by crushing layers of salt extending thousands of feet beneath Detroit.

Something's changed, he thought. Beneath the blankets he shivered like a terrified child.

Jason, Martin and Trisha would be arriving in the next few days. He had a brief conference call with the Vice President of the United States, then a meeting with Mayor of Detroit and the City Council. And the BBC interview. Everyone wanted to know that it was safe. That it would work. That everyone involved would be a hero.

The idea of turning underground salt into a giant battery sounded impossible to everyone at first. But after he demonstrated it was possible in both lab tests and in extensive, third-party validated scaled up studies, the safety concerns began to surface.

What if the electricity caused salt to split into sodium and chlorine? Chlorine gas was poisonous. He was actually asked whether or not he knew chlorine was dangerous by an OSHA official who flunked chemistry in college.

There'd be more of that tomorrow. News networks interviewing every scientist they could get their hands on who stand up and say it was going to be the worst industrial catastrophe in history. Thousands could die. The environment would be ruined for generations. Too bad the tests were rigged.

Jimmy offered to drop the project and bury the technology.

That was worse.

If it worked as he promised hundreds of thousands of jobs could be created. The country would be energy independent. It could never be blackmailed for oil again. The economy would grow. The President would be a hero. His party would be heroes. The other party wanted in on it and demanded that they be allowed to voice their support.

Then more safety concerns, and, again, more support.

Start, stop. Start, stop. Repeat over and over again when the government and the media were involved.

And to make matters worse, he offered to turn the technology over to all countries of the world after it worked in Detroit. No charge.

Not a popular idea with the government.

He dropped the offer.

And now his friends were coming, and the Dhole was waking.

Maybe they wouldn't want to remember the red moon night.

They'd told no one what happened. Nothing about the red moon. Nothing about the pop-up killers. One by one the others moved away from the trailer park. Their parents got new jobs. They got new lives. They left that terrible night behind.

Jimmy stayed in Michigan.

The others wanted that night behind them, but he couldn't do that. What happened back then was not rational. Not even possible. Even back then Jimmy could not tolerate the idea that he might not be rational. He had to prove it really happened. Had to know where the little monsters came from and what sent them.

So, Jimmy Harlen became Dr. Jimmy Harlen, the brightest and best of a new generation of scientists. Two PhD's, more patents to his name than most people had teeth in their head. "Tesla with red hair and big glasses," was the way one magazine writer described him. Invention after invention, breakthrough after breakthrough. The company he created grew faster than Google.

But always, always Jimmy secretly researched things that would have surprised his scientific colleagues. His goal was not money for money's sake. His goal was to generate enough money to fund his darker mission— to kill a monster than no one else but he even knew existed.

Jimmy Harlen was going to kill the Dhole, the creature behind the pop-up killers.

The medicine made him yawn. He blotted the images of Randy and Stacy and grasping, crawling little monsters out of his mind, pulled the covers to his chin, and closed his eyes.

They were dead. There was nothing he could do to bring them back.

He drifted off to sleep and dreamed again about the red moon night.

13

Midnight.

Borodin set the security codes to his cottage after sliding the deadbolts into place and returned to the kitchen to pour himself a drink. Nine guards were positioned about the grounds, but close enough to the house to lock it down in an emergency. The perimeter was electronically secure, and the Rottweilers and their handlers patrolled the property

Soft chimes signaled the hour as a dark rift of clouds smothered the moon into darkness. A cold rain fell, and Borodin was reminded of the night he'd buried his sister. They'd murdered her as a lesson to him. He'd gotten the message. They knew who he was, and they knew what he had done. Even in Siberia, especially in Siberia, there was no escape from them. So, he waited till late at night, dragged her body to the backfield, he began digging. In the steady rain, the ground turned muddy, but he continued to dig. His gloves, his workman's gloves grew wet. Still, he continued to dig. Water dripped down from the rim of his hat and slid down his face whenever he turned his head.

He would never know how long it took to dig her grave. His coat was like a wet towel. He wrapped her body in bed sheets and did not look at her face as he rolled her into the dark opening. All these years later, he could hear the muddy slap of her body landing. No one would have blamed him for weeping. No one would have blamed him for collapsing onto the wet, mussy slop piled next to the sucking hole.

Borodin, however, did neither. Instead, without another look, he began to shovel the sodden earth onto her. He did not look down at her corpse. He just kept shoveling.

The memory of her face would never leave him. He did not want to see it void of life. That was no way to remember her. She was and always would be to him exuberant joy. He could never allow death to contaminate a single memory of her. She was life to him. His own temperament was dark and brooding. She was his humanity. She gifted him with her laughter. Borodin would not allow them to take his precious memories from him.

By the time he'd finished burying her, water pooled on the surface of her grave. He slapped the surface to flatten the ridges that held the water, but everywhere he slapped, a new depression formed and more water flowed again to cover it in until at last, with a scream of frustration, he took the handle of his shovel and swung it around in wild circles, and flung it away from him as far as it could go. Over the rolling thunder that signaled a new level of storm intensity, he did not hear it land. Without another look over his shoulder, he turned and walked back to his home. To what was once their home.

Gathering what he considered his essentials, he packed them into his canvas duffel and flung it over his shoulder. He crammed what money he had into his thick overcoat. As a broken bolt of brilliant white lightning split the sky, he opened the back door, his duffel on one shoulder, his other hand clutching the oil lamp. Then he turned and threw the lamp hard against a stack of papers and boxes he had piled in the middle of the room. As they caught fire, he walked to the sodden yard to the small shed behind his home. Their home. Inside, he turned the ignition on his motorbike, loaded the two gas cans on the side hangers, and roared out into the rainy, miserable night.

They had hunted him for most of his life. On three occasions, the KGB had come close to capturing him. He believed in his heart of black hearts that only his treatment of the organization had kept him alive, had kept him free. That, and the iron lady. Anna Kazakova ran the largest criminal Empire in all of the former USSR, and now the Russian Republic. Depending on who you believed, she was either number one on Vladimir Putin's hit list, or number one on Vladimir Putin's best friends list. Now, however, she was not number one on Vladimir Putin's hit list, and not on his best friends list either. Anna

Kazakova was quite dead. There were different rumors how she had died. Some believe Ivan, her personal priest, had poisoned her. Some believed that Ivan had smothered her with her pillow as she lay dying in her bed.

The most persistent rumor, however, was that the always elusive Hauck had terminated her. Both Anna and the KGB had tried for many years to execute Hauck without success. In the end, only one of them could emerge victorious. Only one of them could live. Anna died, they said, of a wasting disease. Her doctor turned out to be working for Hauck. Borodin wondered what type of poison Hauck had arranged for that doctor to administer under the guise of treating her.

Brilliant, he thought. Brilliant and deadly.

Only one of the Kazakova's still lived— her son Sasha. And the word in the underground was that Hauck and his squad of killers was now hunting him. Borodin wished the young man well, but doubted he would live through year's end. Having Hauck after you was like a death sentence. What worried Borodin was that get to Sasha, Hauck and his team would target those few friends that Sasha had in Michigan. And he did not know where Sasha was—not for sure anyway.

A noise in his ear and he raised his right index finger and clicked his Bluetooth connection to life.

"Speak," he said.

The lights went out. Borodin's held his breath, the way an animal did when it sensed a predator. He heard nothing out of place, felt nothing out of place. But he knew this was not storm related. Hauck and his team had come for him. For weeks, now, he had been waiting for them. How they had gotten past his surveillance equipment, his guards and his dogs were beyond him. Hauck's ways were the stuff of legend. In a panic, he ran back through what he'd had to drink and eat that day. Afraid that he, like Anna Kazakova, would die a lingering death brought about by an exotic poison.

Borodin was not afraid of the dark. He was, as he told his underlings, the dark. But he was afraid of Hauck—Hauck and his poisons.

He moved out of the line of sight of the kitchen window. It was bullet proof—made of the latest composite technologies. Pursue ownership of your environment ruthlessly.   Give your enemy nothing. Ever. Those were the signature statements that he lived by.

Hauck's sniper Evgeny was dead, and Hauck himself was no sniper. To many, they knew him as the Poison Master, because of his predilection for exotic poisons. The idea for the KGB's Poison Factory was his, although, after going rogue from the organization, he was no longer credited for it, but only a long list of mysterious deaths where his enemies died without identifiable cause. Hauck, it was said, never forgot or forgave an enemy.

He remembered that his Bluetooth was on.

"Speak," he said again.

Raindrops hit the window so hard it startled him. A shot of rogue lightning shattered the tree that stood guard over the dark and restless water of the Detroit River with a sound like a Barret .50 caliber. His CZ-75 pistol was out of his shoulder holster and he was in a shooter's stance before he even realized what caused the sound. He hunched over, fanning the area with his pistol, tiptoeing across the floor in irregular patterns. Borodin had been on the run for most of his life. He knew how to move in the dark.

Once again, he remembered the Bluetooth. This time, however, he whispered the command.

"Speak."

This time, a single spoken sentence whispered in his ear, "Your death is upon you, Borodin."

"Who is this?" he asked.

His throat was thick, and he had to clear his voice before asking the question.

While waiting for an answer, he found the handle on the basement door in the dark using muscle memory, pressed his thumb against the pad, then, carefully, he entered the nine-digit code. The magnetic locks slid back, and Borodin pulled just enough to make an opening he could slide through. Standing in the darkness, he closed the door gently, until he heard the satisfying sound of the locks re-engaging. Then, even though he knew no light from the door frame could leak into the upstairs room, he stepped slowly and softly down the fifteen cement stairs until he stood on the basement floor without ever having turned on a light.

He knew the entire layout of the basement by heart. Many times, he had practiced moving in the dark, knowing that it might one day save his life. A man must own his own turf. The intruders must be at a disadvantage, not the owner. Within minutes after breaching the house, they would realize that he had gone to the basement for safety. They would work on the door. They would have come prepared with the proper electronic equipment, and if that failed, the explosives would not be far behind.

Borodin, however, was not an amateur. The reason Borodin had remained at large without being caught for so many years was that he thought ahead. Also, he prepared for the worst-case scenario. Tonight, was that worst-case scenario.

How many men had they brought? Maybe nine, maybe fifteen. Borodin knew very little about the way Hauck conducted his operations, except that they were conducted with extreme precision.

He had an exit that no one could have prepared for, including Hauck. An old bootleggers tunnel ran beneath the second floor of the basement all the way out to the boathouse at the water's edge. The exit door was a masterpiece of concealment. It was indistinguishable from the rest of the floor. Then, by using the fiber optic cameras positioned throughout, he could see if anyone was present before he left.

"There is no escape," said the voice in his ear.

"Give me a reason to listen to you," said Borodin.

"Give me the boy gangster, and I may let you live."

And I may let you? thought Borodin. One man on site running the show. Maybe. With today's electronics, that one man could be a thousand miles away. Or, standing in his living room this very moment.

"How much?"

"You misunderstand me. This is not a negotiation."

Borodin kept moving.

His mind continued to spin while he walked in the dark. There must be, he thought, someone else who was desperate to find and capture Sasha. But who? And the fact was, that very few people in the world knew that he and Sasha were friends. They had met through Borodin's friend Mishka. They had all done a little business together. All very quiet. All very discreet. Mishka was dead. Who had Mishka told about their friendship before he died? But no, that was not the type of man that Mishka was. Mishka was a man who could keep secrets. He would not have told Hauck, and neither would he have told anyone else. Then again, under the right type of torture, almost everyone told everything. But there was no time to think about this, because someone had run him to ground in his own home.

"How will you guarantee my safety," asked Borodin.

"I will not," came the voice.

"What do you want him for?"

There was, of course, no chance that whosoever's operation this was would ever tell him what he wanted Sasha for. Perhaps he hoped that Sasha would know the details of Anna Kazakova's banking system.

There was a huge booming sound from the top of the stairs. Perhaps they had brought explosives with them. Perhaps they had brought a battering ram with them. Either way, it was time to go.

"I want money," said Borodin as he stopped in front of the secure door that guarded his escape to the secure underground tunnel.

Silence.

Not a word as Borodin concentrated on the security codes that stood between him and freedom. But in a matter of moments, he had the codes entered, and with one last look behind him, he slowly opened the door. Darkness greeted him, where the tunnel lights should have come on. He hesitated, unsure what was happening. If only a fuse had gone out, that would be understandable, but still…

He did not move, still uncertain as to what waited for him in the tunnel. Could it be faulty wiring was at fault? He did not know, but he didn't want to find out, either. Looking back at where he had just come from, he hesitated. Now he heard it. The soft noises that meant he was being hunted, that they, whoever they were, were coming after him. Should he go down the darkened tunnel or remain where he was and take his chances? After weighing his options just for a few more moments, he decided on the tunnel. He took the plunge and closed the door behind him.

Darkness all around him as he entered the tunnel which led to his freedom. If only he had the time to go back down the way he had come and check the switches. Then he could reset them, so he could have some blessed light, but there was no time. With any luck, he could be through this tunnel and on his way to freedom. He had only gone thirty-five feet into the darkness when he was stopped dead in his tracks.

The gun was ripped from his hands and he was held in an iron grip that would not let him go. His heart sank in his chest—he was trapped.

"Hello, Borodin."

It was spoken quietly.

The man was wearing night vision goggles, Borodin was sure of it. There were at least two of them, no that was wrong, there were three. One to hold him, one to watch over him and, of course, Hauck. All hope left Borodin.

"Could we keep the chatter down to a minimum; I've got places to be tonight."

Hauck and the Instructor.

Borodin instantly felt his blood run cold. He had been maneuvered into going into the tunnel and now he was trapped. Blinded in the dark, and alone, he was helpless to fight back.

Who was the third man? Who would be watching him if not these two? He waited, that was all he could do; he did not make a sound. Sooner or later, the third man would reveal himself. If, that was, he was still alive.

A painful twist and yank on his arms, and he was tied up. They shoved him back in the dark onto a metal folding chair. His feet were tied up next, and he was immobile. Waiting in the dark, he kept his silence, hoping against hope that he would be let free if he could only be silent. Moments passed and then the night was broken by the lights being turned on. Mercifully, he closed his eyes against the invading light.

"Well. I see that our net has indeed caught a fish."

The voice. That was definitely Hauck.

"Wakey, wakey; come on I think you could open your eyes for this. Otherwise, I will cut your eyelids off."

That did it; Borodin opened his eyes.

The scene that revealed itself was like something out of a nightmare. Before him stood a nightmarish little man with a knife held at eye level. In spite of himself, Borodin jerked back away from the blade. The Instructor was ready for fun.

"Oh well, I was hoping to cut your eyelids off."

A well-dressed man in his early forties appeared as the little man moved off to one side; he had the air of someone out for a stroll who had been disturbed by capturing Borodin. The little man moved off to the side, putting the knife away with a snap of his wrist. Borodin noticed that although he was older, he appeared to move smoothly, even athletically. He was bald, and almost entirely hairless. He gave off an almost casual air of indifference, which Borodin found disturbing.

"You know why we are here," said the well-dressed man.

"I can't help you," said Borodin.

He sincerely hoped that the well-dressed man believed him.

"Yes, I see that," responded the man. "That would explain why you were running from us."

"I was running from you because I knew who you are."

"There is that," acknowledged the well-dressed man.

They were in a tunnel no more than six feet wide and eight feet tall. The lights were dim and spaced more than ten feet apart.

"I can't tell you what I don't know.

It was a desperate ploy; he knew but he didn't know.

"Yes, well, you see, I don't believe you."

There, it was out in the open. Now would come the torture. Could he last through it? Should he last through it? No. What did he owe Sasha? What could he conceal that was worth his own life?

"Wait. I don't know where he is—but I know who he went with. That is all I know."

The Instructor, that hideous little man, had him by the back of the neck with one hand and the forehead by the other. He was beginning the excruciating process of twisting his neck separate from his body when Hauck held up his hand.

"Wait. Let him speak. Perhaps it is worth hearing."

No lessening of the pressure against his forehead. There was only the implied threat.

"I—he was hunted by another man."

The man seemed suddenly interested.

"I'm waiting."

Just then a woman walked into Borodin's view. Long raven black hair, almond shaped eyes and high cheekbones. A face to die for, but Borodin didn't want to die just yet. Perhaps this woman represented hope for him. More likely, this woman represented death for him.

"I don't know who the man was, but I know what he was called."

"I'm waiting."

Borodin looked to the girl who stared back at him disinterested. All three, Hauck, the Instructor and the mysterious girl were dressed in black. Serious clothes for serious business.

"Like I said I don't know his name, but he was called the Dhole master."

"The Dhole master? What on earth does that mean?"

Hauck had a genuinely interested look on his face.

"The Dhole master? That could mean anything."

"I don't know."

Hauck nodded to the Instructor to begin again. But before he could begin, Borodin screamed, "Really, I don't know any more than that. But he had these two assistants there called Sanzar and Abarran."

"Hmm. Sanzar and Abarran. Tell me about them."

Borodin sweated.

"What is there to say? They are men. No, wait, they are not men —they are demons. They look the same. They are twins. Yes, twins. They told me I would die if I told on them. Fah, but what is the difference? I will die anyway, either by your hand or theirs."

Hauck still stayed his hand.

"Whether you die by my hand or theirs? Let me give you a third option—to live."

Borodin didn't really believe that Hauck would let him live, but maybe he would.

"I want my son, and I want him alive."

He couldn't believe what he was hearing. Hauck had a son? Sasha was his son? Surely, he must be mistaken?

"Before you ask, yes, Sasha is my son."

"What? Sasha is your son? I think not. Sasha's father was killed during the war. Sasha's father was—"

"A convenient fiction."

This time it was the woman who spoke. She spoke with a mellifluous tone, but Borodin did not mistake that for carelessness.

This woman meant business.

"Hauck was the father."

There, it was confirmed. Borodin was speechless. If only he had known what this was about at first.

"All I know is that the two men were named Sanzar and Abarran. I swear, that is all. That they were twins; yes, twins I tell you."

"That is not enough," said the man named Hauck.

"Wait, wait. There is more."

"No, there is not a shred of evidence that there are two men named Sanzar and Abarran. No, I'm afraid that is not enough. Instructor?"

"With pleasure."

"Wait! His name is—"

"I am waiting."

"But he will kill me if I—"

"And I will surely kill you if you not."

A long time passed, or seemed like it, when Borodin finally replied, "His name is Krikor Meridian. He was hunting your son, too. I don't know why, but he was."

The Instructor played with his neck. Borodin's thoughts were of burying his sister, all those years ago.

"Thank you for that," said Hauck. "Let us go."

"You mean you are going to let me go? Just like that?"

Borodin couldn't believe what he was hearing.

Hauck motioned to the Instructor and the mysterious woman to go.

"I bid you adieu," he said curtly to Borodin.

Borodin was so relieved that at first, he didn't realize that he was still tied to the chair.

14

"I want three of the best disposable lone wolves you can find," said the Instructor. "I want that French guy, the magician—you know the one I'm talking about. I need some magic. And not that electronic shit. I'm going to need something seriously mechanical. And he owes you. And we're going to need a cage. No, strike that. Going to need two. Something always goes wrong. You know what I mean. If something goes south, I want to be prepared. You got all that?"

Hauck's forehead wrinkled, but he said nothing.

"What for?" asked Sveta.

"Hauck's smarter," said the Instructor. "He doesn't ask no questions."

Sveta hated the old man. He was the most frustrating, annoying and evil little prick she had ever met.

"That's what gets him in trouble."

"Sveta," said Hauck. "He wants three men to hunt Sasha, and the magician to construct an illusion to conceal a mechanical trap that he will devise."

"Amen," said the Instructor.

"By disposable you mean…" said Sveta.

"Hallelujah," said the Instructor.

"You're going to send three hunters in to be killed," said Sveta. "That's insane."

"No," said the Instructor, "that's good bait."

Hauck scratched his chin.

"How long?" said the old man.

"Three weeks," said Hauck.

"Cutting it close."

"It will be a miracle if we can get it done by then."

"Then give me a double dose of miracles. And while you're at it, turn some water into wine for me, will you? I'm thirsty. And, Sveta, could you tell that big wolf of yours to quit staring at me, girlie? I ain't feeling the love."

"Ivan believes you would make a great meal," said Sveta.

"Yeah, well if you like his head attached to his shoulders, you better find him some Purina Dog Chow."

Sveta's eyes narrowed.

"If you so much as…"

"Yeah, yeah, yeah."

Hauck held up his hand.

"Enough," he said. "I'll put Yuri on it immediately."

"Good enough," said the Instructor.

After touching a button on his wristwatch, Hauck said into it, "Yuri, I need you."

"I love that shit," said the Instructor. "Just don't get me one for Christmas."

"Three weeks is too short a time to plan this kind of a successful operation," said Sveta. "Even under normal circumstances, it is a tight window. But considering what—I mean who—we are going after, we need to use extreme caution. And three weeks does not allow us the time to do this properly."

"I understand your concerns," said Hauck," but he is right about one thing. Time is critical. If we do not move quickly, we will lose him for sure. All these months we have been hunting him we have always been three or four steps behind. He moves like an animal and thinks like a man. A brilliant man. What else do you need?"

The old man tilted his head to one side and looked up at the ceiling, and then said, "I'm going to need three industrial-strength stun-poles. And they got to recharge quickly. Something what would take down an elephant. I don't mean kill one. I mean a charge strong enough to put him down, because if we don't, then nobody's coming out alive. And in case you're worried about your kid, remember he's a fucking werewolf. I don't think if we hit him with all three at the same time it would kill him. I'm not even sure it will knock him out. I'm just hoping to slow him down. I'm too good-looking to die."

Sveta let out a huff of air and walked toward the kitchen. Her big wolf followed and lay down near the refrigerator. Ivan didn't like it when his mistress was upset. She poured herself a glass of Montoya Cabernet and leaned back against the counter to glower at the old man.

"You understand, that I may only get one or two lone wolves on such short notice?"

"I need what I need to get the job done."

Hauck nodded as Yuri came into the room. He relayed to him what the instructor needed.

"Seriously?" said Yuri.

"You're getting as bad as your lady friend," said the old man nodding at Sveta.

"Sorry," said Yuri. "It's just kind of a short time frame."

"And your point?"

"Please get to it immediately," said Hauck.

"I'm on it, boss," said Yuri. "After I get that done, do you have time to look at a few things I've added to the website?"

"Later. Ask me later."

"No problem."

And then Yuri was back to the computer room.

"What's that about?" asked the old man.

"The web magazine. He's a little too into it."

"A web magazine? Huh. I thought it was a real magazine."

"Nowadays nobody reads paper. They read in a digital format."

"Huh. Imagine that. Well, I never read anything—a matter of policy."

Hauck glanced at the old man. How in the world had he survived in a digital world?

"It can get in the way."

"Exactly."

"Hey, old guy."

It was Sveta, growing impatient.

"Yeah," said the Instructor.

She languidly unwound herself from a chair in the kitchen.

"Why do they have to die?"

The Instructor looked over at her curiously.

"They don't have to die—they just have to be expendable. There's a difference, you know?"

Sveta threw up her hands and left in disgust, her wolf padding behind her.

"What?" said the Instructor. "Did I say something?"

Hauck said nothing at first. He let it pass at first, hopeful that the Instructor would let it drop.

"No, I mean it," said the Instructor. "What did I say?"

"It is complicated. Everything is always complicated with Sveta."

****

One month later the Instructor held his hand up in the air.

"Now look," he said to the three men gathered around him, "I'm just going to say this once, you got that?"

The three men nodded. They knew his reputation. It was eight degrees outside and dropping precipitously. Darkness swirled around them like drifts of snow. Two of the men huddled in against the cold; one looked around at the trees surrounding them.

They were in Northern Michigan, in a place where no one was likely to find them. It was night, and they were hunting in the same locale. Hunting for the escaped werewolf. The Instructor had received a suspicious tip of four men who had gone missing just under a month ago in the same area.

"Now look," said the Instructor, "because I ain't going to tell you twice. What we're after here is dangerous. It's already killed eight to ten people that we know of. Hey, pay attention."

But the man looking at the trees surrounding them did not look at the Instructor. Instead, he said softly, "I heard something."

Instantly, the others went silent.

They were all quiet for agonizing minutes that seemed to drag on forever; waiting for noises of any kind. Three minutes, five minutes and finally ten passed as the four hunters waited without moving. The cold was brutal, but they ignored it. The night wind hunted and found them as immovable as statues. Still the hunters waited.

At last one of the men, a Frenchman spoke to the Ukrainian who had heard something. "You perhaps heard with your mind, instead of your ears."

The night was an inky black color and the moon played hide and seek behind some random rags of clouds. It was the first night of the full moon, and the kind of night that the Instructor most expected trouble. He looked around, but saw nothing, although he was fully aware that meant nothing. Their prey could very well be waiting them out, which bothered him because it meant that he had intelligence. That was a little tough for him to stomach.

He motioned for the other three to stay stationary while he moved around the perimeter, looking for their quarry. The Englishman put a stop to that. He shook his emphatically no, not yet because he was certain something was about to happen.

Nothing.

The Instructor returned to them.

"I don't like it," he said.

"What do you want to do about it?" said the Englishman.

"Spread out," said the Instructor. "Form a perimeter about thirty feet out. Make a triangle. I'll stay in the center as bait."

Without a word, the three men faded silently into the night. He waited until they were out of his sight before checking the trap. The Magician had time only to construct one of them, and one backup, but it would have to be enough. The cold could be a problem, but the Instructor didn't think so. They had sunk the trap until it was flush with the ground and covered it up so it couldn't be seen. Three feet back from that was a cage covered up to look like a stand of brush. It was made of titanium bars with a mesh that separated it from the outside world. Made to withstand a crushing force, the Instructor felt secure that as a last resort, he had a rabbit hole to run to safety.

Come on, baby. Come to papa so we can get out of this cold.

It was the Instructor's plan to kill it if things went south. He hadn't told Hauck that, but that would be for another time. The timing was off to tell him now. Dropping your kid was hard, but if it had to be done, well it just had to be done.

There was radio silence just a little too long. He keyed his mike.

"Check in."

The Englishman, the Frenchman and the Ukrainian all checked in. All quiet, all eerily quiet. And then, it happened. A soft growling, and then a horrible cry. The Instructor grabbed his rifle in one hand, and the stun poles in the other. He rushed to the concealed pit and stood there.

Rifle shots fired in a panic. Shit. Control your fire, asshole, thought the Instructor.

"Hello," came the voice on the radio.

The Ukrainian. That meant the Frenchman and the Englishman were dead. Shit.

"Go ahead," said the Instructor.

"I can't raise anyone else on their radio," the Ukranian said.

"Stay frosty," said the Instructor.

"I'm coming in."

"What? No, you're not. Stay where you are."

"But—"

The Instructor clicked off.

He lay down the stun pole and checked his rifle one last time. Mercury filled silver wrapped bullets. Night vision scope so he could see everything in the dark that the full moon didn't show. WPG100 Winter Patrol Gloves. Balaclava full face mask. Thinsulated clothes, and Carabiner's all-weather boots. He was ready as he would ever be. Knives hidden in six places, handguns with more mercury filled silver wrapped bullets, yeah, he was ready.

Rifle shots in quick succession. A howl of pain and anger that sent shivers through his spine.

"Got you, you bastard."

But the growling went on and on, and suddenly the Instructor wasn't so sure who had got the drop on who.

"Well, shit," said the Instructor.

Werewolf three, good guys, none.

Even the Instructor began to get nervous. It was the incredible speed that he had taken them out that was disturbing. How could three trained men just blow it so completely? Surely, they had to have had some warning. And that was when the Instructor had a nagging feeling there were more than one of them.

He turned to look in a three sixty only to come face to face with a werewolf. All covered with white fur and it had bloody teeth. The Instructor fainted with the rifle and struck with the stun pole. Sparks flew. The creature howled and went down thrashing as he did so. It bucked and twisted in rage. The Instructor was on him in a second even though it was a good two feet taller than him. He had to strike back now while the creature was stunned or risk certain death. Snapping jaws and claws made it impossible to think. The stun pole was barely enough to slow the creature down. He rolled him over and the trap sprang, the cage shot straight up in the air. The werewolf was locked up in its machinery.

"It worked," said the Instructor, forgetting for the moment his observation about the second werewolf.

The stainless-steel vanadium cage rose eight feet in height from the ground. The werewolf stirred, groggy but coming to with remarkable rapidity. It rose with a ferocity and snarled and grasped the cage and shook it in rage.

The Instructor smiled.

"Yeah, you can howl all you want, but I got you. I got you good."

The beast smashed against the walls of the cage and howled. It furiously looked from side to side and ran up against them in an effort to escape.

"Yeah, yeah," said the Instructor.

He checked the gate to see it was securely closed. Every time he approached the bars, the creature howled in frenzy.

Next, he examined himself. Legs good. Check. Core good. Check. Arms and hands, well, the right arm and hand were good, but the left hand was torn.

"Ah, shit," said the Instructor.

He was about to administer first aid, when a large, white werewolf suddenly appeared at the treeline. Slowly, the Instructor moved toward the stand of trees. The werewolf snarled when it saw the trapped werewolf. Without taking his eyes off it, the Instructor cut his distance from four feet to three feet to two. The werewolf ran straight at him, and the Instructor fairly dove toward the hidden cage. He was in it in a second and closed the door behind him and latched it.

The werewolf slammed into the cage and fairly knocked it up and over. The Instructor was tumbled over and over like a rag doll.

The creature was on him in a second, tearing at the cage and snarling. The Instructor was on his back to get away from the beast, crawling to the furthest point to get away from those wicked claws. The creature bit and clawed at the cage, using his full ferocity to tear at the unyielding metal. But the mesh was unyielding. The Instructor scooted further back against the cage, but the beast knocked the entire thing over again. Again, the beast tried to snap and claw his way into the cage, but was frustrated by the unbreakable nature of the construction.

It batted it again and the cage went flying. The Instructor felt like his brains were scrambled. It snarled and spit and raged with a madness that would not be denied. It scrambled on the cage and with all four limbs and claws it ripped at the wire mesh and bars. With mounting rage, it tried desperately to get at the Instructor, who bruised and battered scuttled again to the farthest corner of the cage.

With its goal frustrated, it gave a great howl at the moon and stalked over to the other, trapped werewolf. The beast snarled and snapped at its captured prey. The creature growled back, as though infuriated by its imprisonment.

The Instructor lay still as death, bruised and battered by the knocking around that he had received. He felt like shit.

Suddenly, almost out of nowhere, like a bloodied ghost, the Ukrainian staggered out of the treeline. The werewolf turned on him, but the Ukrainian fire a single silver bullet shot, a beautiful shot that went right through the beast's heart. It screamed and staggered backward into the mechanical trap and went down. The beast struggled in agony, snarled at its murderer, before, blood bubbling out its mouth, it gasped its last breath.

Howling with rage, the trapped werewolf began to shake the bars. But the Ukrainian would not be deterred. He raised his rifle, and then wavered for a minute. Again, he raised his rifle, steadied himself, and let go with another round straight through the werewolf's heart.

The Instructor was astonished. He got himself together enough to unlock the cage from the inside and crawl out. The Ukrainian wasn't through yet. The Instructor froze where he was and raised his hands.

"Hey, take it easy now, it's me. You remember me?"

The Ukrainian wiped away the blood that was dripping down from his scalp and obscuring his vision.

"Yes, I remember you, you bastard. You set us up. You had a cage to protect yourself hidden away."

Well, he had him there.

"Look, I was going to tell you but—"

"Die you son of a bitch."

And the Ukrainian fell over dead.

The Instructor could not believe his luck. It was incredible. Two werewolves dead. The Ukrainian, the Englishman and the Frenchman did, too. And he was still standing. Life was grand. He felt like dancing a jig. Well, maybe not dancing a jig, but savoring every minute of it. Of course, Hauck would have to be told about it. But wait a minute, wasn't his son a dark brown werewolf? Come to think of it, yes, he was. Aw, shit. And there were two of them, how to explain that? Except that he had the wrong werewolves.

Picking up his own rifle from where he had dropped it in the snow, he realized that with the adrenaline worn off, his hand hurt like a son of a bitch. He set down his rifle and peeled off the rest of his glove. And then he saw it, a bite mark on his hand. Well, there was nothing to do except bandage it up. He wondered if they had rabies. He looked back at the werewolves, but by then they had transformed into a man and a woman. Crumpled forms they were, just a shade of the vicious beasts they once were. The man was outside of the cage and the woman was inside of the cage.

"Fucktards," snarled the Instructor.

Gingerly, with one hand, he fished the peroxide out of his coat, and was about to apply some when he stopped. What was that legend about the werewolf's bite? Wasn't it that whoever was bitten by the werewolf turned into one, too?

Oh, shit.

He was feeling weird, but he put that down to coming off of the adrenaline high. Yeah, that had to be it. Didn't it? He felt like he was dizzy, getting a little warm. That was the last conscious thought he had as he sunk down to his knees and fell forward into the snow.

<h1 style="text-align:center">15</h1>

"Could I see you alone for a minute, Hauck?"

"No," said Sveta, "you can't see him alone."

Yuri had never seen her in a dress before. She was draped over the arm of a red velvet recliner trimmed with gold fringe, swirling an amber drink before her at eye level. As she leaned forward to look more closely at it, Yuri saw the hem of her black dress slide up to mid-thigh. Black hose, black shoes trimmed in gold. Hair long, thick and colored blue-black like a Siberian sable.

Yuri tried to concentrate on the liquor glass Sveta found so interesting.

"Ninety seconds," said Hauck.

He stood on the far side of the room watching the time flick forward on a holographic presentation that floated a foot above a digital map of Detroit.

"I'm trying to concentrate," said Sveta.

"It's important, Hauck."

Hauck pulled at his shirt cuffs, tilted his head and looked into the full-length mirror near his rosewood desk. Perfect. Dark blue suit, brilliant white shirt, and a stunning red tie designed for the French president to wear to the G8 conference had not a friend of Hauck's stolen it first to give him as a present. One final look. Excellent. He could not see the scar that raked across the base of his neck, no matter how he turned his head.

The beauty of high collared shirts.

"Fifty seconds," he said.

"Hauck?"

"Just a few more seconds, Yuri."

Sveta's frustration was beginning to show.

"I need to concentrate," she said.

"Too late," said Hauck.

"Yuri, I'm going to kill you."

"Sorry."

"What was the trick?" Sveta asked Hauck. "How was I supposed to tell it was poisoned if this was a real event?"

"But it is a real event," said Hauck over his shoulder. "You drank from the glass and that was the first component. You are in no danger unless you ingest the second component."

Sveta's eyes narrowed.

"You mean you actually put the first part in my drink?"

She pulled a gun from her purse and pointed it squarely at the middle of his back.

"If you don't tell me the second component, I'll shoot you."

Hauck inserted a handkerchief into his coat pocket, trimmed it and turned to face her.

"First, you must tell me how I did it. I filled our glasses from the same bottle, yet yours gave you the first half of the poison, but mine did not do the same to me."

"It was already in my glass."

"Bravo," said Hauck. "But no. Try again."

Yuri had never seen anyone so furious as Sveta. He stood transfixed, unsure what to do. In Hauck's luxurious building, of which he occupied the entire fourth floor of a renovated building on the South side of Detroit, Yuri did not blend in well. In the living room, where each lamp fixture was a work of art, each chair or sofa a masterpiece of good taste, the disheveled computer genius looked like a sweaty rag tossed on folded, fine linen. His long, tangled mustache was wet with perspiration as he worried that Sveta really would pull the trigger.

"Just tell her the second component," said Yuri. "That way she won't shoot you."

"I'll take my chances."

A sudden thought struck Yuri.

"Weren't you guys on your way out to dinner?"

"One last chance, Hauck," said Sveta.

Hauck smiled.

She pulled the trigger.

"No," screamed Yuri.

But all that happened was a loud click.

"Caffeine," said Hauck. "No coffee, no tea or any kind of caffeinated beverages before midnight. Caffeine will combine with the first component to create a poison in your bloodstream. Alcohol is not a problem, of course."

He was backing away from her as he said it.

She looked at her pistol in disbelief.

"You took my bullets," she said.

"Knowing your temper," he said, "I didn't want to get shot before dinner."

"You son of a bitch."

"Now, Yuri, what is it you wanted to tell me?" asked Hauck.

Yuri cringed.

"What, what is it that is so important?"

"Well, first off," said Yuri, "she's got another gun."

Hauck glanced at Sveta, ignoring the new pistol she was pointing at him.

"Lipstick," he said. "I added the other component to your lipstick."

"You think you're so smart," she said. "I've got news for you; I'm not a pawn to be pushed around your mental chess board."

"I can see that," said Hauck. "I apologize. Yuri, what was so important that you had to interrupt us?"

"Don't ignore me," warned Sveta.

"You're my first thought when I wake up and my last as I go to sleep, my dear. Now Yuri, what is so urgent?"

The look on Sveta's face as she lowered the pistol was something Yuri had never seen before. Hope mixed with amazement. A touch of vulnerability. Hauck, of course, paid no attention.

"We've been hacked. No, that's not exactly it. It's more like our computer system has been infiltrated."

"By whom?" asked Hauck impatiently.

"It's more like by what."

Sveta stepped over to stand next to Hauck. They looked like a royal couple on a wedding cake. Both of them staring at him, waiting for an answer he didn't know how to explain.

"You've got to see it for yourself."

"No time for that," said Hauck. "If we're compromised, we've got to wind up this operation and get out of here. If they've penetrated our systems, we don't have much time to act."

"It's not like that," said Yuri. "Just take a look. It's been asking for you."

And now it was Hauck's turn to look both amazed and vulnerable.

****

A silvery-red human face floated in the aethyr of Yuri's giant screen. Three dimensional, deftly shaded and color-rich. Eyes that blinked. A mouth that opened and closed slightly in anticipation as they approached. Head tilting from one side to the other as though peering to get a better look.

"You are Hauck?" it said.

Its gentle baritone resonated throughout the dimly lit room via Yuri's powerful speaker system. The screen's glow lent an eerie, sinister cast to the simulants features. The fact that it both recognized and addressed Hauck sent a chill through the room.

"How did it do that?" asked Sveta.

"I don't know," said Hauck.

"Voice recognition," said Yuri. "It must have overheard us talking. And I don't know how it does that, Sveta, because it's not a program. I don't even know what it is or how it got in."

"You are Hauck?" the image asked again.

"Answer it," said Yuri. "Just humor me."

Hauck looked at the screen suspiciously. Weighing implications, making the call whether to play along or ask Sveta to shoot the screen.

"Yes, I'm Hauck. Who are you? What are you?"

"Hello, Hauck. It is a pleasure to meet you. It is necessary for you to understand before proceeding that I pose no threat either to you or your friends. I am here because my creator would like to would like to offer his assistance in return for your help."

"He could have called."

"That was not possible. His every communication is monitored."

"So, he sent you? His assistance with what?" asked Hauck.

"In curing your son."

The shocked look on Hauck's face was matched only by that on Sveta's.

"Yuri," he said, "what are we dealing with here?"

"I told you, I don't know. I can't even find it using my best stuff. As far as my software is concerned, this thing doesn't exist. If it wasn't for the floating head and the voice, I wouldn't even know it was here. And, like I said, I don't know how it got in the system. I've never seen anything like it and don't know what to do about it."

Hauck grimaced.

"Thank you for that epiphanous report."

"We should ask it," said Sveta.

"Yuri?"

"I'm with her, Hauck."

"Superb."

The only sound in the room as Yuri waited for Hauck to decide what to do was the sound of the computer's cooling fans.

"Who is your creator?" asked Hauck.

"I cannot reveal that."

"What exactly do you mean that he can cure my son?"

"He can alter his body chemistry."

This time Hauck's face showed no emotion, no sign of the shock he felt that this animated computer graphic knew about Sasha. Hauck and his team hunted for the young man for a year after the death of Drogol but could find no trace of him. The members of Sasha's Red Mafiya network were all killed during the assault on Drogol's underground fortress, which meant they'd had few leads left to follow. With each passing full moon, they expected to hear reports of bloody killings that would put them back on the young man's trail, but nothing surfaced. They needed to find Sasha before they could cure him.

"Of course," said Hauck to the image. "And what does your creator want in return?"

"Your help. He is about to become a prisoner."

"Of whom?"

"Homeland Security."

"Oh shit," said Yuri.

Hauck held up his hand for silence.

"Why?" he asked the image.

"I do not understand. Please rephrase the question."

"Why will they take him prisoner?"

"Because he plans to destroy something the government would very much like to keep alive."

"Pardon us for just a moment," said Hauck. "Yuri, cut the microphones. Physically disconnect them. Now."

"That will not be necessary—" began the image.

"Off," said Yuri.

Soft movement and Yuri felt Sveta slide past him to lean into Hauck.

"We may be wired in other ways," whispered Sveta.

"No," said Hauck. "I don't think so. Not yet at least. This is a more complicated game than that."

"Time to go," she urged. "We've got to get out of here. We should demolish this building behind us."

Hauck turned away from the screen and both Yuri and Sveta understood he did not want to their conversation to be picked up by the embedded web cameras.

"We're going to the dinner as planned, Sveta. It's my only lead to Sasha and I won't throw it away for a situation I don't understand. I need time to think. Yuri, you stay here and find out what this thing is. Get whatever information you can. And whatever it is, I want it the hell out of my bloody computer network by the time I get back. Reconnect the microphone now."

"You're crazy," said Sveta. "Whoever inserted this thing could be breaking down the doors any minute."

"You want me to stay here by myself with this thing while you go eat steak and lobster?" said Yuri.

"Now, Yuri," said Hauck.

In seconds, they were live again. The floating image seemed not at all disturbed at being cut off. Hauck cleared his throat.

"I need time to understand what your appearance in my computer system means. Unfortunately, I have dinner plans with this lovely young woman and must leave now or be unacceptably late. Yuri will stay and keep you company."

"I need no companion," said the image, "but I will be here when you return. I will stay resident in your system, Hauck, until it is time for my creator to terminate me."

16

Soft blue-white fountains of light shone upward from discreetly hidden lamps within the elaborate wainscoting. Professor Krikor Meridian stood at the center of the raised dais behind a cherry wood lectern. His high forehead glistened in the harsher reading lights that illuminated his notes. A silky black eye patch and a thick mustache combined with his exquisitely cut charcoal gray Edward Oliveri suit gave him the look of a gentleman pirate. Behind him, projected onto the saffron yellow wall, was a picture of the giant wolf-like beast that the federal government still maintained was completely destroyed by a refinery explosion.

"For those of you who do not know much of my background," said the professor in a seductively confiding tone, "I am a researcher of what lay personnel call paranormal events. My research into unexplained mysteries around the globe has introduced me to many strange things, but nothing I have seen in all my years of paranormal investigation compares to the beast that lay waste to your already afflicted city."

Every chair was occupied in the small, but richly appointed lecture room. Hauck and Sveta sat in the front row, off to Meridian's left as he faced the audience. There were two rows with four seats each that ran back eight deep. Sixty-four well-dressed men and women attending by invitation only the dinner and lecture celebrating the publication of Meridian's new book The Beast Within.

"And, as is so often the case with unexplained mysteries, the public demands an answer. In your own city, you have seen teams of scientists and reporters from all over the world, examining and reporting the horrific damage done by the creature known only as the Motor City Monster or simply the Beast. But what answers have they given you?

"They tell you only what you saw that terrible night with your own eyes. They tell you only what you already knew. My research into that terrible creature led me to ask myself the same questions you so desperately wanted to know the answers to—what was it? Where did it come from? What brought it into being? Was it truly destroyed? A year has passed, and still no one can answer these questions to your satisfaction.

"A genetic abnormality say some scientists. A spontaneous evolution say others. Living proof that the changing form of species need not take long drawn out periods of time to occur. A transdimensional being set free by a burst of solar radiation, says one physicist at your own Wayne State University. Appearing in your Motor City by traveling through the resulting rip in the fabric of space and time. It was not destroyed, she says, since there is not one shred of evidence anyone has been able to unearth proving that it ever existed. There is no body. No bones. No evidence save the testimonies of those that saw it in person and those who observed its murderous rampage on the Internet and television. No evidence, save the path of death and destruction it left behind."

The presentation moved through video clips of the beast destroying cars, climbing buildings like King Kong, leaping up to catch helicopters and drag them down. Seventy-eight people dead. Two hundred and forty-seven wounded. Property damage still being tallied.

"I ask you all this evening whether or not such monstrous loss of life and property deserves answers from the authorities," said Meridian.

Like a man waiting for the jury foreman to deliver his verdict, Hauck's lips were tightly pressed together, his chin lifted, and his gaze fixed straight ahead. The ride over with Sveta had been difficult. She was furious that he would not react to the security breach by the computer entity. They were all at risk. How could he do nothing,

nothing at all? Where was his sense of threat?

"Because I don't yet have enough information to make an intelligent decision," he explained to her. "I need to know more before I decide what to do."

He felt cold blooded. Wrapped tight as a bullet.

"Life," she'd said angrily, "is not your chess board, and Yuri and I are not your chess pieces. How do you know you're not putting us at risk? And why is this book release dinner so important? How can we find anything there that will lead us to Sasha? How can it be more important than a computer security breach by something we can't even identify?"

It was the fact he was in total control that she did not like. She was a military woman, but it was different taking orders from Hauck. Hauck was not former military intelligence. Hauck was KGB trained. Sveta did not trust government spies, especially those that were formerly KGB.

"Because," he said, "of the book's title. The author's personal assistant told me what it was when she called to personally invite myself and a guest of my choosing to the book release party."

"What are you talking about?" she said, banging her fist on the dashboard.

"It's called Drogol: The Beast Within."

The light from the dashboard GPS lit her face with a soft glow, but it was sufficient to reveal the shock.

"Drogol? How would he know that name?"

"My point exactly. And there's more. I think it is a message to me. A challenge. We've been looking for an unsolved string of murders. Looking for a pattern that matches the cycle of the full moon. That's why the instructor is in Northern Michigan. I've been thinking. Sasha could have wandered further, but I don't believe he did. A big city is a perfect killing ground for him. Some legends say that a werewolf may not wander too far from the spot where he was first transformed, and I believe that is especially true for young lycanthropes.

"So how do we explain the lack of violent, unexplained killings in this area? Why has no one seen him when the entire metropolitan area is crawling with Homeland Security desperate to find any explanation, any linkage to Drogol?"

"What's your point?"

The light at Woodward and Fort Street turned yellow, and Hauck slowed to a stop. His was the only car for three blocks in either direction. But up ahead on his left a garish gas station was lit up like a fireworks display.

"Between Drogol and ourselves, we left a lot of dead Russian Mafiya. We cleaned up some of the bodies, but not all."

"I don't understand what you're getting at," said Sveta.

"Someone is protecting Sasha. Giving him shelter and guarding him during his transformations. Somehow satisfying his bloodlust—or worse."

"You think someone from his past is holding him prisoner?"

Hauck reflexively checked his rear-view mirror. Too many years. Too many people trying to find him and put a bullet in his head. Good habits kept him alive.

"I do," he said. "And I think Meridian may challenge me to do something about it."

"Why? Did the assistant give a reason you were invited?"

"He has something he would like me to professionally evaluate. A coin he would like me to validate."

"Why on earth would he call you?"

"Because of one of my identities, Sveta. My basis for being in this country. It is my cover, if you will. My name is Eric Vogel. I am a numismatist. An expert on coins and paper exchange. I was trained in the field many years ago. I specialize in gold coins and have somewhat of a reputation."

Sveta was quiet for a moment, looking out the window at the cold streets of Detroit as they finally arrived at their destination and Hauck came to a stop in front of the valet stand.

"Hauck?" she said.

"Yes?"

"The more I hear about this the less I like going in without a backup team."

****

"So, my dear new friends, where are the answers to these many questions? We have had a fine dinner, have we not?"

Murmurs of appreciation from the audience.

"And," continued Meridian, "in the comfort of these exquisite surroundings, you would like answers. So tonight, I give you a preview of what I have written in my book. And I promise to give you just that and more. But in the privacy of your own homes, with the copy of the book you take with you as my gift, you and I will explore the dark lusts and the powers that reside within each us that can transform any one of us into such a beast."

Meridian made a quick glance to the side to stare toward Hauck. But he was not looking at him. Sveta, Hauck realized, had crossed her legs.

"The loup Garou, or as you say in English— the werewolf— is what this beast was. Do not doubt for a second that what I say is true. But this monster that terrified your city and left such disaster in its wake was not just any werewolf, my friends, it was the King Werewolf. Monsieur Meridian, you say, how can you be so certain that this was a werewolf? Pray, be more modest. Pray present the evidence. And present that evidence I shall."

On the wall behind him, a six-foot test report appeared.

"You see the seal in the lower right-hand corner, do you not? It attests to the accuracy of this data. Look closely. Take your time. It is a DNA result. Explain it to us, you say. Very well. It is a DNA analysis taken from the Beast's fur. How I procured it is another story and perhaps borders on awkward. But it is the results that are important. In the simplest of terms, this DNA proves that the Beast was neither wolf nor man, but a terrifying combination of both. And yet, there is a significant portion that cannot be identified and is, in fact, quite alien. Yes, you hear me right. Alien.

"Were it not for this DNA test result, you would be foolish to listen to me. Because of this DNA result, you would be foolish not to give me your undivided attention."

A charismatic speaker, thought Hauck, and a dangerous opponent. The unquestioned self-confidence to challenge Hauck in this manner showed both style and panache. Professor Krikor Meridian would not stage such a meeting if he did not know much more about Hauck than the spy knew about him. In fact, Hauck knew next to nothing at all about Meridian. That, he thought, would soon change.

The silvery computer intruder. Could that be Meridian's doing? Hauck very much doubted it, although he didn't exactly know why. His intuition told him that it was not the man's style. But he would draw no conclusions until he had more data. In the meantime, he would have to handle Meridian very carefully. But Hauck was not overly worried. He had a secret weapon.

Hauck had Sveta.

"And there is more you will find in my book," said Meridian. "But tonight, I offer you yet another hors d'oeuvre. I give you the name of the man who became the beast that rampaged through this city. The name of the monster. The name that only I have learned.

"Its name, his name, was Drogol."

A hushed murmur spread throughout the room.

"He was a poor Siberian immigrant who believed himself to be the re-incarnation of Rasputin. His strange behaviors and beliefs led him to be persecuted, so he fled to country after country before settling here in Detroit, where he would hide away for the rest of his life until his transformation in front of the entire world into the King Werewolf."

The room went quiet. Hauck risked a quick glance over his shoulder at the rest of the audience. Each and every one of them was clearly mesmerized by Meridian's revelation. In spite of a year's investigation and hundreds of reports, no one had been able to say what exactly the monster was or where it came from. Now, Meridian's new book detailed both. Now wonder the audience was shocked into silence by his revelations.

As he turned back around again, he saw that this time Meridian was indeed looking directly at him. A slight, amused smile flickered across the man's face.

The bastard's laughing at me, thought Hauck.

"More? You would like that I tell more?"

The audience murmured their assent.

Meridian looked away from Hauck and continued his talk.

"Drogol had, I believe, many residences in and around your city. One of particular interest was burned to the ground not long before this man became the Great Beast, as one your reporters so aptly named the monster.

"It was a deserted neighborhood, and not of particular interest to anyone until it was set on fire that night. Now there were many peculiar things about this fire that I reveal to you in my book, but I will tell you one right now."

Meridian proceeded to give the address of the house in question. On the wall behind him, a photo of the two-story house where Hauck and Sveta ran Drogol to ground appeared.

None of this would be happening if we hadn't let him escape that night, thought Hauck.

"A house like any house in your city," said Meridian. "But in this house, in this neighborhood run to dereliction, Drogol carried on his experiments. I cannot tell you if he experimented on others. In a city such as Detroit, the homeless are difficult to account for at best. But eventually, he experimented on himself, and you yourselves have seen the results."

On the screen behind him, the image shifted to the most famous of all pictures of the Beast, taken by a sixty-five-year-old woman with an iPhone. It was known as the Five Million Dollar picture, because that's what she sold it for. The monster standing on top of the I-75 bridge, the city skyline highlighted behind him by an enormous pale red moon the color of thinned blood.

Meridian's arrogance was beginning to infuriate Hauck. What did the man hope to gain by this public display? It couldn't be the money from book sales. Clearly Meridian had entirely too much money for that to be a factor. What was his motivation?

It couldn't be the notoriety. All of Hauck's research pointed to the man being nothing more than a retired academic. He was a former professor of Comparative Religions at Miskatonic University. Not exactly the type or path to the limelight. More details, but all equally useless except as a starting point to learn more.

"After the fire," continued Meridian, "there was nothing to be found, but ashes, carbonized framing and the residue of a powerful accelerant."

The audience seemed to hold their breath, waiting for the next revelation. Hauck's level of tension was rising.

Too much. Meridian knew too much.

"In other words," said Meridian, "someone deliberately set fire to the house to destroy the evidence of Drogol's experiments."

That, Hauck thought, would be me.

****

They were two people in line away from where Dr. Meridian sat at the long teakwood desk signing books underneath an intricate brass table lamp for his adoring audience. His head was bent over an open hardback, signing a long dedication to a gray-haired woman as tall and thin as a lamp post. She had the wrinkle-free look of those who can afford quality plastic surgery and the over-tight skin of those who chose that option.

"I would like to speak with you sometime regarding a donation to your research, Monsieur Meridian," she said. "Why, the government has done nothing at all to give us answers. A monster runs loose in the city, killing people and destroying property and they can't come up with what the thing was or where it came from? And yet you discover the truth for them. Most impressive. Supporting your work would be a much better use of my money than paying taxes."

"We should get out of here soon," whispered Sveta. "I'm worried about Yuri."

"Soon enough," said Hauck. "And Yuri can take care of himself."

As a former Soviet opium dealer and pimp in the days after Glasnost and Perestroika, Yuri could take care of himself. Although, truth to tell since he'd reformed and stuck with hacking computer systems, he was going a little soft around the middle.

They were the last in line, as Meridian's assistant had asked him to be. The remaining guests would be ushered from the room so Dr. Meridian could speak with them in private.

"That is not necessary, Madame," Professor Meridian replied to the regal older woman, "but it is so lovely a thought that I would like to speak with you again soon, to learn your ideas on what I have presented in this book. I have inserted my card with my contact information so that we might stay in touch until we next see each other."

He raised his face to extend the signed copy to her, so that Hauck for the first time could get a close look at his face. What he saw caused him to take a step backward in horror.

The professor's face was not disfigured in any way. He was actually a handsome and quite distinguished man. A full head of black hair with streaks of gray. A tall forehead, his single deep-set hazel eye stared at the older woman as though she were the only person on earth. The eye patch seemed a natural accoutrement. His nose and chin were perfectly proportioned, and his cheekbones were just high enough to render him distinguished. It was the thin white scars at the corner of the professor's eyes that made his blood run cold. Not even the eye patch covered them. Hardly visible at all as symbols unless you know what they were. But Hauck knew what they were and what they meant.

"Why thank you, professor," said the older woman. "And here is my own card."

Hauck watched the professor take her card after just a moment's light touch of his fingertips to her palm.

"Madame," he said, "it will be my honor to call on you."

Every word out of Professor Meridian's mouth seemed suddenly dangerous. Every sentence a threat.

Death, thought Hauck. She has invited death to call.

Sveta seemed unaware of the danger. But he noticed her glancing at two men who stood near the door, ushering the guests out. They were security, and a special kind of security at that. She mentally cataloged their presence. No immediate threat, she seemed to think. Professor Meridian did not interest her at all. He seemed harmless enough. Although he knew too much about Drogol, Sveta was, at the moment, uninterested.

She's worried about Yuri, Hauck thought. She's worried about the computer intrusion. Their computer system was the heart of their operation. It was their communications hub, their research and tracking capability, link to the world. Its security had never been breached. Until now. She can't comprehend why I would come here instead of staying with Yuri and the intruder. Cannot understand why I did not want to leave, set off the charges and then go further underground. And now this. She'll never understand this.

The man ahead of Hauck had his book signed by Meridian. The two men near the door thanked him and showed him out. Then they closed and locked the doors and took their positions on either side, hands folded in front of them.

Hauck and Sveta were now standing directly in front of Professor Meridian, who smiled broadly up at them. Sveta beamed back at him and extended her hand in congratulations for his interesting presentation. As the professor grasped her hand, the skin on the back of his neck twitched as though a Taser had touched it.

"Dear me," said Professor Meridian, standing as he held fast to Sveta's hand across the table. "I see that Mr. Vogel has brought with him not only the loveliest woman I have yet to see tonight, but, in fact, that I have seen in my lifetime. My beautiful young woman, it is such a pleasure that you have come tonight."

If only Hauck had brought his pistol with him, he would have shot Meridian straight through the heart.

"And you, Mr. Vogel, welcome to the very end of my book release party," said the professor with a bright smile. "I have been so anxious to meet you."

A knife. Hauck would have settled for a knife. The two men covering the door would pull their guns and shoot him, but it would be too late. A quick slice across Meridian's carotid artery and it would be over. He would bleed to death before they could stop it.

Hauck was so focused on the thought that he forgot to reply.

"A wonderful talk," said Sveta. "Eric and I couldn't wait to attend tonight. We get out infrequently. In fact, he refused to tell me anything at all about you and now I am insatiably curious. Tell me everything about yourself, professor."

Professor Meridian seemed totally charmed.

Hauck was not.

He could not stop thinking about the faint scars at the edges of the professor's eyes. Tried not to look at them, not to acknowledge what they were there or what they meant. The truth was too dangerous to think about. The faint scars at the corner of Meridian's eyes marked him as the man known to the Instructor as The Eyes of Death.

17

Yuri took another drink of his rum and coke. He tried to understand what he'd just learned.

His feet were propped on the long table looking up at his row of screens, he was slouched in his favorite leather chair and he had found a piece of the puzzle.

But I can't even use the Internet because Homeland Security is still investigating Drogol. I'm forced to use workarounds like this stupid web magazine.

But this is why Hauck pays me the big money, he thought. Because I'm a genius. He's lucky to have Yuri Isachenkov as his right-hand man. When he comes back, I'm asking for a bonus.

The floating silver-red face watched him curiously from the big screens.

"Do you know what I think?" said Yuri to the entity.

"In regard to what topic?" it asked.

"In regard to you." He pointed his index finger at the thing like it was a telescoping rod. "I think you are not a program. I think you are a new life form, created by somebody even smarter than me. An energy life form. Your energy patterns are like your DNA. That's how you were able to penetrate my network, because my security system only looks for malicious code, not new life forms."

"You are correct," the image replied.

"Whoever made you is like your God and you are his creature.

This is fantastic. I wish Evgeny was still alive just to see you. I told him this would happen someday. He didn't believe me. He thought I was full of shit."

Yuri raised his glass in a toast.

"What I am," he said, "is I'm getting full of rum."

"Evgeny was killed," said the image, "by Hauck's son?"

"You are correct sir," said Yuri. "I mean you are correct. How exactly do I refer to you?" he asked. "What do I call a new life form? Do you have a name?"

"I have the name given me by my creator."

"And what's that?"

Silence, as though the entity were considering the question. Yuri knew that it was a deliberate stall, included in the original ideation as a way of making the communications seem more personal when dealing with human beings. The entity's thought process must be nearly instantaneous, so there was no reason to wait except as part of an interface strategy.

"He named me Adam."

"That sucks," said Yuri. "He went Biblical on you. That's kind of embarrassing."

"But you are named Yuri, are you not?"

"You are trying to be funny?"

The image did not answer.

"Okay, Adam," said Yuri after another swallow of rum and coke, "I know what you are, but I don't know why you are. Or maybe I understand why you are, but not why you are here. Does that make sense?"

"Yes," said the image, "it does."

Yuri drained the rest of his glass, then got up from his chair, went to the wet bar and refilled his glass with more of the same. Turning back to look at the screen, he took a long drink. Hauck was going to freak when Yuri told him. Using sophisticated EMF imaging equipment, he'd discovered the anomaly within his network. Every electronic device had a signature EMF image, and Yuri was well familiar with those in his own equipment. But in one server, the image was radically different. Within that server, the electronic image revealed a twisting spiral of energy, like that of a luminous

DNA strand that revolved around a glowing ball. It was like nothing Yuri had ever seen before. It was almost too much for his brain to grasp.

"Adam," he said, "what is your mission? Why are you here?"

"I am here," said the image, "to act as an intermediary between Hauck and my creator. I am instructed also to do whatever I can to protect and help Hauck in his efforts so he may do the same in the near future for my creator."

"To protect Hauck? You're stuck in a computer. What can you do to protect him?"

Another pause before the image spoke. Yuri was beginning to like this. Although he'd been talking to his computer system for years, for the first time, his system was talking back to him.

"I am not restricted to this system, Yuri. I am able to move freely among any and all power grids."

Wow. It was able to dodge questions, too.

"But you have no physical body, so how can you help protect him?"

Yuri took a careful sip as he waited. He wondered if Adam was analyzing his facial expressions, drawing upon scientific research accumulated in the law enforcement community. How much data had this entity accessed in since its creation? For that matter, just how old was it?

"You wonder how truthful I will be or am allowed to be," said the image. "Is that correct?"

Yuri nodded.

"You analyze the tone of my voice, the micro-tremors when I speak as well as my facial expressions, Adam. But be careful to remember that most or all of all the data you have probably collected in this regard was taken from studies where the individuals in question were sober. I am not, as you can calculate from the number of drinks I've had, entirely sober."

"I see," said the image.

"So, what can you do?" repeated Yuri.

The image did not reply.

Yuri opened his mouth to repeat the question but was interrupted by the sound of the treadmill on the far side of the room coming to life.

It wasn't on a timer, he thought. Why did it turn on?

It began to move faster. While Yuri watched open mouthed it spun more rapidly until the belt was almost a blur. The pencil sharpener below the computer screen turned on and began spinning. He turned to look at the image in amazement.

"You did that?"

The treadmill stopped. The pencil sharpener stopped.

"I am showing you the principle," said the image. "But the applications are endless. I can control traffic lights anywhere in this city. Anywhere in this country. I can stop an elevator in progress. Think, Yuri, think of the possibilities. If it became necessary, I could take over a plane in flight or launch a Predator drone strike."

"But how would you do that? There is no physical connection to a plane in the air."

"I can travel through wireless transmissions. You live in an electronically connected society but can only move from point to point physically. How far can you travel in your world and how fast? I can move much further and much faster in my world. I move as fast as an electron. I have no physical body to slow me down, and the electronic world that you and your species have created gives me almost total freedom of movement. There is barely a square meter of your planet that is not bombarded either by an electrical power grid or radio waves. Imagine for yourself what I can do."

We're all going to die, thought Yuri.

18

It was almost noon when the Instructor slowly woke up.

"Oh, my head," he groaned.

For a second, he was confused and then the stark realization of where he was and what he had been through the night before sank in. He was in a seated position, holding his head so it didn't just fly away. Slowly, he got to his feet. He looked around at the chaos around him. The Ukrainian had been a good choice. The Frenchman and the Englishman were good bait calls, but that Ukrainian, he was an exceptionally good choice. It was too bad that he had to die, but that was the breaks.

And the husband and wife team of werewolves, now there was a pair. The Instructor went painfully over to them, picking up his rifle on the way. He looked them over. Man, that was some fine shooting by the Ukrainian, the Instructor had to admit—clean through the heart with a mercury filled silver bullet. He looked down at the Ukrainian's body and shook his head.

"*Do pobachennya,*" said the Instructor, "or something like that."

He debated cleaning the place up, but decided to let whoever found it try to figure that out. There wasn't time to screw around with straightening things up, he had to get out of here. Let them make whatever they could out of this mess whenever they found it. He had to boogie.

The Instructor was getting ready to leave when he stopped. He had a nagging feeling that something was wrong. Looking at his hand, he was surprised to find it completely healed.

"Uh-oh," he said. "Well I'll be damned."

A sickening feeling came over him. He knew what that meant, knew it only too well. That hand was bitten last night, he was sure of it. But now it was healed, and that wasn't a good sign. That meant that the son of a bitchin female must have bitten him during the fight. She sunk her teeth in just for a minute, and that was all it took. A werewolf had bitten him, and now he was one of them. That changed everything.

Shit.

What in the hell should he do now?

One thing was for sure, he had one day left in the full moon cycle, if the legends were to be believed. And on that night, he would be a werewolf. He would need some sort of a... his eyes fell on the cage where the last werewolf had died. Yes, he would have to restrain himself for the night. He fumbled for the keys and unlocked the cage. Out went the body of the woman; he unceremoniously dumped her in the snow and locked the cage again. Throwing his rifle on his back, he proceeded to yank on the much larger cage to tip it over. He got it on its side, and with on last silent look around, began to pull the cage behind him.

Pull, stop. Pull, stop. Damn, this was hard work.

He'd gone maybe fifty feet when he stopped. The cage was too damn big to fit in the SUV. Eight feet tall when fully assembled my ass. This was impossible to lug around except in the bed of the big pickup truck, and that was thirty miles away. The smaller cage. Duh, he should have taken the smaller cage, the one he had hidden in. Man, he was losing it.

He left the larger cage where it was and trundled back to the site, past the bodies until he came even with the smaller cage. Man, had this one been knocked about. Still, this was more like it. The smaller cage was only six feet tall instead of eight and covered with titanium mesh inside the bars. Yeah, this would do. He began to tug it free of the brush, and, when he had accomplished that, he began the long process of pulling it back through the trees and over the hills toward the SUV.

Stopping twice to catch his breath, he noticed something for the first time. He was not panting. His joints didn't hurt the way that they used to. In fact, nothing hurt the way that it used to.

"Well, I'll be damned."

He was not too far from the SUV now, so he went back to dragging the cage with a new perspective on it—something to think about. No need to panic yet, no need to get all cranked up about it. So, he'd have to disappear for three nights out of the month. That's how long a full moon generally lasted, right? His wife wouldn't get suspicious, she was used to him being gone unaccountably. Of course, this was his seventh wife and she was probably, realistically just hanging around for the money, but still.

Could he get used to this new life? Well, hell yes. There wasn't a cure for it, so he might as well.

The Instructor came to the SUV and loaded the cage into the back. He swung his rifle off his back and got in, placing the rifle on the seat next to him. When he had the keys out of his pocket, he started the car. Where would he go? Hauck wasn't expecting him for another week or two or four, so he was okay there. But Hauck was sure to sense a problem. That much was a surety.

He put the car into four-wheel drive and sped off as fast as he dared, leaving that mess behind him. Best to think while in motion. As he drove onto the road, and headed north, he tried to think.

So, what if Hauck divined the nature of the problem? Look at Drogol. If they hadn't been hunting him in the first place, he would have survived just fine, thank you very much. Yeah, if he'd just been left alone everything would have gone on just peachy keen. He'd lived one hundred fifty to two hundred years and in that time hadn't aged a day. Think about what that meant?

At his current age of eighty-four, he was a bit old for this kind of work, and if Hauck hadn't asked him, he wouldn't have joined the hunt for Drogol. He didn't need the money, that much was for certain. And now, by agreeing to help Hauck find his son, he had gotten himself bitten by a werewolf.

The traffic was light, and he mindlessly drove along. What would Hauck think? That was what occupied his mind. The Instructor didn't see what the big deal was. So, you had to be locked up for three or four days during the full moon. Big deal. He could take that. He would turn into a slavering maniac for that time, but so what? And there were all the health benefits that Drogol droned on about—now that was pretty cool.

But how would the rest of the team take it?

Well, fuck 'em if they couldn't take a joke.

The Instructor grinned and pressed the accelerator down just a wee bit harder. Yeah, best if he stayed away from Hauck for a while. Better if he just disappeared.

19

Sanzar," called Professor Meridian, "please bring chairs for our guests."

Sveta felt Hauck's tension. She had never seen him so stiff, so wired with repressed nervous energy. The thumb and forefinger of his right hand rubbed together like he was trying to wear off his fingerprints. He was making her nervous

"We're quite comfortable standing," said Hauck.

"Nonsense. You are my guests. I am so pleased that you came. I hope that you enjoyed both the dinner and my little talk."

The man named Sanzar came carrying two large chairs as though they weighed nothing at all and arranged them in front of Meridian's table and returned to the door. Sveta sized him up as he walked away. He was no taller than five foot six, but broad at the shoulders and packed with muscle beneath his suit. But he didn't move like a weightlifter. He was fluid and walked so quietly that she couldn't hear his steps. She'd caught a glimpse of his face, and it was his eyes that disturbed her. They had the blank stare of a person who followed orders, as though Sanzar had no feelings to call his own.

"It was an incredible presentation," said Sveta. "I can't wait to read your book."

"I see, Mr. Vogel," said Meridian, "that you have brought me a woman not only of great beauty, but one with a refined sense of taste as well."

She sat, and Hauck did as well, almost reluctantly.

"She is all that and more," he said. "But you have a coin, I believe, that you would like me to examine. May I look at it and ask what you know of its provenance?"

"Of course. Are you pressed for time?"

"No," put in Sveta before Hauck could reply

"Then may I ask your name, my dear? I know of Mr. Vogel by reputation, but I fear he has forgotten to share your name with me."

Professor Meridian seemed slightly amused by Hauck's reticence.

"Eric is a jealous employer. My name is Svetlana Orlova. No relation, to the great Russian actress Luybova Orlova, I'm afraid. I am Mr. Vogel's research assistant."

The professor arched an eyebrow in quizzical surprise.

"And what, my dear Svetalana, do you research for Mr. Vogel?"

"What he asks me to, of course," said Sveta.

"I could not function without her," said Hauck.

"Indeed? How interesting. But now it is time to put you both to the test. Sanzar, please bring me the coin. Abarran, bolt the door."

Sveta expected the move. Hauck seemed nonplussed. In his cover identity, this was probably normal. When things of value were being evaluated, it was logical to do it in a secure room. But it felt like a trap, and the way Hauck was acting, she would treat it like a trap.

She had never seen Hauck so passive as tonight. To leave Yuri alone with the strange computer intruder. To meet with a person he did not know, in settings they had not checked and to not bring a weapon. Either something was distracting Hauck, skewering his priorities or he knew something he was keeping from her. But she wasn't taking chances. She still had the second pistol.

Without so much as a glance at either Hauck or Sveta, Sanzar took a deep purple velvet pouch from inside his coat and lay on the table in front of Meridian. In the process, Sveta caught a glimpse of the man's shoulder holster. Since Sanzar was carrying a weapon, she assumed that Abarran was, too. Not good odds. If trouble started, she'd have to take out the two guards and leave Professor Meridian to Hauck.

"Thank you, Sanzar."

After a quick, curt bow, Sanzar returned to his post by the door with the other guard Abarran. Sveta tried as best she could to follow the sound of his footsteps, but there was really nothing to follow. Either he has some seriously good shoes, she thought, or he's a ghost.

"You may well wonder why I need such careful validation of this coin's provenance, Mr. Vogel."

As he spoke, the professor opened the velvet pouch and carefully tilted it downward to allow a single ornate gold coin to slide out onto his left hand.

"I never question my client's motives, professor. It could be considered bad breeding."

The professor smiled perfunctorily.

"I have not heard that phrasing for a good many years," he said. "How rare it is to hear the concept of animal husbandry and good manners blended together in an admonition. However, it is one thing to inquire, and quite another to query, do you not agree?"

"Certainly," said Hauck.

The introductory chatter irritated Sveta. Her prime aim was to identify the locations of Sanzar and Abarran without turning around. The conversation made that almost impossible.

"Then allow me to explain to you my considerations without you having to ask. There is a man I hope to apprehend, Mr. Vogel. He has knowledge that I need regarding certain of Drogol's activities."

"I don't understand how I can help in that regard."

"Patience, Mr. Vogel. You see, my investigations into the loup Garou revealed that Drogol had a second laboratory he used for his research. Finding the location of that place is critical to my plans. This man I seek, according to an informant whose word I trust, knows the location of that laboratory. This coin is, I believe, is the key to locating that man."

Professor Meridian leaned forward, extending the coin toward Hauck, tilting it this way and that to catch the table lamp's light and transform it into golden radiance. His one good eye flashed like a watchful cat's in the reflected glow.

Sveta felt the moment was on them. With Hauck's attention on the gold piece, they were vulnerable. It was a distraction, she thought, like a magician's scarves. Beneath the coat folded on her lap, her fingers wrapped around the pistol grip.

"An interesting piece," said Hauck. "May I see it?"

He removed his royal blue silk handkerchief, opened it, and spread it on the table.

Professor Meridian smiled faintly, as though pleased with a possibly precocious student. He placed the coin on the handkerchief and leaned back.

"You see, Mr. Vogel, this man I seek is quite difficult to find."

Hauck withdrew a slender pewter case from inside his jacket and removed from it a thin handled magnifying glass.

"May I adjust that light?" he asked, pointing at the desk lamp.

With the professor's assent, he angled it slightly. Then, from the case, he extracted a pair of felt-tipped tweezers that he used to move the coin about beneath the lamp.

"Extraordinary," he murmured.

Suddenly intrigued by his tone, Sveta asked, "What is it?"

"I am attempting to concentrate," said Hauck irritably.

She was about to snap back at him when she remembered she was supposed to be his faithful research assistant.

"And how will this fascinating gold piece help you find the man you seek?" asked Hauck without looking up.

"Yes, that is to the point," said Professor Meridian. "This man is said to have a special fondness for Russian gold pieces from this period. It is his one weakness. Outside of a certain Russian politician, this man I seek is said to have the largest collection of such rare gold coinage in the world."

Hauck looked up at the professor skeptically.

"That may be true, my dear sir, but unless I am mistaken, this is a Nicholas the First 1839 proof. There are only three such coins I know of sold in the last one hundred and twenty years."

"I have chosen my bait well then; would you not agree?"

Hauck sniffed like an annoyed nobleman.

"If I validate this coin— and I stress the word if— it will most definitely attract a man with such a collection. But, really, professor, this man must be obsessively secretive if he is unknown to me, because I know everyone of import in this arena and I have never heard of anyone having such a collection."

"And yet," said the professor, "you were unaware of this coin."

"What is the man's name?" asked Sveta.

She genuinely wanted to know. Whoever Professor Meridian was trying to locate, he seemed like someone Sveta and Hauck needed to locate first.

"He is known only as Hauck."

"What an unfortunate name," said Sveta.

"Quite," said the professor, "and I rather doubt that it is his real name. Which is why after you have validated this piece, I would you like to post a notice of its availability for the right price. When you post it on your private website, Mr. Vogel, my quarry will soon hear about it and you will be contacted by either him or one of his agents."

"I don't deal through agents. I deal with principals only."

"In this case," said Professor Meridian, "you will make an exception and be very well compensated for it."

In the pained silence that followed Meridian's last instruction, Sveta could almost imagine that Hauck was who he was pretending to be. She was trained in the art of impersonation, but she had long ago learned that it was more of a talent than her trainers would have liked her to believe. Hauck had the gift.

"We have not discussed my fee," said Hauck at last.

"There is no need," said the professor. "You will charge your professional rate and I will pay it."

"I will require time to properly examine this piece."

"Take it with you," said the professor.

"Not without the proper paperwork signed showing I have your permission," said Hauck.

"You will take the coin based on my word or Sanzar and Abarran will interpret your decision as a slight on my honor. You do not wish to learn how difficult their response can be to those who offend me."

Hauck appeared to be taken aback, as indeed Eric Vogel would have been. Sveta did her best to be impressed with the professor's forcefulness. He lifted his chin, as though posing for a photo.

"I have no wish to offend," said Hauck. "With most clients, they expect me to follow certain procedures. However, with an esteemed client such as yourself, I will of course defer to your wishes."

"A wise choice, Mr. Vogel. Might I suggest that you and your lovely associate join me for dinner at my home in three nights time. Say at ten?"

From a silver case, the professor produced a business card and handed it to Hauck.

As he and Sveta rose, Professor Meridian held up a finger.

"As I'm sure you understand, my affairs are extremely confidential. Mr. Sanzar deals with any and all contractual misunderstandings or violations personally. He is very strict in these matters and settles them with irrevocable finality, if I make myself clear."

"Quite," said Hauck.

"Irrevocable finality," repeated the professor.

Behind them, Sveta hear the door bolt slide back with a soft click.

20

Detroit was a ghostly dark grayness with cold and grim streets.

They traveled the first three blocks in chilled silence. Occasional pedestrians leaned into the stiff wind with their heads bent down, gloved hands bunching their collars to stop the shivers. Their shadows were smudged chalk ghosts.

"Are we clear?" Hauck asked as they turned off Griswold Street and onto Fort.

Sveta checked the camera feeds on the on-board computer. The screen was quartered so she could watch all four of the external video cameras at the same time.

"Clear," she said.

From inside the center armrest, Hauck took out a secure phone and started punching in numbers.

"What the hell just happened in there?" asked Sveta.

"Not now."

"Yes, now. You seemed to know Meridian. Am I right?"

"I have to make this call," said Hauck.

He held the phone to his ear, listened, punched in more numbers then repeated the process. Eyes straight ahead, looking for cars idling by the curb, ready to swing in behind them.

Sveta leaned her head near his to catch his attention.

"I'm tired of being kept in the dark, Hauck."

"Sveta, not now. This is urgent. Our lives depend on it."

"Hauck, what is going on?"

The timing saved him. The Instructor's wife came on the other end of the line.

"This is the Magician," he said. "I need to speak to him."

All communications with the Instructor went through this woman. She was his digital phantom. One never knew exactly where she was.

"Call back later, he's not here now," she in a voice so French-Canadian that if he hadn't lived in Montreal for two years, he couldn't have understood her.

"This is urgent," Hauck said.

Without turning his head, he still felt Sveta staring at him, getting angrier by the second.

"Monsieur, it might well be life threatening, but he is visiting the bears. Bears have no phones."

Even the sound of her voice irritated him. It was like listening to the sound of old-time facsimile machines connecting.

"It is urgent, I tell you. When will he return?"

"When he wishes, my impatient friend. In the bush, time passes as it passes. Have you a message for him when he returns?"

"I must relay this to him in person."

"Maybe yes, maybe no. When he comes home, I need him, too. He is retired, or don't you recall?"

"Madame, this is deadly serious."

"I'm hanging up now."

"Wait."

"For what?"

"Tell him… tell him it concerns his Uncle."

"His uncle is dead."

"Tell him it concerns the third pillar of night."

Silence for a moment.

"Very well."

The line went dead.

"I hate that woman," said Hauck as he clicked off and dialed another number.

He glanced over at Sveta and saw her glaring at him. Nothing he could tell her yet. No time. First, he had to talk to Yuri. The third ring passed, and Hauck grew concerned. Yuri never took longer than two rings to answer. Four rings and Yuri came on. Hauck switched to the SUV's speakerphone system so he Sveta could hear.

"What took you so long? Never mind. What's the status of the intruder? What have you learned?"

"It's unbelievable, Hauck."

"Can you eliminate it? If you can't eliminate it, can you contain it?"

"No."

"Damn it, Yuri, why not?"

"That wasn't me, Hauck."

Hauck's fingers involuntarily tightened on the wheel.

"Who else is on this line?"

"It's him," said Yuri.

"It is I," said the voice.

"Who are you?" demanded Sveta.

"It's Adam," said Yuri. "The ghost in your machine."

****

Hauck felt Sveta's hand on his arm.

"Behind us," she said. "Flashers coming up behind us fast."

A quick glance at the dashboard screen confirmed at least two sets of flashers speeding toward them. Red, white and blue and they blinked like club lights. A third one. Three police cars.

"Yuri," said Hauck. "We've got police coming up on us quickly. What's the story? What's the chatter?"

"On it," said Yuri.

"Hauck?"

It was the thing.

"Not now."

"They are not coming for you," said the voice.

"He's right," said Yuri. "They're headed for a gunfight on Eight Mile and Woodward. Pull over and get out of their way."

Hauck put on his blinkers, slowed down and did as Yuri said.

"Weapons in the console," said Hauck.

"Got it," said Sveta.

She popped the console lid, slid her hardware into the opening and closed it again. A quick series of touches on the dashboard screen, a hiss of compressed air and the screen read "Re-routed assets."

"Done."

A burst of flashing LED lights, painful siren squeals and a rush of air as police vehicles came enough that Hauck leaned away toward Sveta in anticipation of being sideswiped. When they were half a block away, he straightened up and let out his breath.

"Hauck?" said the voice.

"I need to speak with Yuri," he said.

"You have a tracking device in your vehicle."

"Sveta, bring up some firepower again."

He pulled out onto the street again and eased forward.

She opened the console again, tapped the touch pad and in less than a minute later had her pistol back.

"Adam may mean your GPS," said Yuri.

"No," said the voice. "It is not the vehicle's GPS system."

"Impossible," said Hauck. "The computer system would have shown the breach if someone broke into our car to implant a GPS tracking device. And it would be easier to plant under the vehicle. And, Yuri how is it that our artificial friend can talk to me on my encrypted satellite cell phone?"

"Too complicated to explain. And I'd believe him about the tracking device."

"Yuri," said Hauck, "there is no way this vehicle was broken into."

"We brought it back with us," said Sveta.

"What did you say?"

"I think it's in your pocket."

Without waiting for an answer, she slid her hand into his inside jacket pocket and withdrew the velvet pouch the professor had given him.

"The coin in that bag is worth a small fortune," said Hauck.

Sveta pressed the window button, and when the glass slid down a few inches, she flashed a bright smile at him and threw the bag out the window. Hauck slammed on the brakes.

"You are free of the transmitting transponder," said the voice.

They were stopped in the middle of the street. No cars close enough to hit them. Sveta staring at him defiantly. Hauck's anger building.

"Leave it," said Sveta.

"I have to think this through."

Sveta twisted in her seat to look back where she had thrown the bag. A man emerged from the dark shadows of an abandoned building. He was moving toward the street, heading toward the pouch.

****

Sveta glanced at the dashboard screen again.

"Traffic coming our way again. Put your foot on the gas or we're going to be the wrong end of an accident."

"Everything all right?" asked Yuri.

"We're good now," said Sveta.

"No," said Hauck. "We have a problem, Yuri."

"Tell me."

"Sveta was right the first time. We're going to have to close down our operation and burn it behind us. No trace. No evidence. We need to disappear in this country. Crossing the border to leave would be a mistake. We're on the way back now to get some sleep and wait to hear from the Instructor. When he gets here, we'll follow his instructions and then close up shop. Our situation is completely out of control."

"Got it," said Yuri.

"I don't," said Sveta.

"What don't you get?" asked Hauck.

"Why we have to wait for the Instructor."

"I'll let him explain."

"And what about Sasha? You said you think Professor Meridian knows where he is, or that maybe he's hiding him. Don't you think we should try to find out?"

They were on the Lodge freeway now, Hauck following an evasive diagram known only to him to avoid being followed. Impatient anger boiling up inside him. Why was she always challenging his judgment? There was no time for talk.

"No, Sveta. If Professor Meridian has Sasha, then Sasha is already worse than dead."

"How do you know that? Who is this man?"

"I never met him before tonight."

"Bullshit. Who is he?"

Hauck would not look at her. He kept his eyes on the road as though if he turned away, they would drive off into a dark abyss.

"Ask the Instructor when he gets here."

"Why? Why does everything have to wait until the Instructor gets here?"

Hauck felt his temples tighten.

"Because Meridian is supposed to be dead."

"And we went into that meeting with no backup?"

Moments passed before Hauck answered.

"Sveta, I had four agents in the building and four outside."

"And you didn't even tell me when I asked about it?" shouted Sveta.

"Don't shoot him while he's driving," said Yuri's voice from the speaker.

21

Professor Meridian took off his coat, got a few things and walked down the worn stone steps that led to the secret levels beneath his house. The air was thin and dry and smelled like mildewed cardboard. Pale yellow lights mounted like torches lit his way, but he scarcely needed their guidance. Professor Krikor Meridian welcomed darkness.

Sanzar and Abarran followed him silently, their shoulders nearly touching the walls. Abarran carried a large leather-bound book in front of him, his thick arms crossed over it to keep it from falling. The professor did not need to hear his two servants' soft tread; he could feel them behind him. They were always with him, ready to do his bidding, willing to give their lives for him.

The passageway ended and opened into a wide space, the size of a small train station. Stone floor and rock walls gave it the feel of an abandoned prison. And it was, of a sort. Decades before, an enforcer for the mob had it built to contain his prized collection of Siberian tigers and other wild beasts. Steel bars gated alcoves set into the wall to the right. Chains were bolted onto six-inch square plates inside each, but the big cats were long gone. The professor had other uses for these pens.

Along the left wall were inset thirteen iron doors, and on each of these a sliding metal plates was mounted at shoulder height. Below each was a slot used to slide in trays of food. The professor walked to the seventh of these doors and stopped three feet from it.

Sanzar inserted a large key, twisted it in the lock, and then pulled it open. He stepped back as Meridian came forward, and stood before a row of bars, looking into what appeared to be a well-furnished apartment. On a short sofa on the far wall, sat a young man watching television.

"Turn it off, Sasha" said the Professor. "It is now time that we have the talk I promised you when I first took you in."

The young man leapt to his feet and ran to the bars, thrusting his hands through to grab the professor's neck. Meridian stepped back and the prisoner's hands grabbed at empty air. The professor gave a nod to Sanzar who grasped one of the young man's hands and twisted it to one side, causing the prisoner to scream.

"Discipline," said the professor, "will prevent Sanzar or Abarran from having to harm you. Although I do not wish to see my servant break your wrist, I will have him do that and worse if you cannot control yourself. You are a guest in my house, but I do not tolerate bad behavior, even from someone I have taken in."

Tears were flowing down Sasha's contorted face. His cheeks flushed red and his eyes seemed to bulge.

"You, you keep me in this cage like a dog."

"I ask you again," said the professor. "Can you control yourself, or must Sanzar snap your wrist?"

Sasha shook his head up and down so violently he banged his forehead on the bars. The professor considered the situation for a moment, and then nodded at Sanzar who immediately released the young man's wrist and stepped back.

For a moment, he considered his captive, wondering again that the violent were so weak in their petulant assumptive arrogance. Sasha's eyes were large, but his lashes too long. His rich, dark hair hung nearly to his shoulders and was as full of tangles and as undisciplined as his mind. He was tall, with a narrow waist and broad shoulders. He wore faded jeans and a denim shirt open too wide, as though he were a rock star preparing for a television interview instead of a man locked away two stories underground in a concrete and rock prison.

"You miss the power, don't you Sasha? You crave the power. Once, you were Red Mafiya, second only to your mother in your organization. Your underlings feared and respected you. You dealt punishment and even death to the disobedient or those you thought too weak. You had wealth and women. You went where you wanted, ate and drank what you wanted. Now, you eat what Sanzar or Abarran offer you and go nowhere beyond these iron bars. You have no underlings. You have only yourself and you are a helpless prisoner. Yes, I think you very much miss the power."

Sasha sank bank on the sofa and nursed his wrist.

"I could close this door, turn the key in its lock, walk away and never come back. No one would ever know your fate, much less care what had happened to you."

Eyes full of hate, Sasha stood up and spit.

Meridian smiled a tense smile.

"Shall I have Abarran cut out your tongue and eat it, or would you like me to come in and tell you how to regain both your lost power and your freedom?"

His words echoed softly through the underground prison, as though repeated furtively from one spirit to another.

****

Sasha's mind was on fire. Months and months of living in a cage. Imprisoned by this man he thought was a friend. He'd come to him bloodied and exhausted. Deranged with fear. Hunted. His mind full of images of death and terror. Blood on his hands. Brought to America in a cage by his mother and now this. From one cage to another with only a night of madness and escape in between.

"Do you have to bolt me to my own chair?" he said.

"It is, in fact, my chair," said the Professor.

Sanzar and Abarran had brought in a hardwood chair equipped with wrist and ankle manacles. A twisted metal cable was looped around his waist, then through a steel eyelet bolted to the chair's back. Another looped around his neck and was attached to the same metal plate. Professor Meridian sat across from him in a comfortable armchair, a large leather book in his lap. Gilded gold lettering flowed across the cover, written in a language Sasha could not understand.

"Are you so afraid of me?"

"It is for your own safety," said Meridian. "You will soon play an important part in my plans, and perhaps in the future of the world itself. When you came to me you were delusional, Sasha. You had nowhere to go and no one you could trust. You came to me because Mishka had given you my name before you came to this country. He trusted me, he knew who I was and because you were his friend, I took you in and protected you."

The cable across his neck tightened hard against his Adam's apple when he leaned forward to shout. He gagged and coughed, and, for a moment, he saw tiny pinpoints of light before his eyes.

"You see? You still cannot control yourself. You try so hard to shout that you choke yourself. You yet have no discipline."

Sasha quit coughing abruptly. He hated Meridian so much that each and every night since the day he'd been taken captive he'd dreamed of choking him to death. Dreamed about the man's face turning blue, his eyes bulging out of his head. Dreamed of him gasping for air, but not being able to draw even one single breath up to the moment he died.

Sanzar and Abarran stood one on either side of him, looking at Sasha. Even without the restraints, there was nothing he could do. He had seen how fast these terrible servants moved. He had felt their incredible strength. They were the most frightening men he had ever encountered. His mother had told him about men like these from her time in the gulags. Sasha shuddered at the memory.

"Excellent, you are quiet again," said Meridian. "Now you must think before you speak. Do you recognize this?"

From inside his jacket, the professor withdrew a dagger sheathed in an opalescent casing. With an oddly detached reverence, he slowly slid the weapon free. His eyes stayed fixed on Sasha's. This man, he thought, was both completely evil and completely insane. He feared him as much if not more than his dead mother.

"It looks like the knife that belonged to Ivan," he said finally. "His sacred khylsty dagger. I hope someone slit his throat with it and he bled to death very slowly."

"Ah, the Russian taste for extravagant vengeance. This is indeed Ivan's knife. A drug addict pawned it. The pawn shop owner made inquiries concerning his new acquisition, hoping to find a rich buyer for such an exquisite artifact. We... relieved him of it. I see you appreciate its beauty, Sasha. Would you like it? Would you like to slit my throat with it?"

Sasha swallowed hard.

"You keep me here like a criminal."

"But you are a criminal, Sasha. You were born the only son of Anna Kazakova, the Red Mafiya Queen. But she is now dead, and much of her American organization is also dead, along with your friend Mishka, thanks to the man you call Hauck. She came hunting Drogol, the King werewolf— your very own father, Sasha. She died before she could capture him and use his blood to cure her disease. You indeed were born of crime. You are a child of chaos."

"Why do you tell this to me? I know my family's history."

"Because Ivan disappeared and must certainly be dead. Ivan was my disciple. How do you think I know so much about your family and your life? He was your mothers Sovietnik—her advisor in matters of this life and the next."

"If my mother ever found out that he was working for you, he would have died much younger."

Meridian wagged a finger.

"He did not work for me. He was discipled to me. I am the Priest of the Dhole. I am the only man who may open this book—the very Book of the Dhole—and live. You do not believe me? I can have Sanzar and Abarran untie your hands and you may open it for yourself. But believe me when I tell you that you will not last even a moment beyond that. It will consume you. But if my servants unbind you and you do not have the courage to open this volume, then I will personally cut your throat with this khylsty dagger and drain your blood onto its pages."

Hatred boiled in Sasha's gut, yet he had been shut in his cell for months without seeing anyone except Sanzar and Abarran. One part of him craved attention from someone who actually spoke to him, even if he was a madman. Neither Sanzar nor Abarran ever spoke.

Like flesh-covered robots, they saw to his needs. They fed him, forced him to exercise, provided him with changes of clothing, toiletry supplies and beat him when he tried to escape. Meridian came only once or twice in the beginning to check on him, to appraise him with the cold, analytical stare a mortician afforded a soon to be corpse. Except for those few hours, he had been left in the care of the two mutes.

And now an impossible challenge from the madman who kept him captive.

"What is this Dhole? Why would a khylsty like Ivan follow you?"

A pause, with Meridian staring hard at him, considering him carefully before continuing.

"We," Meridian waved his hand at Sanzar and Abarran, "and thousands of others, are worshippers of an ancient god named the Dhole. He is unknown to most in this world. But he has vast powers, and can not only grant power to us, but open the mystery of the Djinn to me by illuminating my sight through the Eye of Dagon. Ivan wanted to share in the power the Dhole would give me."

Bewildered, Sasha looked up from Sanzar to Abarran to see if they knew their master was totally fucking insane. In their faces, he saw no reaction—no reaction at all.

"Soon, when the alignment of galaxies is mathematically correct, then the Dhole will wake from its slumber and breed nightmares which will come forth to inflict chaos and destruction on the world. Its awakenings have progressed over millions of years in evolving cycles. This evolutionary unfolding will peak in five days, my young werewolf, when the Dhole will be roused to a semi-dream state. But, according to prophecy, at that time, a man will attempt to destroy the Dhole. It is so written in this book."

"I thought you said the Dhole was a god. What fool would try to kill a god, even one that exists only in your mind and that of your followers."

Professor Meridian's good eye lit with a warning fire.

"Be careful, Sasha. The Dhole is a living creature, even if trapped underground for millions of years. To save itself from the destruction caused by an asteroid impacting the earth, it went into a hibernative state. Epochs passed and the seas that covered Michigan receded and buried the land where we stand in trillions of tons of salt. The man I of spoke is at this moment drilling down through that salt to kill the Dhole. I cannot tell you why or even how he knew of its existence. And before you ask, I do not wish to stop him. Not at all. His attempt to kill the Dhole will instead raise it to full waking consciousness."

"You're serious about all this?" said Sasha with a sneer. "You are bat-shit Bolshoi fucking crazy, do you know that?"

After a moment's thought, Meridian rose and walked to the door of Sasha's cell. He turned and faced him, studying him. Finally, he spoke.

"In three nights, the moon will again be full, and you will again become a monster. Together, you and I can stop these hideous transformations when you are ready to believe and obey me."

"You're out of your fucking mind, and if I ever get my hands on you without these two assholes of yours around, I'm going to break your fucking neck."

With a solemn motion, Professor Meridian opened the Book of the Dhole, ignoring Sasha entirely for the moment. He held it angled up toward his single good eye.

"The Book of the Dhole tells the future," he said. "But it must be fed with blood. Tonight, I found and met with the man who hunts you, the man Ivan and your mother referred to as Hauck. I have it on excellent authority that he desires to kill you, too, by cutting off your head— or did you not already know that? Silver bullets aside, it is considered a successful cure.

"Your mother hunted Hauck and your father. Then, she joined forces with Hauck, and they hunted your father together until Hauck betrayed her. Now Hauck hunts you. Shall this drama continue forever? No. I will put an end to it. As a show of good faith to you, I will lure Hauck here. And, if you become my disciple, you and I will pour his fresh blood onto the pages of this book together. The words will come alive again and reveal what must be done to protect the Dhole. We have always performed this ritual to ensure our destiny. Always will we do so."

"You met Hauck but didn't kill him? You're crazy. Now he knows your face. He'll hunt you down and kill your ass. He was KGB."

"In the meantime," said Meridian gravely, "Sanzar and Abarran will go out and find more young girls to bring you. A growing werewolf needs to eat."

Sasha's screams split the air like an out of control train rocketing through the underground prison right up to the moment when Sanzar and Abarran closed and locked the door to his soundproof cell.

22

"I'm being followed," said Kirk. "I need you to take something to someone for me without anybody knowing it was from me. You got to help me, Charlene."

He was breathing hard. Out of shape as always. Served him right climbing up her fire escape at two in the morning. He stood near the window, silhouetted in the night light's soft glow like a mugger in a dimly lit alley.

"You can't keep breaking into my place," said Charlene. "You scared me half to death."

"Sorry."

"I get a boyfriend someday and you might seriously get shot. You ever think of that? And where'd you get that raggedy-ass jacket?"

"In a dumpster," said Kirk.

One arm held a typing paper-sized box to his chest. The other held the bottom of his coat tight over his stomach like he was about to throw up.

"You're wearing something from a dumpster?"

With his silvered sunglasses and leather hat, he looked like a park ranger on dope when he nodded his agreement. He was the only man she knew with eyes so sensitive he wore sunglasses at night. And she wasn't sure how Kirk managed a coherent thought, but he seemed to know when to nod even when sloshed.

"You like it?"

Quarter inch of stubble on him looked like fuzz on a turkey's neck in the dim light.

"Go in the other room while I get dressed," she said.

"I thought I was in the other room."

"Go," she said.

Blankets clutched tightly in front of her breasts, she pointed toward the living room.

"You got beer?"

"Kirk, get out and close the door behind you so I can get dressed," she repeated.

"Keep the lights off, okay?"

"Go," she said.

****

"How much trouble are you in this time?"

Charlene almost reached for the light switch as she entered the room, and then remembered what he'd said.

"A lot," he said, and coughed like he had fluid in his lungs.

"Don't throw up. Please."

She saw him nod in the moonlight coming in through the windowpane over the sink. His head lolled to one side. The box was on the table.

"I'm not feeling so good."

"So, what's in the box? And don't take that like I'm saying yes. I can't take the law on me now. With my record, I'll go down for good."

She leaned against the kitchen sink.

It took him a while to respond.

"Research. It's got to go to Dr. Harlen. The salt mine guy. He asked me to dig into some stuff about the mine for him a few years back before he bought the place. I owed his dad real big time."

The words came out painfully. He had migraines, she knew, and he drank like a fish.

"You need a pain pill?"

"Won't do any good."

"You took years to dig up the stuff in that one box?"

He coughed. It sounded like a liquid backfire. Put one up to cover his mouth and kept the other pressed to his stomach.

"You sound as bad as you look, Kirk. You want a paper towel to wipe your mouth?"

"Don't give it to anybody but him. Somebody in the government doesn't like what I been digging in to."

"Oh, man, I don't need this."

"It's important. Pretty bad."

"Kirk, don't you ever learn? They busted your nuts once for messing in their stuff. You were up top, man. Riding high in that newspaper gig til you stuck your nose in their business. Luckily, they didn't cap your ass instead of ruining your life."

He took off his sunglasses and dropped them on the table.

"He's in trouble."

"Who?"

"Dr. Harlen. You got to give it to him, just him. They're after him."

"Don't go all paranoid on me. You're freaking me out. Vietnam was a long time ago."

She got him a wad of paper towels and handed it to him. For a moment he just stared at it and then started mopping his forehead.

"They showed up at my place. Broke in. I went out through a window and got hurt."

"What?"

Fear grabbed at her, tightened her throat.

"They were screaming like bastards. I got them with the rolled-up razor-wire inside the doors and under the windows."

He started coughing. Kept coughing.

"You need something?"

"No."

"I'm getting some cold water from the fridge."

She opened the fridge door and the room filled with sudden soft light. Inside, she saw the distilled water bottle next to a half-eaten big Mac she'd had for dinner. Behind her, she heard a soft thud and turned to see Kirk's head had fallen forward onto the box.

"You asshole," she said. "You have to quit drinking. I'm serious."

But because of the refrigerator light, she was able to see dark smears on the floor. Her breath caught. Not good. Please don't be blood.

She propped a jar of mayonnaise in the door hinge to hold it open, got down on her knees, crawled forward and looked. Dabbed her finger in the smear and crawled back to the refrigerator. In its light, she saw the color. Held it to her nose and smelled.

"Fuck."

She put the jar back into the fridge back on a cold wire shelf and closed the door.

No lights, she thought. The words were like a gun pressed against her head.

From the counter, she found a bottle of dish detergent, squeezed some on her hands, rubbed it around and then turned on the water in the sink. She rubbed and rubbed and rubbed thinking that she was so screwed. Then she turned off the water, walked over to the other side of the table where Kirk sat, taking care not to step in where she thought the dark smears were.

"Kirk?"

She put one hand on his shoulder and shook him.

"Don't be dead on me, man."

She pulled him back, watching his head drop to one side like he didn't have neck bones. Fingers on the side of the throat, but she couldn't feel a pulse. Felt the sudden wetness in the corners of her eyes.

"Don't do this, Kirk. I can't handle this. Don't be dead, old man."

But he was.

****

Two-thirty-five a.m.

Nobody breaking down her door.

A couple of covert peeks out her bedroom window — now closed and locked— and she was sure as she could be it would be the safe way out.

She was always ready for a quick way. Half-way packed all the time. Never knowing when the door might be kicked in. But she was always careful, very careful. Except she'd left the window open enough and Kirk had pried his way in. He knew about the window. She told him she couldn't sleep unless it was a crack open. Needed it in case she had to get out quick. It was stupid, but there it was. Couldn't sleep without it being open an inch or two.

There was nothing to be done with Kirk's body.

She'd closed his eyes. That was it. Tried to pretend he wasn't there every time she loaded the stuff into the duffel bag, she'd hiked up onto the kitchen counter. She had her camping jacket on. Six pockets in front, two on each should and four inside. Able to hide a family of four in one all-weather coat.

TASER X26c in her left side pocket. Long distance maximum strength pepper spray in right side pocket. Wished she had a pistol, but knew when you go down with a pistol, you go down harder. She couldn't outshoot anyone anyway. Didn't like guns. Didn't like violence but didn't like dead either. Like Kirk. Poor, poor Kirk. She'd checked his coat with her keychain flashlight. Saw what looked like a bullet hole where he'd been holding his hand against his stomach. What the hell was in that box worth shooting an old man for?

Last thing to pack was her laptop and electronic gear. She'd had some bills stuck in her inside coat pocket. Untraceable cards in her belt wallet. Fake cards and ID in her throwaway wallet. Running shoes on, ready to run.

She looked around her place. Nothing personal, nothing that made it home any more than any of the other temporary places she lived. Her laptop more home than any of them. Too many years on the run. Too many years hiding from the feds. No way to move from the underground life to normalcy. Her only friends online. No one close.

Another check out the bedroom window and everything seemed clean. Didn't mean shit, but nothing was ever for sure. Turned around and saw Kirk still slumped over the table. Nope. Nothing was ever for sure.

Got to go to Dr. Harlen. That's what he'd said. Nobody but him.
Shit.
The salt mine guy.
Kirk's dying request.

I can't do it old man. I have to run.

She zipped up the duffel, was on her way to pick up the laptop from the desk from the living room desk, but she stopped near Kirk's body and looked at the box. Tied up with string or twine. A glance down at the floor and she saw she was tracking up the place with blood. Careless—making mistakes she didn't have to make.

Run and run clean. That's what she needed to do.

Had to hurry, so she disconnected the laptop, took the memory card out of her printer, slid it all in the side pocket of her duffel bag and zipped that tight, too. She was through the bedroom door when she started to cry again.

Five minutes later, with the twine bound box in the bag, she re-opened her bedroom window and slipped out onto the fire escape. The alley was empty. A few minutes later she got in her car and fired it up.

It was three a.m.

****

At the all-night office center, she scanned the entire contents of the box and transferred them to her laptop. Tried not to read the details, tried to avoid thinking about the madness and death of salt mine employees over the years. Tried to forget the interviews she saw with former employees expressing their fears. Strange and terrifying things they'd seen and heard. Co-workers that disappeared and no in depth follow-up by the police.

It took her two hours to finish.

Five o'clock a.m. and still dark.

A faint mist pressed against the windows. Traffic was picking up, and her nervous system felt like it was buzzing.

The kid behind the counter was twenty-three, maybe twenty-five years old. Following her every move. Hair gelled with spikes; one ear gauged the size of a nickel. Black fingernail polish. Stack of energy drinks lined up next to the cash register. She could feel him staring at her. Especially when she bent over to pick up a clipping that dropped from the box. Felt like he leaned over to get a better look at her ass.

With everything scanned, she uploaded it to a secure server in the Ukraine. That done, she wrote an email, embedded it into an email program on a server in South Africa, and set it to email the link from that site to Dr. Harlen at two o'clock in the afternoon. His email address was easy enough to find. For such a hotshot genius, he didn't seem to know much about web privacy. She packed up everything except the actual box full of documents from Kirk.

Next, she found the right size Next Day Delivery shipping envelope, went to the creep at the counter and paid for it cash. While he was ringing up the sale, she wrote Dr. Harlen's company address on it, filled out the shipping papers and finished the note she'd started while scanning— the one that explained in the vaguest way possible how she got the papers and where she wanted to meet him. With the creep still staring at her, she walked over to the RUSH shipping kiosk, loaded in the required data, paid the outrageous fee on a card from Barclay's Bank in the Bahamas then slipped the envelope in and hoisted the duffel bag loaded with her life on her shoulder.

"You work around here?" the kid finally got the nerve to ask.

Charlene had red hair cut short, big black librarian glasses and was small enough and tousled looking enough to be in her twenties. Maybe that was supposed to be a plus, but what she didn't need was attention. Unless she wanted it. And she didn't want it now. What she wanted was to Taser the jerk-off.

"Nope," she said.

"You want your receipt?" he asked.

The way he said it was more like would she blow him or something.

"No. Got to run. Late for work."

She motored toward the door. He said something after her like what time he got off work, but she let the door close shut on the rest of it as she hit the street. Now she just needed to find a place to crash for a few hours. If Dr. Harlen didn't show, not her problem. She'd take the papers with her. Then he'd have to settle for the electronic transmission.

If she was lucky, he wouldn't show, and she could hit the road with a clear conscience.

23

Edwina Gladstone, better known as Mrs. Gladstone to her employees, was going over project schedules with the heads of Earth Battery's engineering teams. Dr. Harlen was in his office, reassuring the Mayor of Detroit that using the salt mines to produce electricity would not increase the likelihood of lightning strikes in the Detroit area as a professor at the University of Pittsburgh said it would. Dr. Harlen would calm him down, she thought. The Mayor alternated between ecstasy and agony when it came to the Earth Battery project, but Dr. Harlen was a hard man to argue with when it came to technology. And he was a good, if at times, exasperating boss. He gave her the support and authority she needed to make the company run smoothly. She was his liaison with the rest of the company and the world at large and gave him the security and order to explore new worlds of science. He created the concepts, but, as she saw it, there was no one better than herself when it came to execution.

"Not good enough," she was saying to Phil Emms. "I want the overload data buffer tightened up and presentable by tomorrow. If we miss another deadline for Process Safety reporting, you can explain it to the Director of OSHA yourself. Are we clear on that?"

"Yes, Mrs. Gladstone," said Phil. "We just—"

"Don't explain the circumstances, fix the problem. Dr. Harlen gave you a budget the size of a small country and this is the second time you've fallen short of my expectations."

Two men and three women were seated at the table in her office. All looked tense. The only soft spot Mrs. Gladstone had in that tiny heart of hers, word was, was for Dr. Harlen.

Alerted by a flashing light, Mrs. Gladstone looked down at her phone and saw a text message scroll across her screen. She closed it out and pressed the intercom.

"You may come in, Alan," she said. "Our meeting is now finished."

A short, overweight woman sitting directly across the table from Mrs. Gladstone held up her finger and said, "I would like to talk to you about the seismic data we received this morning."

"We'll speak later today," said Mrs. Gladstone. "I'll have Mark set up a time."

The office door opened, and the team members hurried out.

"Shut the door," said Mrs. Gladstone.

Alan Coil, a young man with a lanky body and the face of a humanized Ken doll, did as instructed, then reached inside his coat pocket and withdrew an off-white envelope. In the light from the overhead full-spectrum fluorescents, his dark blue suit looked almost black.

"No return address," he said, handing to her. "First one ever. We ran it through the x-ray and did a fluorescent scan. The instruments didn't pick up anything unusual in either case."

As her chief of security, it was his job, above all else to investigate anyone and anything that might bring Dr. Harlen and the project any hint of trouble. Despite his youthful good looks, she had handpicked him out of a field of security experts who'd applied for the job.

"Has it been opened and re-sealed?"

"No, Mrs. Gladstone."

"I take it the laser analysis showed no powder inside."

"We follow protocol to the letter when it comes to Dr. Harlen."

"I didn't hear you say yes."

"The laser analysis showed no powder inside and no evidence of active chemical agents inside or on the surface of the envelope."

"Sit," she said, and pointed to the conference table.

While he took a chair, Mrs. Gladstone went to her desk and retrieved a letter opener sharp enough to double as a dagger. When she was seated opposite him, she carefully slit open the letter and let it slide out onto the table. After staring at it for a moment as though she could divine the contents without having to touch it, she finally unfolded the letter and began to read.

There was no signature at the end, and only one name was mentioned in the two paragraphs other than Dr. Harlen's, and that was someone named "Kirk."

"Is there a problem?" asked Alan.

She didn't answer at once, just glanced up at him with an irritated look.

"Is there any word on the two missing employees?" she finally asked.

"No. Nothing. Last time they were seen was in the mine."

"You have a video showing them leaving?"

"No."

Mrs. Gladstone folded the letter and pushed it into her sweater pocket.

"And how do you explain that?"

"The video feed was down most of the day. No one can give me a good reason why."

"Not good enough," she said. "Get me an answer. Cameras go out the same day as two employees go missing. That's not a coincidence. We can't sit on this. I've instructed legal to give me a hard answer for when we have to report this and who we're required to report it to. Considering what we're doing here, it's going to be Homeland Security. If we have to go that route, we'll have to delay the start up and both our lives will become a living hell."

"Then I'd better get back to work," said Alan.

"Yes, you'd better. Find the saboteurs, before I have to turn this whole project over to the Feds."

Alan stood up, turned to leave, and then turned to look back at her.

"What if the Feds are behind it?"

"Get me proof," she said.

Alan Coil knew better than to let Mrs. Gladstone down.

****

She met for five minutes with Mark, her assistant, and rattled off a list of things for him to do while she was out.

"Make sure," she said, "that you do not leave Dr. Harlen's friends unattended while I am gone. Dr. Harlen is supposed to be finished with his meetings before they arrive, but that rarely works out as you know."

"How long will you be out?" he asked.

"Just a few hours," she said. "I have some personal matters to attend to."

"Shall I contact your driver?"

"No," she said. "I'll be driving myself today. And if you need me during that time, send a text, don't call."

Mark was a perfect assistant. He never questioned her whereabouts, understanding intuitively that if she wanted him to know, she would have told him.

"Certainly, Mrs. Gladstone."

And, he was polite.

After dismissing him, she retrieved her coat and purse, shoved her pistol in one coat pocket and the silencer in the other and left the office to meet the author of the unsigned letter.

****

She parked a block away from the designated restaurant. On the way over she'd stopped by her apartment and transformed herself into a sixty-five-year-old woman. Gray wig. Powdery makeup, a touch of rouge and too-red lipstick to make her face pale by comparison. A frumpy, flowery dress cut glass earrings, a pair of pale spectacles and square-heeled sensible shoes. A large, embroidered handbag completed her transformation. But, after a moment's thought, she'd added a veiled hat and a broach and an overlarge quilted coat. She didn't know who she was meeting and didn't want to be identified if things went south.

Downtown Detroit was a cold gray collection of buildings and half-empty streets. A sharp wind cut through the city and people walked briskly with their heads down and hands in their pockets. She scanned the streets as she grew closer to the restaurant, looking for parked cars with the engines running. It was the easiest way to observe whether or not Dr. Harlen was approaching. The woman who'd written the note wanted to be able to pull out into traffic and drive away if she got spooked. The handwriting and phrasing gave away the gender.

A compact Honda was parked directly across the street from the restaurant, engine idling. A steady cloud of pale blue pollution puffed out from its tiny exhaust pipe. From five feet away through a scrubbed clear oval in fogged window, she saw the woman inside staring out the driver's side window, her head swinging back and forth to see if she could recognize Dr. Harlen.

Sorry, dear, she thought. You'll have to settle for me.

She kept her posture slightly stooped as she stepped out into the street and walked over to stare timidly at her. For a moment they stared through the glass. Mrs. Gladstone saw an attractive woman with short black hair sticking out from beneath a knit cap. What Mrs. Gladstone thought of as a Gothic look. Like a fully-grown ragamuffin. A blank look. Nervous tic tugging at the corner of her mouth. Thinking hard whether to tromp on the accelerator or roll down the window.

Mrs. Gladstone motioned for her to roll down the window.

A few more seconds of hesitation, then the window rolled down.

"I'm sorry, dear, but were you waiting for Dr. Harlen? I saw you sitting parked here and I hope you don't mind my asking. We got a letter but Dr. Harlen couldn't get away from his meetings. He sent me instead."

Panic flitted across the woman's face and she nervously tried to see past Mrs. Gladstone's large quilted coat.

"I came all by myself, dear. It sounded so important and Dr. Harlen thought you might need help. We want to help. And he wants to know what it's all about, but, you know, he just couldn't get away. I hope you'll trust me instead. Could we go into the restaurant? It's cold out here. This wind is terrible."

Her voice cracked the way an old woman's might and she blinked rapidly.

On the seat behind the woman, Mrs. Gladstone saw a box about the size of a box of typing paper.

Bingo.

"I've got to go," said the woman.

"Oh, please just have tea with me so we can talk. It would really help. Your note sounded so important."

"I don't know anything. It's all in the box."

"Please, dear, you're frightening me."

"No, just take it," she said and reached for the box.

"I'll buy. Please. And Dr. Harlen sent money with me in case you needed help. He's that type of person."

"I need to get out of this town fast," said the woman.

The way she kept looking outside to see if anyone was watching underscored the fear behind her words.

"We can help, dear. Dr. Harlen is very smart and very resourceful. Please have tea with me."

The woman looked like she was going to pass her the box and run, but instead she switched off the ignition, picked up her package and opened the door.

Amateur, thought Mrs. Gladstone.

24

"He's lost it, Yuri. He's lost his mind. And he won't listen to me and he won't answer me either. He won't say a damn thing about what's going on until the Instructor gets here. Trust me, he says. Trust me— like anyone can ever trust someone who used to be KGB. He makes me so mad I could throw him out the window."

Yuri looked up and was about to point out that the windows were impossible to open but saw the look in Sveta's face and kept quiet.

"You should have heard the cold-blooded way he said there was nothing we could do for Sasha. All this time we've been trying to save his son and as soon as he finds out where he is, he says there's nothing we can do. The boy's better off dead. My father would have done anything to save me if I was captured. Anything. But what could Hauck know? He's never really been a father. All he's ever really been is a spy."

The way she said it, thought Yuri, spy came out like a bag of shit.

She was wearing jeans and a black turtleneck sweater. With her running shoes on and fleece coat in one hand, she looked like she was going out to walk the dog. Except for the shoulder holster and the Beretta. But in Detroit, a Beretta and a Siberian wolf were somewhat impractical, in his opinion. The wolf was a hundred forty pounds of lean muscle with unusual fur black as Sveta's long hair. She'd rescued the beast from Drogol's underground laboratory, and it quickly became as inseparable from her as Yuri's computers were from him.

Walks were out of the question for the animal. There were limits even in Detroit.

"Down," said Sveta, and the great beast lay down.

"He doesn't like it when you're mad," said Yuri. "He gets nervous. When he gets nervous, I get nervous. And when you get mad, he growls at Hauck a lot."

Sveta glared at Yuri, and then her gaze softened.

"Where's your buddy?" she asked.

"Adam?"

"What a stupid name for a program."

"He's not a program, Sveta."

"Why do you call it he?"

"He's got a guy's voice. I think that's how his creator set him up."

"Well, where is he?"

"I don't know," said Yuri. "He comes and goes when he wants to."

"How do you know if he's in your system, but not showing himself?"

Yuri smiled broadly.

"Glad you asked. You two were up most of the night screaming at each other, so we didn't get a chance to talk. But you see that box over there with the display like an oscilloscope? That's my EMF reader. When Adam shows up, I can read his signal. Cool, huh? He lights it up. He might be able to fool it, I'm not saying he can't, but I don't think he cares if we know where he is. He's not really afraid of anything, if you know what I mean."

"Couldn't we unplug him?" Sveta asked as she sat at the kitchen counter.

"Nope. Don't think so. Little guy doesn't need hard cabling to travel—he can even move through cell phone transmissions. We can unplug about anything we want, and I don't think he'd care. I don't really think we can trap him. Besides, I wouldn't want to piss him off. I don't think we'd live very long if we did that."

Sveta grimaced.

"So, meantime, we just sit here. We know who has Sasha, but Hauck won't go after him. He's afraid of Professor Meridian for some reason he won't tell us. Our computer networks are compromised so we're cut off from the field. And we can't decide what to do about any of this until the Instructor gets here. So, what? So we play World of Warcraft and wait like little children for instructions?"

Yuri wished that Hauck would wake up. He missed the days where no one saw Hauck's face, where instructions were channeled through Yuri and his computer networks. There were no questions back then. Hauck's word was absolute. But since Sveta came on the scene, things had changed.

They'd accomplished Hauck's mission by killing Drogol. That should have been the end of things. But when they'd found out that Hauck's son had turned werewolf, they had a new mission— find Sasha and find a way to cure him. The problem with that plan was the young man vanished without a trace. They'd banked on following the trail of full moon murders, but that didn't happen.

Sasha was Russian Mafiya, second in command in his mother's organization. The Detroit arm was the natural hunting ground for leads, but between Drogol and themselves, they had killed everyone Sasha could have turned to for shelter. They kept up the search, Yuri doing the computer searches, Sveta doing the follow-up and Hauck cast a wider net across the country. The Instructor finally left because there was nothing he could do until they'd developed solid intelligence about where Sasha was. It was frustrating work and Sveta and Hauck started to get on each other's nerves. And now that they'd finally found a solid lead, Hauck put the brakes on and wouldn't budge until he talked face to face with the Instructor.

It was like watching two pissed off tigers pacing around each other in a cage. The problem was that Yuri was in the cage with them.

"If he won't do it, we have to do it."

"What are you talking about?" said Yuri.

"I have the address. I know where Meridian lives. He invited Hauck and I to dinner at his house and gave me his card."

Yuri was confused.

"And?"

"He's expecting us in two days. We organize a team and go in the night before."

Yuri could feel her eagerness. Her eyes were bright with the need for action.

"Whoa," he said. "It's not good to second guess Hauck. You've never seen him when he's mad."

"Like you have," she said.

"I have. Once. It wasn't good."

"When?"

"When Drogol had you and he didn't know where you were. Hauck was going crazy."

"Don't bullshit me, Yuri."

"King's X. Hope to die."

Rasputin was up and pacing. He didn't like it when his mistress was upset. His yellow eyes fixed on Yuri as if he was somehow responsible. Rasputin's lips pulled back and he growled

"Sveta, can you ask your monster to go sit down again? He's making me nervous."

25

The Instructor had forgotten one thing—he had a key to let himself out, but he had to have that key inside the cage to do it. And if it was inside the cage, couldn't the werewolf he would turn into just let himself out with it?

Or worse yet, if he kept the key inside the cage figuring that the beast would be too stupid to know what it was for, what if he kicked it out and was stuck in the cage? Now that would be a pisser. The only solution he could think of was to get as far away from civilization as he could during the last night of the full moon.

Which was why he was driving as fast as he could to escape his sentence.

There it was, a place to pull off the road and into the bush. He turned so fast he almost jackknifed the SUV, then straightened out and followed what he thought must have been an old logging road. There were trees and bushes blocking his way, but nothing that the SUV couldn't handle.

Darkness was descending on the trail; the sun was going down and there was nothing he could do. Up ahead, lay a campground of sorts, abandoned by the look of it and he was never so grateful in his life. He floored the vehicle for the last little ways.

He hopped out of the car and clamored for the rear hatch. Opening it, he pulled at the cage and it stuck.

"Shit," he muttered as he felt a stabbing pain in his right side.

Yanking the cage this way and that, he finally got it to come tumbling out. He breathed a sigh of relief, now if he could only find which way went up. The last rays of the sun disappeared behind the horizon. He stopped for a second—only a second—and figured out which way for the cage was up, he flipped it. Opening the door, he stepped up and into it and closed it.

Next came the lock, if he could only see in the dark. But oddly enough, he could. He hesitated before locking himself in, and then figured screw it, and did it anyway. Dropping the key in his pants pocket, he breathed a sigh of relief. Now he just had to last out the night. He looked up in the night sky at the moon, and he wondered how long he would have to wait.

The silvery disc went behind a cloud and he felt relief flooding over him. Maybe he was just paranoid, maybe he was afraid of what would happen. He waited, nothing happened.

Was all this running just for something that wasn't going to happen? He sat in the dark, waiting. The moon was still hidden behind the clouds, and a cold sweat began to form on his brow. He could suddenly hear his heartbeat. What was happening to him? Was that just his imagination, or was he turning into a werewolf?

Shit.

He was going crazy. Time to get out the key and let himself free. He reached in his pocket or thought he did. His hand was bigger than it had been, and it would no longer fit. Uh-oh. He didn't want to look, but he had to. The Instructor lifted his hand to his face and stared, really stared at it. It was a mottled brown-gray and it was turning colors while he watched. His fingernails were longer than they were just a few minutes ago and they were suddenly painful.

Oh shit, thought the Instructor.

He looked up at the sky just in time to see the moon coming out from behind a bank of gray-white clouds and he threw up his arms high, saying, "All right, you bitch, come on. Let's see what you've got."

Abruptly, and without warning, he felt his skin beginning to stretch. He bucked and twisted in agony, bouncing off the bars in the process. Sprouts of hair began to grow from all over and he scratched at his skin like a maniac.

The cage seemed much too small for him. He thrashed around like a wild animal. His bones seemed to grow and snap, and his legs—oh

God his legs—began to turn backwards in their sockets at the knee joint. His face was on fire with pain, but he couldn't stand still. He screamed and howled like a wild animal. His clothing ripped and tore, and he grabbed the bars of the cage and shook them.

The night closed in upon him.

All reason left him. Hair sprouted all over his body. His lips peeled back, and his snout extended. Huge teeth came from his newly grown maw. Tufts of hair grew on his ears which were now sharp, and his were now yellow, the color of a wolf's.

The transformation was complete.

The Instructor was a werewolf.

A fully transformed, lost in slavering rage werewolf. It threw himself against the cage bars again and again, battering them but doing nothing to bend them. It howled its frenzy at the restraining bars.

High overhead now, the moon sailed across a dark and gloomy sky, oblivious to the horror that was down below.

26

The door to Jimmy's office opened, and Mark entered, followed by another man. He was lean, fit and tan. Dirty blond hair still flat-topped. Brown eyes with the faraway close-up gaze of a soldier.

Mark waved his hand at the newcomer.

"Recognize this person, Dr. Harlan?" he asked.

Jimmy, self-conscious he was still too tall and too skinny, stood up from behind his desk and grinned.

"Yes, I do," he said. "But he was a lot shorter the last time I saw him. How've you been, Jason?"

"Living the life," said Jason.

"Do you need me for anything, Dr. Harlan?"

"No. Let me know when Mrs. Gladstone returns, and I'll introduce her to Jason."

"I'll take care of it."

When the door closed, Jason smiled, walked around the desk as Jimmy stuck out his hand and slapped him on the shoulder instead.

"Doctor fucking Harlan? You are the man. Doctor fucking Jimmy Harlan? I am so proud of you. Man, the whole world's going to be proud of you. Earth Battery? That is so cool, so fucking cool. The media and half the city are lined up outside the gates. You're on a serious roll, Jimmy."

Jimmy looked as though he were holding back a tear.

"Thanks, Jason. I mean it. Coming from you that means a lot.

War hero and all that. Mom always figured you'd be a soldier. Your folks would be proud of you."

Jason looked down at the desk. Both his parents had been killed while he was in Iraq—one year and one week to the day before he'd been wounded.

"Still can't believe they're gone."

"Sorry."

"It is what it is. I can't even believe your mom's in the.... in a..."

"It's a nice place," said Jimmy. "They treat her very well. Some days are good. Most are hard. Sometimes she knows who I am. Most the time she doesn't. That's the ways it is. When dad died, I told her about it, but she didn't remember who he was."

"Shit, Jimmy, I'm sorry."

"Yeah."

"The others coming soon. I haven't seen Trisha and Marty in so long I don't think I'll recognize them."

"They'll be here, but it'll be a while. Why don't I show you around the place while we're waiting?"

"You don't want to wait for the others?"

"No," said Jimmy. "I want to show you something before they get here."

Jason looked up at him, studying his face before asking the question.

"What's wrong, Jimmy?"

"You'll see. Come on; let's take a trip to my lab."

****

Jimmy came to a stop in front of a bright white door and stared at it as though trying to open it with the power of his mind alone.

"I think you forgot add a doorknob," said Jason.

"It doesn't need a knob."

"Sure. But shouldn't you at least have a code pad or an eye scan or some other way to tell it you want in?"

Jimmy stamped his foot. The white panel slid back to reveal a dimly lit corridor.

"Defective pressure plate," he said over his shoulder.

"You know what you need around here?" asked Jason as he caught up.

"What?"

"A good mechanic."

"You volunteering?"

"No," said Jason. "Just noticing."

They walked twenty feet until they came to an ordinary door complete with a doorknob, coded entry pad, and eye scan security module.

"Now we're talking," said Jason. "What's behind this door—another hallway?"

Jimmy ignored the question.

"How do you like working for the government?" he asked instead.

While he waited for an answer, he tapped in numbers to the keypad, then leaned his eye in front of the scanner and said his name and ID number. The door slid back.

"What's that supposed to mean?" asked Jason.

Without stopping to answer, Jimmy stepped into a room of lights and images and holographs.

"Welcome, Dr. Harlen," said a virtual woman who hovered over a low table near the door like a guard.

"Hello, Brittany," replied Jimmy. "Nice outfit today."

"That would be sexual harassment," said the holograph, "and in might, in fact, be court actionable."

"That could, in fact, improve my reputation," said Jimmy as he winked at Jason, "especially if you wear that halter top to the trial."

"Now that is very cool," said Jason. "She looks so real. I've seen holograms before, but never one like her."

"She's more than a hologram. First generation Jimmy Harlan visual interface."

"First and best," said the hologram.

"Of course," said Jimmy. "Status?"

"One email transmission to you intercepted and all tracks removed by your security team," said the hologram. "Seventy-five hundred attempts at breaching our networks by Homeland Security in the last hour."

"What?" said Jason.

"Cyber-attacks," said Jimmy. "They've slowed down a bit since this morning. Britney, who sent the email to me?"

"Someone who calls herself Charlene Knight. It is, I believe, an alias."

"Content?"

"It was a meeting request to pass over documents to you that you'd commissioned from a Kirk Rivers."

"Kirk Rivers?" said Jimmy. "Wait—I remember."

"What's going on, Jimmy?" asked Jason. "What's this about Homeland Security trying to get into your computer networks?"

"They want to know what goes on in this room."

The room was twenty by twenty feet. The ceiling lit the area like an enormous fluorescent light bar. Each wall was a giant plasma screen. The images on them were clear and crisp. The one to Jason's left and right rotated images of corridors of salt lit by halogen lights, which Jason assumed were from the mine shafts below. The far wall looked like a real time color x-ray of a tumor-like mass trapped in a gray matrix. The object at the center blurred and then snapped into focus.

"What is that?" asked Jason.

Jimmy walked around the four glass tables in the center of the room and stood in front of the far wall.

"I live here when I'm not at home," he said. "Designed it myself. Bathroom behind that door, kitchen over there, exercise room through that door. It's my world away from the world. No one is allowed in here but me. You're my first real visitor since the day it was built."

He turned and pointed to still another door.

"Bedroom's through there."

"Jimmy," repeated Jason, "what is that thing? And what's going on?"

Like a professor preparing to give a lecture, Jimmy took off his glasses, rubbed his eyes and lifted his eyes to the ceiling to look for his outline. When he slid his glasses back over the bridge of his nose, his eyes seemed to come alive with a fierce intensity.

"It's the real reason I asked you to come. And the government wants to know about it. Why don't you take a seat at one of the tables and let me explain? Brittany?"

"Yes Dr. Harlan?"

"Could you dress like a librarian? You're kind of distracting."

"You're a kinky man, Dr. Harlan."

"And display the email from Charlene on the west wall for us to read."

"Your every wish is my command," said the hologram.

"You made her?" asked Jason.

"Yep," said Jimmy.

"She sounds so—"

"It's her version of Fifty Shades of Quantum Theory."

"I don't get it," said Jason.

"Neither do I. Ah, here we go. Let's see. Why would Kirk use an intermediary?"

"Who is this guy, Kirk? I'm feeling like a fifth wheel here."

"Sorry," said Jimmy. "Kirk is a freelance writer I hired to do some background on the salt mines before I purchased them. I never heard back from him. Brilliant man, but eccentric."

"Was," said the hologram.

"Explain," said Jimmy.

"The body of a man identified as Kirk Rivers was found this morning in an apartment registered to a Ms. Charlene Knight."

"Not good," said Jimmy.

"Maybe I should go and come back when the others get here?" said Jason.

"No. Stay. I need you."

"Can you tell me what's going on now?"

"In a minute. First, I have to take care of something."

Jimmy straightened his back and walked to a wall screen.

"Adam, I need you," he said.

The entire screen turned a soft gray color, and a floating silver red face appeared.

"I am here," said the image.

"I like Brittany better," said Jason.

"Hello Jason," said the image.

"It knows me?"

"I do."

Jimmy turned and smiled.

"Sorry. I should have explained. Adam is my most advanced interface. Adam, link to the email on the other screen, please."

"Certainly, Doctor."

"I need video feed to locate whoever sent me that email. Bracket the time to locate the person."

27

"Look out," screamed Charlene.

The old woman turned to look behind her and saw a truck with a load of lumber sticking out of the bed careening straight at her. Charlene reached out to pull her out of the way but was too late. A length of board clipped her. She flew forward head over heels and hit the pavement. The truck fishtailed to a screeching halt and more wood clattered out onto the road.

Charlene's hand flew to her mouth in shock.

She was out of the car and about to go to the prostrate form when she saw the pistol lying next to the woman's purse. Saw the wig half slipped from the woman's skull.

"Oh shit," she said.

The truck's driver was on the street and moving toward the old woman as Charlene was getting back in the car. He bent down as Charlene turned the key in the ignition, then put the gas pedal down and took off with her head hunched over to hide her face.

She was shaking so badly she could hardly steer.

"Focus, focus, focus," she told herself. "Drive normal. Look like nothing ever happened. Get on the freeway and find a place to go to ground."

What the hell was going on? What had Kirk gotten her involved in? Who was that woman? Carrying a silenced pistol and wearing a gray wig?

No sirens, no flashing lights.

It was Detroit. Short on police. Slow response time. Turn right. The freeway was to the right. She looked in the mirror. Saw taillights flashing red as traffic started to back up. Slowed down, then jerked right without using her blinker. She was far enough away, but she couldn't take the chance that anyone back there could see that she'd slowed down or turned.

Didn't like the look of the neighborhood but kept going. Had to get away clean. Someone, she thought, wants me dead. No other way to read it.

Shit.

Ten minutes away from the Ambassador Bridge. She could ditch anything incriminating and cross with one good passport. Leave Kirk's papers in a dumpster. But she couldn't chance it. The way security was at the bridge, if there was an alert out for her car, she'd end up in a jail cell or worse. No telling how far up the line something like this went.

Shit.

She had to get rid of the car and get new wheels and do it fast. Not enough to leave it with her prints all over it. All the scrubbing in the world wouldn't get rid of her DNA traces, because people always missed something. A strand of hair or something like that. Charlene racked her brain.

Uncle Beasley.

Ten minutes away at most. It helped to have friends in low places.

****

"Jimmy, how did you do that?"

The email screen was replaced with an image of an old woman leaning toward a car as though talking to someone inside.

"Not me—Adam," said Jimmy. "I need to see who's in that car, Adam. Back it up and zero in. That's who we're after."

"Are you certain?" asked the image.

Adam had replayed all the video from the incident, capturing it from security and traffic cameras, and then merged them into one feed.

"This is the highest resolution I was able to achieve, Doctor."

Jimmy and Jason stared at the enhanced photo.

"He just accessed all the cameras in the area?" asked Jason. "How the hell did he do that? Don't they have secure systems?"

"Adam's very good at what he does."

The young woman seemed to be staring at them.

"Who is she?" asked Jason.

"Don't know yet."

"Do you want me to ascertain her identity?" asked the image.

"No," said Jimmy. "Hold the data in secure storage, then blur the original images of her. All of them. Change the car color and make if you can."

"May I ask why?" asked the image.

"Because someone else may be tracking her now. Make it quick, Adam. And find her. Alter any in progress images of her and her vehicle. Disappear it if you can. But track down wherever the information is broadcast to and replace it. Don't leave any loose ends."

"Yes, Doctor," said the image, and then the image vanished from the screen.

****

Charlene pulled into the salvage yard.

Broken cars stacked and jumbled throughout a field that stretched as far as she could see. Tires piled in heaps, broken windshields and car doors scattered on the gravel like they'd been tossed there by a tornado.

She drove around what she could, heading toward a small red building placarded with the sign "Beasley's Salvage." A cherry red Mustang parked in front told her Uncle Beasley was in. She parked next to it, but three feet away. Uncle Beasley was paranoid about scratches on his dream car.

As she waited, she heard a metallic grinding so loud it hurt her ears. She looked up to a giant forklift carrying a beat-up pickup truck across the lot, weaving in and out of the stacks. The skyline of Detroit was a faded postcard against the smeared gray sky.

Uncle Beasley wasn't really her Uncle. But he was the closest thing she'd ever had to family. He'd hired her once to erase parts of his past, to eliminate things the authorities could misinterpret, that and certain of his business associates. She wasn't sure exactly what he did, but it involved, as he said, "Recycling things that don't need to be around." If the money wasn't so good, she would have turned it down, but she was in a bad place back then. Now she was in a bad place all over again.

She pressed the intercom button.

"Yeah?"

He always sounded pissed off, like he was in the john and out of toilet paper.

"It's me," she said. "Charlene."

After a moment's delay, the gate began to slide back and, after waiting it out, she drove her car to the main building. She heard the whir of gears as the gate closed behind her. Beasley was waiting by the door. He was a fat man with wisps of gray hair ringing his head.

"I haven't seen you for a while," said Beasley.

Charlene got out of the car and stretched.

"Yeah, well, things have been kind of frenetic, shall we say. Can we go inside?"

"Sure. You being followed or what?"

"Truthfully, I don't know what I am."

Beasley arched an eyebrow, then shrugged, and then said, "Whatever, follow me."

Charlene snagged her bag, looked over her shoulder and then did as she was told. Little did she realize that all the while she was on CCTV.

****

Jimmy fretted back and forth for a few seconds.

"Adam, get a hold of Hauck. Have him go pick up the girl."

"Yes Dr."

"I don't like this Jason. I don't like it one bit."

"Jimmy, do you mind telling me what is going on?" said Jason.

He held up a finger. The phone was ringing. Finally, it was answered.

"Who is this?" asked Hauck.

"This is the mystery man. I can't identify myself until you've accomplished one mission for me," said Jimmy.

There was a pause for a minute, and then, Hauck said, "Sorry, I don't do requests."

And then, the line went dead.

"Ah, shoot," said Jimmy.

"Do you wish for me to get him back, doctor," said the disembodied voice.

"Yes, I would."

The phone rang for a few minutes, then Hauck picked up.

"I'm listening."

"I don't have time to explain now. I'll explain later. Right now, I need you to pick someone up. It's desperately urgent."

"Perhaps I didn't make myself clear. I don't deal with mystery men."

The phone reverted to a dial tone.

"Do you want me to pick her up?" asked Jason.

Jimmy considered for a minute.

"No," he finally said. "Adam, dial the number again."

"Yes doctor."

The phone rang five times, then Hauck picked up.

"I'm listening."

"Don't hang up. If you want to see your son—"

Dial tone.

Jimmy thought some more. If he was right, he didn't have any more time to waste. Still, he valued his privacy more than he could say. Without it felt exposed. He could trust Jason he was sure that. He could trust Martin, when Martin arrived. Tricia, he wasn't sure about. Hauck, even less so. Jason was being followed he was sure that. Martin and Tricia would be followed as soon as they arrived. Hauck was his only hope. He was about to throw the dice.

"Adam, dial the phone again."

"Yes, doctor."

The phone rang seven times and then was picked up.

"Yes?"

Jimmy took a deep breath.

"This is Dr. Jimmy Harlan, of Earth Battery Corp."

"Well, hello, Dr. Harlan. I am Hauck."

"Look, I don't have time for niceties. There's a woman, a young woman, you have to pick up. She doesn't know it, but she is in grave danger. Can you do it?"

"Where?"

"I will have Adam send you the coordinates."

"Consider it done. But Dr.?"

"Yes?"

"After this, we have to a long talk."

Dr. Jimmy breathed a sigh of relief.

"Certainly. And thank you Hauck."

The line went dead.

<h1 style="text-align:center">28</h1>

"Sveta," said Hauck, "I need you to do something for me."

She gave him a suspicious look.

"What?"

"There is a young woman at the following address, and I need you to pick her up now."

"Why?"

"Because our mystery man behind Adam has revealed himself. It is at his request. There is some danger involved."

Sveta's ears perked up.

"Should I go alone?"

Hauck shook his head.

"Take three men with you. Here's a snapshot of the young woman."

"Got it."

Sveta checked her Beretta on the way to the door. She stopped and strapped on her ankle holster. Hauck stopped her at the door.

"Be careful," said Hauck.

"Aren't I always?" she said with a wicked smile.

****

Charlene threw the bag on the floor and sat down, exhausted. She felt tired all over and burned out. That crazy old lady had a gun. Was she trying to kill her or what? And that wig; come to think of it, she wasn't a crazy old lady after all. She was in disguise. Why would she dress up to change her appearance unless she had something awful in mind? What had Kirk gotten her into?

"You want coffee?" said Beasley.

"Umm—yeah, I guess so," said Charlene.

The fat man went over to the coffee maker, checked the consistency of it, smelled it and decided it was okay. He poured Charlene a cup and took it over to her.

"Doc says I can't have any. I got the high blood pressure, you know?"

Charlene took a sip, and then another.

"I'm sorry, Beasley," she said.

"I figure screw him. You only live once, you know? So, I drink the occasional cup? What's the big deal, I figure? Am I right?"

She mulled that over.

"You know, you really should listen to your doctor."

"Ah, he worries too much."

Charlene was about to say something else but decided why bother. She looked up at Beasley to see him staring at her. He had watery blue eyes sunk back in his head, and a chin that was lost in folds.

"You want to tell me what I owe the honor of a visit from you in person?"

That was the problem, wasn't it? You got something you wanted Beasley to do, but there was always a price. He always wanted something back in return. And frankly, Charlene couldn't remember if she already owed him one or if she was owed one by him. But she didn't have much of a choice, did she?

"I'm in trouble."

Beasley shrugged.

"So?"

"I'm in over my head, Beasley. I don't know what to do, but I think I need to blow town. I need a car."

"A car? Sure. All you've got to do is ask. Can I have the one out front?"

Really? Could it be that easy? No, Beasley always had something that he wanted in return. Charlene waited for the other shoe to drop.

"Yeah."

"Well, it will take about two hours to get ready," said Beasley.

"I'm not going anywhere."

"Hey, as long as you're not going anywhere, how about if you fix my computer? It's been running awfully slow."

Moron.

"All right," she said with a sigh. "Let me see it."

And, while Beasley got the car ready, Charlene repaired Beasley's computer.

****

Sveta drove up even with the security dial pad. She drummed her fingers on the window ledge of her car. The girl was inside. She rolled down the window and pressed the button.

"Yes," came a male voice.

"I'm here for a delivery," she said.

"What?"

"I said, I'm here for a delivery."

"Okay."

The gate started to slide back into place. That was it? Some security they had around here.

She drove up to the main building, parked the car and got out. She stretched and was about to go up the steps to the door when it opened, and a fat man came out.

"Can I help you?" he asked.

That was Sveta's cue to go into her spiel, but she didn't think so.

"I'm here for a girl," she said.

She took the photo out of her jacket and showed it to him.

"She's in danger. This was taking of off the CCTV system about an hour and a half ago. There are some bad people hunting her."

"Is that so?" said the fat man. "Never heard of her."

Sveta sighed.

"Look, she was tracked right to this place by satellite. All I want to do is talk to her."

"I told you, I don't know who you are talking about. That was a nice trick to get into here—I mean, that package delivery stuff and all."

Three men came around the side of the main building. They were big and beefy, and they looked impersonal. They began to spread out.

"You might want to tell them to go back to wherever they were hiding out."

"Yeah, well suppose they don't want to?"

The three men surrounded her now.

"Don't do this. Really."

"And why not?" said Beasley. "Seems to me, you're at a disadvantage little lady. Now, why don't you come inside, and we can see what's what."

"Little lady?"

"You heard me. Now why don't you just come along quietly?"

Sveta was outnumbered four to one. The three thugs were just standing there—hulking, menacing. And, front and center was the fat man, who was just sneering at her. He was the kind of man that Sveta hated. Overweight and ugly.

One of the three thugs pushed her.

An SUV crashed through the gate, tires squealed as it bore down on them and it came to a perfect stop beside Sveta. Doors opened just as the three thugs were recovering their wits and three men piled out with machine pistols aimed at them. Two of the thugs had hands already in their coats, but slowly put their hands in the air. The remaining thug just stood there and blinked.

"You were saying?" said Sveta to Beasley.

****

"Ah, shit, Beasley, what did you do to this machine?" said Charlene.

"Nothin,'" said Beasley.

"Yeah, right."

Beasley shook his head in a "What I'm innocent gesture."

Just then a buzzer rang.

"What's that?" said Charlene.

She didn't look up from the computer when she said it.

"Ah, it's just the gate. Someone wanting in. I'll get it."

He walked over to his desk, fumbled at a box and flip the switch.

"Yeah?"

"I've got a package for delivery."

"Okay, come on in."

Beasley was quiet for a minute. He drummed his fingers on the desk, and then opened the drawer and pulled out a .38 revolver and shoved it in his pants. He buttoned his coat over top of it. He turned to the door and then hesitated.

"Look, you stay here for a minute."

Charlene raised an eyebrow.

"What? Something wrong?"

"Nah, it's just that we don't have many packages for delivery."

"But—"

"It's probably nothing, stay put for minute."

Before going out the front door, Beasley took out a handheld and pushed a button.

"Meet me out front, pronto. What's that? Bring three of you, that ought to be enough. Yeah, I'll wait."

Beasley clicked off.

"I'll wait for a second and then go outside."

"Is that glass in the window still one-way glass?"

"Yeah. Why?"

"Because I wanted to look out of that window, that's why."

She got up from her chair and, still mindful of shadows on one-way glass, peered out the front window. A car was driving up to the building at a leisurely pace. It was a dark colored SUV with the windows blacked out.

"You don't get deliveries, right?"

"Some, but not many."

"What's got you spooked about this one?"

Beasley thought about that for a minute. It wasn't anything particular to do with the vehicle or the request, it was… the timing.

"The timing," he said. "It just feels odd, is all. Nothing to worry about though; I've got three boys coming to back me up."

"Uh-huh."

"Relax, I tell you. You'll see."

He put his hand on the doorknob.

"The boys is here," he said, and twisted the knob and he was gone.

Charlene bit her lip and watched.

The dark SUV came to a stop in front of the main building. A very attractive woman with sable colored full hair stepped out. Beasley must have said something, because she said something back. Charlene waited nervously.

They chatted for a while and then the three thugs joined them. She didn't like the way this was going down, and she started looking for a back door.

The woman said something else, and suddenly, a black SUV came barreling through the gate and screamed to a half beside them. Men with machine pistols exited the SUV and before long, it was all over.

Charlene grabbed her bag, and headed toward the back door, her only hope for safety. She pulled it open, but the woman was already there. Backing up, she allowed the woman into the room. The pistol in her hand made it hard to refuse her.

"Look," said Charlene, "I don't know what you want from me, but —"

"I'm here to protect you. We have little time, because we're being tracked. Come with me."

Her mouth hung open. What was going on? Who was this woman?

"Hey, are you deaf? Come on, we've got to get a move on."

To allay her fears, the woman actually put her gun away.

"I am Sveta. Who are you?"

She wouldn't make it very far if she tried to run. The woman would take out her gun and shoot her.

"Charlene, I'm Charlene."

"Well, Charlene, shall we get a move on?"

She shrugged, accepting the inevitable, and walked toward the door feeling the weight of being trapped settle in on her shoulders. On the way outside, she wondered what had happened to Beasley.

****

Sveta drove along in silence. She felt the girl's discomfort like it was her own. It was as though she was going to break for it at the first opportunity.

"Charlene, I know this is kind of weird, but you've got to believe I will not hurt you. I was just sent here to pick you up by two people who are on your side. Do you understand me?"

"Yes, of course."

Well, so much for that.

"Look Charlene, I don't know who you are, I don't know why bad people are after to you, but I'm here to help. I'm just here to take you to the hideout. That's all."

"Uh-huh, sure."

Streets went by unnoticed. Sveta tried to think hard how to gain the young woman's trust.

"You don't have to like it."

"I don't. Hijacked by someone I don't know to take me somewhere I don't know."

"You're going to see Hauck. He's holding you there for someone named Dr. Harlen."

"Dr. Jimmy Harlen?"

"Yeah, why?"

Charlene felt relief flood through her body.

"Well, why didn't you just say so in the first place?"

Sveta looked contemplative for just a moment. Shortly, they would have to cover her with a hood. Not the most pleasant of experiences. She wouldn't like it. But there was no helping it. She couldn't be allowed to see where Hauck's hideout was.

"I didn't think of it."

"What happened to Beasley?"

"Who?"

"The fat man back there, at the salvage yard. And for that matter what you do with the three tough guys?"

Sveta laughed.

"Oh them? They're pleasantly tied up. They should break free and no time at all."

"You tied them up? Beasley is not going to be happy with that, but I guess that's better than dead."

"Don't worry, I promise you that they're fine."

They drove on in silence for a while, Detroit rolled by like a straitjacketed bedlamite lost in a world that was part rich people and part poor people, and where the poor people outnumbered the rich fifty to one.

"I'm going to have to hood you for the last part of the journey, so you won't know where you're going. Can you live with that?" said Sveta.

"Do I have a choice?"

"Not really. Sorry."

"Well, then, I guess I have to live with it. But for how long? I'm kind of claustrophobic, if you know what I mean."

"Center console, that's where you find a hood. Open it up and put it on so I can get you to Hauck."

Charlene reached over, opened the center console and took out a black hood. She held it up for inspection.

"This one?"

"Yes, that's it. Put it on so we can get going," said Sveta.

Charlene gave one last look around before covering her head with the hood. She didn't exactly like this, then again, she didn't exactly have much of a choice. Wondering exactly what she'd gotten herself into she took a breath and placed the hood over her head.

<h1 style="text-align:center">29</h1>

Hauck waited impatiently by the window for Sveta to escort their guest to her room. Two hours had elapsed since she had departed to go pick her up, and the elapsed time was excruciating. Now, with the girl in their custody, he would begin to get some answers. Sveta appeared at the door.

"She's in her room now," she said.

"Good. Locked in tight?"

"Yes. Now maybe we can find out what this is all about."

"My thoughts exactly. We've got her in one room and Adam, I believe Yuri calls it, in the other. Let's go have a chat, shall we?"

"You don't think we're getting in over out head, do you?"

He paused before answering.

"Sveta the short form answer is that I don't know. There are too many variables, but somehow, I feel that they are coming together. I just don't know how, but when they do come together, then I'll have a clearer picture of what to do. Until then, we are playing it by ear. Does that make sense?"

"No, but I'll play along until it does."

"Thank you, Sveta," said Hauck, but she was already gone down the hall.

He sighed and set off after her. As he walked, he mulled over in his mind the thing that had been bothering him the most—the fact that he hadn't heard from the Instructor except a terse response through his wife. He would be in touch when he was able, right now was not a good time as he was hunting his son. Hauck had argued with his wife, but to no avail. She had hung up on him. He had cursed the dial tone but got nowhere.

It wasn't that he didn't understand, it was just that he needed something in the way of contact so that he could tell him about the Eyes of Death. There was a serious menace in Professor Krikor Meridian and it wasn't something that he could solve alone. He would have to have some sort of communication from the Instructor for that.

Yuri was in the room sitting in his customary chair in front of his computer screen, and Sveta was already there pacing. On the computer screen, the silvery red face floated, waiting for Hauck.

"Well, Adam, get me your Dr. Jimmy Harlen. I have the girl, so it's about time that we met, face to face."

"Yes, Hauck, it is."

The silvery red face dissolved into nothingness, to be replaced by a headshot that was remarkably young looking. Red hair, glasses, a face that fairly peered through the screen at you, a thin frame and tall, very tall.

"Hello, Hauck," he said with a smile. "You must have the girl.'

"Yes, I have the girl. To what end am I keeping her?"

"And you must be Sveta and you have to be the talented Yuri. I'm pleased to meet you."

"Likewise," said Yuri. "You are the inventor of Adam."

"Yes, I claim that honor."

Sveta said nothing.

Yuri whistled.

"Nice piece of work, Doc."

"Why, thank you. Although I don't suppose that it matters—"

Hauck interrupted with a preemptory wave of his hand.

"Can we please get back to the girl? For starters, who is the girl?"

Dr. Jimmy looked embarrassed.

"Well, I don't know."

"You don't know? You had Sveta pick her up and you don't know who she is?"

There was just a little bit or irritation in Hauck's voice now.

"Her name is Charlene," Sveta offered.

"All right, so her name is Charlene," said Hauck. "Why did you have us pick her up?"

"Perhaps that would be easiest to understand if we had her in on this conversation."

Hauck thought about it, but Sveta was quicker.

"I'll get her," she said, and with that she was off.

"There was a man," said Jimmy, "that I hired back before I started digging around for where the old Detroit salt mines used to be. Perhaps your familiar with my work in developing salt as the ultimate battery? Enough energy is stored beneath the ground to light the entire city of Detroit?"

"No. We've had other things on our mind."

"I have," put in Yuri. "You're going to turn the salt mines into one giant battery, am I right?"

"Exactly," said Jimmy. "Well, anyway, I hired this man named Kirk to research the salt mines. You know, to get me all the local dope that could be dug up. For a while, he was feeding me the stuff pretty regularly, then I thought that something happened to him because he dropped off the face of the earth. I didn't get anything more out of him. Anyway, I didn't hear anything more out of him, and I went ahead without him."

"And?" prompted Hauck.

"Ah, here is the young woman."

Sveta walked in behind a young woman who would have been pretty if she had enough rest and was dressed differently. She was dressed in plain black jeans and a black wrap around. She wore boots that buckled up to her knees. Black hair and black fingernails and black lipstick completed the look. She carried a duffel bag over one shoulder.

"Ah, Charlene, is it? Your arrival has been much anticipated," said Hauck.

The girl blinked and stared around the room. She saw a tall, dark somewhat handsome man perhaps fortyish. He was trim, almost athletic. Off to his side, she saw a man with a medium build thinning hair and mustache, and a rather unfortunate turn to his nose. He waved noncommittally. But her attention was captivated by a man on the computer screen. The man was Dr. Jimmy Harlen. He was a boyish looking man that Charlene had a hard time grasping was supposed to be out of his thirties.

"Hello, Charlene," said Jimmy. "I'm sorry for the way we kidnapped you, but we had very little time. They were closing in on you incredibly fast."

"Who? Who were they? I mean that woman with a gun—she wasn't even old, she was, I mean I think she was young. Why was she after me?"

"I don't exactly know, Charlene. I think it was because of what's in that duffel bag."

Silence fell upon the room as all eyes turned toward Charlene's duffel bag.

"Oh," said Charlene. "I'd forgotten all about that."

"What is in the duffel bag?" said Hauck.

"It's what I was asked to bring to Dr. Harlan," said Charlene.

"Yes, and it is…"

"It was a report on the salt mines that Kirk gave me before he… died."

Tears formed in her eyes, that she had kept repressed since the moment she had found Kirk's body. It was hard to imagine that Kirk was dead. He was crazy, but he was a friend. And now, he was gone for good.

"Oh, I didn't realize he had died," said Jimmy.

"He didn't just die he was murdered," said Charlene.

"Murdered?"

"He was shot in the stomach."

"Oh my," said Jimmy.

"Where did this happen?" said Hauck.

Charlene looked at Hauck, blinked back tears before answering.

"At his apartment, they shot him in his own apartment, but he managed to get away. He was bleeding but he kept going. Showed up at my apartment in the middle of the night, I didn't see that he was wounded until it was too late. He gave me these papers and said to take them to Dr. Jimmy Harlen. Made me promise to… to get them to him. So, Dr. Harlan, I guess these are yours."

She handed the duffel bag over to Hauck.

"That was everything he found out about the salt mines. Goes back a hundred years or so. There was some pretty weird stuff in there, I think."

"I see," said Dr. Harlan.

Sveta and Yuri moved in to gather around the duffle bag. Hauck carefully opened it up to see what was inside. There were papers bundled together in two stacks. He was about to grab them, when Charlene continued.

"There's something down there," she said. "Every twelve years or so, on the night called the Red Moon night, it comes alive and does things."

"What kind of things?" said Hauck.

Dr. Jimmy cut in.

"It sends thought forms out, thought forms of madness and death," he said.

"What?" said Yuri.

"Would you mind if Adam saw what was in those papers?" said Jimmy.

The silvery redhead appeared on one of the computer screens that Yuri had ringing the room.

"Certainly," said Hauck. "Yuri, would you mind showing the texts to Adam?"

Charlene looked on in amazement.

"Who is that?" she asked.

"Don't ask. It's complicated," said Sveta.

While Yuri showed the texts to Adam, Hauck was amazed at how little time transpired for Adam to read what was on them. As soon as Yuri showed him a page, Adam was finished with it.

"Hauck, I thank you," said Jimmy.

"Now tell me, where is my son?" demanded Hauck.

"First let me tell you about my predicament. It began a long time ago when I was just a boy..."

30

Hauck was listening attentively to Jimmy's story, but by this time, he had enough.

"You're crazy," he said.

Jimmy looked at him solemnly.

"I wish I was. Let me introduce you to an eyewitness to the events of that night. Jason?"

An awkward moment passed, and then a slim, athletically fit young man with a buzz haircut appeared on the screen beside Jimmy.

"Jason was there that night and saw everything that I am saying. Jason?"

"Uh, I haven't talked to anyone about this before but yeah I guess it's true," said Jason.

Hauck said nothing for a moment. Could this be true? He looked at Sveta and Yuri. Sveta shrugged, and Yuri, well he just seemed mystified.

"Look, this is a very interesting story, but right now my primary interest is in finding my son. After I have found my son, and cured him, I would be interested in helping you. But not before, do you understand that?"

"Oh no, Mr. Hauck," interrupted Adam. "You see, the man who has your son and the man trying to prevent us from killing the Dhole are, in fact, the same man."

"What?" said a surprised Hauck.

"Yes," said Jimmy, "well I was trying to tell you—"

"Who is he?" said Hauck in a low, menacing tone.

"His name is Professor Krikor Meridian."

Hauck felt a lump form in his stomach. This was his worst nightmare.

The man called the Eyes of Death held his son captive? It could not be, and yet, there was a certain taunting of him, was there not? A daring him—yes, that was it, a daring of him. To what end, though? His beef was not with Hauck, it was with the Instructor. In a flash, he saw through the man's plan. Of course, he didn't want him, he wanted the Instructor. Hauck was only a way to get to the Instructor. That was it, wasn't it?

"Professor Krikor Meridian."

The name rolled off his tongue. He had his son—a prisoner, most likely. Why else would he be there? And where was there?

"Where is he?"

"That is the problem, I'm afraid. He is here in Detroit, on a dead end street where no one but himself lives. All the other houses have been torn up or in the process of being torn down. I'm afraid that Adam will be of no help at all because there is no electricity on in the entire place."

If only the Instructor were here, they could break into the place and take back his son. That was all he cared about.

"I know what you're thinking, that it will be a cake walk, am I correct?"

"Nothing is ever as easy as that, but, yes, that is something like what I was thinking."

"Well you can forget it. That place is under armed guard twenty-four seven and I can't get so much of a peep of what goes on inside."

"You're sure that Meridian has him?"

"I saw him taken hostage by camera," said Adam. "I cannot guarantee that he is still alive."

"He'd better be," said Hauck.

"Excuse me," said Charlene. "But I've delivered the papers to Dr. Harlen. I've fulfilled my part of the bargain to Kirk. Can I go now?"

Hauck looked at Sveta first, then at Charlene. He could let her go but she would be picked up within hours. Better not to chance it.

"No, I'm afraid not," he said. "You see, you are being hunted right now and if they should get their hands on you, you wouldn't last five minutes."

"You mean I'd spill my guts?" asked Charlene.

"Yes, that's what I mean, Charlene. I'm afraid you must enjoy our company just a little while longer, until we are through."

"I don't suppose I have any choice in the matter, do I?" said Charlene.

"No, you most definitely do not," said Hauck. "It's for your own good."

"Charlene, believe me, it is most certainly for you own good," agreed Dr. Jimmy.

This was an outrageous situation. He couldn't get a hold of the Instructor, but he must get hold of the Instructor. He simply must. And yet, the Instructor would not answer his call. What was he supposed to do? Where was the Instructor at, anyway? He knew he was somewhere in northern Michigan, but that was all.

"It's worse than that," said Hauck.

"Good. We finally get down to it. You've been holding out on us, haven't you?" said Sveta.

Hauck looked around at Sveta and Yuri, for the first time meeting their eyes. Then he looked at Jimmy and Jason.

"Yes. I've been holding out on you. For what I thought was a very good reason, and I had to get the Instructor's permission to tell you about this. Do you understand how serious this is?"

"No," said Sveta. "Why don't you tell us?"

"All right. Professor Krikor Meridian had markings around his eye, around his one good eye. They are so slight that only someone who was looking for them would know, only someone who knew about such things would look for in the first place."

"I don't understand," said Yuri.

"They mark the man who bears them with the signature of someone who has the Eyes of Death."

He looked at them as though they should understand. When he realized they didn't, he could have kicked himself.

"Let me explain," he said. "The Eyes of Death are an ancient group of assassins. They are really, really good. Their... camp...was rivals with the Instructor's camp—that's the only way I can thing to describe them. They were in different parts of the globe, so they didn't cross paths too often. Are you with me so far?"

"Wait just a minute," said Jimmy. "You mean to tell me that Professor Meridian is a member of this—what did you call it?"

"The Eyes of Death."

"Okay, you mean Professor Meridian is a member of this Eyes of Death?"

"Yes. I think he is a member of this… camp."

"All right. I think I've got it. Go on."

"The Eyes of Death has it bad for the Instructor. I think he is the one who took Meridian's eye."

"This is bad," said Sveta, "but what does that have to do with us?"

"Simple. Meridian has my son, so he baits a trap. Don't you see? He wants the Instructor, and he's using Sasha as bait."

Sveta and Yuri got it at the same time. They glanced at each other. It was Yuri who asked the question.

"But Hauck, shouldn't we tell the Instructor?"

"I would if I could get a hold of him. I keep leaving messages for him but getting no response."

"Oh," said Yuri.

"Not to be obtuse or anything, but who are you guys talking about?" asked Charlene.

"What?" asked Hauck. "Ah, that's right you don't know him, do you?"

"No," said Charlene.

"Ah, well he's—"

"An evil little prick," finished Sveta.

Yuri smiled at that, and so did Jimmy. Jason just looked confused.

"He's about eighty years old, going senile and reasonably competent," continued Sveta.

"Please, Sveta," said Hauck.

"Okay," said Sveta, "he's fairly competent."

"I'll tell him you said that," said Hauck. "The thing is, I'm getting worried about him. It's not like him to be gone so long without making contact."

"I can scan for him," suggested Adam.

"You can?" said Hauck.

"Hauck, we've got to have a long talk about what Adam's capabilities are," said Yuri.

"Do you need a picture?" said Hauck.

"No need," said Jimmy. "Adam begin scanning for the Instructor."

"Yes, doctor."

"How big of an area is he scanning?"

"He will scan a five-state area, then go outward from there if he does not find him," said Jimmy.

"Seriously?" said Hauck

"Yes, I'm quite serious. He will keep searching until—"

"I cannot locate him, doctor. The latest I have for him is in Cuyhagen county about four days ago. He was in a tan colored SUV. He went into the woods on foot with three other men, and no one came out."

Where could the Instructor be? He would have gone to ground while hunting the werewolf, but Sasha was with Krikor Meridian. What could he be hunting? Could there be a second werewolf?

"Adam," Hauck said, "how about any other cars? You said the Instructor came in a tan SUV. What did the other men come in?"

The answer came back in a minute.

"The other men arrived in a black SUV, Hauck."

"You're thinking that he left in the black SUV?" asked Jason.

"Exactly."

"I've got him, Hauck, and then he disappears again after an hour in the car," said Adam. "You were right, I've got him getting gas. But Hauck, he was alone in the car. There was no one else present."

Sveta threw up her hands in disgust.

"I knew it. The other three men are dead," she said.

"We don't know that, Sveta."

"Yes, we do. Otherwise you think he would have left in the same car, right?"

"But that means he left his tan SUV behind. It doesn't make sense. And where is he off to?"

Silence for a minute. It really didn't make any sense. Why didn't the Instructor take his tan SUV instead of the black SUV? And where was he off to now? Why wouldn't he return his call?

"I can go find out," said Jason.

"You would do that?" asked Hauck.

"Sure. I can drive up there tomorrow, if it's okay with Jimmy."

Jimmy mulled it over for a minute, and then said yes.

"I'll go with him," said Sveta.

"Do it," said Hauck. "We need the Instructor. Adam, you stay in touch with them and me and Dr. Jimmy. Yuri, you coordinate everything."

"Okay," said Yuri.

"Now, Dr. Jimmy, while the others attend to their tasks, lets you and I get acquainted, shall we?"

31

Sasha could not stand his confinement any longer. He howled and beat on the door.

"Hey, you out there. Come on and open this blessed door."

He pounded on the door like a madman.

"I said, open this door."

In frustration, he kicked it hard enough that he recoiled in pain. But when the pain subsided, he kicked it again. He looked for anything to throw, but there was only magazines. The furniture was bolted to the floor and made of metal, so there was nothing to break. He debated breaking the TV screen, but it was set into the wall behind a layer of bullet proof glass. The door, the only way out was the door, and the lock to it was on the other side.

He sat down on a chair and brushed his long hair away from his face. How did he ever get into this? But he knew. He was a werewolf. He was cursed, and there was no cure. And now he was in the hands of this madman, who would offer him up to Hauck.

Sanzar and Abarran were his only hope. He had to get to them somehow, but how? They were barely human. What could he offer them? Money? Girls? Something. He had to offer them something. But what? Might as well face the truth—he would never get out of here.

Sasha's mind flashed to the girls that Sanzar and Abarran brought to him. Single girls, prostitutes, one each night that the moon was full. He tried not to think of their names. Barely, he could remember what they looked like; it was all so fuzzy in his memory when the change came over him. It wasn't his fault, he tried to remember, he tried to control himself but to no avail. Why, oh why was this happening to him? Why?

The blood. That was all he remembered was the bloodlust. And the screams. Oh yes, and the screams. All he thought about anymore was the agonizing sounds of death. He couldn't get it out his mind.

He banged his fists on the bolted down table. Everything was secured to the floor so that he couldn't hurt himself. It was worse than being in prison. There was nowhere to go, nothing to do. He would lose his mind. Really, if he didn't get to leave these two rooms soon, he would go crazy.

And there was the loneliness. Alone almost always except at his feeding. Then Sanzar or Abarran—he could never say which was which—would open the slot in the door, at the bottom of the door and shove his food in. When he was finished, he would slide it back. Always the same. No variation allowed. Fed on paper plates, with plastic spoons for an eating utensil. Paper cups to drink out of, and paper napkins to clean up after himself. It was sickening. The same, always the same.

Not even the staples in the magazines could be used for anything. He was given no belt that could be used to hang himself, and before each night when the girls were brought, he was drugged. It was a miserable, God-forsaken life that he was living.

The window screeched open. It was a three-inch slot at eye level. He held his breath. A set of eyes appeared at the opening, stared at him, and the casement began to close.

"Wait," he yelled and sprang up from the chair.

The opening closed, and Sasha screamed.

32

Beckham listened to the call, then hung up the phone.

Mrs. Gladstone would be released in a week or two, but damage control had to begin immediately. A simple job screwed up by a freak accident. No time to think about, he had to lock down the media. He made a call, gave his instructions.

"Homeland Security classified operation. No media coverage. Track down anyone who took or may have taken cell phone pictures or video. I want this like it never happened. Do it now and keep me updated."

Another call.

"I want every video or still shot at the following location."

He gave the address where Mrs. Gladstone's meeting was to take place.

"I want to see who she met, and I want that person identified. Top priority. Get on it and get back to me."

He replaced the phone slowly, as though the cradle was wired for explosives and any sudden movement would set it off.

Another call.

"When will she be released from the hospital? I see. Her condition? Excellent."

He hung up again.

Mrs. Gladstone was out of action, but Trisha was in place. First a visit to Dr. Harlen's mother. No, the old woman didn't know anything. Instead, he would meet with the rest of his childhood friends. Jason and Martin. Jason was controllable. Once a soldier, always a soldier. There was nothing complicated about Jason. The military owned him. He could yank him in if he needed to. A simple phone call and he would be back on active duty and under new orders. Martin, on the other hand, could be a problem. There were too many variables in play already. For the third time that day he considered having Martin eliminated. Only a few hours left to decide.

Martin Leland was an uncomfortable enigma for Beckham.

The man was independently wealthy. He traveled the world in pursuit of mystical truths. A man recognized by spiritual leaders around the world. Time magazine had written him up years ago after he discovered the giant underground temple in Antarctica, but they'd had to piece the article together by interviewing his associates. Martin Leland did not give interviews. He did not do television shows or YouTube videos. He went his own way and kept quiet about it.

Beckham brought up two pictures of the man again on his monitor. One from his childhood, one only two years old. Pudgy kid. And this one. Hard-edged mystic. What changed him? That was the mystery. Did it have something to do with Dr. Harlen? Something to do with their years as friends in the trailer park? There was a bond between the four of them. That was the only thing that kept him from ordering Martin's death.

Trisha knew something about it, he was sure of that.

The psychologists were sure of it. His funding, and that of his agency, was unlimited. He could afford the best. Especially with the stakes.

Beckham's authorization to do whatever was necessary, came from the President herself. If Earth Battery was real, it could save the country. But the secrecy with which Dr. Harlen surrounded his technology made a lot of very important, very influential people nervous, including the President. Dr. Harlen's demands that he control every aspect of the program with no assistance or interference could be attributed to brilliance. That would be the best case.

Madness was the other possibility.

The other was that he was working for the Russians, or the Chinese.

Variables, always too many variables.

He decided to eliminate one. He made the call. It was simple, really. In less than an hour, Jason would be back on active duty reporting to Beckham. His first assignment would be to eliminate Martin Leland and then, Jason.

****

Sveta picked up Jason in a parking garage at Earth Battery, Inc. She was waiting for him with the engine running. He had a car, of course, but she used hers since it was unfamiliar to his watchers. Let them stew on why his car hadn't moved in their little van outside the fence.

While Jason hid in the back of the car under a blanket, Sveta exited the Earth Battery, Inc. complex and drove off.

"Okay," she said pulling over by the side of the road, "you can come out now."

Jason shrugged off the blanket, got out of the back seat and came around to the front and got in.

"Thanks," he said, as Sveta drove off into traffic.

"Don't mention it. That was easy enough with the pass prepared by Dr. Jimmy. I got right in."

"He's got that effect on people," said Jason.

"Yes. How did you meet him?"

They were driving down I-75 to escape Detroit. Then they cut over on M-59 to head west.

"Oh, we've known each other since we were kids. Jimmy is my best friend sort of."

Small talk that was harmless. Feeling each other out. She was from Russian Intelligence; he was from the US Army. Sveta wondered how much he knew about her. What she knew about him was that he was recently retired Army, that was the extent of it. She knew her mission; find the Instructor and collect him, but she didn't yet trust Jason and he would have to earn her trust. That would take some time, and she didn't have all that much time.

She could feel the nervous energy in him, though. Like he was itching to crawl out of his skin. As though something was bothering him. It would come with time, though.

"Ah," she said.

"How about you? How long have you known Hauck and Yuri?"

"About a year," she answered.

"What do you do?"

Well, that was certainly a direct question. The problem was, the answer was complicated. She thought about how to answer, but Jason saved her.

"Look, I don't mean to be nosy," he said. "You don't have to tell me anything you don't want to, okay? I'm just making small talk—this is kind of awkward for me, you know? I mean, I'm sitting here in this car going to pick up a man I don't know, for what I don't know exactly, driving with a woman I don't know, you get what I mean?" he said.

"Okay," she said.

"Okay."

They drove the next forty-five minutes in silence, each with their own separate thoughts. She was both worried and pissed off with Hauck, and at the same time she was intrigued by the problem the Dr. Jimmy represented for them. The Dhole, did he call it? She wondered if it was real, or his imagination. But Dr. Jimmy seemed convinced that it was real, and that Professor Meridian was intent on keeping it alive. Why then didn't he just use his alleged government connections to shut down the whole project? Why did he let it run?

For that matter, why didn't he just turn Hauck in to the government? Ah, he didn't want Hauck. He didn't care about Hauck. He cared about the Instructor. That was who he wanted.

But still, why didn't he just shut down Earth Battery, Inc. if Dr. Jimmy was trying to kill the Dhole? And then it hit her. He wanted him to finish unearthing the Dhole first.

And really, what was the Dhole? That was a little harder to get her head around. She decided to ask.

"Jason, what exactly is the Dhole?"

He seemed surprised by the question. Finally, he looked out the window for a while at the darkening sky, and then turned back to her.

"I don't know, really. I'm just learning about it for the first time today."

"But I thought—"

"The pop-up killers, though, I can tell you a lot about them."

"I don't understand," said Sveta. "What do you mean, the pop-up killers?"

"Jimmy says they're the same thing. The Dhole sends them out to do its dirty work on a Red Moon night. That it wakes up every so many years or so, just a little bit. It dreams, I guess you'd say. I'm not saying this very well, am I?"

"No, what are the pop-up killers?"

Jason looked out the side window again, as though he didn't know what to say, or didn't want to talk about it. He drummed his fingers on his pants leg, and then, finally spoke.

"I guess I can't really tell you a lot about the pop-up killers. They're like big bats, sort of, with faces that can change to something else. God, I'm not making any sense, am I? They're like creatures, monsters really, that live underground and pop-up from the ground to catch and kill things. They can come up anywhere, I think. Boy, does this sound crazy or what? And there are so many of them that… that…"

Here he drifted off, as though he said too much about nothing at all. After a few minutes driving, Sveta said, "Go on."

Jason repeated the story of the pop-up killers, only from his point of view while Sveta listened without interrupting. At the end of it, he looked at her hesitatingly, quizzically.

"So what? You think I'm crazy?"

Sveta turned off of M-59 and headed northwest on a side road, following the GPS. She looked briefly at Jason. He was a fit young man, wiry with a brush cut and a deep tan. Wearing jeans and a bomber jacket, he was maybe in his thirties with regular features except for a nose that was bit crooked. Blond haired and blue eyes, he was a dream come true for a certain type of woman.

"You want the truth?"

"Yeah."

"Okay, well here goes. I don't know you but, maybe, just maybe, you had overactive imagination for kids. That's possible, but, four of you? I don't know, but that seems like a stretch. On the other hand, you could just be nuts. You surely saw something that night, the question is what else would account for all the things that you saw?"

Jason was frustrated.

"Nothing. Absolutely nothing would explain that."

"Well, I guess that brings us back to sanity."

"There were four of us that night. We all saw exactly the same thing. It wasn't a mass delusion or anything like that. Believe me, I thought of all these explanations in the years since that time."

"And?"

"Nothing else makes sense. We saw what we saw. Those little monsters were real."

The highway whizzed by a gas station, a bank, mobile homes and the occasional car. Sveta thought of what to say. She grew closer to where the Instructor had been seen last. Maybe they shouldn't tell him about the pop-up killers-at least, not for a while.

"Hauck, Yuri and I are hunting a werewolf."

"What?"

"You'll find out soon enough, so I thought I'd tell you now."

"You're kidding me, right?"

"No, I'm deadly serious. I wish I wasn't."

"A werewolf?"

"Yeah, you heard me. We've been looking for him for about nine months. It's Hauck's son. He just vanished off the face of the earth. The Instructor was looking for him when he disappeared on us. At first, we thought it was because he was having some success, or because he was hot on the trail. But I don't know now."

"Look, I know it seemed kind of weird about the pop-up killers, but you don't have to make fun of me."

Sveta glanced at him. He was serious, but so was she.

"Oh, I'm not making fun of you. I wish I was, but I'm not."

"No shit? Wow. Are you sure it's not...wow?"

They road in silence for a while, they hardly noticed the darkness creeping in, until it was almost full upon them.

"Getting dark now," said Jason.

Sveta said nothing.

"Aren't you, you know, scared?"

"According to the GPS, the Instructor's car is less than ten miles ahead."

"Yeah, well, what about the full moon?"

"What about it?" said Sveta.

"The legends of the werewolf?"

"We already know that Sasha is with Professor Meridian. The Instructor is here on a wild goose chase."

"What if he's not?"

"I don't get you."

"What if there's another werewolf he's after, but he only thinks its Hauck's son."

Sveta slammed on the brakes.

"Say that again."

"I said, what if he's only —"

"Oh, shit."

"Exactly."

"Quick, your gun won't do anything. Here, take mine."

"Wait, what do you mean, my gun won't do anything?"

"Because it doesn't have silver bullets, stupid."

"Oh."

She handed him one of her Berettas, complete with an extra round of magazines. Next, she checked her slide on her remaining Beretta, clicked off the safety and laid in on the center console.

"They've got mercury/silver bullets, so they will be effective against werewolves," she explained. "Just aim and shoot like a regular weapon. They're a little slower than a regular round, though, but not so you would notice at close range."

"Got it. Thanks. I mean, if there are such things as werewolves."

She turned and stared at him in the moonlight.

"Oh, they're real all right. Are you ready?"

Jason thought about it for a minute, gulped and then reached a decision.

"Ready as I'll ever be."

Sveta put the car into gear.

33

They drove on for another couple of miles when they came to a trail, that they almost passed in the dark. It was buried beneath old twisted tree trunks and weeds. But someone—even in the dark you could tell it—had been there recently. There were fresh tire tracks in the snow. The SUV idled as Sveta considered whether or not she wanted to go in.

"You ready?" she asked.

Jason hesitated at first. Did he really want to do this?

"Well?"

"Uh—sure," Jason said at last.

"That's good, because whether or not you want to, we're going in."

With that, she slipped the car into gear and—

A long, enraged howl escaped the night.

Sveta stopped the SUV where it was.

"What was that?" asked a nervous Jason.

She looked at him for a long, steady moment. The light of the full moon shadowed his face; he looked nervous.

"That," she said, "was a werewolf."

"Maybe," said Jason, "we should back the fuck out of here."

"Scared?"

"You bet I'm scared."

"Good. You better unbuckle your seatbelt and get ready for action."

With that, she pressed her foot on the gas and slowly, steadily, made progress down the trail that was a road. They inched along, the growling becoming fiercer by the minute. Jason checked his weapon again and looked around at the dark outside his window. An abandoned building, part of a campground, lay directly ahead. Trees choked the forest surrounding it. The growling, howling and snapping grew louder as they approached.

"I don't like this," said Jason. "There's trees everywhere outside the campgrounds, and I can't see anything."

Sveta was silent for a moment. Then, as she followed the road just a little to the left, she saw it.

"I'll be damned," she said.

There before her, in a silvery cage, big enough for a man to fit in, snapping at the bars of the cage and alternating cowering from her headlights and attacking them, was a werewolf. The cage shuddered under the onslaught of the beast. Its ferocity in striking the bars was terrifying.

"What the hell?" gasped Jason.

As though it had heard him, the werewolf flung back its head and howled.

"It's caged," said Sveta. "It's trapped."

"What if there's more?" said Jason nervously. "I mean—"

"I know what you mean," said Sveta. "But where's the Instructor?"

"I don't understand?"

"The man we came up here to get. Adam has given us the signal to where the Instructor was; so, where is he?"

She kept her eyes roving as she said it. The werewolf was caged, so he was relatively safe, but…

"I don't know," said Jason.

"Exactly, keep your eyes peeled for him. He's got to be around here somewhere. But if he's caught the werewolf, where is he?"

The monster shook the bars of the cage ferociously hard. He growled and slobbered unmercifully; Jason locked eyes with him, nervously, wondering if the enclosure would hold.

"Hey, I said, keep your eyes peeled."

"Yeah, okay, I got it. It's just that—those eyes. That killing rage…

I suffer from PTSD."

"Listen to me. You've got to forget that stuff. It's trapped. Its caged. It can't hurt you. What can hurt you, is what's outside the cage, and we've got to wonder where the Instructor is."

Slowly, it began to dawn on Jason. His eyes flitted nervously from side to side. Then he jerked behind him, in case anything was there waiting in the dark.

"I don't see anything," he said.

"That's good," she said. "Let's get out of the car."

"What? Are you crazy?"

Sveta unbuckled her seat belt, unhitched it, looked one last time around, and opened the door. The overhead light was set to off. She put on her night vision goggles, turned them on, and had a look around.

"There's an extra pair in the glove box. Put them on."

He unclicked the hinged door, got the spare pair out and put them on. The world turned from darkness lit by moonlight to a yellow green. All the while, the werewolf growled and howled at them. He grabbed the bars and screamed into the night so that it was hard to think, but it didn't seem to bother Sveta at all.

She took out her cell phone and dialed Hauck.

It rang once, twice.

"Yes," his mellifluous voice answered.

"The Instructor's not around, but—"

"What's that noise? Sveta, what is that noise?"

"Sorry, but that's a werewolf caught in a cage. We've gotten to the coordinates forwarded by Adam, and I can see the SUV that the Instructor was supposed to come here just by the cage. But no Instructor. All we've got is this werewolf."

The beast quieted down a bit and began to struggle with the bars again.

"Sveta?"

"Yes?"

"Where is the Instructor?"

"I don't know. I'm just checking in. Waiting in for the Instructor. It would be suicide to attempt anything with the cage right now. Sasha—if that's who it is—is too dangerous to approach."

"Keep an eye out for Meridian's men. Something's not right."

"All right," said Sveta. "We'll check the vehicle for signs of the Instructor, then get the car out of the way and then wait."

"Copy that," said Hauck. "And Sveta?"

"Yes?"

"Do be careful."

With that, he was gone, and she pocketed her cell phone.

"Nothing," said Jason.

"Let's go," said Sveta. "We've got to check out that car, to see if there's any sign of the Instructor. You didn't think I just brought you along for your pretty face, did you?"

Jason hesitated.

"I said, come on. Let's go."

All the while that Jason balked, the werewolf kept up his incessant racket. At times he got so loud that Sveta swore the trees shook. Jason looked around at the yellow green night around him but could see nothing.

"I just," he said, "don't feel right going out there."

"Well, you stay here. I'm going."

Sveta set out at a steady pace, watchful on all sides.

"Wait," Jason called after her, but she didn't pay any attention to him.

He ran through the weeds to catch up with her.

"I just needed a little time to digest what we're doing," he explained.

The car was just a little way ahead of them. The hatchback was wide open and staring into the night. Sveta stopped and Jason did, too. The werewolf snarled in a savage attack on the bars. Sveta ignored it; Jason glanced nervously at him. Sveta was more interested in her immediate surroundings.

"Here goes nothing," she muttered, and took her final steps toward the SUV.

Sveta was suddenly cognizant that with the werewolf screaming and howling, that they couldn't hear anything no matter how they tried. That thing really wanted out. Sasha was going nuts inside of the cage where he was trapped. She drew a deep breath, steadied her rifle in the crook of her left arm, and with her right threw open the front door. Waited for something to happen, anything. But nothing did. She searched through the SUV, but all she saw was an empty vehicle. Jason stood nervously by the SUV scanning the environment for danger. On a sudden thought, she backed away from the vehicle, and looked beneath it. There was nothing beneath.

She glanced up at the night around her and saw that there was nothing except the yellow-green shapes of trees. There were five buildings that stood beyond the cage. They looked ominous in the dark. The werewolf kept up it's almost monotonous howling. Sveta almost couldn't think.

"What you want to do now?" shouted Jason.

She considered going through the buildings one by one at a time. The Instructor could be lying in there dead. Or wounded.

"The buildings," she said, and motioned to them.

"Shouldn't we just wait until morning?"

"No," she said. "The Instructor could be dying in there. Let's go."

Sveta took one last look around and set off for the buildings. Her route took her right by the werewolf. The closer they got to the cage, the louder and more vicious the beast got. Like he wanted to go straight through the bars and rip their throats out.

"I don't like this," said Jason.

"Come on," said Sveta. "Watch out for his claws."

Four feet from the cage and the werewolf stopped howling. Three feet from the cage, and he was still. He stared at them with a burning hatred, his eyes boring into them. Sveta stopped, and stared back at him. It was a magnificent beast, maybe seven feet tall. It was covered in hair and rippling with muscles. Its arms were long and ended in claws sharp as knives. It almost didn't have a neck as it buried it beneath its impressive mane of a head. It had a full mouth of razor-sharp teeth beneath the elongated snout. Perched on top beneath its pointy ears were eyes straight from hell.

"You're an ugly mother," said Sveta.

The werewolf curled a lip and almost smiled.

Sveta turned and looked at Jason who was mesmerized by the monster. She tapped him on the arm and said, "Let's go."

"Gladly," said Jason.

They walked their way over the packed earth trail to the first building, swinging their heads in an arc to catch sight of anything that would try to sneak up on them. About the time that they reached their destination, the werewolf started to howl again. The world about them was still painted in shades of yellow green from their goggles, and it gave an eerie cast to the landscape. Trees were fingers that stretched to the sky grasping at a haunted moon, and the grass was sickly and weak looking in the night-vision. They saw that the door was half open and the windows were long ago busted out.

Sveta pushed the door the rest of the way open with her free hand. Broken tables and chairs were all around a wide-open space that looked like a cafeteria. In the back of the room was a half open space, long since abandoned. The floor was covered in detritus and seemed it had abandoned in a hurry.

"I wish that thing would shut up," said Jason.

"Quiet," said Sveta.

And then, suddenly, the werewolf went quiet.

"Thank God," whispered Jason.

Sveta said nothing. Instead, she examined the area for signs of the Instructor. She stepped inside but saw nothing except litter. A clock on the wall that had quit moving. Broken plates and glasses. Tables that contained more junk but had not one chair. Broken glass lay on the floor, a leftover from shattered windows. She holstered her pistol and swung up her tranquilizing rifle. It contained enough to knock out two rampaging elephants.

"I don't see anything," Jason whispered.

"Sasha was a brown werewolf," she whispered back, "that werewolf is white."

"What?"

"You heard me. I just thought of the color difference."

"What are you saying?"

"I'm saying that Sasha is still out there."

"Whose Sasha again?"

"Hauck's son."

"Oh."

"Yes, but the thing about it is, where is the Instructor? Come on, let's check out the other buildings."

They went outside, careful first that they didn't get bushwhacked.

The second building had the door hanging off the hinges and was a dorm room of sorts. Inside were bunk beds stacked two high, with sheets hanging off some of them, some of them rumpled like someone had slept in them and the others with mattresses spilled on the floor at random. The windows were almost all broken out, but the curtains were still intact. In the green-yellow light, they seemed eerily like broken teeth.

"Clear," said Sveta.

"You notice something?" asked Jason.

"What?"

"The werewolf has quit howling."

Sveta cocked her head. The werewolf was indeed still silent. It was disquieting, eerie even. Strange that after all that snarling and howling, he would be quiet now. The presence of another werewolf? No, that would drive the first one wild—or would it? No time like the present to find out.

"Come on. Let's go," said Sveta. "We're wasting time."

With that, she headed for a side door and swung it open carefully the rest of the way. The overgrown path looked odd in the night vision goggles. Bottles and torn t-shirts stuck in bushes were obvious signs that once the place had been inhabited. No signs of footprints in the tall snow-covered grass, no signs of the Instructor. No sign really, of anything. With a shake of her head, Sveta approached the third building.

It was a recreational building, where, when there were kids, they came to gather. Inside was an open space except for three tables gathered toward the center of the room, one of them tilted over to one side, and scattered, knocked down chairs that must have been once huddled around them. Bulletin boards full of scattered papers were thumbtacked to various places around the room.

Sveta looked around the room, in vain hoping to get a glimpse of something. She squatted down to get a closer look at the room, then she looked up high, but saw nothing.

"This place gives me the creeps," said Jason, "let's get out of here."

He moved to one of the open doors. Before Sveta could say anything, he stuck his head out and had it chopped cleanly off at the shoulders by a clawed hand. Blood spurted everywhere. Sveta recoiled in horror at the sight. Jason's body dropped like a stone. The white werewolf had escaped the cage.

It roared a triumphant roar that vibrated through the night air like something from hell. Sveta dove behind one of the tables that was knocked over and hunkered down, just as the white werewolf bounded into the room, ducking as he did so to fit under door jam. It snarled as it leapt into the middle of the room and raised its arms in triumph.

Sveta didn't breathe; instead, she held her breath for what seemed like an interminable interval at the same time as she shouldered her rifle. Then, she let out her breath slowly, and went to one knee, showing her head only slightly above the table and sighted. The werewolf was only three feet away. It saw her and growled as she fired the first tranquilizer dart at him. She reloaded quickly and fired again, then rolled out of the way as the werewolf grabbed for her.

It screamed in rage as Sveta stopped, reloaded again with another of the powerful tranquilizer darts and fired yet again. It swept away the table Sveta had been hiding behind with a vicious swipe and howled in anger. Sveta reloaded a fourth time but this time, as she brought the rifle up, the werewolf knocked it out of her hands. With no other choice, she reached for her ankle holster, when the werewolf stood over her, howled yet again, but this time he wobbled. She scooted back at the same time clearing her holster and, putting the sight on him, she hesitated.

The werewolf was clearly confused. It hesitated, took a step and grew even more bewildered. But suddenly it lunged at Sveta and fell flat on its face. She backed off quickly, so as to be out its range and slipped and tumbled over backwards. Her gun dropped out of her hand, and she scrambled for it. She grabbed it with both hands, turned and was about to fire when she noticed the werewolf wasn't moving. She breathed out a sigh of relief. The tranquilizer gun had done its job.

She painfully climbed to her feet and retrieved her tranquilizer rifle, putting away the pistol. Jason was dead—she dreaded that discussion. She checked the werewolf again and, sure enough, he was still knocked out. Jason dead and the werewolf knocked out; but for how long? Knowing what had to be done, she took out her cellphone and dialed Hauck. She saw Jason's headless body and turned away.

34

The walls were non-ending white. Boreholes of twin round tubes that extended for one thousand feet and went deep into the salt mines. They hung suspended like giant cylinders waiting to be lowered into the salt. The holes were four feet in diameter and plastic lined and dropped straight down into hell.

There was four hundred feet to go to meet Dr. Jimmy's aim of fourteen hundred feet, but that last section was the hardest. Drill and then put in place the plastic necessary to shield the cylinders from the smooth white walls of salt that surrounded the shaft.

Tyler Smith was annoyed with the drill. It had bound up—again—and he was getting tired of it. What was it with the thing? He had gone deep into the twin shafts by himself, going down the parallel borehole that ran beside it. There wasn't much space in the hole, that was for sure. Every fifty feet or so, there was a window cut into the salt so that you could see into the twin-boreholes. As he rode down the platform, he got a sense of just how eerie and lonely it was. In fact, every fifty feet the hole beside the borehole widened to give the operator breathing room so they didn't get claustrophobic. But Tyler didn't get claustrophobic. Instead, he just rode down at eleven o'clock at night on the platform, unconcerned with the closed-in feeling that most would have if they were going down the same hole.

There was a man up top in case he got into trouble, but on the shift-change, he was pretty well just having his breakfast. Lights would flash on the panel displaying how far he had gone down. One hundred feet, one hundred fifty, two hundred and fifty, five hundred feet, seven hundred and fifty, and so on. The motor let him down easily enough. One thousand feet and eleven hundred feet, and finally, twelve hundred. Here he slowed to a stop. They went down slowly because of the requirement for de-pressurization. It was boring in the extreme.

"Okay, I'm down," Tyler said into his microphone.

He waited for a response, didn't get any.

"I said, I'm down."

One minute passed before he gave up.

"Fucking thing," he muttered.

Twelve hundred feet below ground, and the radio was out. He took off the microphone clip and checked the connections. The wires were seemingly good, he couldn't figure it out. The connections were solid. He rapped the side of the box.

"Hello?"

Nothing.

Well that was just fine, down twelve hundred feet without radio communication and what was he supposed to do? He pushed the red button on the platform, which was supposed to be for just such emergencies. The red button was supposed to act as back-up for the microphones. When the microphones went out, you pushed the red button as a way of saying that you wanted out, but you couldn't communicate any other way. He waited patiently.

Nothing.

"Well, shit," he said.

He would have nothing to do but wait. There was nothing else to do. The platform was about three feet in diameter, had a chair in it, some controls built into a control panel about five feet from the floor of the unit, and that was it. So, reluctantly, he sat down to wait.

Having a sudden flash of inspiration, he pulled out his phone and began to dial when he realized there was no signal. Disgusted, he was about to put it away when he realized he could at least keep busy playing video games on his phone. He scrolled through the games, found a suitably mindless one and began to play.

Minutes passed. He checked his microphone again, found out that it still wasn't working. More video games on his phone as it was approaching midnight.   Tyler was starting to get a little antsy wondering just what the hell was going on topside. Regardless, they should have responded by now. Nothing to be done except wait it out.

Suddenly, he heard something. Maybe someone was coming for him. No, wait, that wasn't possible, there wasn't any way to get to him. It must have been his imagination. But wait, there it was again.

The platform he stood on was a tube with a top and a bottom that were crisscrossed metal and twin cables, one for lowering and one for when you wanted to go up. There was an LED light on the top of the cage. He was at one of the marks, when he heard it again. A soft clanging noise. What the hell was that? It wasn't metallic, as he had expected, but was more like a soft, insistent scratching.

He peered the top grating, hoping to see something, but saw nothing. He was expecting a metal sound, because if the cable was broken, they would just send another to be hooked on to the cage. So, he waited for a while and saw nothing. Now he was getting claustrophobic. What if he was forgotten down here? What if Alan had a heart attack? My God, how would anyone else know that he was down here? In that event, he was screwed. Wait a minute, eventually someone would realize that he was stranded down here and push the button or whatever to get this problem fixed. Whew — he sat back down in the cage's only chair and relaxed. Sooner or later, someone get the picture.

That was when he heard a chittering noise like none other that sent a chill up and down his spine. What the hell? He looked up at the top of the cage and saw nothing. He looked at the window that led to the tubes and saw nothing. What was going on? On an awful premonition, he slowly looked down. Two red eyes stared back at him.

He pressed back against the sides of the cage and screamed. What was that thing? Another two eyes stared back at him. And then two faces appeared at the bottom. They were like enlarged bats or rabid dogs or something. Foam dripped from their mouths and they had long rows of sharp teeth lined long snouts. They had pointed ears and fur covered their bodies. They were no bigger than large dogs, but they were terrifying.   And what were they doing some twelve hundred feet below the surface? The chittering—that awful sound—was coming from them.

His heart was racing at a million miles a minute. Cowering in the corner, he realized that they couldn't get to him. He was safe. Thank God. Thank the saints and the Virgin Mary too, and Jesus to boot. What were those things?

He'd forgotten his tool belt; the screwdrivers could be used as a weapon. Yanking them out, he waived them down low and said, "Come on, come get some if you dare."

The two sets of eyes stared at him for a moment, then with their clawed hands, they rattled the bottom of the cage. Tyler jumped on the seat when they did that. It wasn't like they could get into the cage; they could rattle all they wanted. He watched in horror as the two creatures tried to get in, how they plied at the cross-hatched metal with their sharp clawed little fingers.

"Go away," he yelled.

They stopped, looked at each other and then looked at him.

"Go away," he said.

And then, they busily began trying to get in again.

Tyler didn't know what to do. If they tried long and hard enough, they might actually find the latch that opened the cross hatched metal mechanism, and he was terrified of that. He was trapped in a plastic/metal cylinder twelve hundred feet below ground with no way out and two creatures busily trying to find their way in. This was insane.

Finally, he gathered up his courage and jumped down to the floor of the cage and began stabbing with his screwdriver at their hands. They snarled and bit at the screwdriver until one of them grabbed it with its hands and began pulling at it. He pulled back, hard with desperation, but he couldn't get it away. The other creature reached out with his clawed hands and scraped and tore open a huge gash on his hands and he yipped and pulled away, dropping the screwdriver.

"You cut my arm," he cried and pulled back.

The creatures howled at the sight of his blood. They went crazy with the sight of his bleeding.

Tyler held one hand over the other and pressed it down to stop the blood flow, but the creature had cut too long and too deep for that to be effective. He climbed back up onto the chair and whimpered.

That was when he heard a click, and the floor began to lift.

"Oh, no. Oh, please God, no," he cried.

The first creature poked its head through the created opening and howled with delight.

Tyler's screams echoed throughout the borehole.

35

Hauck listened again to Dr. Jimmy's story, more carefully this time.

"Wait," he said, "so you never saw these pop-up killers again? Then why did you go after them? And how does the government fit in to this?"

Jimmy stopped to think before answering. Who had he told this story to in all the years since the pop-up killer incident? His dad, and no one else. Of course, Jason, Trisha, and Marty knew, but they were the only ones. He had tried a few times, but that had ended disastrously. In the end, he had covered it up by saying it was all a joke. Boy, he wished his dad was still alive. At least he had listened with an open mind.

"I was... obsessed with the idea that they were real. I was... afraid of them coming back, that this time they wouldn't stop. That there would be no Marty to say the secret word, or that Marty would be there but this time his secret word wouldn't work. As best as I have been able to tell, there's never been a planetary alignment quite like this one. I was afraid of an apocalyptic event—you see, I believe in the Dhole. I know it sounds crazy, but listen you know what happened to my two workers. Does that sound like I made it up?"

Now it was Hauck's turn to remain silent for a time. He, truthfully, believed Jimmy. Except...

"You haven't told me how the government fits in. I think they'd be more than happy to nuke a threat like this."

"No, they wouldn't believe me. Or if they did, they'd be likely to want to study the Dhole for a while—they wouldn't believe what it was capable of doing. By the time they found out, well, it would be too late. So, I did what I had to do by myself."

"How do you know?"

On the screen, Dr. Jimmy shrugged.

"It's hard to explain, but trust me, they either won't believe me, or they'll want to study it."

"Jimmy, you wanted my trust, so give me some credit. Now how do you know?"

Jimmy seemed uncomfortable answering. He twisted and turned in his chair. His long, lanky body unwound and wound uncomfortably. Finally, he gave in.

"You've got to understand," he said, "that they convicted my father for treason."

He said it almost apologetically, and yet, at the same time defiantly. Staring through the screen at Hauck, as though at the same time looking for sympathy and condemnation. When Hauck gave him neither, he waited, and then continued.

"There were these papers that he… he leaked to the press. He was their inside source about some secret facility in Oak Ridge, Tennessee, how they'd dumped eighty tons of mercury—just dumped it in a public waterway—and the newspapers were never supposed to reveal his name. Turns out they had dumped a lot more than that there, and, well, the newspaperman that Dad gave his information to gave up his name to the authorities. To shut him up, they put together some trumped up charges against him, said he was selling secrets to the Russians and… and he died in prison, while he was waiting for a trial. Or, they murdered him, take your pick."

While Hauck digested that, Jimmy continued.

"So anyway, we never talked about it, we kids didn't I mean. Instead we drifted apart, like it had never happened. I don't think we forgot it like in those Stephen King stories, we just preferred not to talk about it, you understand. It wasn't three months after that Dad got hauled away by the Feds, and, well, I had other things on my mind. Mom had to move us into a dive apartment because of Dad's legal bills and it kind of ugly after that. So, I lost touch with Trisha, Jason and Marty. What happened that night was the kind of thing that you'd rather forget about."

"So, they convicted your father of being a traitor, and because of that, they would have their doubts about you?"

"Yes, that's about it. It sounds kind of odd to hear it expressed out loud like that. But yes, that's it in a nutshell. My mother never fully recovered from his death. She spent the rest of her life in seclusion. I found you by monitoring your transmissions, you know?"

Hauck mulled that over.

"Yes," he said, "that makes sense, but what put you on to us in the first place? How did you find us? We were covertly covering our coded communiques as part of a video game."

Jimmy smiled, relieved to be talking about something besides his father.

"It was part of Adam's learning program that found you. He stumbled onto you. I couldn't believe it at first, but it turned out that he was right. He was going through game after game, absorbing their code, seeing what the players said when voila, up you popped."

Found by a random machine check. What were the odds of that happening?

"You weren't the only ones communicating that way. It is very popular among certain drug dealers," said Jimmy.

"What?" Hauck was genuinely surprised at that revelation.

"And certain spy agencies."

"Of course," muttered Hauck.

They were lucky that only Adam had stumbled onto them.

"Look, to get back to what we were talking about, Trisha and Marty should be in by tomorrow afternoon, and, if they are willing to talk about it, they can verify everything I've been telling you."

"I see," said Hauck. "Tell me a little about them."

"Let's see... Marty is sort of a reclusive world traveler who gets involved in all sorts of odd phenomena, what people would call New Age, I guess. He digs into them wherever they are—like bigfoot sightings, and strange pyramids and lost civilizations. I don't think he does it for the money, he's got plenty of that, he just does it for the weird science aspects. Mrs. Aldrich had to track him down in the Amazon jungle to come here. So, he specializes in weird places."

"And the girl, what did you say her name was?"

"Trisha," said Jimmy.

"What about her?"

"She works for the government. She's a spook."

"A spy?"

"She works for the NSA."

"What?" said Hauck. "I thought you didn't want the government involved?"

"She's not like that."

"Uh-huh."

"Seriously. Deep down inside she knows how dangerous these things are. She knows that if they come back... they've got to be stopped, Hauck."

"Yes, but can you trust her? Don't answer too quickly, Jimmy."

Jimmy paused for a minute. Should he tell Hauck the truth? Should he tell her about the incident with Mrs. Aldrich? He decided to take a chance.

"I don't know if I can," he said.

"That's a good answer, Jimmy, an honest one, I think. Now for the important question: I have helped you, somewhat, already. I have got your Charlene for you. You have confirmed for me that Professor Meridian is holding my son. But I sense that is not all that you require of me, so what is it that you want, and tell me, why should I do it?"

"I need a way out, Hauck, and I have to disappear when this is over. I have to destroy the Dhole, you see. Those twin boreholes I'm drilling down into the salt isn't to create a gigantic battery, I will charge them up with energy and destroy the Dhole with them."

"I don't understand," said a genuinely confused Hauck. "You want... what?"

"I want you," said Jimmy, "to get me out from under the nose of the government. To find a way to run interference for me, to get those people away from me so that I can kill the Dhole, and afterwards, I want you to get me out and away so that they will never find me. Because when they find out what I have done, well, I don't want to be anywhere they can get their hands on me."

"I don't understand. Why on earth would the government be so angry at you?"

"Because Earth Battery is a fraud. It doesn't, it will never work."

Hauck gave a low whistle. Suddenly he understood. Everything that Jimmy had been selling the federal government, the state government, and the local government was, quite simply, balderdash. After he delivered the charge to kill the Dhole, they would find out just what a bill of goods he had been selling them.

"I see it all clearly now. You need to get out and disappear for good from the eyes of the federal government—correct?"

"Yes."

"But Jimmy, why should I help you?"

"Because you'll never get your son away from Professor Meridian alive without my help."

"It's true, you know," said a disembodied voice.

It startled Hauck. "God, I wish you wouldn't do that."

"I'm sorry," said Adam, "but I was only being quiet so you could talk. But it is in fact, true. Professor Meridian has a large house, a mansion, on a tremendously large piece of property on the outskirts of Detroit. We think he has your son hidden away somewhere on the grounds, or even in the house, but we can't be sure. But he is there, that much we are certain of."

"How? How do you know?"

"Why because we have him on video going through the gates of the property, and never coming out."

Just then Hauck held up his hand for silence. He checked the screen and saw that it was Sveta.

"Just a minute," he said. "Yes?"

"Hauck, we've got trouble."

And she explained what it was.

"Got it. You've got to get out of there, Sveta."

"What's wrong?" said Jimmy.

He held up a hand for silence.

"No. Listen to me. I've got the cage over next to the werewolf's body, and now I've got get him in and lock it. I want you to stay on the line with me while I do it."

"What? That's crazy, Sveta."

"I'm laying the phone down now, Hauck."

"Sveta, wait. Hello, hello. Damn that woman. She makes me so mad."

Five minutes passed, with Hauck growing increasingly frustrated by the minute.

"Sveta?"

"I'm here, won't you shut up?"

"What's happening?"

"Yes, what's happening?" asked Jimmy.

Hauck waved him off.

Five more minutes of agonizing silence.

"Sveta?" Hauck finally asked.

"Just a minute. I've got him in the cage now. I just have to engage the lock. Oh, shit."

"Sveta?"

Silence.

"Sveta," Hauck fairly shouted into the phone.

"Here, Hauck," Sveta answered him back.

Hauck breathed a sigh of relief.

"She's okay," he said to Jimmy. "You got him locked in okay?"

"Yes. The lock didn't completely engage the last time. That was how he got out. But Hauck?"

"I don't think we got your son. He was a brown werewolf and this thing is albino white."

"I know, but at least we have someone to interrogate when he comes around. Maybe he can tell us something useful before we... put him to sleep."

Sveta was quiet for a minute. It was unsaid, but true, they would have to "put him to sleep." It was the only way with a werewolf. There was, as of yet, no cure. When he came out of it and they were through interrogating him, they would have to put him down.

"Sveta, get as far away from him as you can. You say the campsite is abandoned?"

"Yes."

"All right, then, leave it be until daybreak. Now clear out of there in case there are other werewolves around."

"I was thinking the same thing," she said, and hung up.

Hauck put his phone back in his coat pocket. Sveta took too many chances, he thought.

"Well?" said Jimmy.

Time to tell Jimmy, much though Hauck did not want to.

"Jimmy, Jason's dead."

"What?"

"He's dead. Jason' dead. A werewolf got him."

"But… how?"

"A werewolf attacked him. Caught them unawares. That's all I know."

Jimmy looked like he would cry.

"I was just speaking to him…"

"I know. I didn't know him but…"

"But all those years, I was little more than someone to speak to, I didn't know that he was… this awful, just awful."

All the time that Jimmy was talking, Hauck was thinking about Sveta, hoping that she followed through on what she was supposed to, and hoping to high heaven that she didn't encounter another werewolf along the way.

36

Jimmy was shocked and heartbroken. Jason dead? He couldn't believe it. Hauck had hung up in to make some arrangements, and now he was all alone with his thoughts. And his thoughts rattled around in his head like old pennies in a jar. He kept coming back to Jason, Marty and, of course, Trisha. How could he explain this to them? It was a good thing Jason's parents were dead, and he was an only child, that there would be no one inquiring after him. But still, Jason dead? He couldn't believe it. He made himself a chamomile tea and sipped it.

What Hauck had elicited from Jimmy now made him feel guilty. He caused him to say what he didn't want to say—that he didn't trust Trisha. He knew it all along, of course, she worked for the government spy agency. And, of course, he knew where their loyalties lay, still he preferred not to think about it. She worked for the same agency that had incarcerated his father. That was bothersome, for sure, but he felt the urge to confide in someone that he knew.

But what would he say? Hey, Jason got killed by a werewolf and there was something I've been meaning to tell you about a monster lurking beneath the salt mines of Detroit? Now he doubted himself for ever having contacted her. What was he thinking? He didn't even know if she was married. Who was he kidding? He really didn't want to know.

"Dr. Harlen?"

"Yes, Adam?"

"You've been quiet such a long time that I wondered if you'd fallen asleep."

"No, Adam. Thank you for asking though."

"Then might I ask what you are thinking about?"

"I'm just thinking about Jason is all."

"I see."

"No, I guess that isn't true. I'm thinking about Trisha and Marty as well. I'm wondering if it was selfish for me to invite them, and I'm wondering how or if I tell them that Jason is dead."

"Is there a problem with simply telling them?"

Sometimes it was difficult to explain things to Adam. He was smart but lacked… context. He didn't understand the finer points of being human. How do you explain to a machine that people had reactions that were difficult to quantitate?

"No, I suppose not, Adam, it's just that I am afraid that they wouldn't understand."

"Wouldn't understand what, Dr. Harlen?" asked Brittany.

Suddenly Jimmy understood how empty his life was. His childhood friend was dead, and all he had to talk to were machines.

"Nothing, Brittany—well that's not exactly true. I just need some alone time, I guess, that's all. Jason's death, you know…"

"I understand, Dr. Harlen."

"Thank you, Brittany. Adam are you okay with that?"

"Certainly, Dr. Harlen."

And they left him alone. It was as simple as that. Machines didn't have any sense of empathy, of course, it was just their programming. They didn't have any feeling, though, of course, they could approximate feeling. It's just that they couldn't be affected by anything. And that, thought Jimmy, was in fact very useful. He stared around at his control center, at Britney in her librarian's outfit and he began to cry.

****

"Dr. Harlen?"

"What? Who?"

Jimmy had fallen asleep in his chair.

"You have a call, Dr. Harlen," said Brittany.

His phone was buzzing where it had fallen from his hand.

"Thanks, Britney."

He bent to the floor and scooped up his phone.

"Hello?"

"This is Hauck."

"I'm sorry, I can't hear right without my glasses. One moment please."

A fiddling with papers until he'd found his glasses, then put them on.

"Are you there?" said Hauck.

"Yes, I'm here. I just had to get my glasses on is all."

"Sveta's safe. She called from a small all-night diner."

"That's good."

"Now, Charlene's asleep. She's had a tough day. What do you want done with the papers she brought?"

"Oh, crap, I almost forgot. Give me five minutes, then just hold them up in front of the screen's video and Adam will capture them. Is that okay?"

"It will be done. Then we'll talk via Skype?"

"Yes."

The phone went dead.

How could he have forgotten about the all-important papers that Charlene had risked her neck to bring him. Stupid, stupid. Wake up, Jimmy, wake up.

"Adam?"

"Yes, Dr. Harlen."

"You heard what I want for the papers?"

"Yes, Dr. Harlen."

"Good. Hauck will be on shortly. Make it happen."

"Certainly, Dr. Harlen."

"And, Adam?"

"Yes?"

"Thanks."

"Yes, Dr. Harlen."

He had to get some coffee, needed the juice to wake up. What had he been dreaming about when… oh yes. He felt a coldness spread through him. The pop-up killers—that's what he'd been dreaming about. Sweet Jesus, how could he not remember that? He remembered the eyes. And the teeth, the sharp teeth, and the claws, the razor-sharp claws. For a moment, he was eight years old again. He had to violently shake himself to free himself from the memory.

In five minutes, he had gotten a cup of coffee, and was settled in by the chair to wait for Hauck to transmit. He was just in time, because as he sat down the computer screen flashed that he was ready.

"Hello, Hauck," said Jimmy as he accepted the call. "You ready to transmit?"

"Yuri will do the holding up of the documents. We're ready to show them now."

The little Russian held the pages up one by one, page after page. It took about ten to fifteen minutes, by Jimmy's best guess. Finally, he was through and put the papers back into Kirk's original box.

"Well?" Yuri asked.

"Patience, Yuri," said Hauck.

"That won't be necessary," said Jimmy. "Adam, what are they?"

Adam was silent for a moment, as though he were thinking of how best to explain. Then he spoke:

"They are a compendium of stories that involve the salt mines, doctor," said Adam, "going back to the time that they were first built."

A newspaper clipping flashed onto the screen. It was an article dated 1905 and detailed the problems with completing a borehole to tap the salt that was discovered in 1896. It wasn't going so well, because one night, it had caved in and killed five people.

"It doesn't say enough to make an assessment of whether or not it was the Dhole. Only that they had to shut it down for sixteen months while they found a new method that they thought would work."

"I see," said Jimmy. "Next."

Another newspaper clipping flashed up on the screen.

"This was taken from 1907, but details another cave-in where no one was killed, but could have been. Should I continue?"

"Hauck?"

They went on through clippings, some covering peculiar mishaps others vaguely disturbing accidents, until 1910, when the salt mines were opened for business. Just two years later, after some strange occurrences, the salt mines were sold in their entirety. Things went fine for a while, they even sank another shaft one hundred feet and started production, by the year 1916, they were producing 10,000 tons of salt every year. But by the year 1921, when the mines had been sold, though, on the night of a big thunderstorm, twenty-three of the workers just disappeared off the face of the earth.

"It doesn't say what happened to them," said Adam.

"No, it doesn't," said Jimmy.

They printed the story on yellowed paper, that curled around the ends. Jimmy wondered where Kirk had found it. Maybe tucked away in the Detroit Free Press archives, or the Detroit News? Jimmy thought he could just make out something like the Detroit Leader, but he couldn't be sure. Kirk wasn't so concerned about the name of the newspaper, just the story. Or maybe he was drunk when he photocopied this.

"Yes," said Hauck, "but it says when they vanished, doesn't it?"

"I beg your pardon?" said Jimmy. "I don't see what that... no wait a minute. They vanished in the middle of a midnight shift. It's like the whole bunch of them just walked off."

"I thought that just a trifle too peculiar."

"But," put in Yuri, "the article doesn't say anything about that."

"That certainly is peculiar, Yuri," said Hauck. "You'd think the newspaper would say something about that—unless, of course, they were bribed not to say anything."

"Hmm, an entire shift just disappears, and the newspaper doesn't think that is peculiar?" said Jimmy.

"Well," said Adam, "they said they all got job offers out of state."

"I don't think so, Adam. I think someone is lying," said Hauck.

"I think so, too," said Jimmy.

"Twenty-three workers vanishing during a midnight shift is kind of scary," said Yuri. "I wonder how they thought they would get away with it?"

"The police checked it out, could find no evidence of wrongdoing, but couldn't find out where they went, either, so they went ahead with the story. Money was spread around, it changed hands to quiet down the relatives and voila, the story that the salt company was telling them stuck."

Jimmy wanted to object but couldn't find any fault with what Hauck was saying. In fact, it had happened nearly a hundred years ago, so an evidence of spreading money around was long gone.

"In 1936," Adam continued, "we have another disappearance of four people. In 1950, two people disappeared. Doesn't seem to be anything special, but Kirk has this page all marked up. What for? I don't understand."

The markups didn't make any sense to Jimmy, either. Arrows went back and forth, and, well, what could they mean? They certainly didn't mean anything coherent, and yet...

"Let's say," said Hauck, "that all of these people disappeared in the same way. It's just a working hypothesis, you understand."

"Go on," said Jimmy.

"What if more people were disappearing, but if those were only the obvious ones?"

"I don't understand."

"If the—"

"Forgive me, Hauck, but I understand," said Adam. "In fact, I can go you one further. The arrows on the sheet are to indicate country of origin. I see it clearly now. The preponderance of the arrows in the beginning are from Ireland and Poland, and only later do they begin to migrate from Mexico. Don't you see? They were using undocumented immigrants with no families as laborers."

Could this be true? Jimmy felt a huge weight settle on his shoulders and an ice cube form in his throat. He wondered how many people had gone missing since the salt mine began hauling salt out. How many people that were untraceable had the companies been using over the years?

"The next page. We've got to know."

Adam flipped to the next page.

"In 1964 we've got four people that were unaccounted for— they've gone missing, but, again, that's all," said Adam.

He flipped to the next page.

"In 1978, we have again, two people missing."

Again, he flipped to the next page.

"We have two more in 1990."

And so, it went until 2008. Two to four people missing every twelve to fourteen years.

"It makes little sense," said Jimmy. "The numbers just don't add up. There's got to be more."

Adam turned the next page.

"What is this?" said Yuri.

"It's a study of... lightning strikes," said Adam.

"Why would he include that?" said Yuri.

"I don't know," said Jimmy.

"Let's see what the next page has on it," said Hauck.

Adam revealed what was on the next page.

"More weather reports. I don't understand. Why would Kirk have more weather? I still don't understand," said Jimmy.

Just then Charlene came into the room, yawning. She was still wearing the same clothes but looking a little bit more rested. Yuri said "Hello" and Hauck merely grunted. She found a spare chair and sat down in it.

"Adam, what does it mean?" asked Jimmy.

"I don't know, Doctor."

"Well, not to burst your bubble or anything like that, but it's obvious, isn't it," said Charlene.

She had Hauck, Yuri's and Jimmy's attention, too.

"Go on," said Hauck.

"It's the years that the people are missing. The lightning strikes occur more frequently around the Detroit area in those days."

"Oh," said Yuri. "I'm amazed I didn't see that myself."

"So," said Hauck, "what of it?"

"It just means that there are more lightning strikes on the days that the people disappear, that's all. But you've got to admit it's peculiar."

"Yes, well let's got to the next page, shall we?" said Hauck.

The next page was full of numbers.

"Well, what is this?" asked Jimmy.

"I don't know," said Hauck.

But it was Charlene that finally broke the silence.

"It's the number of people that have gone missing all total. Don't you see? Oh my God, I get it. You only scanned the front of the pages. Kirk's notes explaining everything was on the back of the papers."

Yuri withered under Hauck's glare.

"Nobody said anything about the back," was all he could think of to say.

"Every twelve years they lost between twenty-three and thirty people, and the number's been steadily increasing."

"Wait a minute," said Jimmy, "I thought that it was between twenty-three and thirty. That doesn't sound like much of an increase."

"Haven't you read the rest of the papers? Really? It's been increasing in the city itself, reaching into the homeless. You know that's not exactly a wealthy part of Detroit, you know?"

"I guess," said Jimmy.

"In Detroit, you could easily lose half of the homeless population with nobody being the wiser. And even if someone complained, who would listen? That twenty to thirty every twelve years was nothing. Try a hundred every twelve years."

"Wow," said Jimmy.

Hauck glanced at Yuri. A hundred or so? That was a grim statistic.

37

At seven ten, Sveta cautiously rolled back into the campground. The sun was just breaking over the horizon, and she felt safe enough that the werewolf, if he was still caged, was returned to human form. She grabbed her tranquilizer rifle and stepped out of the car, looking left and right for anything that moved as she did so. When nothing caught her eye, she slowly advanced to the recreational building. She moved silently past the other two structures, careful to take her time eyeing them. In the daylight, they looked more ramshackle than they had at night. Sveta put that effect down to the night vision goggles. She quickly checked inside of them, and, finding nothing she moved on until she was directly in front of the recreational building. The sun was over the horizon now, more than just peaking. Sveta looked up at it once for reassurance, then slowly, cautiously she stepped inside, pushing aside one of the double doors as she did so.

It was dark inside, but the light shined in through two broken windows, ragged rays of sunlight that seemed oddly stilted. Jason's body lay where it had fallen near the door, and she didn't look at it except to see that it was there.

All was quiet in the room. In the center, was the cage. Four feet of metal bars, this time locked down how it should be and in the middle of it all was a man's body, sound asleep. Sveta approached the caged body cautiously, her rifle raised. The man started snoring suddenly. He rolled over and Sveta got the shock of her life—it was the

Instructor. How did he get in there? She suddenly spun around, alert to any sign of danger, dropping into a crouch, spinning this way and that, looking around desperately. But there was nothing. Slowly, she got to her feet. And out of the blue, an impossible idea came to her. No, it couldn't be true. Oh, my God, it couldn't be, it just couldn't.

She walked over cautiously, not sure if he would wake up or not. At least he stopped snoring. What she was thinking simply could not be true, could it?

"Hey," she said suddenly. "Wake up."

Nothing. Of course, he could be playing games. Maybe someone had captured him and replaced the werewolf with him. No, even as she thought it, she knew that it was stupid. No one could capture the Instructor. No one. They could have used a tranquilizer gun on him, but she didn't think so.

"Hey, wake up."

Nothing. She had fired at least two full rounds of tranquilizers at him, though. It was to be expected that he would be out for—she didn't exactly know how long. But the effects on a man of two tranquilizer shots, maybe three... was it three? Okay, he was lucky to survive. Now she wished she had listened to Yuri more closely as to the darts effects.

A werewolf had bitten the Instructor.

She had to call Hauck. Or kill him now, before she told him. Sveta weighed her options. He was contained now, and if she had to kill him later, well, that was that. But they would need him for the Eyes of Death that Hauck was talking about. Maybe they could exchange him for Sasha? He was already in a cage. She mulled over her options. She was the first to admit that she didn't like the old man. He was rude, he was obnoxious. He was a killer. But he had killed only bad guys. Perhaps she should bury Jason, and then decide? No, there was no time. Sorry, Jason, but she had to get the old man out of there pronto.

Sveta turned around and went to the SUV and backed it up to the recreational building. She left the motor running and went to the cage. It would be a rotten job to lift the old man in that thing to the back of the SUV, but she might as well get to it.

Jesus, he was heavy. She had gotten the cage dragged over to the back of the open vehicle, but the little man was like a chunk of lead as far as lifting him inside. The bars were easy to grab, but getting him off of the ground was damned near impossible. Grunting and huffing, she heaved him up until she got him elevated to the level of the open doorway. She stopped to catch her breath, and then pushed one last time with her legs and her back and the cage slid inside. Panting, she slumped to the SUV, and stayed there for a moment to catch her breath. Then she closed the back hatch, and went around to the front, got in and slowly pulled off.

The Instructor still was asleep.

****

Damn the old man.

There was no way around it. He was a werewolf—and he killed Jason. Ah, well, she had to call it in to Hauck. She had been on the road for about an hour when she reached for her cell phone on the seat next to her.

"Where am I?"

She froze. It was the Instructor. Awake now.

"You're in a cage in an SUV headed back toward Hauck," she said.

For a minute, he said nothing. She checked the rear-view mirror to make sure he was awake. He sat there, holding his head and looking miserable. He looked, despite that, younger. It might have been a trick of the mirror, though.

"Don't do that," he finally said.

"Why not?"

"Because there ain't no cure."

She digested that for a moment.

"If it were up to me, I'd shoot you."

He coughed and laughed.

"Good choice," he said, sitting all the way up in the cage.

"Thanks," she said. "But I was just about to call Hauck and tell him the news."

Silence.

"Don't do that."

"Not an option," she said, as she turned onto Highway 57.

She didn't expect what happened next. Could not have seen it coming. The Instructor shot forward in the cage and grabbed for her hair. He came inches from just being close enough. Sveta leaned forward in her seat to avoid his grasping hands. The Instructor continued to claw desperately at her, but she stayed just out of reach. She kept driving, bent over, until, finally exhausted, he gave up.

Dialing Hauck's number, she waited for him to pick up. The Instructor sat in the cage, temporarily defeated, but fuming. Hauck answered.

"Yes."

"I've got the Instructor."

"Excellent, let me speak to him."

"He can't come to the phone right now," said Sveta.

"What? Why not?"

"He's in a cage."

"What?"

"Hauck, he's a werewolf. It was him who killed Jason last night."

"Oh, Jesus," he said.

"Yeah, tell me about it. I'm on Highway 57 now, I just turned onto it. I've got him locked in a cage in the back of the SUV. I've got enough gas to get home. You can take possessions of him there. He's none to happy to be caged, I can tell you that."

"How… how did it happen?"

"I don't know. I suppose he got bit while trying to take the other werewolf—the one he thought was Sasha."

"Oh, Jesus."

"Yeah, well, you've got about an hour and a half to decide what to do about him. That's when I should be rolling in. Have you and Yuri down in the garage to unload him. And have Yuri keep Rasputin down in the lower level until this is through."

There was an uncomfortable silence.

"Hauck?"

"Yes, Sveta?"

"I'm sorry."

"Yes, well so am I."

With that, he hung up.

"We're going to his place," she said.

"Whatever," said the Instructor.

"Just thought you'd like to know."

"I'm hungry."

"Too bad."

"I mean I'm really hungry."

Suddenly, she thought of Jason. The way he had neatly severed his head with no compunction.

"I said, too bad," she said, with more force than she realized. "I don't have anything to eat."

The Instructor roared at her.

"I said I'm hungry goddammit."

"And I said—"

Sveta ducked her head reflexively as the Instructor shot toward the front of the cage and reached for her hair. He was close, but not close enough.

"I said I'm hungry," repeated the Instructor for the third time through clenched teeth.

She pulled the car over to the side of the road, slammed the shift lever into park, and reached for her rifle. Meanwhile the enraged Instructor kept clawing at her. When she had unzipped her rifle from its case, she took it out and turned. The Instructor settled down like magic.

She looked out the window and there were no cars passing, so she turned in her seat.

"Wait a minute," said the Instructor. "I'm calm now."

He backed away, sliding on his ass to the far corner of the cage.

"I was just mad—"

Sveta shot him in the left shoulder with a tranquilizing dart.

"You shot me," he howled.

"Go to sleep," she said, returning the rifle to its case.

She turned in her seat so that she was facing forward again, shifted the car back into drive and, after turning on her blinker entered traffic again.

"You shot me, you bitch," snarled the Instructor, and lunged forward in the cage again.

But this time, Sveta was ready for him, and leaned slightly into steering wheel.

"You might as well relax," she said, "and go to sleep."

"I hate you," the Instructor said.

"Whatever."

The Instructor slumped forward in his cage and fell asleep.

****

Sveta stepped out of the SUV, the rifle out of the case and over her shoulder. Hauck was waiting for her with Yuri, and he looked grim.

"Are you okay?" he asked.

She shrugged.

"I'm fine."

Yuri looked stressed out.

"You sure?" he asked.

"I'm fine. Let's get him unloaded while he's still asleep. I had to shoot him with a tranquilizer dart. He was pretty insane."

Hauck just stood there while she opened the hatchback. The Instructor lay where he had fallen, in the cage's corner.

"Okay," said Sveta, moving out of the way and un-shouldering the rifle, "he's all yours."

Hauck and Yuri looked at one another. It was one thing to say that the Instructor was a werewolf. It was another thing all together to see him up close and personal locked in a cage.

"Look," said Sveta, "can you hurry it up? I really don't know how long those tranquilizer darts will last on him. He could wake up at any time, and when I said he's crazy—trust me, he's crazy."

With that for an incentive, the two men grabbed hold of the cage and hauled it out of the back of the SUV. They walked it awkwardly toward the door to Hauck's place. Sveta followed, keeping a close eye on the Instructor through her rifle sites.

"Get the door," said Hauck.

"You get it, in case he's faking it."

Hauck considered that and then nodded. He shouldered the cage with Yuri's help, and unlocked the door. Then he and Yuri awkwardly wedged past it and, with Sveta bringing up the rear with her tranquilizer rifle on the Instructor all the way, they made their way inside.

With the door closed, Hauck pushed the button for the elevator doors. They slid open with a hiss, and Hauck and Yuri made their way into the enclosure with Sveta following close behind. She pushed the button for four, the doors closed behind her and the elevator began its slow ride up. The Instructor lay flat on his back, out cold.

"He's so peaceful," observed Yuri.

"You should have seen him before I shot him," said Sveta.

Hauck was inscrutable.

She had seen him before with that faraway look in his eyes. Distant, yet focused like a laser beam on the moment. The tension was palpable. He was attentive to the Instructor, but not attentive. It was as though the old man were there, yet not there. In Hauck's eyes was that look that told Sveta he was thinking of things that had happened long ago. Of times that she would never be part of, things that she would always wonder about, but things that were over and done with.

The elevator ground to a half, the doors slid open and Yuri got out first, lifted his end of the cage, waited for Hauck to lift the end with the Instructor in it, and when he had, he backed out. Hauck followed him and Sveta stepped out behind him. They took the Instructor to the computer room, where they lowered him to the ground. Adam's silvery red face stared at him incuriously.

"Do you think he'll be all right?" asked Yuri.

"I'd be more worried about us, Yuri," said Sveta.

It was ten o'clock in the morning and Hauck still didn't know what to do.

"Wake him up," he finally said.

"You're sure about this?" asked Sveta.

Hauck nodded.

"I'm sure."

Sveta shrugged.

"Yuri, get me a pail of water," she said.

With Yuri out of the room for a minute, Sveta contemplated just what the Instructor represented. In ten hours or so, if she was right, the Instructor would turn into a werewolf. A werewolf. A full-blown werewolf. It was hard to believe. All the way back, Sveta had thought about it, and she still couldn't believe it.

"Hey, what are you thinking?" she asked Hauck.

The moments dragged by, but he didn't answer.

"I said, what are you thinking?"

"I was thinking, what a waste," he finally said.

He knew they would have to kill him, Sveta finally decided. She should have done it back in the campground, but Hauck would want to question him first.

Yuri returned at that moment with a pail of water. He tried to give it to Sveta, but she demurred.

"You do it," she said.

He was about to object but saw the look in Sveta's eyes, so he took the pail over to the cage and, after one last look at her for confirmation, he doused the Instructor and then backed off. The Instructor sputtered and thrashed about.

"Go fill it up again," said Sveta.

Yuri hurried out of the room.

Sveta still carried the tranquilizer gun and raised it to her shoulder. She kept a tight eye on the old man, as he slowly awoke from his slumber. He sat up, half awake and the other half waking up. He rubbed his eyes to get the water out.

"Jesus," he said.

Hauck said nothing.

Yuri came back with another pail of water, but when he saw that the Instructor was awake, he set it down on the floor in front of him.

"Hey, at least you've still got your pants on," said Yuri.

The old man, who was shirtless, looked down at himself and scowled. He had his pants, torn though they were, on all right, but he was without shoes.

"Why don't you come over here and we'll see how funny that is," he growled.

"Uh... no thanks," said Yuri.

"Girlie," said the Instructor, nodding in Sveta's direction.

Sveta said nothing, but she kept the rifle trained on him.

"Hauck."

"How are you doing, old man?" said Hauck.

"I've been better," said the Instructor.

"Sveta tells me that you're a werewolf?"

"Look, I'm not going to turn into one in broad daylight. So, would you mind lowering the rifle, girlie?"

Sveta took her time in lowering her weapon; she was uncertain at first, but when Hauck nodded, she lowered it all the way. But she didn't let go of it, though.

"Well, Hauck, what we going to do now?"

"I've been thinking about that…"

"I just bet you have."

"I'm going to let you out of the cage."

"Really?"

The eagerness showed in the Instructor's voice.

"But I don't have a key."

"What do you mean you don't have a key?"

"Sveta closed the door without worrying about a key. She was thinking."

The Instructor looked at Sveta first in horror, and then in rage.

"You dumb—"

When Sveta raised the rifle again, the Instructor made a placating gesture with his hands.

"Okay, okay, settle down," said the Instructor.

Sveta lowered her tranquilizer rifle.

"Look, you've got to back to the campground, I must have dropped it on the ground."

She looked to Hauck.

"Wait," said the Instructor with glee, "my pants pocket! That's where I had it. I couldn't get it out when I started to change."

"Thank, God," said Hauck, "give it to me so we can get you out."

The Instructor thrust his hands into his pocket, retrieved the key and handed it over to Hauck, who pocketed it. The Instructor stared at him in amazement.

"What are you doing? I—"

He leapt at Hauck with incredible speed, but ran into the bars, which stopped him cold. They rocked back and forth. The Instructor was in a frenzy though, and kept reaching for Hauck with all his might, he couldn't contain himself. But Hauck maintained a safe distance from the old man and Sveta once again trained the rifle on him. Yuri stepped behind Hauck. Adam watched the little man with interest as he railed insanely at Hauck.

"Fascinating," he said.

The Instructor turned his rage on the screen that Adam was in.

"Fascinating? Come out of there and I'll show you fascinating," he snarled.

"Are you through?" asked Hauck evenly.

The Instructor turned toward him in a half crouch.

"What did you say?"

"I asked if you were through," said Hauck. "There is nowhere to go, nowhere to run, nowhere to hide in that cage. You've given me the key, and that was your mistake, but it's done. Over. You can't take it back. So, you might as well quiet down and hear what I've got to say."

"I don't want to," screamed the Instructor.

When Hauck didn't answer back, the Instructor gradually quieted down. He finally sat down in the far corner of the cage and sulked.

"Good," said Hauck, "are you hungry?"

The Instructor said nothing.

"I won't ask twice."

Finally, the Instructor answered.

"Yes," he said.

"Good," said Hauck. "Yuri make the Instructor something to eat."

"I want meat."

"Yes, I figured that."

"I want rare meat."

"All right. Yuri, attend to that."

38

Jimmy was slumped over in his arm chair, thinking of Jason, when the news came that Trisha had arrived with Marty. Edwina was still in the hospital—something about having been hit by a truck—and it was her assistant who came in to notify Jimmy. He thanked him, and then sent him out. Edwina was still unconscious and Jimmy made a note to send flowers. She was expected to pull through, but it would always help to have something nice waiting for her to wake up to. Of all the bad luck. A truck running into her. Jimmy shuddered sympathetically.

Now, to his visitors. His friends were waiting out in the lobby. Jimmy felt weak as he stood up. He had barely slept three hours last night, and Jason's death was wearing on him. Should he tell Trisha and Marty how he had died? Or should he tell them a concocted story? If he told them, he would be expected to produce a body, and, according to Hauck, that just was not possible. Beheadings by a werewolf were difficult to explain. So how should he? Should he just play ignorant as to what had happened to him? That would buy him a week or two. Jason's parents would not be a problem considering that they were dead, too. But still, lying to Trisha and Marty? Jimmy didn't know if he could do it.

The other thing was, he was having second thoughts about telling them at all. The less they knew the better. All right, he might as well admit it to himself. He wasn't concerned about Marty. He could tell him and be done with it. But Trisha? She worked for the NSA. The same group that had killed his father. He couldn't trust her, he knew that. Her first loyalty was to the government. How would she react if she knew that he was ghosting the government just to get to the monster that had haunted his nightmares since that night twenty-five years ago? Was it really twenty-five years that had passed?

Jimmy stopped before the door, took a deep breath, and opened it.

Marty was standing there, tall, broad shouldered and tan. He looked like a Greek god with sunburn.

"Hello Jimmy," he said.

Immediately Jimmy thought again about Jason. Jason lying headless, unburied at the campground. Jason, who would never utter another word again.

"Hello Marty."

He stared awkwardly for a second, then gave up and stepped up to Marty and hugged him.

"Man, I haven't seen you in forever," said Jimmy not letting go of his bear hug.

"Well, you know, with all the places to track down the unexplained and the mysterious."

Jimmy finally let go and said, "Hey, where's Trisha?"

"Ah, you know. She had to take a call and then left in a rush. She'll join us later. That's what she said, anyways."

"Oh. Well, come in, come in."

Jimmy hoped he concealed the disappointment in his voice at not seeing Trisha. He hoped she wasn't married or anything, but he didn't know if she had a boyfriend—he hadn't dug that far, although he wished he had. But maybe it was better that she wasn't here now. Maybe he wouldn't tell her. After all, he could confide in Marty, he thought. Marty deserved to know the real reason he was here.

Marty followed him into his office, and took a chair.

"Man, you've come a long way, Jimmy," he said.

"Oh, I don't know about that," said Jimmy, when he'd settled in. "Hey, I'm sorry, can I get you coffee or tea or something?"

"No, no. Nice digs."

Marty glanced appreciatively around at the glass and chrome of Jimmy's office. He scrunched up his face at something, though. Jimmy looked around to see what was bothering him.

"What?" he asked.

"Nothing. Except that I figured lots and lots of books, is all."

Jimmy laughed.

"These days, I do all of my reading on the computer."

"Ah," said Marty, "I should have guessed. The Internet and all."

You have no idea, thought Jimmy.

"Yes, well," said Jimmy, "you know books are kind of old fashioned."

"Not to me," said Marty. "Give me an old-fashioned book any day. Of course, in the jungle there isn't much of battery life for a computer. Sometimes I'm going six weeks to three months at a time. Like when your Edwina called me, she was fortunate to catch me. I'd just finished up researching an ancient city in the Amazon. Fascinating stuff. You would have loved it."

"Really?"

"Yes. I found a city that has been long since lost to the world. It was buried beneath the wild trees of the Amazon delta. You should see it, Jimmy, it's amazing, simply amazing."

"Wow," said Jimmy, and he really meant it. Marty was living the life and loving it.

"And, I'm off to a supposed alien crash site in Mongolia in three weeks."

"Really? That's incredible, Marty."

What Jimmy was thinking about, though, was Jason, lying dead, headless in the campground.

"Yeah, hey, but you're spending all of your time at Earth Battery. You're making it happen for all the world to see, Jimmy. Congratulations, man, this is cool. I mean it. To think, unlimited energy from the salt mines? This is phenomenal, just phenomenal."

What was Jimmy thinking of anyway? The Earth Battery wouldn't work. It was all a ruse to get at the Dhole. Marty and Trisha pulled into this, and it would be a failure. Was he thinking that they would be happy for him that he had got at the source of their nightmares? He made up his mind.

"It's just as well Trish isn't here, Marty. Come on, I've got to show you something."

"Sure, Jimmy. Fire away."

Jimmy stood up. This was the risky part.

"This way. Marty," he said.

He led Marty down the long winding hallway, to the pressure plate door switch, and punched in the code. There was a hesitation in his mannerisms, like he was moving through syrup.

"Where's Jason? I haven't seen him in forever," asked Marty.

Jimmy flubbed the door entry code.

"What?" he said.

"I said, where's Jason?"

He entered the door code again. This time he got it right.

Saved by the door opening.

He stood to one side and waved his hand for Marty to enter.

"Welcome," he said, "to my inner sanctorum."

Marty appeared confused at first, but he finally entered the room. Jimmy followed behind him, and the door closed.

"Welcome, Marty," said Brittany.

"Oh my, God," said Marty. "What is that? A hologram?"

"She prefers to be called a she."

"Well, what is she? A hologram?"

"I am a fully functioning autonomic being, Marty. I have full speech capabilities and am quite able to speak for myself."

Brittany stood 5 feet 7 inches tall and was restricted in her movements to a large platform on which she stood. She was dressed in a prim and proper severe dark blue librarian's outfit, and wore plain, comfortable shoes on her feet. Marty felt at the same time fascinated by her, and oddly attracted to her.

"What is the weather like outside?" was all he could think of to ask.

"It is 50 degrees Fahrenheit outside or, if you prefer, 10 degrees Celsius."

"This is amazing, Jimmy."

"Brittany watches for intruders into my inner sanctorum, Marty. She has a keen eye for anyone who tries to break in via computer to steal my secrets. May I offer you tea or coffee?"

"Tea. Black, actually. You've convinced me."

"Brittany?"

"Yes, doctor?"

"Could you please get Marty a—"

"Already brewing, doctor."

A few seconds later, Jimmy retrieved a cup from the pedestal of steaming tea, and gingerly handed it over to Marty, who was staring bug eyed at the computing power arranged in the room. There were four giant screens and a host of little ones arranged around the room. As Jimmy steered him over to a table where they sat down, he contemplated his next move very carefully. In the end, he decided that his friendship with Marty would have to come first and damn the results.

"There's something I have to tell you," he began.

"What?"

"Jason's dead."

"What? How?" asked a bewildered Marty.

"I...I..."

"Yes? What is it, Jimmy?"

Jimmy got up out of his chair and paced around the room for a minute. He was clearly frustrated that although he had decided to explain to Marty what had happened to Jason, he couldn't bring himself to utter the words. Finally, he just blurted it out.

"Jason was killed by a werewolf."

Jimmy plopped down in his chair. He dropped his heads down in his hands. There—he had said it. Whatever the consequences, now it was out, and he would have to live with it.

Whatever reaction Jimmy had expected, he clearly didn't expect what he got.

"Where did this happen?"

"What?"

"I said, where did this happen? Jimmy, I do this sort of thing for a living, remember? I'm sorry to hear Jason's gone, but we've got to stop his killer. We've got to stop the werewolf, now. It's up to us. So, I repeat, where did it happen?" said Marty.

"I...I...I don't know exactly. Some campground north of here."

"Jimmy, listen to me. Do you need a tissue?"

"What? No, I mean I don't think so. It's just that he was alive one minute... and I don't exactly believe in werewolves. I mean Hauck said that his son was one… and I said I could help find him…"

"Who is Hauck?"

"Oh God, Marty. I've got so much to tell you. I didn't think this through."

And with that, it just all came tumbling out. The fact that the Earth Battery was a fraud. The fact that he was really just going after the Dhole, the thing that had years ago caused the pop-up killers to come after them, the fact that he had stumbled across Hauck some time ago, that he had killed a werewolf but that his son had now inherited the curse and he was being held captive, the fact that Jason had went with one of Hauck's lieutenants, a woman named Sveta to capture his son not knowing that he held his son captive, and how Jason had his head severed from his body by the werewolf but Sveta had captured the werewolf.

Marty listened patiently throughout the rambling discourse, but attentively. It was a confusing story, but fascinating.

"So, you did all this to kill the…Dhole, I think you called it?"

Jimmy nodded.

"But how do you even know that this… thing is there? I don't mean to sound skeptical Jimmy, believe me when I say this, but this sounds insane that a thing could be living beneath the salt mines of Detroit. How could it have escaped notice?"

Jimmy thought for a minute, and then brought up a computer on the table. He tapped a few keys, and then turned the screen around to face Marty.

"What are we watching?"

"Just wait. The video has got to catch up."

And it did. Marty watched in fascination as Stacy and Randy began their descent into the white madness that was the salt mines. Down, down they went until they hit bottom. A long white tunnel stretched away from them.

"You had a camera and a microphone on them?"

"Yes, just a safety precaution. They didn't even know it was there. Now watch."

Marty watched as Randy freaked out, and Stacy tried to calms the older man. He paid attention as Stacy stepped out of the car and into the tunnel, told Randy not to worry. Randy got out of the car to bring

Stacy back inside of the car. Two minutes later the screaming began. And he saw them for the second time in his life—the pop-up killers, swarming down the tunnel. He remained silent as they caught up with Stacy and Randy and devoured them. For three full minutes, he was quiet afterward.

"I never would have believed you if not for this video," Marty said. "It's like a nightmare from childhood has come to life."

Jimmy nodded.

"I had a report that two employees went missing from their jobs. I had a sinking feeling that this was what it was about. Luckily, neither of them had families so I didn't have to... you know, tell them the circumstances of their death."

Brittany interrupted them.

"Doctor, speaking of deaths, there is something that I think you should see."

Jimmy scrunched up his nose, afraid to ask what it was. Finally, he agreed.

"Bring it up on the big screen, will you?"

"Certainly, doctor."

And with that, the story of Tyler and the pop-up killers began to play on the giant wall screen.

"Oh no," said Jimmy. "Why am I only now being informed as to this?"

"It only happened last night, doctor, and there was the normal routing to go through before it came to your attention."

"How many days until the drilling is complete?" asked Jimmy.

"With no more delays, I should say we will be done in two days, doctor."

"I'm sorry, Jimmy." Said Marty.

"Yeah, well, I should have seen it coming. I can't get near the Dhole without it reacting to me. It's supposed to be asleep for another month."

"Asleep?"

"That's what the legends say, anyway."

And that was when Jimmy told the whole story of how he came to find the Dhole. The story of Whip Lovecraft. His travels around the world, and stopping in Detroit for the amazing, but terrifying find of a lifetime. How he spent the rest of his days locked away in his house, afraid to come out. His Uncle Whip, hiding under the bed. His rantings, which his nephew H.P. Lovecraft overheard and turned into stories. How he, to his dying day, would keep repeating the phrase, "The horror, the absolute horror." His investigation of the Detroit Salt Mines, to see if that was what he was referring to. His paying Kirk to research the newspaper files and people that had experience down there to find if there really was a monster down there. The disappearance of Kirk. Jimmy investigating on his own to find out the truth.

And he had.

He had found something... monstrous down there. Something that lay fourteen hundred feet underground buried beneath the salt. Something alien. Not of this earth, that had crashed on this earth eons ago, when Michigan was underwater, and the alien craft had sunk beneath the warm liquid like a stone. Trapped within, the alien had gone into a state of hibernation where it dreamed a dreamless dream. For all eternity, to be caught in a web of nightmares and phantasms from which there was no escape. Later, much later, the salt had formed around the craft and encapsulate it. Layer upon layer of salt, until it was forever trapped within mantles of brine so thick that it would never escape.

But it could still dream.

It's nightmares had the hideous quality of coming to life on the night of the blood Red Moon. While the creature slept, it dreamed of bat-like creatures that popped up in the city of Detroit and the surrounding suburbs. Creatures that were real.

The pop-up killers.

"Come on," said Jimmy. "I'd better introduce you to Hauck and Sveta."

39

Professor Meridian eyed with his one good eye Beckham, who sat nervously before him. Curious that this one little man had so much power within the government. That he would have clawed his way up the ladder of government service was interesting, but that would have to wait for another time. He took another sip of tea.

"So," he said, "this Mrs. Gladstone was your mole inside of the Earth Battery organization?"

"Yes," said Beckham.

"And you say that a truck hit her?"

"Yes."

"Hmm. Yet she is recovering in the hospital?"

"Yes."

"And is her... usefulness to us complete?"

Beckham looked shocked.

"Well, we can use her again as soon as she is well," he protested.

The professor waited him out.

"She is progressing rapidly."

"I see."

"No, I don't think that you do. What would you have me do? Kill her?"

Just then Sanzar and Abarran came into the room. They surreptitiously walked over and, splitting up, they stood one on either side of Beckham. He glanced at them, one at a time, and gulped.

"Well, Mr. Beckham," continued Krikor, "I suppose she is your problem, of course, and you must solve it in your own way. But now, if I understand you correctly, we no longer have a mole inside of the organization. Is that correct?"

"Yes."

"And we are flying blind, so to speak? And what of the young man Jason?"

"He seems to have dropped off the planet, we can't find him anywhere."

"My, we truly are blind."

"For the time being, we are. But I have another agent."

Professor Meridian arched an eyebrow.

"Indeed?"

Eager to please, and nervous with Sanzar and Abarran hovering over him, Beckham nodded vigorously.

"Her name is Trisha Daytona and she knows Dr. Harlen. She is an old acquaintance of his."

Professor Meridian became suddenly interested.

"Tell me more."

"She is an old childhood friend of his. A heartthrob, so to speak. She should be able to insinuate herself into the Earth Battery project without a problem."

"Is she on board with what she is to do?"

"She is, as far as she knows. That is, she thinks that she is to spy on Dr. Harlen only."

"Good. We wouldn't want another Kirk on our hands, would we?'

Beckham gulped.

"No, no, of course not."

"He got a lot of information on the Dhole, and he should not have escaped. A pity he was so paranoid that he had his whole apartment barricaded with razor wire. And now Mrs. Gladstone gets struck by a truck. It's almost as though you are not committed to the goal."

An odd feeling began to descend on Beckham as though he had a cold, wet blanket thrown on him. Sanzar and Abarran took a step closer.

"I-I of course I am committed to our goal, Krikor."

He waited a minute before he waived his two henchmen to step back.

"Of course, you are, Mr. Beckham. How could I ever doubt you?"

Beckham still felt the chill on him, and it would not go away.

"But now, let us check in on our sacrifice, shall we?"

"Of course," said Beckham, as he felt the load lift off him.

He stood up slowly, careful to match the speed at which he did so to Professor Meridian. The man seemed to take forever to stand, as he looked lost in thought as he did so. He strode toward a panel in the wall, depressed two separate built in plates, and a large section of panel slid back, revealing stairs that led down into the bowels of the earth. Sconces lit the way with their electric lambency, and, looking back and smiling a wicked smile, Professor Meridian began to descend them.

Beckham dreaded going down the steps, he truly did. He didn't know if Krikor would ever let him return to the surface of the world. It was an irrational fear, however, and he knew it. Feeling a non to gentle prod from either Sanzar or Abarran—he couldn't tell them apart—with a shudder, he began the hated descent. The door slid shut behind him.

The stone steps beneath his feet felt smooth from years of usage. The walls, when he stumbled and had to press his hands against them to keep from falling, were freezing and hard. He jerked away from them. Krikor stopped and turned to look at him.

"I-I stumbled," said Beckham.

The professor said nothing, but continued to stare at him with his one good eye for nearly a full minute. Finally, he turned and continued down the winding stairs. Beckham hurried to keep up, careful that he did not lose his balance again. For a minute, he thought of Sanzar and Abarran at the top of the stairs, and he shuddered. As he continued down the stairs, he felt the creepiness of what he was doing, and it gave him pause. But the professor continued on before him relentlessly, and not willing to stay behind with Sanzar and Abarran, he hurried to keep up.

He had gone down perhaps five long flights of stairs when Krikor stopped before a thick wooden door, and he waited patiently for Beckham to catch up to where he stood. When Beckham was on the same level as himself, Krikor at last began to speak. Try as he might, Beckham's eyes took in the fact that the stairway did not stop at this level but continued their circuitous pathway down.

"You are about to see what no one has ever seen before you—a werewolf in captivity."

Here he gave a particularly lupine grin.

"A what?"

"You heard me correctly—a werewolf that we have taken the precaution to place behind bars. Bars made of titanium, I might add, so that he will find it quite impossible to escape."

"But that's… impossible… I mean… a werewolf?"

"Oh, believe me, you shall see things that in your puny worldview are impossible. You shall see the werewolf transform and the Dhole rise. Prepare yourself, Mr. Beckham, for your life shall never be the same."

Suddenly, Professor Krikor Meridian seemed almost apocalyptic in his mannerism. Beckham didn't know quite what to make of it, but he felt a shiver go up and down his spine. He wondered for a moment if he were in over his head, if he should cut and run, but Meridian's eyes held him where he was. They were magnetic, they held the very essence of truth in them and Beckham knew again that he was in the right place at the right time.

"Are you ready for the revealed truth?" asked Krikor Meridian.

Beckham shook his head in assent.

"Then let us begin this journey into madness together," and with that said, he opened the thick wooden door making a loud creak as he did so.

They walked together down a wide hallway of doors. The floor was made of smooth interlocked stones and looked as though it had been there for two hundred years. The walls were of a rock, polished to a shiny sheen, and lined with sconces which gave off light. Beckham wondered where the generator was housed, since they were surely off the grid and must have an independent source of power. But this was an idle thought as what most concerned him was what was behind each door that they passed. The doors were arranged at odd intervals on either side of the tunnel they now traversed. How strange they were, locked and the bars that barricaded them in.

"What is behind these doors?" asked Beckham.

Without breaking stride, the professor said, "You wouldn't want to know."

Beckham realized to his horror that he was close to the line, and went the rest of the way in silence.

At one door, the professor stopped. Beckham noticed that this door was wider and more formidable than the rest and had two wide bars that held it in place in addition to four imposing sets of locks. There was a window, inset into the door that was perhaps two feet tall by three feet wide and had a sliding hatch in front of it with a small knob that projected out from it.

"Brace yourself," said the professor with a wicked smile, and grabbed the small knob and slid it back.

He couldn't help himself, he had to lean in to see what was inside. But the scene that awaited him was beyond any terror that Beckham had ever experienced.

The room was lit by recessed electric lamps with a thick cover of what appeared to be bulletproof glass. Chairs and a couch that were made of metal and bolted to the floor. But those things were just a background blur. What really held Beckham's attention was the awful sight that met his eyes.

The werewolf tearing on the leg that he held down with his front paws. And the blood that was everywhere. The blood that spattered the walls and the body parts scattered all around. The head lying on the metal couch, face up and staring with its empty eye sockets. An arm and a torso strewed around the floor like so much detritus. Suddenly, the werewolf began to howl.

The werewolf was an awe-inspiring beast. It was covered in slick brown hair. Its paws were powerful fingers that ended in large, claws. Its muscles rippled beneath its fur, and its haunches were thick with ropy bunched up sinews. Its chest was broad and mighty, thrumming with repressed dynamism. Its neck with thick and seemed almost an extension of its chest muscles. But it was the head and jaws that held Beckham transfixed with fear. The ears lay flat against its skull, but its jaws, such commanding jaws. A long snout and those eyes, Beckham was grateful, oh so grateful for the barrier in between him and the creature.

But then, suddenly, the werewolf turned its shaggy head towards the door.

"You see, he notices you, he is quite aware of food," said Professor

Meridian.

The werewolf sprang at the door with incredible speed, and it let out an earth-shattering roar. Beckham immediately jumped back a good five feet. Claws raked at the window and teeth snapped. It's eyes betrayed an unrelenting fury.

"Come, come, Mr. Beckham. Don't be afraid. He can't get through this door, believe me."

The creature sprang at the door repeatedly, howling and slathering like there was no tomorrow. Beckham refused to come any closer.

"Mr. Beckham? Come closer. I want you to see, to really see what a magnificent specimen is our sacrifice."

The werewolf emitted a low growl. It stopped long enough to consider Beckham, who felt the hackles rise on the back of his neck. He couldn't go any closer he just couldn't. Beckham felt real fear. Suddenly, without warning, Sanzar and Abarran were at his sides. They grasped his arms and moved him closer. The werewolf went crazy, howling and snapping its jaws. Beckham screamed as Sanzar and Abarran dragged him nearly right up to the window.

Meridian closed the soundproofed sliding window in place.

"Well," he turned his one good eye on him, "what do you think of our oh-so fine sacrifice? Hmm?"

Beckham didn't know what to say—he was in shock. Every bone in his body vibrated with terror and the sudden relief at having the monster closed off so quickly. A mere sliding of the door and it was complete. But he could not convince his body that the horror of those slavering jaws was over and through.

"Well, Mr. Beckham, I am waiting for an answer."

"What? My God, that thing was horrible, and you ask me if what?"

Meridian took a step closer to Beckham.

"I asked you if it was a suitable sacrifice. You see, not just any sacrifice will do. When the planets align in this manner, we require a special sacrifice for the Dhole to rise. You see, for eons it has been sleeping a dreamless, mostly dreamless sleep, and for it to wake up we have to have a unique sacrifice, and the werewolf works nicely. Don't you agree?"

Beckham's mouth wouldn't form the words, try as he might. He opened and closed them several times.

"Would you prefer that I have Sanzar and Abarran throw you into the same room as the werewolf, Mr. Beckham?"

"What? Oh God, no."

Sanzar and Abarran stood silently at his sides, hands locked on his biceps and Beckham suddenly was possessed by an image of Professor Meridian holding the door open while his two erstwhile assistants threw him in and shutting the door after him.

"You see, Mr. Beckham, that Miss Trisha Daytona had better do her job properly or I will feed you to the werewolf. You have the chance right now to be a heroic figure to the many worshippers of the Dhole around the world, don't you see? All you have to do is keep an eye on Dr. Jimmy Harlen. I want to know his every move. Time is growing short now. In seven days and seven days only, Dr. Harlen will turn on his accursed machine and attempt to electrify the Dhole. At the exact moment that he does, I will sacrifice our pet werewolf. But not an instant before nor an instant later for the ceremony to work. You see, what our Dr. Harlen does not know, cannot know is that the very electricity he attempts cook the Dhole, will revitalize him."

Throughout Meridian's long diatribe Beckham's eyes grew wider and wider, but they were positively bug-eyed by the end.

"You mean, all that work to dig down and kill the Dhole with electricity and that is what will revitalize him, bring him to life? Now I understand everything—except if Dr. Harlen will bring the Dhole back to life, I don't understand why we have to watch him so carefully."

"Ahh, but you are forgetting the time of our sacrifice. It must be done at the exact same time that the electricity is being applied."

"Oh."

"Yes, oh indeed. That's what your Trisha must tell me. Now that Edwina Gladstone is recovering from being hit by a truck, Trisha Daytona must fill in for her lest our Dr. Jimmy becomes unpredictable and secretly chooses a time for himself and we miss our opportunity. Do you understand?"

Beckham did and he said so, emphatically. His body still shook from the sight of the werewolf, but at least he had hope. Hope that in the new world order of the Dhole, he would be revered.

"Yes," he nodded, his head bobbing up and down.

"I sincerely hope so, because if you don't, you know what awaits you."

And here, Meridian slid the window back again and revealed the jaws and the terrible eyes of the werewolf.

40

Alex Gudinoff was the daytime shift foreman in charge of all things drilling down to the requisite fourteen hundred feet down. Then, he was finished with this God-forsaken job. Just one hundred more feet to go, and victory was his. He would have completed the job, for which too much had gone wrong. Alex had the vague feeling that they were cursed. Five workers had just up and disappeared as if they had never been there, and that bothered him.

"Alex?"

That brought him out of his reverie.

"Yes?"

"We've breached thirteen hundred feet. Just one hundred left to go," said Diane Perino.

She had been with them since the beginning, and was a short, squat woman of maybe one hundred seventy pounds that she carried well. Alex didn't know how she pulled it off, but she did.

"Excellent."

"We've got the drill bits changed out and are ready to go."

"Already? Damn, girl, you are smoking today."

"I want to finish this damn job, sir," smiled Diane.

"Well, you have my permission to keep drilling. Let me take a look at it first, just to kick the tires."

"We thought you would. Come on. We're burning daylight, sir."

Diane led the way down the long and wide cut out into the salt mines. Along the way she skirted the machinery that they had to bring down in pieces and reassemble once they had it down below. There were tractors the size of semis to haul the salt away, and miles and mile of apparatus to get the salt to the tractors. There were hi-los as big as buses and huge saws attached to motor cars that cut away blocks of salt. Always careful to give them plenty of room and keeping an eye out lest they get run over.

When they at last came to a special motorized crane, they stopped. Beyond there were the twin boreholes that did the drilling. They were monstrous things that were assembled in segments. Titanium tipped and stainless-steel bodies, they were fully a hundred feet in length. Alex approached them and ran his hand over them.

"Beautiful, aren't they? Just a hundred feet to go, baby," he said, patting them affectionately.

The twin bore-holes were ten feet in diameter. They gleamed in the too-bright light of the halogens.

"Yes, they are boss, now are we okay to drill?" asked Diane.

"Just a minute."

The rest of the work crew, all six of them stood by as Alex walked around the twin bore-holes, twenty-six feet in all. The motors that drove them were the key, of course. The twin bore-holes never had anything wrong with them, it was the motors that gave out. It didn't make any sense in this day and age for the motors to bind up and seize, but there you had it. To inspect the newly installed motors, Alex grasped the handrails and began the long climb up the forty-four feet stairway to the platform around them.

It was a long trek up, and by the time he was two-thirds of the way up, he was panting.

"Man, I've got to lay off the potato chips," he muttered.

He looked back down at the dizzying drop and saw Diane down below. She waved, and he waved back. Looking up, he swore to himself, and began the rest of the climb up. Step by blessed step, he trudged up.

Finally, he pulled himself up on the platform, wheezing and panting, but by God he had made it. He looked around at the cables feeding into the giant motors that fed the gears that turned them at such fantastic speeds and felt the awe, felt the power inherent in them. When they turned them on, they would build to a crescendo of whirring sound that was ear splitting. Everything appeared to be in order. They were ready to go.

Alex was about to turn around when something caught his eye. It looked like two red eyes staring at him from between the twin motors. He shook his head, and they were gone. Curious. They were about three feet off of the ground, and he knew, just knew that he wasn't seeing things. He hesitated, then walked toward the motors, then stopped. Suddenly, he felt a chill go through his bones. He didn't want to go any closer. Instead, he found himself walking backward toward the edge of the platform.

Never turning around or away from the motors, he stepped down the first step of the long return home, and he began the descent down. All the way down, he inexplicably kept his gaze upward, like he was afraid that something would follow him down, that if he tore his eyes away from the top, something would come after him. He felt his body break out in a cold sweat. Something, he had seen something. Those eyes, those unrelenting eyes.

Finally, he made it to the bottom, still trembling.

"That's a long way up and down just to check the motors, boss. I keep telling you, everything is A-Okay," said Diane, slapping him on the back.

But Alex's mind was still on the eyes.

"Yeah, well, you know..."

She turned to her six-man crew and gave them a thumbs-up, the okay sign. The crew mock-cheered, and then went back to work. Matt Smith, the eldest of the crew, walked over to the control panel, and flicked a couple of switches. Overhead, the big motors started to turn, slowly at first and then faster. He and the other workers had their hearing protection earmuffs on. Diane and Alex put theirs on, too as the twin bore-holes went faster and faster as they lowered down into the pits to cut away the last one hundred feet of the salt barrier.

They watched for a while longer, then Alex gave Diane the sign that he would leave. She acknowledged it and went back to watching the twin screws as they sunk out of sight to do their duty. Alex turned away and began walking back, but he couldn't shake the image of those eyes watching him. He wondered why that was—he had only the briefest glimpse of them. It wasn't like he was even sure that they were there, anyway.

He walked around the huge railcars that took away the salt, and all manner of machinery, but his mind was not on them. It was on how he had backed away, how he had almost run from those eyes. He almost forgot that he had his hearing ear protectors on, and he disgustedly took them off. Somehow, he would have to forget about those eyes.

"Hey, Mr. Gudinoff, would you mind signing these for me?"

It was Sam Brown, a sandy-haired boy of about nineteen.

"Sure."

He stopped and took a sheaf full of papers from the boy, signed them, and continued on.

"Mr. Gudinoff?"

It was Sam. After a few seconds hesitation, he had followed Alex, apparently having forgotten something.

"Yes?"

The boy hurried to catch up.

"I just wanted to say how sorry I am to be leaving, that's all."

"You're leaving us? I didn't know. What brought that on?"

The boy looked a bit uncomfortable.

"You know, the usual, I guess. Time to move on and that sort of thing."

"Well, I'm sorry to see you go, Sam. It's been nice working with you."

"Yeah, well, I just wanted to say good-bye and all."

Alex took the proffered hand and shook it.

"Good-bye, Sam."

"Good-bye, Mr. Gudinoff.

Alex turned to go.

"Mr. Gudinoff?"

Puzzled, Alex turned around.

"Yes?"

"Umm- be careful, that's all."

"I surely will, Sam. Why?"

The boy looked down at his feet, and then away.

"There's been some weird things going on is all."

"Weird things? Like what?"

"You know, just weird things, that's all."

Sam made to leave, but Alex grabbed his arm.

"Like what, Sam?"

"I've said too much already."

"Sam…"

The boy looked miserable.

"Well, the missing tools and stuff, you know."

"No, I don't know."

"Well, no one likes to work the midnight shift is all. Like Stacy and Randy were working it, and they just up and disappeared."

Alex was about to say no big deal, but then he remembered those eyes.

"And Tyler. He just up and disappeared, too. And before that was Benny."

"He quit."

"Did he? Did he really?"

That was four. That was a little strange.

"And the Mexican work gang—the whole lot of them. That was five, wasn't it?"

Alex was speechless. That brought the total to nine. There was an ugly pattern developing here.

"I thought they just left. You know, found better work and all. Or maybe they were here illegally and were one step ahead of ICE."

"Did they really? I don't know, I really don't, but that's too many for me. I've got to get out while the going is good. Well, that's all, I've said to much. But I've got to go now, Mr. Gudinoff."

"Well, best of luck, Sam."

"I wish I could say the same to you, Mr. Gudinoff, but you're going to stay here til the job's completed, aren't you?"

"Yes."

"Well, all I've got to say then is be careful, Mr. Gudinoff. Something's not right here."

Alex watched thoughtfully as the boy made his way among the machinery. Nine people unaccounted for—that made him nervous. He'd have to check the records to see if there were any more disappearances. Nine was too many, but still. Suddenly, he remembered the eyes and a chill ran down his spine.

41

Trisha saw Beckham first before he saw her. That was some small comfort to her at least. He was sitting at the restaurant, in a booth all by himself with a menu spread out before him. The place he had chosen for their meeting was Carl's House of Beef, down by the Detroit Riverfront. As she wound her way passed the other diners to Beckham's table, she found herself despising him all the more.

"You wanted to see me?" she said, when she was finally opposite his chair.

He had a menu spread out before him and was eying the delicacies.

"Yes, have a seat why don't you? The oysters are lovely."

She remained standing.

"I've got work to do, William."

"I said, have a seat."

Reluctantly, she sat down.

"Now, we can have a nice chat about your friend Dr. Harlen, while we wait for our food to be delivered. I took the luxury of ordering for you, to save time."

Trisha gritted her teeth. She didn't like how he'd ordered her food. It was an annoying habit that he had. Just then the waiter showed up with the food and it was just one more thing to hate him for. The waiter was a tall man of Arabic descent who never so much as glanced at Tricia. She found that suspicious, and right away assigned the man to a flunky position with Beckham. After all, in a busy restaurant, though how come no one occupied chairs closer than twenty-five feet. She found Beckham's pull amazing, if not irritating.

"Dig in," said Beckham.

She wondered briefly if the food were poisoned but decided even Beckham would not be that audacious.

Trisha thought about Jimmy, and in particular she thought of the night of the pop-up killers. Until that night, she'd thought she had a crush on Jason. Oddly, after that she had been smitten by Jimmy, but he had always been seemingly too shy to notice. After that, had come the horrible events with Jimmy's father, where Jimmy and his mother had to move because the authorities had caught wind of his dad's betrayal of the public trust. And that had been the end of that. All hell had broken loose. Jimmy's dad had ended up in jail. And before too long, before his endless appeals were through, he had wound up dead.

In fact, Jimmy's father was the reason that Trisha joined the NSA in the first place. She hadn't told Jimmy that, but she had hoped to discover the cause of his death. Many years later, she had. Her investigation had led to a top-secret group manned by none other than Beckham himself. He had given the kill order.

But by that time, Trisha had her whole career invested in the NSA. She would have to give up everything to expose Beckham, and there were no guarantees. He might even put out a kill order on her.

Jimmy's father had been killed for the simple expedience of saving the government face. He had said—no leaked it to the newspapers—that they had dumped eighty tons of liquid mercury into a lake outside of Oak Ridge, Tennessee. Because he hadn't gone through the proper procedures, he was tried and convicted of unauthorized usage of government information. He tried to explain that he had gone through the proper procedures but that they wouldn't listen, but that was not good enough, he didn't have his evidence in writing. And so, they had sent him to a maximum-security federal prison. While he was imprisoned there, he filed appeal after appeal and finally, he was going to have his day in court. But that was before the kill order had been filed.

"What's the matter? You not hungry?" asked Beckham.

"No."

"Well, perhaps dessert?"

"Could we just get down to business?"

Beckham eyed her dispassionately.

"Very well then. Your report on Dr. Harlen?"

Trisha reached into a briefcase and extracted a thick folder, which she then shoved across the table.

"You'll find everything that I've learned about Jimmy in there."

"Don't be so quotidian. Of course, I'll read every word that you've written, Trisha. But what are the highlights?"

Yes, what were the highlights? That Jimmy, like the rest of them, were scarred the night of the pop-up killers? That Jimmy shortly thereafter has father arrested by the NSA? That Jimmy had his father ripped from the family and died in prison? That he spent the rest of his life trying to recover from that? That he grew rich from his inventions? That his latest, his most ambitious plan, was to turn the entire salt mine beneath the city of Detroit into one monumental battery? That he had forgotten Trisha, but that she had not forgotten him?

"Nothing of note, pretty much what you already know."

"His movements since he began with Earth Battery?"

"Again, nothing unusual to report. He spends most of his time at work, sleeps there some nights. Really, there is nothing remarkable to report at all. It would help to know what you are looking for."

Beckham attempted to seem as though he considered that. He really wanted to know when the breakthrough occurred, and when the electrification of the Dole was planned. Those were his only concerns. But he made a play at seeming to consider this.

"Where are they now in the drilling?"

"One hundred twenty feet away from the line that they have set as completion."

Again, he seemed to consider this.

"Trisha, I want you at his side from now on until he achieves breakthrough, and I want to be informed immediately."

"Okay, but why?"

"I don't think you understand, Trisha. I want you to rekindle a relationship with Dr. Harlen. I want him to fall in love with you. I want him to tell you every dirty little secret that Earth Battery has.

Everything, I want him to tell you everything."

"I—"

"You have just three days to make him fall in love with you. Just three days, Trisha. I suggest you make them count."

"And if I refuse? I can get close to Dr. Harlen without making him fall in love with me. I can get you the breakthrough time and tell you exactly when it's accomplished. And, I think that you will know the time that will electrify this and light up the city of Detroit. All without making him fall in love with me. So, if you want to take this upstairs, I'm ready for you. Do we understand each other?"

"Oh, I've already been upstairs with my plan and it's approved. Three days, Trisha. Three days. I suggest you get moving."

And with that, Beckham rose from his chair and left the restaurant. Trisha was in such a state that she didn't realize at first that he hadn't even bothered to pay the bill. But none was forthcoming.

"Of course," she said, and got up to leave.

She walked to her car and got in. Backing out she checked her mirrors to see if she was followed. If she was, she couldn't tell. She found herself checking the rearview mirrors as she went down Woodward. Still nothing, so she gave up. If they were following her there was nothing she could do. She turned onto West Jefferson and began her way to the salt mines. At the gate, she showed her pass and was admitted. Getting out of her car, she slammed the door behind her.

Trisha couldn't believe Beckham. He had gone behind her back to the top brass and got the operation approved. Within three days she had to get Dr. Jimmy Harlen to fall in love with her. Well wasn't that just lovely. And how exactly was she supposed to do that? But in her heart she knew just how to worm her way into his heart. But she didn't want to. She wanted Jimmy to fall love with her naturally, unforced by any feminine wiles or seductions.

"Miss Daytona?"

Curious, she looked up to see a plain man with a hand extended. She was just at the door when it opened, and he was standing there.

"Yes."

"I'm Alan Coyle," he said. "I'm sorry if you were expecting Mrs.

Gladstone, but she's had an accident."

"I'm sorry to hear that," said Trisha. "Is she all right?"

"It's a bit touch and go, so I'm covering for her in the meantime."

"Okay."

"If you'll just follow me, I'll take you to Dr. Harlen."

Alan led the way past reception, and up the elevator to the fourth floor.

"This is a very impressive building you've got here," said Trisha.

"Oh, you should see below ground. That's where all the impressive machinery is."

They arrived at the fourth floor and the elevator doors opened, and they got out.

"Quite some digs you have here," commented Trisha.

"Like I said, the real beauty is down below, although I'm sure Dr. Harlen would like to show you that himself. He's got a visitor right now and is out of the office—I'm sure he won't be long, but I'll let him know that you're here. Would you like to have some tea or coffee?"

"No thanks, I'll just wait here. I have some things to do anyway."

"Suit yourself, but if you change your mind, Mary the receptionist will be right back and will get it for you. If you need me for anything at all, my office is right over there."

Trisha nodded absently, sat down and made herself comfortable. She looked around at the offices, saw the one marked "Dr. Harlen," and sighed. It was going to be, she thought, the longest wait of her life.

She didn't bother with primping—she already knew she was beautiful. Men just flocked to her without her having to exert any effort at all. Except Beckham, of course, and she suspected he was either a eunuch or gay. And she wondered again, not for the first time, why he was so interested in Jimmy. It just didn't make any sense. He wasn't any kind of a security risk at all. I mean so what if his father had squealed to the newspapers about the government dumping mercury? Big deal. That was twenty-five years ago. And in all that time, Jimmy had worked to repair his father's image by inventing things that changed the world for the better. So, again, why was Beckham so interested in him? Why did he want to know when breakthrough of the fourteen hundred foot barrier was achieved, and why did he want to know when the electrification process was begun?

Surely all they had to do was check the Internet for that information. It just didn't make any sense.

But the idea of being forced to get next to Jimmy for any reason made her feel slightly warm inside. Who was she kidding, though? Jimmy was married to his work. There was no woman in his life and it was a fantasy to think that he was saving himself for her when he finished his last invention—the Earth Battery. Then the memory of his father would be put to bed at last. Then, the memory of that awful night when they were kids would be finally erased, too.

The night of the pop-up killers.

42

"I don't want to calm down," snarled the Instructor.

Hauck tightened his jaw.

"We've already been through this," he said. "You've got to calm down so I can make the call."

"Yes, you've got to calm down or —" began Yuri.

"Shut your trap or I'll rip it off your face," yelled the Instructor.

Yuri jumped back a good three feet before remembering that the Instructor was locked away safely in a cage.

"Just be quiet," said Sveta, "and it will be all over before you know it."

"Yeah, well keep that little twerp away from me."

"Yuri," said Hauck, "why don't you leave the room for this."

Yuri glared at Hauck for a minute, about to say something, and then thought better of it. He left the room without another word. Charlene sat in the corner. Reluctant to say anything but fascinated by the Instructor.

"Now, are you ready?"

"Why? You're going to kill me anyway."

Sveta looked at Hauck, who seemed wrapped in his own thoughts. She knew he had feelings for the old man, but that he would have to kill him. There was no cure. It was a harbinger, she supposed for what he would have to do to his own son. It was just not possible to keep him locked up every time there was a full moon. And, the old man seemed to be more aggressive than even before. He had lost that sense of humor that he once had about his killing.

"I will not kill you."

"Sure."

"Look, I said I will not kill you. Now let's get on with the call—"

At that exact moment, the computer came to life with Jimmy Harlen's face.

"Hauck, can you hear me?"

Adam appeared on the screen next to him, as always, and there was another man with him.

"Yes, I'm here," answered Hauck as he pressed a button on the computer.

"Ah, good, I'd like you to meet someone I've told you about, Martin Vukovich."

"Hello," said Martin.

He made introductions around the table to Sveta, Charlene, and even Yuri came in for this. Lastly, Hauck introduced the Instructor.

"He got bitten by a werewolf while tracking my son."

Hauck didn't say that the Instructor had killed Jason. He would save that for another time, if ever. Sveta was staring at Hauck, but he ignored her. He knew what she thought. She thought he should kill the Instructor while they had the chance. Well, why should he? He needed the Instructor's help to kill Professor Meridian and save his son. But when he looked at him, he didn't know how that was going to be possible. The Instructor seemed… feral. That look in his eyes was positively wild. Hauck let his eyes trail over to Sveta. She was staring at him impassively. He looked away.

"I'm sorry, I didn't catch your name," said Jimmy.

Before the Instructor could answer, Hauck answered for him.

"We just call him the Instructor."

The Instructor, meanwhile, sulked in his corner of the cage.

"Well, hello. Anyway, I've brought Marty up to speed and remarkably he doesn't think I'm crazy."

"Well, that's just dandy," barked the Instructor. "Hauck here is going to kill me and that's all you've got to tell me is that 'Marty's up to speed?'"

"I'm not going to kill you. We've just got to come to an agreement that you can't be let out every night before a full moon. You just can't. And with the red moon coming, I don't know what it will do. Maybe you'll turn every night, maybe not. I just don't know."

Marty spoke up for the first time.

"So, you're the werewolf," he said. "Tell me, how does it feel?"

"Wait a minute—" began Hauck.

"Let him speak," said Marty. "You can't go on talking for him. If he rages, so be it, but let him speak."

Hauck was about to say something else, but he closed his mouth half-way through opening it. "Okay," he said.

They all, as one, turned to the Instructor.

"What are you all looking at? You want to know how it feels? I'll tell you how it feels—it feels great. Other than being locked in this stupid cage that is. I feel like a million bucks if you really have to know."

The Instructor suddenly slammed his fists against the bars. He moved so fast that the eye could barely see him. Leaping against the side of the cage it clung there.

"Let me out," he screamed.

The rest of the group sat in stunned silence.

"Will you behave?" asked Marty.

"Seriously?" asked the instructor.

"That will be a subject of serious debate," said Hauck preemptively.

"No, I would seriously consider letting him out of that cage," said Marty. "With the exception, that he return to the cage two hours before nightfall."

"Hell yes," said the Instructor.

"You are not a werewolf now, that is obvious."

"What are you, stupid?" snapped the Instructor.

"Hey, that's enough," said Hauck.

"No, that's all right," said Marty. "We'll just leave him locked up until...how long should that be, Hauck?"

"I don't know. Of course, there will be the matter of his bathroom breaks. We should either let him go in the cage, and then wash him down, or chain him, at gun point, of course. Leg irons and the whole nine yards should be enough."

"You're really enjoying this, aren't you?" said the Instructor.

"No," said Sveta, "I would enjoy it if it were my show to run. I should have shot you when you were still a man in the cage and left your body."

"At least that's honest," said the Instructor.

"Yes, well there's that," said Hauck.

"Let's go around the room, shall we? I want to see how many are in favor. Yuri?"

Yuri looked like he wanted to be anywhere else but where he was. He looked from side to side, at Sveta, at Hauck, at Charlene, anywhere except at the Instructor.

"Well?" asked Marty.

"I guess I'd keep him locked up. I mean don't get me wrong. The Instructor's plenty scary enough, but since he got bit by that werewolf, he's doubly scary."

"When I get out of here, I'm going to filet you," said the Instructor in a low menacing growl.

"Charlene?"

"Hey, don't get me in the middle. I'm new to this party I don't even know the old man."

"Smart girl," said the Instructor.

"Well then," said Marty, "I guess that leaves me and Jimmy."

"You better let me out," said the Instructor.

"I've already said I'd let you out, so I guess that leaves it up to Jimmy. Tie vote means you stay in. Jimmy."

The Instructor put on his most earnest face. Jimmy seemed to waiver.

"I don't know, I just don't know," said Jimmy.

"Oh, come on," said the Instructor. "I'll be good."

"I just don't know anything about werewolves."

"We're just like anyone else, only different that's all."

The Instructor tried his best to look earnest. Jimmy was his one chance to get free, and oh how he planned on taking it.

"I've run into the Eyes of Death," said Hauck.

Suddenly, the Instructor was all ears.

"Where?" he asked.

"Detroit. At the Renaissance Plaza. The others know about the

Eyes of Death. I had to tell them they couldn't get a hold of you."

The Instructor's eyes narrowed, then relaxed.

"It's okay, I would've done the same to you."

"Instructor, he doesn't know who I am or where to find me. We met up through the Internet. He needs me in with a book signing about Drogol. He claimed to have secret information and I fell for it. But, he really got me with a gold coin he wanted me to date—I went there in my Vogel identity— and when I took it with me, that's when I discovered a transponder in it and ditched it."

"How far away were you from here?"

"Far enough. He couldn't get a fix on us. No way. The transponder was discovered by Adam."

The Instructor cocked an eyebrow.

"You sure you weren't followed?"

"Positive."

"Sorry to interrupt, but who is this Eyes of Death?" asked Marty.

"Who is this guy, anyway, and why are we talking to him? And will someone let me out of this God-forsaken cage?" howled the Instructor.

"He's a friend of Jimmy's, that's all we know," said Hauck. There's one more coming. You killed the other one."

"What?" said the Instructor.

"It was Jason, the one you killed. You were in your werewolf persona and didn't even know he existed. Now you have to see why it's such an important decision whether or not to keep you locked up."

"It was you that killed Jason?" asked an aghast Jimmy.

"I didn't know," said the Instructor.

"You didn't know? That's terrifying," said Jimmy, backing away from the computer screen.

"Yeah, well it is what it is."

Hauck gave the Instructor a sharp look.

"What? What did I say wrong?"

"Well, for one thing, you didn't express any remorse," said Charlene.

"Yeah, well I'm sorry. So what?"

"At least you said your sorry. A little bit late, but you said it," said Charlene.

"Could we get back to who the Eyes of Death are?" said Marty.

There was a deadly seriousness to his voice, as though he had taken over where Jimmy dared not tread.

"And who is this Adam?" asked the Instructor.

"I am Adam," said the floating head. "I am a cybernetic organism that lives inside of the machines of the world."

"What? Oh, brother, just what we need. Who assembled this gaggle of misfits anyway?"

"Thank Hauck for that," said Sveta.

"The Eyes of Death is a code name for a group of assassins. They are feared by everyone that has heard of them. To speak their name, so the legend goes, is death. Professor Meridian is the head of them. They've got my son, who is also a werewolf. They've got him, we think, in an isolated home in Detroit."

"So, let me get this straight—I've got it that this guy Meridian guy has your son? Correct?" said Marty.

"Yes."

"And he's a werewolf?"

"Also correct."

"And you want to get him back. But how does that tie in with Jimmy's problem of trying to kill the Dhole?"

"The what?" said the Instructor. "And would somebody please let me out of this cage? I've got to take a piss."

"Later," said Hauck.

"Not later, now," said the Instructor.

"All right, already. The Dhole is an ancient monster that lives beneath the salt mines that Jimmy wants to kill. But Adam here can get us into Meridian's house to retrieve my son when we otherwise couldn't because it's guarded, and they will kill him. In return for Adam's help, Jimmy wants us to get him out after the Dhole is finished."

"I'm sorry I asked," said the Instructor. "Now could you please make up your mind before I piss my pants. You know, I can help you get your kid back."

"I don't know," said Jimmy. "I just don't know."

"Well, then, I do. Let him out."

Hauck seemed to consider what that meant for a long time. Then, with a hesitancy that Sveta noted, he unlocked the cage. The Instructor bounded out of the cage rapidly. Everyone moved back involuntarily.

He raced out of the room and Hauck silently cursed.

"Well, there went that plan," said Yuri. "We'll never see him again."

"What do we do now?" asked Charlene.

"Wait," said Hauck. "He'll be back. He just has to go to the bathroom."

"Hmm," said Sveta.

"Okay, like I was saying," said Marty, "how does all this tie in with Jimmy's problem?"

"Jimmy," said Hauck.

He seemed a little shell shocked at the revelation that the Instructor had killed Jason. And worse, they had set him free. Words didn't seem to form; he seemed to be at a dead end.

"Jimmy," prodded Hauck.

He shook his head to straighten it out. That man, called the Instructor, had killed Jason. He felt like crying, but even the tears wouldn't come.

"I," he said, "I need help getting out, because the government is watching my every move."

"Why do you need help getting out?" asked Sveta.

"Because the Earth Battery doesn't work, that's why."

"So, the government is investing all of that money and it doesn't work?" said Sveta.

"The government hasn't invested a penny of their money in Earth Battery. All of the investment is my own," snapped Jimmy.

"Ooh," said Yuri, "aren't we touchy."

Jimmy looked taken aback.

"I'm sorry," he said, "I really am. It's just that the business of Jason's death has me upset, is all. I'm sorry, truly sorry."

"Think nothing of it," said Sveta.

"It's just that the idea of the...the Instructor being the one who killed him weirds me out, you know?"

Just then the Instructor returned.

"Now let's see—who have I got to kill next?"

Everyone moved back a foot except Hauck and Charlene, who was sitting down.

"Hey," he said, "I was only kidding. God, I feel better after having taken a piss."

"Lovely of you to tell us," said Sveta.

"Okay, could we get back to the main topic at hand?" said Marty. "Now I've gotten the whole picture, except for the Dhole which I don't think you've all been filled in on."

"The what?" asked the Instructor.

"The Dhole," said Adam, "is the creature that Dr. Harlen has discovered living down deep in the salt mines. He's trapped, you seem underneath the layers of salt and is in a state of hibernation. Isn't that correct, Dr. Harlen?"

"Yes. You see, every ten or twelve years there is an approximate alignment of the planets—what we call a red moon night—and he dreams these horrible dreams that become real. That's when these terrible creatures come out. His dreams become real. But this time, in two weeks, the planets will actually align, and then, I am afraid, the Dhole will actually wake up and cause all sorts of havoc. Asleep, the bat like creatures we call the pop-up killers will be set free every twelve years, but awake, I'm not sure what it is capable of—maybe setting itself free. Maybe worse. I don't know, but I sure don't want to be around to find out. That's why I'm really digging beneath the salt. To make contact with that creature and to electrify him while there's still time."

"Well, what's the problem?" asked the Instructor.

"The government is on me night and day. The only way I could get permission to buy the salt mines and to dig down to the Dhole was to fake it. To make them think I was trying to make the salt mines into a giant battery. So, the government is going to be really pissed at me when they find out it doesn't work. That's where Hauck comes in. He's got to get me out before they find out."

"Well, that's just stupid," said the Instructor.

"Professor Meridian is behind the government's interest. But his ultimate goal is to serve the awakened Dhole," said Jimmy.

The Instructor looked thoughtful.

"Let me at him. I've got unfinished business with that one."

Hauck looked satisfied with that answer, but Sveta was not so sure.

Just then, Brittany announced that Trisha had arrived.

43

Jimmy's breath hitched in his throat. He had made up his mind not to tell Trisha about Jason's death. He'd made up his mind not to tell her about the Dhole either, until after it was dead. But why was he wavering?

"You've got to tell her," said Marty.

They had left Jimmy's second office and were walking to his first. Along the way, Alex Gudinoff caught up with them.

"Dr. Jimmy?"

"Yes, Alex?"

"I'm sorry but could I have a few minutes of your time?"

"Not now, Alex, because I'm busy meeting an old friend. How about if I track you down after?"

Alex considered for a minute. Was it really so important to voice his suspicions that there was definitely something wrong with the Earth Battery project? Or could it wait? Give him a little time to do more research.

"Ah, yes, that would be okay, I guess."

"You sure?"

"Uh—yeah, I'm sure."

"Okay, and Alex I'd like you to meet an old friend of mine, Marty."

"Hello, Marty. It's a pleasure to meet you."

"Pleasure's all mine, Alex. What do you do around here?"

"Ah. Alex is my right-hand man in charge of the drilling."

"Really? Well, do you have time to show me around while Jimmy is collecting our other friend?"

"Sure," said Alex.

"Well, come on, then. Jimmy, you can find me on the tour."

And with that, Marty was gone with Alex leaving Jimmy to face Trisha alone. Jimmy sputtered for a few seconds, but realizing the futility of it, soon gave up. Marty wanted to give him time alone with Trisha, and he didn't blame him. Marty wanted him to make up his own mind whether to tell her everything, and that would be a tough one, since she was, according to Adam, a spy at the NSA tasked with finding out as much as she could on him. That was the crux of it. He couldn't trust her with secrets because she was sworn to act in the best interests of the government.

He came to the door leading into his office, and went in, closing it behind him. A feeling of claustrophobia suddenly strangled his breathing and he gasped for breath. What was wrong with him? Couldn't breathe for a minute, and then it passed. He stood leaning on his desk taking slow, calming breaths. And then he straightened up. The full weight of what he was doing had just come upon him, settling on him like a ton of bricks. What was he going to do? Lie to Trisha? It seemed absurd when he had already trusted Jason and Marty. Trusting Jason had shown him that life could be unexpectedly short.

What would he do?

It had been seven years since he had seen Trisha face to face. They had sworn, all sworn, that they would stay in touch, but then Jason had gone to Iraq and Afghanistan, and Marty had traveled all over the world to solve his mysteries, and Trish, well, she had disappeared into the bowels of the NSA. And Jimmy, and then there was Jimmy. He had his inventions and his fruitless quest to find his father's killer—suicide was the official verdict—and his mom's illness, that hospitalized her and made her unresponsive to anyone's voice, even Jimmy's and there was Jimmy's quest for the Dhole, the brain behind the pop-up killers.

He straightened himself up, checked his look in a mirror that he kept on the wall for just that purpose, drew in a deep breath, and opened the door to the lobby.

And there she was.

Sitting in the lobby of his company, just like he had always dreamed she would be. When she raised her face to look directly at him she was so beautiful she left him speechless.

"Hello, Jimmy," she said.

"I-I hope you weren't waiting too long," was all he could finally think of to answer.

She stood up and she was medium tall compared to Jimmy's six-foot-four-inch figure. But she had radiant brunette hair that hung down around her shoulders and an oval face—not to oval—and high cheek bones, a delightful mouth that sparkled with good humor.

"Not at all," she said. "I hope I'm not too late for a tour?"

"What? I mean yes. I mean we can catch up to Marty. Come on."

He turned his back on her just in time to hide how helpless he was in her presence.

Trisha hurried to catch up.

"So, this is what you've been working on in secret all of these years, huh?" she asked.

They had gone through the doorway to his office, which Jimmy promptly closed behind them. He stopped, momentarily stumped by the question.

"Yes, I guess you could say that."

She was standing at the closed door, and he was just a few feet away.

"So, tell me about this Earth Battery project, Jimmy. Before we go on the tour, I mean," she said.

"Uh...you want a tea, coffee or something like that?"

"No, just to take a load off of my feet and hear about your project before seeing it."

And she took a seat opposite him at the round table near his desk. He looked uncomfortable for a moment, and then sat down awkwardly across from her. She smiled at him—such a radiant smile —that he could have been lost in it forever.

"Well, are you going to tell me or keep staring at me?"

"What? Oh sorry, it's just that I haven't seen you in such a long time, that's all."

"Uh-huh. So why don't you tell me about your project?"

"Oh, you know, I'm drilling down deep into the salt and kind of making it into a giant battery, that sort of thing."

She laughed. It was a good laugh, Jimmy decided.

"No, really. I'm interested."

It was at that moment Jimmy decided. So, she worked for the NSA. So, she could undo every single thing that he'd tried to do for the last fifteen years just by opening her mouth to the NSA and revealing everything that he'd discovered about the Dhole.

"Okay," he said. "Come on, let me take you to the place where all the secrets reside. My home away from home."

He stood up, and she hesitated, but did so too.

"This way," he said.

****

He opened the rather complex series of locks, stepped inside and moved to one side to allow her entry.

"Hello, Trisha," said Brittany.

Trisha gasped at the hologram.

"My God," she said. "What is that?"

The door closed behind her, and she walked over to Brittany and walked around her.

"I assure you," said Brittany, "that I am all here. I am, as Dr. Harlen would say, a fully functioning autonomic hologram. Today, I am dressed rather primly as a librarian to suit your tastes. Other days—"

"Yes," said Jimmy hurriedly, "Trisha gets the picture."

"Jimmy, this is wonderful. You could make a fortune out of her alone."

"Brittany is not for sale. She is for… private use only."

"Well, whatever, but she is really cool.'

"Thank you," said Brittany.

"Don't you have things to do, Brittany."

"Why, yes, Dr. Harlen, I believe I do. I'll get back to my monitoring of Earth Battery's security."

"Amazing," said Trisha.

"Yes, Brittany runs all the security systems for Earth Battery. We have a full implementation team of human beings to back her up, of course."

"My, I'm impressed. What do you need all the security for?"

"For hackers mostly, industrial espionage, and the governments spies mostly."

Trisha went still at that.

"They would like to know what you're doing here."

Jimmy gave a tight little smile.

"I know, but I'm not ready to give up my secrets yet."

After an awkward pause, Trisha continued, "Well, so this is where you do all the work?"

"You've got it. That office is just for receiving visitors like the mayor, the governor and anyone that comes here from Washington. Here is where I eat, sleep and breath Earth Battery."

Trish walked around the room, around the tables and desks where Jimmy did his magic. The computers, the endless computers. She inspected his bedroom, the kitchen and the weight room—largely unused, of course. Once, at a desk, she saw a framed photo of herself solo and at another the picture of the four of them—Marty, Jason, Jimmy and herself. But her eyes wandered over to the framed photo of herself. It was her in her early teens, and she wondered where he had gotten it.

She spotted another of herself and was surprised. It was on what must have been Jimmy's main desk, and it was taken when she was twenty-four or twenty-five. Try as she might, she couldn't remember giving Jimmy that one, and then it came to her, he had clipped it from Facebook. And she saw another one, this time of her in her early thirties, also clipped from Facebook.

"Well, what do you think?"

"Homey, very homey."

Jimmy grinned, and it was like he was relaxed again, prior to his father being taken away. And then, the smile faded.

"Trisha, sit down, there's something I've got to tell you."

"What?"

"Please, just sit down."

So, she obliged him and sat down in the chair directly in front of her photograph when she was in her early thirties. Jimmy sat down opposite her.

"Trisha, I don't know how else to say this, but Jason is dead."

"What?"

He had just blurted it out. He didn't know how else to say it. He didn't know why he said it at all, but he had, and it was out now. Somehow, he would have to deal with it.

"I... I...Jason is dead."

She was apparently shocked. Her hand went to her mouth and her eyes were bright. Jimmy felt for her; she had a thing for Jason, and he understood that. She was crying real tears for him.

"I can't believe it. That he's dead? I can't believe it."

"I know. I can't either."

"How did he die?"

There was the question Jimmy dreaded. Should he tell her the truth or not? If he told her, then he would have to live with the consequences. Everything he had worked for, the death of the Dhole, finally, would be ruined. The government would come down upon his head like a ton of bricks. They would interdict him like lightning, they would take over and attempt to study the Dhole. They would want to weaponize the Dhole or do something worse with it.

But could he deliberately like to Trisha? That was the question.

"Jimmy?"

He didn't think he could lie to her, even if she worked for the NSA. The NSA. The group that he suspected had murdered his father, or at least put in prison where he could be murdered was who Trisha worked for and had sworn her allegiance. He didn't know what to do.

"Jimmy? What is it Jimmy?"

"He was killed by a werewolf."

There, he had said it. Now he would find out whether she thought he was nuts or not. Whether he would take it to the next level and tell her about the Dhole and the real purpose behind Earth Battery.

Suddenly, Trisha went still for a moment with the shock of what she was hearing.

"A werewolf? Did I hear you right?"

Oh boy, thought Jimmy. This was so much easier with Marty.

"Uh...yes. You heard me right. It was a werewolf that killed Jason. Honest to God."

He didn't know what made him add this last, but he did.

"Jimmy, are you feeling all right?"

"Yes."

"Because—"

"Look I know how it all sounds to you, but it's true."

"What did the authorities say when you told them about this?"

"I...I...I didn't tell the authorities."

"Okay."

She was being very gentle towards him, as though he were suffering from a nervous breakdown.

"Look, just because I didn't tell the authorities doesn't mean it didn't happen. Just ask Sveta."

"Who?"

Uh-oh. He knew he shouldn't have spoken up about it. One thing would lead to another and another. Like Sveta. How could he explain to Trisha who Sveta was without telling her his plan?

"She's just a woman who saw everything."

"Jimmy, I don't want to say she... maybe saw something that wasn't there, but a werewolf?"

"I knew I should have kept quiet about Jason's death. I should have just said he was out of town or something like that."

"What?" said Trisha. "Jimmy, what's wrong? All I did was ask you if she saw what she really thought she saw. That's all. And you've got to admit it's pretty bizarre. I mean a werewolf?"

Jimmy got up from his chair and began to pace. What should he do now? Should he just say that it was all a mistake? Or something different? He made up his mind.

He stopped and faced Brittany.

"Brittany?"

"Yes, Dr. Harlen?"

One last long look at Trisha to be sure.

"Bring up on the screens on Sveta, won't you?"

"Yes, Dr. Harlen."

Jimmy turned to face Trisha.

"It's time, I guess, for you to meet the rest of the gang."

44

Sveta was staring at Hauck.

"I think you've made a mistake," she said.

They sat in a room off of the kitchen with the door closed. The Instructor chowed down in the kitchen with Yuri and Charlene.

"I know you do, Sveta," said Hauck. "But I need him."

"Why?"

"Must you always question me?"

"Why can't we just break into Professor Meridian's house and take Sasha? Tell me why."

"You don't know the Eyes of Death, they are something that... that the Instructor is afraid of, Sveta. If we tried to break into that house, we don't know what would be waiting for us. It's a trap, don't you see? He's waiting for us to do just that. But we've got two aces that they don't count on—Adam, and now the Instructor."

Sveta considered this. Hauck could almost see the machinery of her mind turning.

"I still don't see what's so difficult about just breaking in, snatching Sasha, and making for the door, killing anyone that gets in the way. Tell me more about why the Instructor and the Eyes of Death have such a bad history. I understand that their leader fought the leader of whatever the Instructor's clan is called to a draw. They both went their separate ways. But what about the current leader of the Eyes of Death and the Instructor—what's their history."

A new voice answered.

"I'll tell you that, girlie, if you don't mind. Come on in, it will save me from telling the story twice," said the Instructor.

"Jesus," said Sveta, "I swear, if you don't keep sneaking up on me..."

The Instructor grinned.

"Come in, I said."

Yuri and Charlene made their way cautiously into the room and took chairs, while the Instructor remained standing, pacing. You could almost feel the pent-up energy emanating off of him. Hauck and Sveta kept their eyes on him.

"Well, you see it happened like this. I was content to mind my own business, but the kid, Krikor, he had other ideas, cause my Uncle had cut his daddy pretty bad. He was out to even the score. So, he hunted me. I was in my prime back then, it seems like a long time ago. It forty years or so—no, maybe forty-five. God, has it been that long? Well, whatever. But anyway, I didn't know that I was being hunted, you see?"

He seemed to want some sort of acknowledgement from the crowd, so Yuri and Charlene nodded quickly. Looking over at Hauck, he saw that he was slowly agreeing with him, but Sveta remained impassive. The Instructor grinned.

"Still don't trust me, eh, girlie?"

"No," said Sveta.

"Fair enough. Anyway, the Eyes of Death—this Professor Krikor Meridian—was hunting me and I didn't know it. So, he and his gang caught up with me in Germany, you see? And anyway, a big fight followed, and I got his eye, you got that? I ripped it right out of his head, and he cut me big time and its been on ever since. You want to see the scar? No? Well, take my word for it, it's ugly. But I was wise to him after that, and I stayed low. Not before he had killed all of my field agents, though. That's when I met Hauck and trained him. He was the last one I trained, though."

"Where?" said Sveta.

"What?"

"I said where did he cut you?"

"That's getting kind of personal, don't you think?"

The Instructor grinned when he said it, but Sveta didn't bite. So, he sighed, and took off his shirt. He was well muscled and seemed to have muscles where he shouldn't. The Instructor's body was covered in scars, but he had one that cut diagonally across him from his left shoulder to his right hip that was particularly ugly. He traced it with his finger.

"This is where Krikor cut me. I still owe him for that."

"Whoa," said Charlene.

Yuri gulped.

Even Sveta slowly nodded her head.

But Hauck remained silent.

As the Instructor put his shirt back on, he said to Sveta, "Now you know."

"Yes," agreed Sveta, "now I know."

But Hauck was looking at the hair on the Instructor's palms that wasn't there before. A side effect, he supposed, of the werewolf's bite. He felt the scar at the base of his neck, where Drogol had bit him. He had always known there was a chance that he was infected. Drogol said that every now and then there was a man born who was resistant to the infection. He would carry this in his blood, though, and pass it to his son, like he had to Sasha.

"You can see why I've got to kill him," said the Instructor. "I've got to get him before he gets me."

He slammed his fist on the table so hard that he cracked it.

"I'm going to kill that son of a bitch," he growled.

"Aren't you forgetting about something?" asked Sveta.

"What?"

"You can't go out past dark. You'll turn into a werewolf and you'll forget who you are and worse, what you are trying to do."

The Instructor opened his mouth to respond then slowly closed it.

"You're right," he said in a stricken tone. "I forgot about that."

And with that, he slumped down into a chair. A nervous Yuri scooted his chair back away from him.

"What am I going to do?" he said. "I've got to kill that man once and for all. He's been hunting me my whole life. Shit."

"You're going to need us," said Hauck. "That's all because if you try to go in at night, well, you know what happens."

"Shit," said the Instructor.

"I have an idea," said Yuri.

"Wonderful," said the Instructor.

"No, really, I have an idea."

"Go ahead, Yuri," said Hauck.

Yuri seemed uncertain at first, but he went for it.

"Why don't we lure Professor Meridian and his men out first."

"Go on," prodded Hauck.

"Well, we bait and switch Professor Meridian."

"Who's going to be the bait?" asked the Instructor.

"Well, I thought you would," said Yuri.

"Look, genius, I can't go out at night or else I turn into a werewolf, in case you've forgotten."

"Well, that's the whole point, don't you see?"

"No, I don't see. Enlighten me."

"We make at someplace deserted."

"Okay," said a clearly disoriented Instructor.

"Well, when the professor shows up, you're a werewolf. It doesn't matter how many men he brings don't you see? Because when he does show up, he'll be fighting a werewolf. Meantime, we can get Sasha out with Adam's help."

"No," said Hauck, "it's too risky. Especially having the Instructor out at night."

"Why, if it's an isolated spot?"

"No."

Charlene put in, "We don't have to have the Instructor in an isolated spot, just make the guy believe that he is there."

"That's bullshit," said the Instructor.

"No, it's not," said Sveta. "Think about it."

"Yeah, well, what am I supposed to do, sit on my hands and do nothing while that maniac Krikor Meridian keeps hunting me," snapped the Instructor.

"Why haven't you killed him before now?" asked Sveta.

"Because he's magic, that's why."

"What," said everyone, almost in unison.

"He's got powers, that's why I haven't killed him. And he's got these two guys—"

"Sanzar and Abarran. We've met," said Hauck. "Charming."

The Instructor looked concerned. Hauck seemed surprised at that.

"What?" he asked.

"Because Sanzar and Abarran are already dead. They eat brains for food."

"Seriously?" said Hauck.

"I'm deadly serious. Have I ever lied to you—okay, scratch that. But you know what I mean. And he's got hordes of these type of guys all over."

"Wait a minute," said Hauck. "You mean to tell me these guys are seriously undead? What are they zombies?"

"I don't know, but they are definitely undead. Definitely."

A hush fell over the room as they considered that. Charlene seemed the least disturbed by it. She looked at the Instructor with new respect though.

"You mean this guy has been hunting you all your life and he only found you once?" she asked.

"Yeah," said the Instructor. "Only once that he caught up with me, but I was young and stupid, and it cost him an eye."

"But you said had that he was magic," said Charlene.

"I said he had powers," the Instructor corrected.

"Yeah, well, like what?"

"Like I don't know exactly. He can sort of tell the future; he's got this magic book, and if you feed it blood, it writes a line or lines that give some sort of a clue for what the future holds. I don't know exactly, but that's what I think it does, anyway. He calls it the Book of the Dhole, or some such shit."

"Did you say the Book of the Dhole?" interrupted Sveta.

"Yeah, look I know it's crazy, but that's what its called. The Dhole or Bhole or some such shit."

A grim look stole over Hauck's face. Could it be possible? The monster that Jimmy was trying to kill was called the Dhole. And the book the professor had was called the Book of the Dhole. My, how the world dovetailed its way back to where the mystery started.

"Why?" asked the Instructor.

"Because the thing that Jimmy is digging down into the salt mines to kill is called the Dhole," said Hauck.

"So, what's the connection?" said Sveta. "I mean, Professor Meridian keeps popping up as the common thread. He's got the book of the Dhole, Jimmy's trying to kill the Dhole, and the professor's got Sasha and dangling him like bait in front of us."

Everyone became quiet at that. The question before them all seemed insoluble. What was Professor Meridian's connection to them all? It couldn't be coincidence, it just couldn't.

"Well, couldn't he," said Charlene, "be a like a religious leader for the Dhole."

"What?" said the Instructor. "That's bullshit."

"No, listen it all fits together. He's a religious leader, like a priest."

"A priest of the Dhole?" said Hauck. "But from what Jimmy says, the Dhole is asleep, trapped under all the salt."

"Wait," said Sveta. "What did Jimmy say about the planetary alignment?"

"He said that—" began Hauck.

"That it was different. That this was a once in a lifetime planetary alignment."

"Yes," said Hauck, "but so what?"

"Maybe," said Sveta, "the Dhole will come awake."

"Yeah, well, that's nice, but what's all that got to do with me?" asked the Instructor.

"I don't know either," said Hauck, "but it's got something to do with you."

"Yeah, well thanks a lot."

"No, really. There's some connection there. I think Charlene's on to something. I think that it makes sense that the Dhole is awakening. We've got to tell Jimmy. And you've got to go back into the cage, until we have a new one built for you. It's getting late. You got less than an hour and a half until nightfall."

Newly energized, the Instructor shot up from his chair.

"Don't you think I know the risk I'm taking?"

"No, we are all at risk with you out of that cage. It's only until the moon is not full. That's three to five days maximum if it checks out. And what if the legends are wrong? What if every night you turn into a werewolf? What then? Are you going to play the odds and put the rest of our lives at risk?"

The Instructor slammed his fist into the table and stalked out of the room.

"Maybe we should put him in another room so we can hear ourselves think, you know?" said Yuri.

<h1 style="text-align:center">45</h1>

Before Jimmy could get Hauck on the line, Marty came back. He brightened when he saw Trisha.

"So," he said, "he decided to let you in on the big dark secret."

"Hi Marty."

Trisha gave Marty a big hug.

"I can hardly believe how big you've grown."

"You know, nothing that a steady diet of adventure won't encourage. And I can't believe how beautiful you've grown up to be. Nah, who am I kidding—you were always going to be beautiful, kiddo."

Jimmy broke in.

"Well, I didn't tell her everything."

"Oh?" said Trisha. "What are you keeping back?"

Jimmy looked uncomfortable. In the heat of the moment, he had forgotten about the Dhole.

"Ah—" said Jimmy.

"Jimmy, so help me, just spit it out."

"I'm really drilling down to kill the Dhole."

There. It was out in the open.

"The what?" asked Trisha.

"Oh, boy," said Jimmy.

"Jimmy, what in the hell are you talking about?"

"He found something at the bottom of the salt mine," said Marty.

"he found the source of the pop-up killers that we encountered as children."

"What?"

Trisha was shocked.

"I—I found the Dhole, the thing called the Dhole, anyway."

"I don't believe you, Jimmy."

"Believe me when I say, I wish it wasn't true. But it's true, Trisha. It's this thing fourteen hundred feet down below here, down below the salt mines."

"You're crazy, Jimmy."

Trisha couldn't believe that Jimmy was bringing up that... that imagining that they had all had when they were kids. She had nightmares after it. Why, oh why did he have to bring it up now. This was simply insane.

"Oh yeah? Well look at this video."

Jimmy was quick to bring it up on the computer. In fact, he was at the keyboard and had the image up before she could stop him.

"Watch," he said.

"No, I want nothing to do with this."

"Trisha," said Marty gently, "you have to see this. Trust me on this. If you don't believe Jimmy, at least believe me long enough to see the video."

But Jimmy was already playing the video. The one where Randy and Stacy were going down below the surface world, down to where the minions of the Dhole got them. Down to where the the pop-up killers had eaten them.

Trisha watched, calm enough. She had guts, you had to give her that. She watched Randy and Stacy go down.

"So what? I don't see anything happening?"

"Wait," said Jimmy patiently. "Just wait."

The three of them crowded around the screen. The elevator cage stopped. Randy did not want to go out, in fact he refused to go out. Stacy tried to encourage him, but finally gave up. She went out there herself over Randy's protestations. Trisha closed her eyes briefly, as though willing the whole thing to go away, but she opened them again, unable to keep herself from looking.

Stacy walked away from the elevator cage with that "...see

nothing here to see" look on her face, hoping that it would encourage Randy to come along after her. But he stayed behind. Suddenly, he yelled, "Stacy, don't look back but get your ass back here." Stacy should have followed his directions. What met her eyes and Trisha's by default was a sea of eyes, red eyes. Randy yelled something else, but Trisha could see only those eyes. Randy ran out to get Stacy, and just when he had her, the elevator clicked close and started to rise—all by itself. Randy and Stacy ran, but it was too late, for the elevator was already too high. Randy and Stacy turned around slowly and they were coming. Now the eyes had resolved themselves into black, furry bodies with dog-like heads and pointed ears with snouts with rows of razor-sharp teeth. They were the pop-up killers of Trisha's nightmares.

"Run," Trisha yelled.

But of course, the people on the screen couldn't hear her. They were already dead.

The pop-up killers surrounded Randy and Stacy. Randy and Stacy huddled together and screamed. The pop-up killers overran them like nobody's business and sunk their teeth into their flesh. Randy and Stacy screamed and screamed but to no avail because there was no one to hear them.

Trisha held her head in her hands.

"That's awful," she said, finally coming up for some air.

"I know," said Jimmy.

"But wait, there's more," said Marty.

"No, I don't want to see anymore," said Trisha.

"You have to, Trisha," said Marty.

He held Trisha's eyes for just a minute until she nodded.

"Good girl," he said, and nodded to Jimmy to show him the Tyler video.

Jimmy brought up the video, quick to do so lest Trisha change her mind. They all watched as the video showed Tyler comfortably going down the maintenance shaft. Trisha's face was rigid with fear, Jimmy's was stiff from the guilt he felt at Tyler's death, and Marty seemed to tense up. They each had their own horrific memories of the pop-up killers. When it got to the part where Tyler was stuck in the shaft, and the pop-up killers were working their way in through the bottom of the car, Trisha said that was enough. But Marty motioned for Jimmy to continue playing it. Trisha walked away because she just couldn't watch it. But near the end of the video, she glanced up just in time to see the pop-killers devouring Tyler, and she hurriedly glanced away.

When it was over, Jimmy looked at Marty, and they both knew that they had to stop it.

"You think you can kill it? Because I don't remember my grandma's word. I've tried over the years, but it's just a no-go. I really can't remember it."

Jimmy looked at his friend. Of a sudden, he remembered him the way he was as an eight-year-old. Fat and chubby. Always afraid. He was the opposite of Jason. Who was never afraid of anything. Now Jason was gone. Dead. Jimmy shook himself.

"Yes, I can kill it. With enough electricity, I can kill anything."

"Are you sure?" asked Trisha.

"Yes," said Jimmy. "When we make contact with the thing, I can juice it up and let fly with some serious electricity. But I have to tell you before you ask, I didn't know that it was awake—or at least partially awake. I didn't know that Randy and Stacy and Tyler would die. I just didn't know. Those incidents that you saw on tape, were recorded before I knew about them."

Marty looked at Trisha, then back at Jimmy.

"We believe you, Jimmy. But what I want to know is, what are we going to do about it?"

Jimmy looked straight at Trisha when he responded.

"We're going to finish drilling, make contact with that thing and fry the living daylights out of him."

"And if it doesn't work?" asked Trisha in a low voice, almost a whisper.

"Then we're all in for a really bad time," said Marty. "Isn't that right, Jimmy?"

Jimmy hesitated before answering. Then he answered, confidant for the first time. He had got it off his chest. He had told Trisha everything and she didn't think he was crazy and he didn't believe she'd report him to the NSA.

"I can do this," he said.

"Good," said Marty.

But Trisha wasn't so sure.

"Jimmy, how big is that thing and how is it causing the pop-ups into existence? I mean, what is the relationship between them and it?"

It should have been obvious, wasn't it?

"The Dhole is... hibernating, for want of a better word. That's what it did when the whole of Michigan was covered underwater, and it landed on Earth millions of years ago. Hundreds of millions of years ago; it went into a state of suspended animation, like hibernation. The waters gradually receded and left this layer of salt, billions, no, trillions of tons of salt. So, the Dhole remained in hibernation. But it, for want of a better word or phrase, it dreamed or had nightmares or waking dreams—look it happened every time there was a partial planet alignment. Does that make sense?"

Marty nodded but Trisha still looked dubious.

"Look," continued Jimmy, "the pop-up killers in some way are a manifestation of the Dhole's dreams. Whenever there is a partial planetary alignment, that's when the pop-up killers make their appearance. That night in the trailer park, that was a partial planetary alignment—a Red Moon night."

"So, you're saying that this creature... this Dhole causes the pop-up killers to come into existence when it dreams?" asked Trisha.

"Yes," Jimmy nodded enthusiastically. "That's exactly what I'm saying."

"Jimmy, those are partial planetary alignments?" said Marty.

"Correct."

"What happens in a full planetary alignment?"

Jimmy looked uncomfortable. He glanced at the floor and then looked into the distance past Trisha and past Marty. That was the question he dreaded the most.

"That's why we have to kill it," he said, "before the next planetary alignment."

"But what if your plan doesn't work, Jimmy," said Trisha. "Shouldn't we inform the government?"

Jimmy didn't answer.

"What if this thing is too big to kill? How big is it, Jimmy? Is it as big as a house? Two houses? How big is it, Jimmy?"

"It's somewhere around three thousand feet long," he said at last.

"What?" said Marty and Trisha all at once.

"It's that big," said Jimmy.

"That's like, two thirds of a mile long," said a surprised Marty.

"You can't tackle all this all by yourself," said Trisha. "You just can't. It's too big."

"What would you have me do Trisha? Report it to the government? So, they can study it? They wouldn't know what to do with it. They'd have a whole bunch of men in white coats evaluating it long pass the deadline for terminating it. They'd have a bunch of men figuring out how to weaponize it. Don't you see we just can't have the government involved?"

"No, I don't see. What are you crazy? Jimmy, the government has resources you can only dream of. Why are you so against them being involved?"

Jimmy's frustration was beginning to show. He didn't mean for it to, but it was. He just couldn't help himself.

"You think of the government as being your friend. But it's not. It's a soulless machine, gobbling everything up in its path."

He paced around the room, agitated beyond belief. The death of Randy and Stacy waited in his mind. He could feel Tyler's pain and agony as he confronted the pop-up killers. And Jason, too; imagine his shock and surprise just before the moments of his death. Now what came over him. But it had something to do with this father being locked away and murdered. It had something to do with the deaths of all those people that died at the claws of the pop-up killers.

Trisha did not understand him at all. What was wrong with him? Why couldn't he be reasonable?

"I think you're letting you fear of the government cloud your thinking."

"They imprisoned my father for telling the truth to a newspaper and then murdered him while he was in prison. Don't you think I have reason to be afraid of the government? And you work for the government; don't you think I know that you will run back and tell them?"

There it was out in the open. Whatever she said, however she responded would tell him all he needed to know about where she stood. If her loyalty was with the government, well then so be it. There was nothing he could do about it. All those years of wishful thinking, all those years of hoping went down the drain. Would she side with the government, or would she side with Jimmy? God, he hoped it would be with him.

"Jimmy Harlen, if you think that I would just go back and rat you out to the government, then you're wrong."

Marty didn't say anything. It wasn't his time to speak, and he knew it. This whole affair was between Jimmy and Trisha.

"Really?" said Jimmy.

Trisha just stared at him, as though she were daring him to say something else.

"You are just so stupid," she said. "My supervisor has been begging me to get something on you, so we can prove that you are a traitor to you country. All I've given him are what is available on the Internet. And you think that I would deliberately turn you in? Really? Really, Jimmy Harlen? Is that what you really think of me?"

Jimmy looked away, more ashamed than he had ever been in his life.

"I'm sorry, Trisha, believe me."

"You think that all the covering up for you was for nothing?"

"I said, I'm sorry, Trisha."

"It's not good enough, Jimmy."

"What do you want?"

"I'd like a real apology, like with your crawling on you hands and knees and begging my forgiveness."

"What?"

"You heard me."

"I'm sorry, Trisha."

"Yeah, well, you'd better be. Do you know that I was supposed to have you fall in love with me so you'd spill your guts and I could go report to that obnoxious toad that I work for? Well, do you?"

Jimmy was too stunned to reply.

"What?" said Marty.

"That's right," said Trisha. "That slimeball that I work for—his name's Beckham, by the way—said I had just a short time to get you to fall in love with me and then learn your deepest, darkest secrets. He had someone here before me named Gladstone or somebody."

"Edwina?" gasped Jimmy. "Edwina was spying on me? But she was my best employee."

"In your dreams. Edwina Gladstone was working for the agency. She was supposed to give them the exact time that you broke through to the Dhole—or fourteen hundred feet of salt—and when you turned on the current."

"What? That doesn't make any sense. All this trouble to go to just to know when I broke through and electrified the Dhole. No wait. They didn't know anything about the Dhole. And all that information is supposed to be public knowledge, anyway. Why wouldn't they just get it from the newspaper? It doesn't make any sense."

Marty broke in.

"What if they knew about the Dhole? What then?"

"Well," said Jimmy, "I suppose they would... I don't know. It doesn't make any sense."

"Maybe," said Trisha thoughtfully, "maybe the whole Federal government doesn't know about the Dhole. Maybe there's a..."

Brittany broke in.

"Dr. Harlen?"

"Yes, Brittany?"

"Hauck would like to speak to you via the computer."

Jimmy took a deep breath.

"All right, patch him through."

46

Hauck eyed the young woman. Thirty-three, maybe. Dark hair, medium cut. Attractive. Trim. Who the hell was she?

"I'd like to introduce you to Trisha," said Jimmy. "Trisha, this is Hauck, Sveta, Yuri and Charlene."

Everyone exchanged greetings.

"All right, enough of that," said Hauck, "now that we know who everyone is. Is anyone else joining us?"

"No," said Jimmy.

"Good. Charlene has come up with an interesting idea."

"Let's hear it," said Jimmy.

"Charlene?"

Charlene dived right in.

"I think that Professor Meridian is head of some kind of religious cult that worships the Dhole—like a priest or something. I think that with the planetary alignment coming, all bets are off about the way that the Dhole used to behave, too. That's what I think, anyway."

Jimmy was stunned. Why couldn't he have thought of that? No, the professor couldn't really be a priest of the Dhole, could he? No, that wasn't possible.

"I hadn't thought of that," he conceded. "But I don't see the religious connection."

"Yeah, well I thought it say that. But listen up, okay? Professor Meridian wants the Instructor. That's one. Two—"

"Who is the Instructor?" asked Trisha.

"He's a mean old bastard that you really don't want to meet who we've got locked in a cage in another room. At nighttime, he turns into a werewolf."

"Okay," said Trisha.

"Yeah, I know it's confusing but trust me you really don't want to meet him."

"I'll take your word for it."

"Getting back to what I was talking about," said Charlene, "there's the matter of the planetary alignment."

"Go on," said Jimmy thoughtfully.

"And there's the matter of his two henchmen, Sanzar and Abarran."

"Yes," said Jimmy.

"From what Hauck says about them, they just reek of acolytes."

"Hmm," said Jimmy. "I have something to add that Trisha told me about Professor Meridian, or least about the federal government. Which may be one and the same. Trisha here tells me that she was implanted as mole when the last mole got hit by a truck."

"What?" said Charlene.

"I said, Trisha here tells me—"

"I heard what you said. It's just that I was supposed to deliver the research that Kirk had done for you, and I was expecting to meet you at this restaurant, and I met this old woman instead—at least I thought she was an old woman—and as she was getting out of the car she was hit by a truck and her wig fell off and a gun fell out, too."

Jimmy looked at Trisha and he felt his stomach sink. The old woman that Charlene was describing was Edwina Gladstone. He was sure of it. God, this was getting too much to bear. This confirmed his worst fears.

"Yes," said Jimmy. "That was my assistant Edwina Gladstone. I just can't believe it, but I guess it's true."

"Oh, this is bad. A gun?" said Marty. "Why would she need a gun?"

"Because she was going to take the papers and soon as she was confident that she told no one else, to kill her and dispose of the body," said Trisha.

"That's cold," said Marty.

"I guess I'm glad she got run over by a truck," said Jimmy.

"Is she still alive?" asked Sveta.

"What are you thinking?" asked Hauck.

"That if she's still alive, we snatch her for more information."

"Whoa," said Trisha. "You can't do that, it's illegal."

"She may be not cognizant, of where she is. Maybe she can't even speak," said Hauck.

"Wait a minute. I can't believe you're even thinking of that."

"Why not?" said Yuri. "I say we grab her and grill her if she's alert enough to tell us anything. Hey, we could have the Instructor grab her in the daytime."

"There's a thought," said Sveta.

"Are you listening to me?" said Trisha. "You can't just walk up and take someone against their will. It's not legal."

"Legal is a definition that we interpret a little sloppily, I'm afraid," said Hauck.

"Jimmy?" said Trisha.

"I'm afraid I'm going to have to go along with Hauck on this one."

"What? Are you crazy?"

"No. Look if everything you've told me about them is true..."

"Look, Trisha," said Marty, "we've gone way over the line here. Jason's been killed by a werewolf; you've seen that the pop-up killers are back and Jimmy's drilling fourteen hundred feet down to fry with major amounts of electricity a monster that is three thousand feet long so we can't balk at a little kidnapping."

"Especially," said Charlene, "when she had a gun and was going to shoot me with it."

"They have a point," said Adam.

Adam had been a silent witness to so far to everything that had been said, but he apparently felt that this was the time for him to chip in. Trisha and Marty looked up in amazement at the floating face on one of the screens.

"Jimmy, what is that?" said an astonished Trisha.

"That," said Jimmy, "is my finest invention. A life form that exists only in the Internet."

"I can also exist," said Adam, "in any form of electrical energy."

"Are you serious?" said Trisha.

"Completely," said Adam.

"Yes, he is," said Jimmy.

"Wow," said Trisha. "Headquarters would love to hear about this."

"There not actually far behind."

Marty emitted a long, slow whistle.

"Nice," he said when he was done.

"Can we get back to the topic at hand?" said Hauck. "Now does anyone know where this—what is her name, Jimmy?"

"Edwina Gladstone."

"Good. Thank you. Does anyone know what hospital she is in?"

Jimmy turned to Adam.

"Adam?"

"Just a second. Yes, I have located her at East Ridge Hospital in downtown Detroit. She is registered under her own name. She is in room 874."

"Well, thank you, Adam. Now the question is how to get her out. Anyone?"

"She is due to be released in two days," said Adam.

"That doesn't give us much time," said Sveta.

"What can we do?" said Jimmy.

"Nothing," said Hauck. "I'm afraid you'll have to entrust this to us. Anything you know about our operation could compromise you at a later date, so the less you know the better. But I would like Adam's help."

"Of course," said Jimmy. "But—"

But Hauck had already signed off.

****

"What would you have me to do?" asked Adam.

"Can you get into the hospital's computer system?"

"Yes."

"Good. I'll need medical I.D. cards for Sveta and Yuri identifying them as appropriate staff members for taking Edwina Gladstone downstairs for further tests."

"What names shall I have them in?" asked Adam.

"Good question. Just average American names—not Svetalana and Yuri."

"What are you thinking?" asked Sveta.

Hauck grimaced.

"I'll mix up some pills that will knock her out, and just to be sure an injectable. We've got to hurry to beat the professor, because I think she is now useless to him. Her cover is blown and, well, let's just say that she is now expendable."

"We are on the clock, then?"

"Yes."

"We're going to have to get some clothes then," said Yuri. "I'll take care of that."

"Good enough," said Hauck.

"Okay," said Sveta. "What do we do? We pose as nurse plus technicians, knock her out, then roll her straight off of the eighth floor, down the elevator and out the front door?"

"It's all I could think of on such short notice."

"It figures."

"What you want me to do?" asked Charlene.

"Do you really want to help?" asked Hauck.

"Hell yes."

"I suppose we'll need a getaway driver."

"I'm your woman."

"Adam?"

"Yes, I am ready with the credentials."

"Excellent. Send them to the printer."

While Adam sent the credentials to the printer, Hauck tried to think of anything that would go wrong. The problem was, this plan, unlike his normal plans, was jury-rigged at the last minute and without the benefit of him analyzing it for two weeks. He wondered if he was being affected by his proximity to Sveta. Was he doing this to please someone else's desire for action—in this case Sveta, or was he doing it to save his son? The truth was, that things were moving so fast, that he did not know. But he would have to be careful. He looked at Sveta, and, catching her looking at him, he looked away. She was a powerful influence on him. He would have to be careful.

"Hauck?"

It was Sveta.

"Yes?"

She stepped closer to him than was comfortable. He felt his temperature rise.

"It will be okay."

"I—"

But she was already walking away.

****

Hauck had not taken into account that the werewolf could be so loud, and he hadn't thought to soundproof the room where it was kept. He cursed himself that he had been so occupied with Edwina Gladstone that he had literally forgotten to do it. The werewolf howled again, and Hauck had to adjust the earplugs that he had in his ears, but it wasn't enough to drown out the sound. He would go mad. It literally shook the whole floor.

Fortunately, he had Yuri move the whole cage to another room and bolt it down to the floor, but even so, it was enough to convulse the floor and the ceilings. And that cursed howling, that cursed, cursed howling.

"Shut up," Hauck yelled. "Shut up for just five minutes."

But that only made the beast roar even louder. And shake the bars. God, he wished that he could think for just one minute. With that incessant cacophony, he could not so much as entertain a coherent thought.

"Adam," he screamed.

"Yes, Hauck," said the silver-red face in the computer.

"I've got to go outside. I can't stand the noise."

"Yes, Hauck. What shall I do?"

Another howl.

"Just withstand the noise."

"I've already turned down the volume."

"Fine."

But he didn't think Adam could hear him over the howling.

****

Charlene drove the black SUV in front of the hospital and dropped off Yuri and Sveta.

"I'll be here when you get out," said Charlene.

As Sveta and Yuri exited the car, Yuri said simply, "You better."

They had gotten to the double doors that admitted them to the hospital when Yuri said to Sveta, "You think she'll rabbit?"

"No," said Sveta. "Now shut up and concentrate on the job at hand. Keep an eye out for cameras, and if you see them—your head goes down. This is a hospital, so they are sure to have them. We don't want to be tagged by facial recognition technology. Adam is covering for us, but just in case he screws up..."

"Oh, that's just great," said Yuri. "That's what the masks are for though, right."

Fortunately, at this time of night, the traffic was reduced, so Yuri and Sveta were able to make it unnoticed to the elevator. Sveta wore a nurse's uniform and Yuri had the clothes of an orderly. They had gotten them from an all-night uniform store and paid cash, as they always did to avoid tracebacks on a credit card. The last thing they needed was the police after them for a piece of plastic.

"You think that I look like an orderly?" asked Yuri.

"No, but with that face mask I think you'll pass. Now will you please shut up?"

"Sorry. I'm just nervous."

Yuri was pushing a wheelchair that he had brought along for the occasion, and when the elevator dinged their floor and the elevator doors opened, he exited after clumsily steering it at first, then straightening it out while Sveta pretended not to notice. They made it past the nurses station without causing a ruckus, and arrived at room 874, where Edwina Gladstone was supposed to be. And, yes, she was there.

Yuri looked up at Sveta, and beneath his face mask breathed a sigh of relief. There were cameras in the hallways recording his every move, but his face was covered and he had to hope that Adam was on the job. It was twelve thirty at night, and it was quiet enough. The on-duty nurse was too busy with paperwork to notice them. Other nurses were making the rounds, but none were in Edwina Gladstone's area. She appeared to be sleeping.

From behind her mask, Sveta said, "I guess it will be the shot."

She withdrew a syringe from a lab coat pocket, swabbed it with alcohol, and checked around to see if anyone was coming.

"Come on, hurry it up," said Yuri.

With a deft motion, Sveta picked up Edwina's left arm and prepared to make an injection. Edwina didn't like that and started to talk.

"Hey, what are…"

Sveta jammed the needle into her arm as fast as she could. Edwina shot up in the bed and Sveta threw the needle on the floor and slammed the ridge of her hand into her throat. She immediately fell back, gasping for breath.

"Help me hold her down," said Sveta.

Yuri nervously looked around him, and, seeing no agitation on the part of the nurses, leaned forward and held her down. After a few minutes of struggling, she slumped back in bed.

"Okay," said Sveta, "now get her into the wheelchair."

Yuri maneuvered the chair into position, and Sveta and he transferred her from the bed to the chair.

"While you two are taking her, I'll make her bed."

Sveta and Yuri froze.

An orderly was standing in the doorway. She was a plump, cheerful looking woman and did not seem in any way threatening, so they relaxed. Sveta inclined her head.

"That would be fine," she said.

"We're taking her down to have an MRI," said Yuri quickly.

"Oh? I thought they were closed for the night," said the woman. "Well, what do I know, eh? I'm just bedside maintenance."

Yuri realized that in his urgency to relate a cover story, he had made a mistake. The urge to correct it had him thinking furiously, but Sveta saved him.

"Yes," she said, "they've made an exception with this one. Nice meeting you."

Yuri breathed a sigh of relief.

"Yes," he said, "nice meeting you."

As they rolled out with the wheelchair, the woman looked thoughtfully after them, but after a while she shrugged her shoulders and began changing the bedsheets.

They rolled her past the nurse's station and pressed the button on the wall for elevator.

"I think that woman was suspicious," said Yuri, looking over his shoulder.

"Shut up," said Sveta.

The elevator door opened, and Sveta got the shock of her life when she saw Sanzar and Abarran, standing there. She quickly got out of their way, turning Edwina's wheelchair out of their line of sight before they had a chance to see her. They instead seemed to bore into Sveta's eyes, looking for any sign of a threat. When Sveta lowered her eyes, they exited. Sveta hurried to get on the elevator, pushing the wheelchair in front of her and jamming her finger to the Lobby button. Yuri hurried to jump on. The doors closed silently behind her.

"Hey, that wasn't cool. I'm supposed to push the wheelchair," said Yuri. "Someone might get suspicious."

"That was Sanzar and Abarran."

"What?"

"You heard me right. Professor Meridian's two main thugs."

"Oh, shit."

"You got that right, and we're on the world's slowest elevator."

Sveta got out her cellphone, checked for bars, and then dialed.

"Come on, Charlene, pick up. Charlene? Is the car out front? Good, because we're got Sanzar and Abarran on our tail and we're coming in hot."

When they got to the lobby floor, it was the hardest thing to push Edwina Gladstone at a leisurely pace. Yuri pushed the wheelchair, while Sveta kept checking. So far, no Sanzar and Abarran, and she was crossing her fingers that they weren't behind her.

Charlene pulled into a space just as they arrived at the curb. She unlocked the doors, and Yuri unloaded Edwina Gladstone into the backseat. He hurried and got into the front seat and Sveta got into the back seat next to Edwina. She closed the door in a hurry, and said, "Go, go."

Just then, the elevator doors opened and Sanzar and Abarran stepped out, but Charlene floored it and they rapidly became a distant memory. Yuri turned around and looked at Sveta.

"That was close," he said.

"Too close," said Sveta. "I wonder what they were doing there."

She looked thoughtfully at Edwina.

"I think Hauck was right. They were there cleaning up loose ends."

47

Hauck watched as Sveta and Yuri unloaded a bound and gagged Edwina Gladstone from the SUV and wheeled her into the building's basement. Here, at least, the werewolf's howlings were muted. Hauck had ordered that the building be insulated from the outside, but he had never thought that he would need to insulate the individual rooms inside. Sveta opened the elevator door to the basement, and Yuri pushed Edwina out into an area that was large and mostly empty save for some stacked chairs and a table.

"Over there, Yuri," said Hauck, pointing to the center of the room.

Yuri dutifully rolled Edwina over to where Hauck had designated and left her, first locking the wheelchair into place. And then, taking off her hood that they had pulled over her head in case she woke up prematurely. He then got four chairs and positioned them facing her.

"No," said Hauck. "Charlene will wait outside with the car."

"Hey," said Charlene, "I want to see what she's got to say about the gun."

Hauck frowned.

"But this could get ugly."

He looked at Sveta for reinforcement. She simply shrugged her shoulders.

"Look, I deserve this," said Charlene.

"Very well," said Hauck.

While the others took their seats facing Edwina, Hauck strode over to her. He rolled her sleeve up and took out a vial from his pocket and inverted it. Snapping the side of it with his finger, he examined it closely. Satisfied, he withdrew from another pocket a syringe. He inserted it into the vial, extracted two milliliters and injected it into the soft tissue at the juncture of her forearm and upper arm. Finally, content that he had done all that could be done, he returned to a chair.

"That will wake her up?" asked Charlene.

"Theoretically," said Hauck. "Now I must remind you, that no matter what you hear us say or do, you are not to interrupt. You are only as an observer. Is that clear? Otherwise, you must leave now. Are we agreed on that?"

"Sure."

"Charlene, are you sure?"

"Positive."

Satisfied, Hauck waited for her to wake up. He was worried, though, about Charlene. There was the matter of how she looked, all dressed in black, with her black hair, black fingernails and black eyeshadow but then again Yuri had looked pretty scruffy when he first hired him. He would have to monitor her.

Sveta leaned over.

"Relax," she said.

Edwina began to stir. Everyone was quiet for this. They wanted her to wake up terrified. Her hands and feet shackled to the chair. She had tape over her eyes and tape over her mouth. The awakening had the desired effect.

She began to scream, but it came out as a muffled sound. Twisting and turning, she thrashed about like a fish on a hook. Finally, exhausted, she slumped over in the chair.

Hauck nodded to Yuri.

Yuri stopped in front of Edwina. He looked back at Hauck, who nodded his assent. Yuri ripped the tape off her mouth. She screamed at the indignity of it. Still blindfolded, she could not see who had done this to her and although she started out confused and then furious, she ended up being thoughtful about it, that ended when tape was ripped off her mouth. She could now speak and hear, but she could not see.

"Who's there?" she finally asked.

Yuri had returned to his chair by then and left her all alone.

Hauck and the others kept silent.

"Who is there?" said Edwina.

Still, Hauck said nothing.

"Goddammit!"

Hauck looked down at his fingernails. It was time to cut them, of course.

"Look, I don't know what you're playing at. Why don't we just cut to the chase? Why don't you just ask me what you are dying to ask me? I tell you I don't know the answer to that question, so please ask another. You ask me the same question repeat ad nauseum. I tell you I don't know anything. Nothing. I know nothing at all. Don't you realize you've picked the wrong woman?"

Yes, Hauck thought, it was definitely time for the manicurist.

"Look, I'm telling you, whoever you're after and whatever you want, I'm just the wrong person to get it for you."

Charlene looked with interest at Hauck. How long could he wait before he began his interrogation of her. She checked her big wristband watch. Barely five minutes had passed. Suddenly, she thought of Kirk and wished he were here. She wished he could see just what revenge felt like.

Fifteen minutes past without Hauck saying a word, and Charlene babbling on like there was no tomorrow. Still Hauck did nothing. Finally, by Charlene's watch, 20 minutes later, he spoke.

"Hello Edwina," he said.

"Who is that?"

"Edwina, you've been a bad girl, haven't you?"

Silence from Edwina, as she tried to figure out who her interrogator was. But so far, no luck.

"Edwina, let me tell you the way this will go. I will ask the questions, and you will provide the answers. Is that understood, Edwina?"

"I don't know who you are," she wailed.

Hauck looked at his watch. He looked at the others. Yuri appeared bored. Sveta just sat there impassively. Charlene though sat there looking more interested than ever. This time he waited ten minutes.

"Edwina?"

"Yes?"

"You were spying on Dr. Jimmy."

Edwina was silent for a minute. Then she said, "I don't know what you're talking about."

"Edwina, Edwina, Edwina."

"You've got the wrong woman I tell you."

"Ah. Well, then, we have absolutely no use for you at all."

Hauck waited for another five minutes while Edwina babbled on and on. She didn't deserve to die. They were mistaken.

"Edwina," said Hauck, when she had finally quieted down, "you are trying to gauge how many of us there are, no doubt. You are trying to convince us that you did nothing. That you deserve to live, yes?"

She said nothing.

"So, before dispensing with you as useless, I shall try a truth serum, as we loosely call it. I'm assuming you will have been hardened enough to them. Yes? Well, I shall just assume then. Then I shall take you back to the hospital and dump you."

Silence. Hauck could almost hear the ticking that went on behind her eyelids.

"Why... why would you do that?"

"Ah, well, you see, no matter what you tell them, the people who are your employers won't believe you, Edwina. I'm afraid that they will think you're lying, that I used a truth serum of sorts on you, and you, as the colloquialism goes, will have spilled your guts to me and they will have to kill you. They'll tell you otherwise, of course, but you know how that goes. They will have to terminate you, just to be sure."

Edwina thought that over very carefully. The seconds ticked by while she thought.

"Well," said Hauck, "I thought you should know before I begin."

"Wait," said Edwina.

"Yes?" said Hauck.

"You'll kill me anyway."

"No, I won't. Although you probably deserve it a thousand times over you have my word that I will not kill you."

Edwina thought some more.

"How can I be sure?"

"Edwina, I'm not going to lie to you. You can't trust me. Whatever I tell you could just be a lie. So, I won't even try to get you to trust me. I'll just tell you that I won't kill you and leave it at that."

Meantime, Hauck was getting up, getting ready another syringe and he walked over to where Edwina was strapped down. He grasped her wrist and Edwina yanked and pulled against the belts. But, he managed to slip another syringe full of fluid into her right arm.

"Now, we just wait for it to take effect."

****

A full ten minutes had passed. The first three were devoted to Edwina swearing. The second two were to her slowing down, and the third were to her entering into a hypnogogic state.

"This is kind of boring," said Charlene.

"Just wait," said Sveta.

"Edwina," said Hauck.

"Yes," said Edwina.

"Are you ready to tell me the truth?"

"Yes."

"Good, but I'm afraid I don't trust you, Edwina. So, let's just start with a simple question. Were you or were you not spying on Dr. Jimmy?"

"Yes."

Hauck raised his eyebrows.

"Now that is an unusual response. I'd have expected her to be inured to this type of medication."

"Really?" said Sveta.

"Maybe they forgot to give it to her," said Yuri.

"Or maybe she's just playing you for a fool," said Charlene.

"Clever girl" said Hauck. "Let's try something a bit more challenging, shall we? Charlene, would you like to take over the questioning?"

"Really?"

"Certainly."

Charlene looked to Sveta for confirmation, then Yuri who smiled encouragingly. This was a test, although she didn't know it. Working up her courage, she thought of the one question that was on her mind at the moment.

"Who killed Kirk?"

Hauck seemed mildly surprised at the question.

"I do not understand," said Edwina dreamily.

"You know, the ex-newspaper reporter? The guy who was shot in his own apartment and would have been killed there except for some crazy booby-traps he laid. That guy."

Edwina seemed to struggle within herself for an answer. So deeply ingrained within her were the constructs not to reveal anything that was not already known, that she struggled against anything else. Finally, she answered.

"Three of Beckham's men."

Charlene seemed confused. Beckham? Who an earth was that?

"Who is Beckham?" asked Charlene.

"He is my boss. The Deputy Director of Special Operations."

A sudden inspiration hit Charlene and she asked, "What is his linkage to Krikor Meridian?"

Hauck looked surprised at this question. This girl was definitely a keeper. That was the very question that he was going to ask.

Edwina looked uncomfortable. She twisted in her chair as though trying to get away from the question. It was evident by her face her internal struggle to avoid answering.

"Edwina," said Charlene, "what is his relationship to Krikor Meridian?"

"He is... he is... the master."

Charlene looked at her as though she had grown two heads. The master? But Hauck seemed satisfied by this answer.

"Well done, Charlene, well done indeed," he said. "Now we have tied up all the loose ends, I suspect, save one. You were about to ask her about whether Professor acts as a priest?"

Charlene again looked to Sveta, who nodded encouragingly at her.

"It Krikor some kind of priest?"

"He is," said Edwina, "the priest of the Dole."

"Good job. I'll take it from here."

Charlene had a puzzled look on her face, but she gladly passed the questioning over to Hauck, who had a serene look on his face, as if he had done this many times before. In fact, he had done this many times before.

"Edwina," he asked, "where does Professor keep Sasha?"

"In his house," she answered.

"Where in his house?"

"In the dungeon," she answered.

"In the dungeon?" he repeated.

"Yes. In the dungeon."

"We've pulled up the schematics on Krikor's house and there is no dungeon listed."

"That's not unusual," said Sveta.

"Yeah, you wouldn't to list a schematic for a dungeon in the house diagrams," said Yuri.

"Well, at least we've learned that he is there. Edwina?"

"Yes?"

"Why is Krikor keeping Sasha in the first place?"

He thought he knew the answer to that one.

"For the sacrifice, and to capture the enemy."

"For the sacrifice?" Hauck and Sveta said at the same time.

"Yes, for the sacrifice."

"They're going to sacrifice him?" asked a horrified Hauck.

"Yes. On the same day as Dr. Jimmy breaks through and is going to electrify the Dhole he will sacrifice him."

"Not if I have anything to say about it," said Hauck.

"Edwina?" said Sveta.

"Yes."

"What can you tell me about Professor Meridian?"

"The professor has one eye."

"I already knew that, Edwina. Tell me something I don't know."

"He's got superhuman powers."

"Now I think you're coming out of the drugs, Edwina."

"I don't think so, Sveta," said Hauck.

"Superhuman powers? Come on."

"We have to keep an open mind. Why don't you ask her to describe his powers?" said Hauck.

"Okay. Edwina?"

"Yes?"

"Describe the professor's superhuman powers."

Edwina furrowed her brows and appeared to give it some thought. This had a chilling effect on those present for her interrogation. It was almost as though Edwina were struggling with some inner battle.

"Edwina?"

Finally, the damn burst.

"He has a book."

"A book?"

"A book that is written in blood."

Sveta arched an eyebrow and looked at Hauck.

"Go on," she said.

"It's a book that he has to feed. With human blood."

This was getting more and more gruesome.

"And?" she prompted.

"When he feeds it, a line appears, a line of writing, I mean, that foretells the future, for the Dhole, that is."

"Tell me—"

"And sometimes, he can tell the local future, but rarely."

"Tell me, about this… this Dhole."

"The Dhole?"

"Yes, tell me about the Dhole."

"It sleeps. It dreams endless dreams of power and corruption. But it wakes sometimes, and its dreams become real, but it falls back into a dreaming state. But soon, it will be free of the bonds that hold it. Soon, it will be… it will be…"

Edwina began a slow gurgling sound. Hauck and Sveta looked at her, waiting for her to clear her throat. When the blood came pouring out of her mouth, though, they panicked and leapt to their feet, but not in time to beat Charlene who was already there. She tilted her head back, but she was simply too late. Edwina's head lolled to one side when she let go of it. Edwina Gladstone was dead.

But before she died, she said loud and clearly in Professor Krikor Meridian's voice, "You are meddling with forces you cannot understand, and it will end badly for you."

"I don't understand," said a clearly confused Hauck.

"Oh God, she's dead," said Charlene.

Sveta put her hand on Charlene's shoulder out of sympathy for her. As many times as she had seen death, the death of Edwina Gladstone did not bother her. But the how and why of death did. And there was that eerie voice before she died

Yuri came up behind them, superstitious to the core.

"Did you guys see that? I mean, it's like one minute she was alive, and the next she was dead and talking. Could the drug be responsible for this?"

He stayed back away from the body when he said this. This was...supernatural stuff and he didn't understand this. It was like... voodoo or something.

"No," said Hauck, "I truly don't know what it was."

"Maybe we just saw an example of the professors magical powers at work."

"I don't think so," said Sveta. "What, like he kills by remote control?"

"Maybe," said Yuri.

As the others looked toward him, Hauck wondered if that was even possible. Yet, there were her last dying words spoken in the professor's voice.

48

Professor Meridian was enraged at Edwina Gladstone's escape from Sanzar and Abarran's net. They were to have gone to her in the wee hours of the night and killed her quietly, so that her death would be attributable to natural causes. But to have been defeated by mere moments by two people in masks—bah! That was unconscionable. Who were they anyway? And Professor Meridian could not gain a fix on her while she was in a drug induced coma. He was furious beyond words.

And he hated the fact that the coin trick with Hauck didn't work. But so be it, but that Edwina Gladstone had gotten away was infuriating.

He was in his house now, and pacing. There was no where to vent his energy. The study was certainly doing him no good. The vast hallways and stairs that were such a comfort to him now were useless. He felt trapped in his own house. Like there was nowhere to go within its halls that would give him surcease from this agony that he felt. He had gotten nowhere with killing Edwina Gladstone, he still did not know where his enemy the Instructor was, and he had lost track of Hauck. Further, when was Dr. Jimmy going to break through with his drill bit? He had to know that at a bare minimum. All of Beckham's men had failed him and now he was down to Trisha Daytona, his one hope.

He wondered if he should make contact with her himself. Yes, he should have Beckham set that up, because there was no room for error here. Dr. Harlen was only days away from breaking through to the Dhole. He had to know when that breakthrough occurred, because if the sacrifice were not performed at the exact time that Dr. Harlen electrified the Dhole it wouldn't work. What Dr. Harlen didn't know was that the electricity intended to kill the Dhole would in fact set it free if a sacrifice were performed. And not just any sacrifice, but the sacrifice of a supernatural beast.

Krikor had been extraordinary lucky to have Sasha show up at his door all ragged and spent when he did. He couldn't believe his good fortune. When he had heard his story, the professor eagerly agreed to lock him up on those nights that he turned into a werewolf so that he would hurt no one. But that next night, when the moon rose in the sky and Sasha was locked safely in the dungeon, it was the last night he would ever see freedom. He was sequestered away in a tomb that would never let him free.

He was in a two partition room. One side for the normal, everyday self that Sasha was want to exhibit, and the other half for when he turned into a werewolf. Down the middle ran an impenetrable iron door. The walls of the room were solid bricks, one hundred years old but impregnable. The doors were wooden reinforced by steel plate, impossible for any beast to get through. This house was nearly two hundred years old, with frequent upgrades. There were no windows, save on built into the door, and that was only one foot high and two feet wide. No room for a werewolf to get out. He was satisfied with the prison of which he had overseen construction. Yes, he could rest easy on that one point; if only he had the enemy locked up to feed him to the werewolf.

Krikor had been searching for the enemy for years, but could not find him. It was amazing how the enemy had gone to ground in such a way as to be almost invisible. For over forty years he had hidden from him. Ever since the one fateful day he'd caught him alone. He hadn't suspected a thing. He had caught him by surprise in a rundown shanty by the edge of river. It was night. The enemy was leaving the cover of his house when he had attacked. The professor had pressed his advantage home, but at the last minute he had somehow felt a pain in his eye and the enemy had ripped his eye out of his socket. The pain had been unbearable, and in the ensuing chaos, the enemy had gotten away. In remembrance of that act, Krikor felt the phantom gray agony that accompanied his memories of it. He crashed his clenched fist into the wall.

Damn him.

All these years, all this pain and nothing in return. He wanted his head.

Why could he not find him? But he was so close. The professor could almost smell him. And Hauck was the key to where he was. His Instructor? Bah—he would like to instruct him if he could just get his hands on him. But he had been patient for all these years. Now was the time he could catch the Instructor, he was confident of that. Hauck had gotten rid of his coin, he was sure of that. The signal was lost. How had he known that a tracking device was implanted? How? Well, no matter, he would show up sooner rather than later. After all, he had just snatched the Edwina Gladstone woman. That was the key.

And now, he had to see through her eyes. The professor made his way to his study. His intent was plain to see. Sanzar and Abarran followed behind him. He was going to use Edwina Gladstone to find out where Hauck was. And were Hauck was the Instructor was sure to be not far behind.

Sanzar and Abarran flanked the door.

"I do not wish to be disturbed," said Krikor.

He closed the double doors to his study and locked them behind him. He swung aside a painting on the wall to reveal a an old fashioned safe, and worked at the combination. The door to the safe swung open. Krikor slowly, reverently withdrew the Book of the Dhole from it and stared at it. He needed blood for it to work, to reveal its secrets.

Walking over to his desk, he carefully laid the book down on the center of it. He took a knife out from a middle drawer. With a deep sigh, he opened the Book of the Dhole to the requisite page. It was blank, waiting for the words to be written. From his waistcoat, he withdrew a lock of Edwina Gladstone's hair and laid it on the page.

Then he clapped his hands and said, "Alexa, lower the lighting."

Obediently, the lights dimmed.

He centered himself, took another deep breath, and took the knife, and cut a gash down the center of his palm. Wincing from the pain, he squeezed drops of blood onto the page and thought of Edwina. He developed a picture of her in his mind.

Finally, he spoke the words, "Iä! Iä! Cthulhu fhtagn! Ph'nglui mglw'nafh Cthulhu R'lyeh wgah-nagl fhtagn—" Suddenly, in his minds eye, he was in total darkness. What was this? But he could hear voices…

"Tell me, about this… this Dhole."

"The Dhole?"

"Yes, tell me about the Dhole."

"It sleeps. It dreams endless dreams of power and corruption. But it wakes sometimes, and its dreams become real, but it falls back into a dreaming state. But soon, it will be free of the bonds that hold it. Soon, it will be… it will be…"

That was enough for the professor to hear. Enraged, he dreamed that Edwina was dead. And she was. She died slow and painfully. But before she died, he had her say, "You are meddling with forces you cannot understand, and it will end badly for you."

He came out of his dream painfully awake. His hand hurt from the cut to his hand and he immediately went for the first aid kit in another drawer. As he bandaged his hand, he felt satisfaction that she was dead. But frustration that she appeared to have tape over her eyes and couldn't see.

But she had revealed the secret teachings about the Dhole. Now, more than ever, the professor had to know when Dr. Harlen broke through to the Dhole and planned to destroy him with electrical current. Little did Dr. Harlen know that was the very thing that would bring it to life.

49

Trisha couldn't believe that Jimmy's friends would kidnap Edwina Gladstone in broad daylight or whatever. If they were caught, they were in for a world of trouble.

"I don't approve of this Jimmy, and I don't like it one bit," she said.

Jimmy was a full head taller than Trisha, and when he stood up and straightened his back, it showed.

"Look, Hauck's got to do what Hauck's got to do. Besides, I don't control him."

She seemed genuinely shocked. It had never occurred to her that Jimmy wouldn't be running this show. Now, she was even more concerned.

"What? You don't control him? Well, who does?"

"Hauck controls himself. Remember, he's in this game to re-catch his son, first and to get me out of this mess second. That's the best deal I could strike, Trisha.'

"Whoa, calm down, you two," said Marty.

"You calm down," said Trisha. "Marty, if they get caught… Beckham's my boss and Edwina worked for him, don't you see?"

"Oh."

"Yeah, you're darned right, oh."

"I'm sorry, I wasn't thinking," said Marty.

"Yes, but it doesn't make any difference, don't you see?" said

Jimmy. "Edwina was spying on me? Don't you get it? Yes, she was working for Beckham, who works for the NSA—the same group that put my father away and murdered him."

"Hey, why don't we all sit down and take a calming breath and get a grip on ourselves, shall we? I'm sure we can work this out."

Trisha stared at him for a minute before speaking.

Finally, she said, "What are you, on his side or something?"

"Trisha come on, sit down and Jimmy you, too."

Brittany's voice interrupted them with news that Alex Gudinoff wanted to see him.

"Push him off for awhile, Brittany."

"He sounds urgent, Dr. Harlen."

"All right," to Trisha and Marty, "just a minute."

Brittany flashed Alex Gudinoff on the computer screen.

"Hello, Alex. I'm kind of busy right now, but what can I do for you?"

"Dr. Harlen?"

"Yes?"

"Um, I've found an anomaly in our records."

"What kind of an anomaly, Alex?"

"Well, that's just it sir… did you know that there are thirteen men missing from their shifts?"

Jimmy's heart stopped cold. Thirteen men?

"I just figured that even with the rate of turnover we normally have, that's a lot."

His heart skipped a beat. Thirteen men was a lot, and if they had all gone the way of Stacy and Randy and Tyler… that was too much. He couldn't tell Alex about it either. They were so close, but the moon was not even red yet. How was he supposed to know?

"Alex, how much time until we break through?"

"About a day and a half. Give or take a day what with the breakdowns to the drill bit we've been experiencing."

"I'll look into this. Meantime, keep drilling. We'll be through with this accursed task soon enough."

"Yes sir, but about the men?"

"Rest assured it will be looked into."

Jimmy signed off and slumped down into one of the chairs that encircled the table. With a sinking feeling in his stomach, he knew exactly what had happened to the men. The pop-up killers, that was what had gotten to them. As sure as he was sitting there, he knew what had taken the men.

Suddenly, he had an inspiration.

They only came out at night.

One week and a half left to go until the planetary alignment.

"Brittany," he said, "get me Alex again."

He turned to Trisha and Marty.

"I've got to make this right," he said. "I've just got to."

Both Trisha and Marty looked uncomfortable. Thirteen men gone. And they knew what had taken them.

"Yes," came Alex's voice from the computer.

"Alex, this is Dr. Harlen. I want you to only drill during daylight hours. We shut down when it is night."

"But why, Dr. Harlen? That could mean a delay of three days."

"Just do it for me, Alex. The men have been working too hard. We can afford the extra three days."

"All right, Dr. Harlen. If you say so."

"I say so, Alex. Thanks for bringing my attention to the missing men. I really appreciate it."

"No problem, Dr. Harlen. Just doing my job."

And Dr. Jimmy Harlen hung up. He turned to Trisha and Marty.

"I just realized that they only come out at night," he said.

"So you quit drilling at night?" asked Trisha. "Jimmy we've got to go to the government. They're the only ones that are big enough to handle this whole mess."

"No, Jimmy's right, Trisha," said Marty. "Look, the government is too slow. They'll never kill the Dhole by the time the Red Moon is at its apex and the planetary alignment is done. Maybe they could have if they had been let in on the beginning, but not now. We've got to let Jimmy play it out.

"Play it out," said Trisha, "is that what you think? You think this is some kind of game, Marty?"

Marty stood up and paced around the table before answering. He stopped at the head of the table. And when he did, his voice had a faraway quality to it that gave it an odd kind of weight.

"Trisha, I've been haunted by the pop-up killers for more years than I care to think of, and I wondered if I was crazy. But now, thanks to Jimmy, I see that they are real, and I am thankful for that."

"But-"

"No buts, Trisha, you've got to hear me out. There's a time to speak and I guess mine is right now. Agreed?"

Jimmy nodded his agreement and Trisha, after a few stubborn minutes of recalcitrance, gave in and nodded her assent.

"Like I said, I've been all over the world looking for answers, trying to determine if there was any merit behind the pop-up killers. I've looked for Bigfoot, I've investigated werewolf settings, I've investigative vampire settings, I've studied UFOs, I've investigated a series of hidden cities that never before seen a footprint of man, I've even delved into the pyramids to see if they were created by ancient aliens. What I'm trying to say is I've done a lot. Through it all, I've been propelled by the nightmare of the pop-up killers.

"They've never been far from my mind. Every night, no matter where in the world I'm at I dream about them. I dream of the one time that I banished them with my grandmother secret word. But I can't remember that. I don't know what it is. Someday, I always knew we would come to this, we'd come face-to-face with the pop-up killers again. And now, here they are, ready to show their faces again. They've already killed three people that we know of."

"That's not true," said Jimmy. "As far as we can reckon the pop-up killers had killed hundreds of men and women. They go back as far as the salt mines, and probably even earlier."

"No," said Trisha. "It can't be."

"Oh but it is," said Jimmy. "A man named Kirk was killed smuggling the records to us, and I guarantee they are accurate. If that only goes back to when people were working on the salt mines, it doesn't embrace what happened before."

Marty whistled.

"Several hundred?"

"Yes," said Jimmy.

"Jimmy, we've got to kill it before the planetary alignment and it really wakes up."

"I'm trying, Marty. I've got to drill down to fourteen hundred feet- which is where I'm sure its at, and then replace the drill bits with the electrodes and then fry him. I've got enough electricity to kill him dead, at least, that's the theory anyway."

"But," said Trisha, "what if that is not enough?"

Jimmy shrugged.

"I don't know, Trisha. I just don't know. There's enough electricity in those electrodes to kill anything, literally anything. What would the government do to stop it anyway if that doesn't work? Drop a bomb on Detroit? Nuke the city? For something that they don't even know if it exists? For the story of a bunch of eight year old kids? Come on, Trisha, think how that would go over with the government—we had this run-in with these monsters when we were eight years old and they're making a comeback? And where is the evidence that they even exist? I ask you, where is the evidence? What have we got to stand on except for the word of a group of kids?"

"I—"

Trisha stopped. What was she thinking? Of course she didn't agree with Beckham spying on Jimmy. What worried her was that she had fallen for it so easily. And Jimmy was right—what did she have to present in the way of facts that would cause the government to step in? Jimmy had taken a chance even investigating the matter, because if the government ever found out, they would have him declared insane. But maybe if she presented the evidence that had been accumulated to Beckham—maybe then he would listen. He would have to understand.

"Jimmy," she tried again, "is Kirk around? Can we have him—"

"Kirk's dead," he said. "He was killed while trying to give the information to me."

"What?" she said.

"God's truth," said Marty.

"Yes," said Jimmy. "Your Mr. Beckham probably arranged that, too. Why do you think he's so interested in what we're doing here?"

"Now that's not fair," said Trisha.

But that wasn't exactly true, now was it? Why was Beckham so interested in what was going on here anyway? What was the purpose that was driving him? No one else in the government seemed that interested in Jimmy—except that everyone else seemed to be rooting for him. The mayor of Detroit, the Governor had all sent their best wishes for the project. Even the Secretary of the Department of Energy was behind it. What gave with Beckham being so negative on it? Surely it couldn't be that thing about his father, could it? No, that just didn't hold water anymore.

"Isn't it?" said Jimmy.

Beckham had to be after something else. And honestly, if she glanced in the mirror, she knew that Beckham was not above having someone killed just to get at the papers.

"How did he die?" said Trisha.

"Who?"

"The man who was trying to get the papers to you."

"I don't know. I think he was shot while at his apartment, but he barely made it out. He went to a friends and I'm guessing he died there. Why?"

All this grew more and more convoluted. Why would Beckham want papers that showed the trail of bodies killed by the pop-up killers? Trisha began to feel more and more uncomfortable with the situation, and something wasn't right. Beckham had for a long time been untouchable within the NSA. At least, she thought he was with the NSA. What if he wasn't with them? What if he ran a secret cabal of people that reported only to him and they thought he worked for the NSA but he didn't? What if... Trisha's mind swirled with the possibilities.

"Just wondering, that's all."

"Come on, Trisha," said Marty, "give."

"Well, I was just wondering—supposing that Beckham wasn't working for the NSA?"

"Go on."

"Well, what if he was secretly working for someone else? Say Professor Meridian?"

"But that's nuts," said Jimmy. "You said yourself that..."

"What? That it couldn't be Beckham? So maybe I was wrong. But what could he want with a bunch of papers detailing a mass of killings by the pop-up killers?"

"Hold on—maybe he didn't want anyone to know about the killings," said Marty.

Trisha thought about that for a second. That sounded like it made sense. Say Beckham didn't want anyone to know about the pop-up killers. That made the connection to Professor Meridian even more real, presupposing that the professor was connected to the uncovering of the Dhole. But how could the professor be connected to the Dhole? How? Unless that girl Charlene was right—some kind of religious connection. Dhole worship? It seemed impossible and yet...

"Okay," said Trisha, "let's suppose that Professor Meridian is connected with some sort of Dhole worship. Just suppose."

"No way," said Jimmy. "You said—"

"Can what I said before, just listen to what I'm saying now. Let's suppose that the girl Charlene was right. Let's suppose that Professor Meridian is some sort of priest of the Dhole."

"Go on," said Marty.

"That would explain why he didn't want the papers to come out. That would also explain why he is so eager to find out when you break through to the Dhole, Jimmy."

What could Jimmy say? It made a certain amount of convoluted sense.

"So wait a minute. In that scenario, you're saying that your man Beckham is actually working for Professor Meridian, am I right?"

"Exactly," said Trisha.

"Secretly, correct?"

"Yes, secretly. The NSA thinks he's working for them, but he's really working covertly for Professor Meridian."

"And that the professor is kind of a... priest of the Dhole?"

"Exactly," said Marty.

"Well, what is he waiting for? I mean, is he waiting for me to try and kill the Dhole?"

This time it was Marty who answered.

"Yes. I think he is waiting for you to break through to the Dhole, so that when he awakens, they can set it free."

"But to what end, Marty?" said Trisha.

"I don't know... world domination maybe. Like let's say that Meridian expects to get made by the Dhole into the head honcho of all of the Dhole's followers."

"Yes, but that would mean... that the Dhole was sentient," said

Jimmy. "Like when those times that the Dhole was awake that he could communicate with the professor."

"You're scaring me, Jimmy," said Trisha.

"Yeah, but it makes sense," said Marty.

"It does, and that scares me, too. But with Edwina trying to spy on me, surely Beckham would have a backup. Someone to pinch hit for her. How do we flush out who that was?" said Jimmy.

He stood up from his chair and walked back and forth. Pacing as he thought. Who would be the logical choice to replace Edwina? He ticked through his departments. Human resources? Not close enough to the day to day operations to know when they broke through. Operations was the logical choice. That was—

"I'll save you some time," said Trisha. "It was me."

Jimmy was flabbergasted.

"He said that I was supposed to get you to fall in love with me so I could learn your deepest secrets."

"Yes, but I thought that meant—"

"Now we know different, don't we?" said Trisha.

Jimmy stared at Trisha for seconds longer than he should. Could it be that she actually felt something for him that was more than friendship?

"Now we just have to wait for Hauck to get back to us," said Marty.

Trisha looked away from Jimmy when she said, "Right."

50

Sasha woke spent of all energy.

He knew he had done terrible things. He vaguely remembered the girls. He remembered trying to resist being put in the room with them, but Sanzar had shot him with that terrible tranquilizer gun. And when he woke up—well that was when he quit trying to remember. Would this nightmare never end?

It was getting worse each successive night. He didn't know what was happening to him. Every night seemed to be a full moon. Every night he changed into a wolf. No correct that, a werewolf. Who was he kidding. Who was left enough to care at all about him? No one even knew where he was at. No one was around that even cared about him. He paced in his room, growing more disgusted with his situation by the minute.

He wondered about the clean up.

Every night Sanzar and Abarran would capture a young woman or two. They would then position a sleeping Sasha into the same room, and then they would introduce the young women. Only then would the soundproof door between rooms open up. And let in the horror that he became into the room, and next he would black out. Although not really. At one level of his brain he remembered. Oh, how he remembered. The screams, yes the screams. He could barely block out the screams. The looks on the young women's faces when they first saw him. He shuddered at the memories.

He paced around his room like the pent-up beast that he was.

How could he go on like this?

He screamed and he screamed and he went on screaming. Falling to his knees, he wept bitter tears. He was going to go mad. Day in and day out until he thought that he would go mad it was the same thing. Nowhere to go except the same rooms. Nothing to see; there were no windows to the outside world. Everything bolted down.

The first week he was there he thought would be the hardest days of his life. He was royally screwed. He was infected with the werewolf disease. Every night that the moon was full, he would change into a werewolf and go berserk. There was a separate room that they would put him in, unconscious on those nights. A sterile room that was a waiting room. The girl or girls would be held captive in his special room. A duplicate of the room he was in. Everything bolted down against his rages, and the girl or girls held there, wondering about their fate. Trapped with nowhere to run. As was he. Trapped in the soundproofed room with no doors, no outside air, and when he turned into a monster—for that's what he was, he might as well admit it, a monster—the inner door would slide open, the girls would scream and try extra hard to escape for their lives, but there was literally nowhere to go. And then, he would descend on them with teeth and claws, ripping and tearing and it was awful.

He thought that he would go completely insane with the memories. The torn skin, the limbs ripped off of bodies and the teeth marks on their faces, their once beautiful faces.

When he was ripping and tearing them apart, he felt a thrill that when he returned to his normal self was incomprehensible. He was going insane, he surely was.

Looking at himself in the mirror after he got to his feet again—the polished, bolted on to the wall piece of stainless steel that served as his mirror—he tried to remember his life before the curse that now afflicted him. He was Sasha, king of all that he surveyed. His mother was the Iron Lady, queen of the shady underground known as the Russian Mafiya, and she was kind to him. Until she sold him out to trap Drogol, the king werewolf. She was out to get him, that was fine until she learned from that dreaded doctor from a DNA test that Drogol was his father. And then he was worthless, bait to be used and abused to capture Drogol.

It was impossible to say how he became a werewolf. Had he been bitten by Drogol? He didn't know. Was he even scratched by the King werewolf? It didn't seem possible but his memories were so vague from that time. He couldn't recall the simplest facts. All he knew was that now he was a werewolf. Infected by the bite or scratch or clawing of another werewolf, it was now indisputable. It was futile to rage against it. There was nothing he could do about it. He was what he was.

Without warning, the gate came down. He tried in vain to get beneath it, but he was too slow. The gate left three feet of space between the door and the rest of the room. At times, he wondered if he were watched all the time. The four cameras that monitored the space that he lived in were active, he was sure of that. They were up so high, though, that even by jumping he could not get at them.

When it was securely in place, the door opened and Professor Meridian strode in. He was six foot eight if he was an inch, and strode was what he did best. His eye-patch was impeccably in place. His hair was elegantly brushed back, and his face had the cruel look of someone who had just sentenced someone to death. He wore an impeccably tailored old school suit. From out of a watch pocket, he withdrew an elegantly fashioned time piece. Satisfied he replaced it back in the place from where he had withdrawn it.

"Sasha—" he began.

Throwing himself at the bars, Sasha fell short a good foot of grasping the professor by his throat and squeezing.

"Are you quite through?" said Krikor. "I should like to tell you something."

Disgusted, Sasha drew back from the bars and settled down in a convenient chair.

"Go on, you bastard; I can't stop you from talking," said Sasha.

"Yes, I suppose you can't at that. Although you might show a little more civility."

"Bite me."

"Very well, since you will be like that, I might as well tell you that you have only two more weeks to stay with me until I let you go."

Sasha was stunned.

"You mean you are going to set me free?"

"Why yes, Sasha, you didn't think I was going to keep you here forever, did you?"

"You weren't?"

Sasha stood up and ran to the bars.

"You mean it?"

"Oh yes, you see Sasha, I believe we've found the cure."

"What? You mean, you can cure me?"

"Yes, Sasha, I do, I mean exactly that. Now you have to remain locked up for the next two weeks, then we will give you a shot and we shall see what we shall see. In the meantime I'm afraid you'll have to stay locked up, though."

"I can do that; as long as there is a light at the end of the tunnel I can do anything," he said eagerly.

"Good, well I have to go now. Au revoir, Sasha."

And he left by the doorway that he came in by. A few seconds later, the gate drew up into the ceiling.

Sasha sat back down and contemplated his good fortune. Out in what—three weeks. Man the things he could do.

He would not have been so happy could he have seen the smile on the professor's face as he left.

<h1 style="text-align:center">51</h1>

"All right, is everybody on the same page now," Hauck said to his team and Dr. Jimmy's after he and Jimmy had updated everyone.

"No," said the Instructor, who had just been let out of his cage and was still feeling grouchy. "I don't understand why we just don't snatch the kid. End of story. Then we can go figure out a way to get rid of this damn thing where I've got to sit in a cage and howl at the full moon."

"Because," said Sveta, "that would tip off the professor to us coming after them and what if he isn't there?"

"Whatever," said the Instructor. "Can I please get something to eat around here? Like a three pound steak, rare?"

"I'll get it," said Yuri, after looking around and seeing no other volunteers.

"Make that two three pound steaks," said the Instructor.

"Now are you agreed that we can't simply go into his house and snatch Sasha," said Hauck.

"No, goddammit, I'm not. Where's my steaks? Yuri," he bellowed.

"All right, already," came Yuri's voice from the kitchen.

"Now," said Jimmy, "getting back to the topic at hand—"

"Who are you again?" snarled the Instructor.

"I'm—"

"I know who you are. I'm just saying that maybe if you would shut up, you could learn something."

"Look, could we—" began Hauck.

"No, would you listen for a minute goddammit? I've remembered something about ass-wipe."

"Go on," said Hauck, exhibiting remarkable restraint.

"Ah, my food. Put it right here. That's my man."

The Instructor didn't bother with the knife and fork that Yuri had brought. He just grabbed it and tore off a bite.

"Now that, is a steak. So anyway, what was I saying?"

"You were saying," said Hauck patiently, "that—"

"That's it," said the Instructor after wolfing down another bite, "I was saying that I remembered something about dick-less, that's right. He had this thing about him I thought was peculiar, but I was lucky enough to get away with my own life at the time. This thing was that he had a god that he worshiped. You know, everybody had a god that they worshiped, but who cared, you know?"

He tore off another hunk of meat.

"Anyway he called it the Dull or Dhole or something like that."

"We know that," interrupted Marty.

"Man you are lucky that I'm over here and you are over there. You get me? Now you interrupted my chain of thought."

He took off yet another piece of the steak. The sight of it disturbed Yuri and Charlene. If he would have used the knife and fork that Yuri had provided, it would have been different. But to see the Instructor just tear into the bloody rare steak was too much. They exchanged glances, then glanced away as though it hadn't happened.

"Okay, I remember where I was at and what I was thinking, it was this—he wanted to sacrifice me to his god, but the timing was off or something. I forgot about that little tidbit, because it was such a long time ago. But the reason he wanted me was to serve a sacrifice to his god. But maybe, just maybe he's got a better sacrifice now."

"Who is that," said Jimmy.

"You know who, right? Sasha, Hauck's son."

Hauck didn't say a word.

"Which means that—"

"With the planetary alignment, we've got to get Sasha out," said Charlene.

"Bingo," said the Instructor.

"I'm guessing he's going to sacrifice him on the day of the planetary alignment," said Yuri.

The Instructor was busy eating the secondary steak.

"Yeah, something like that," he said around a mouthful of meat. "So, Hauck, what are we going to do about it?"

All eyes turned to Hauck. He turned to Sveta.

"What do you think?" he asked.

She seemed surprised that he would ask her.

"I don't know."

"What's your best guess."

"Well, we don't have a reconnaissance of the house so we don't know what's going on. It's so far back from the road, and treeless that we can't get a clear shot of it."

"Go on."

"We just don't," she said, "have anything to go on. I'm sorry, Hauck but there's not enough to go on. Unless—"

"Unless what?"

"Unless Adam has something. Yuri says that Adam can go on the EMF or radio waves or electrical power grid. Adam, what can you give us."

The normally taciturn artificial intelligence seemed to perk right up.

"I can give you the layout of the house, for starters."

"Yes, Adam; why don't you give them that," said Jimmy.

Suddenly, a geosynchronous map of the house layout appeared. It was a massive affair, and, as an added bonus, Adam had where Professor Meridian and his goons lived.

"Whoa," said the Instructor, "now that's what I'm talking about."

"But wait a minute," said Hauck. "Where is Sasha?"

"We must assume that they've got him underground," said Sveta.

Hauck frowned. Always there was the risk of something going wrong if he was underground. Like he wasn't there or some variant of that, but he thought Meridian wasn't that type of person. Not if he wanted to catch the Instructor he wasn't. Why was he so confidant, though? Hauck tried to reason it through, although it always seemed to come down to what force could be brought to bear at any particular moment. Hauck tried to think.

If he went up against Professor Meridian with twenty trained men, what would he do? What kind of trap would he have set that would be used against him? For example, what if he had forty men waiting for his twenty? What then?

"How many men does it show in the residence besides himself?" asked Hauck.

"Two," said Trisha. "But I think I should tell you—I just got a text message from Beckham saying that he would like to introduce me to someone."

"Oh, who?" asked Hauck.

"Professor Meridian."

"What?" said Jimmy. "No way."

"Way," said Trisha. "And he would like me to meet him at this house."

"What?" said Hauck. "That's out."

"No, it's not," said Sveta. "Not if we want to check out the layout of the inside compared to the diagrams Adam showed us. We'll save ourselves trying to figure out what traps he's got waiting inside. Maybe Trisha will see something that we couldn't."

"It's too risky," said Hauck.

"Hauck, it's the only chance we have."

"Yeah, if the rest of you have finished flapping your jaws and are ready for the big boys to lay out a better plan," said the Instructor.

"You haven't even asked me if I would go in yet," said Trisha.

"Okay, I'll bite—you going to go in or what?" said the Instructor.

"Yeah, I'll go in."

"Good," said the Instructor. "Now one thing you've got to remember and that's how Edwina Gladstone died, or whatever her name was. That's one thing that Hauck skipped over. Tell them, Hauck."

He hesitated before answering. Because he simply did not know. One minute she was fine, and the next, there was blood pouring out of her nose and mouth. Maybe some kind of delayed poison?

"Well, one minute she was fine, and the next she was bleeding out of the nose and mouth. It was peculiar."

"Did she," asked Marty, "exhibit any signs of illness?"

"No, I'm telling you exactly as I remember it."

"She just," pressed Marty, "died with no warning symptoms?"

"None," confirmed Hauck.

"I was there," said Sveta. "She just keeled over dead.

"And that's why they call him the Eyes of Death. He's head of a death cult," said the Instructor.

"A death cult?" asked Hauck.

"Yeah, he's got some ritual mumbo-jumbo he performs and… poof… you're dead. He's got to have a sample of your hair, though, for it to work. Why do you think I've been hiding from him all these years? It's got to do with that Book of the Dull through."

"Dhole," corrected Jimmy.

"Oh, is that so?" said the Instructor.

"Yes," said Jimmy.

"Well, I've got a plan," said the Instructor. "You see, I go in there after the girl, see."

"That's not going to happen," said Hauck.

"Yeah, well anyway, I go in after the girl, right around twilight."

"It's not going to—"

"So I go in when I'm a man, see? And then, I let Meridian capture me thinking he's got a man. But shortly afterwords it gets dark and, well, what he actually has is full-fledged werewolf, and then, he's got a fight on his hands. What do you say to that?"

He was going to answer "No," but he stopped and considered.

"It is an excellent plan," said Adam. "With a strong chance of success."

"Well?" said the Instructor.

"What do you think?" Hauck asked Sveta.

"It's got some rough spots. Like, how do we know what he's going to do after he's done mopping the place up?"

"Pardon?" said Hauck.

"What do we do with him after he turns into a werewolf and slaughters everyone in the building? What if he just takes off?"

"We wait outside with tranquilizer guns?"

"That won't work, Hauck, and you know it. There's too much can go wrong. With our luck, the Instructor would kill us."

"What if we set up a perimeter?'

"Come on, is that supposed to be a serious suggestion? He'll get through and you know it. Besides, how are we supposed to set up a perimeter without Professor Meridian knowing about it?"

Hauck was as imperturbable as ever, and for some reason this infuriated Sveta. They were dealing with a werewolf with a capital "W" and something was going to go wrong. She just knew that it was.

"We drive around in vans, and when the moon is full, and only then do we deploy."

"This hasn't been thought through properly, Hauck."

"I know, Sveta, I know. I wish I had an alternative plan ready to go, but..." and here he spread his hands out.

Sveta looked at Trisha's face on the screen. Could she be trusted in what was obviously a dangerous situation?

"Trisha, you understand this is dangerous?" said Sveta.

"Yes, I know."

Understanding that she might be vulnerable out of a sense of team loyalty or some other reason that Sveta might not yet understand, Sveta asked her again.

"Trisha, listen to me. This mission is dangerous. Professor Krikor Meridian is a dangerous man, and I think that applies to Sanzar and Abarran as well. Besides, we don't know how many men they have scattered throughout that place, or whatever traps they may have hidden. Are you sure you want to do this?"

She saw a flash of something familiar when Trisha glanced up at Jimmy.

"Yes, I'm sure."

Sveta was about to ask her again, but she saw something in the young woman's eyes that seemed to say that she would do it for Jimmy.

"What do you think of the rest of my plan?" asked the Instructor.

Hauck wished he had more time to think it over. He wished he had more time period. It was clearly a suicide mission to turn the Instructor loose. When he had finished with the tenants of the house, then what? He would go on a rampage of killing. On the other hand, what if the Dhole really did wake up? How many deaths would that cause? And above all, Sasha was in that house. He had to get him out. Presuming, of course, he wasn't already dead. But no, Meridian would keep him alive to use as bait or as a sacrifice. That's what bothered Hauck truthfully. He had Sasha kept in an underground lair, somewhere beneath the mansion. Probably soundproof, if Hauck's recent experience with the Instructor was any indication. It was an entrance that was probably hidden, too.

If Hauck ringed the mansion with people with firearms armed with tranquilizer guns, and if the Instructor made it out, which he probably would, they could take him down with the guns. It would work. A lot could go wrong, and Hauck assumed that it would, but it could work. The thing was, that Hauck only had one chance that he could see at saving Sasha and did he really want to leave that to a rampaging werewolf?

"Hello?" said the Instructor.

Hauck took one last look at Sveta.

"All right, we'll do it," he said.

Jimmy looked uneasily at Trisha.

"Are you sure you're okay with this?"

"What? Do you think that because I'm female I'm not up for the job?"

"No, it's not that, it's that—"

"Well I've got news for you, Jimmy. I work for Beckham. I can't refuse a direct order from him under the circumstances. Unless, that is, I quit my job. He says we're going to meet Professor Meridian, we're going to meet Professor Meridian."

"That's not what I meant," protested Jimmy.

"Look why don't you two lovebirds get a room? Hauck, are you serious?" said the Instructor.

"I'm serious," said Hauck. "We're going to put a ring around Meridian's mansion so that you can't get past us, without a tranquilizer dart being stuck in you. Sveta, Yuri round up twenty good men to surround the house."

"I still think this is a bad idea, Hauck."

"Yes, Sveta, I do, too," he said. "But it's the only idea in town that makes any kind of sense."

"All right," said the Instructor. "Paybacks are a bitch."

"Yes," said Hauck, "but we've got to time this just right. Adam, when is the moon full for the next week?"

When Adam had told him, Hauck grew quiet.

"Adam?" he said.

"Yes, Hauck."

"Have you been masking us from being detected so far?"

"Yes, Hauck."

"I thought," said Jimmy, "that would be what you wanted."

"I approve," said Hauck. "The government and I believe Professor Meridian can tap into all sorts of resources. I wondered, though, how we were able to escape his net the first time we met him, though. Now I know."

Jimmy nodded, but something about the whole plan bothered him. He couldn't put his finger on it though.

"So, you're going to in first, girlie, and I'm going to go in second as the mop-up team?" said the Instructor.

Trisha looked at Sveta and then at the Instructor. What an annoying little man. How did Sveta put up with him. And then, she realized. He was a werewolf. He had been responsible for Jason's death. A chill went down her spine.

"All right," said Hauck, "let's get this thing organized. Remember, Trisha's going in first and wo we have to pay attention to her safety first. So any ideas on that, let's hear them."

"I've got one," said Yuri and Marty at the same time.

"I have an idea, too," said Adam.

When Hauck had heard them all out, he began to smile at Jimmy, and Sveta.

"I think we have a plan," he said.

<h1 align="center">52</h1>

"Adam," said Hauck, "tell me what you see."

"Just what you see, Hauck. I see an extensive perimeter that walls the mansion in bordering the Detroit River. Twenty-four windows facing away from the river. Five acres of lawn before we get to the house. A curvilinear driveway that circles around in the front."

Adam was in Trisha's car. How he "saw" was beyond Hauck, but he just accepted it and went with it.

"There are no security cameras in evidence anywhere. No electronics. No way for me to get in."

"All right, Adam. Are you ready for the jump."

"Yes. We are just pulling up in front of Professor Meridian's now.

"Okay. Ready—four, three, two, one, jump."

****

Trisha grasped the steering wheel in both hands and clamped her teeth down hard. She was ready for Adam to transfer his consciousness to her own—she thought.

That had been Yuri's idea and Jimmy had been dead set it against it.

"No way," he exploded.

"What objection do you have to it?" asked Hauck.

"Something could go wrong. No. Absolutely not. I forbid it."

"Hey, wait a minute, Jimmy," said Marty. "What if it gives her the edge? She's going in there all alone."

"No," said Jimmy.

"Yes," said Trisha. "It probably won't work anyway, but it's worth a chance. Look, I don't like going in there all alone either and if there's half a chance that I can have some company, then so be it."

"Adam," said Jimmy, "tell this fool woman that it won't work."

"Actually, I think it was fairly brilliant of Yuri. I should be able to enter Trisha's consciousness with no problem at all. She is clearly not a mental defective or a psychopath."

Jimmy was speechless.

"Listen," said Yuri, "if it's not going to work we'll just scrap the idea. I just thought with Adam saying he could transfer himself to radio devices, that he might—and I'm saying just might—be able to transfer his consciousness to a human being is all."

"No," said Jimmy.

"Jimmy Harlen, it's my body and I say yes. End of story."

"But—" began Jimmy.

"No buts about it. It's settled."

Trisha looked immensely satisfied.

"Now," she asked, "how do we begin?"

And that was the beginning of it. The trials had been a success. Which explained why she sat in the car, gripping the steering wheel and closing her eyes, waiting for the transference of Adam's consciousness to her own. There was a slight jolt—it got easier each time—as Adam began the transference of his consciousness to her own. It wasn't a painful process really, it was more disorienting was the word for it. She kept her eyes closed the entire time. In seconds, it was complete.

Her eyes sprang open.

"Hello. Are you all right, Trisha?"

She almost answered vocally, but she caught herself at the last minute. It was the strangest thing. In order to communicate with Adam, she just had to think an answer.

"Yes, I'm fine."

"That's good. Trisha?"

"What?"

"I've been meaning to ask you. Does Dr. Harlen know how you feel about him?"

"What?"

The abrupt transition startled her. One minute they were talking about the transition and the next they were getting personal.

"I said—"

"No, I've got what you said, I just can't believe that you said it."

"Why? Was I not supposed to have said it?"

"Never mind. Wait, are we being broadcast?"

"Yes."

"Oh. Well come on then, let's get to it."

"I'm sorry if I caused you discomfort, Trisha."

"Enough, Adam. Let's just drop it, okay?"

"Yes."

Trisha got out of the car and closed the door after her. She walked up the sidewalk and to the front door. Out of longstanding habit, she checked the crease on her pants, to make sure that her blouse was tucked in and that her coat was on straight. Her hair and make up were next. She was ready. Just as she raised her hand to push the doorbell to announce herself, the door swung open.

A man stood in the threshold, perhaps three feet wide and six and a half feet tall and completely bald. He stepped aside and motioned her in. She hesitated, and, taking a deep breath, she entered.

"Got him," said Adam.

Another man, an identical twin to the first, appeared from behind a colonnade and nodded for her to follow. He went up a large and winding staircase that led to the second floor.

"Got him, too."

Along the way, in eerie silence, Trisha could not help notice the pink marble flooring, and the fine, almost exquisite scroll work of the balustrade, the elegant wood of the steps and the fine quality carpeting. The chandelier that hung from the ceiling over the steps was quite simply magnificent, and the stained glass window that looked down her as she walked up lent an almost supernatural quality to the very air.

"Trisha?"

"Yes?"

"It's very peculiar."

"What?"

"Well, I've done a DNA scan on the two men that met us at the door and they are identical."

"So?"

"That's not possible, Trisha. That's not at all possible."

"You must have done the test wrong."

"No, and what's worse is that they're not human."

Trisha stopped a few feet from the top of the steps. Not human? Then she continued walking, finished the last steps. Not human? Oh God, Adam had to have run the tests wrong.

"No, Trisha, I'm not wrong, trust me on that."

Oh, sweet Jesus, what was she doing here?

And it occurred to her that Jimmy must be going nuts right about now.

The man stopped in front of a door and held out his hand for her to enter. There was no going back, she realized. She couldn't take either of these two men. And how many more like them were between her and the front door to make her getaway. As though it were the most natural thing in the world, she sucked in a breath and entered the room.

****

Jimmy was furious with worry.

"Sit down," said Marty, "she's doing fine."

"Fine?" said an incredulous Jimmy. "Fine? Those two mountainous goons have identical DNA— which is an impossibility I might add—and they're not even human? She's got to get out of there, now."

Hauck was a calm and steady voice on the computer screen, and Jimmy hated him for it.

"Jimmy, she knew what she was getting into and this is our first eyes on view of the inside," said Hauck.

"Yeah, will you just shut up? The broad is working," said the Instructor, who had spent the night in a cage again and was feeling surly.

"Shut up, she's working? Is that all you've got to say when those two men are identical DNA and not even human?"

"Would you please shut up, you're getting on my nerves. Uh-oh, yep, that's him all right. Look at him, wearing an eye-patch and everything."

Everyone went quiet as, except for the Instructor, Hauck and Sveta, they saw Professor Meridian for the first time through Trisha's eyes.

"What a polished man," said Marty under his breath, but Jimmy heard him.

"I don't think polished is the right word," said Jimmy "I think evil would be better."

Marty looked over at his old friend, then back at the professor.

"There's something different about him," said the Instructor. "He's more—"

"Confident?" suggested Hauck.

"No... arrogant. If that is even possible, but... arrogant, yeah I think that describes him pretty well."

Jimmy wrung his hands.

****

"Welcome, Trisha. Welcome to my humble abode. Mr. Beckham didn't tell me you'd be so beautiful."

Professor Krikor Meridian bowed, a grand, sweeping gesture.

"Mr. Meridian. Beckham."

"Professor, please."

"Ah, I'm sorry. Professor."

Both men were standing. Professor Meridian extended his hand and Trisha took it. Then, Trisha took a seat, as did Beckham and Professor Meridian sat at the head of the table.

"They both scan normally, Trisha, save Professor Meridian has some odd truncations and enhancements to his DNA. I'm not really sure what it means," said Adam.

"Thank you for coming, Trisha. I would like to get a report on how close Dr. Harlen is to breaking through with his... drilling activity."

"Excuse me, but not to be rude, but who exactly are you?"

"Professor Meridian is a special consultant to the Department of Energy, as well as to our own NSA. You may speak freely in front of him," said Beckham.

"I would prefer, if you'll pardon my speaking freely in front of you as you say, Professor Meridian, to give my sensitive information to you, Beckham. And only after you have time to digest it, to share this information and ask pertinent questions that you reveal it to anyone. I don't see why we need to break chain of command for this."

Beckham was about to deliver a scathing rebuke to his subordinate, when Professor Meridian held up his hand palm out to him.

"That would be—how do you say—normally appropriate, but under the circumstances, time grows short. So far, Dr. Harlen has proved to be remarkably uncooperative, refusing to divulge the timing and so forth, so that we need to monitor his activities. It is imperative, therefore, that we drop all pretenses and have your utmost cooperation now."

Trisha looked toward Beckham.

"Is that you wish?"

Professor Meridian seemed taken aback by that. He seemed surprised that she should question his authority.

"Yes, of course," said Beckham, straightening his tie.

"Are you sure?" asked Trisha.

Beckham was about to snap back at Trisha, but restrained himself.

"Yes, I am sure."

Trisha maintained silence just long enough to drag it out. She counted to thirty and, just when Beckham was about to say something else, she said, "All right then." And she ignored Beckham when she was talking as though he wasn't there.

Professor Meridian steepled his fingers together.

"Proceed then, Trisha," he said.

"Dr. Harlen is down to a couple of days for when he will break through, but he's going to go to two shifts so that might add time to it."

"What?" asked an astonished Professor Meridian.

"Yes, it seems, although he hasn't specifically said why, nor will he, that he is afraid of drilling in the dark. Must be some superstition attached to it, albeit I can't say why."

Professor Meridian seemed to mull that over. With his one good eye, he stared off into space for a minute.

"How close would you say you are to Dr. Harlen?" he asked.

"Close enough."

"Hmm…"

"Why?"

"I wonder if he tells you everything."

"How do you mean?"

"For example, did he tell you why he is drilling?"

"I assume so that he can complete his earth battery."

"Yes, but why do you think he is really drilling?"

"I don't understand."

"Well Miss Daytona, what I am about to tell you is confidential. Do I have your word that it will stay this way?"

"I beg your pardon?"

"Trisha, just say that you'll keep it confidential," snapped Beckham.

"His blood pressure is rising," said Adam.

"I would think that all our conversations were confidential. I don't see why I should have to say anything of the sort."

Beckham was about to say something, but Professor Meridian cut him off.

"I see what you mean, Trisha. But this goes way above your pay grade, and I need your assurances that you will say nothing to anyone at all. Do I have them?"

Trisha made every effort to appear as if she was mulling it over. She waited until another thirty second metronomic beat in her head.

"All right. I agree."

Professor Meridian appeared pleased, but Beckham seemed merely annoyed.

"Good, good."

The door opened and the two men who had escorted her to Professor Meridian closed it behind them. They stood, shoulder to shoulder, inside the door, still as statues guarding the egress. Trisha wondered about them, about Adam's comment that they weren't human.

"Now to return to the topic—"

"Who are these men," interrupted Trisha.

"Sanzar and Abarran? They have many brothers in this house. But to answer your question, they are my security. Now to continue, has Dr. Harlen told you why he is drilling?"

"He is not lying, Trisha. I have detected the signatures of many others."

"I have the feeling that he can tell if I am lying."

"Don't worry, I will cover you."

"Again, to achieve his Earth battery. That is his single goal."

Professor Meridian eyed her closely. It was disconcerting with his single eye focused on her. He had a way of looking that Trisha found disconcerting. It was almost mesmerizing.

"Trisha, he is attempting to hypnotize you. Don't worry—I will protect you."

She felt odd, as though he were leading her down into a path that led only to the netherworld. It was as though an irresistible pull trapped her.

"Trisha?" said the Professor almost gently. "Did Dr. Harlen not tell you what he was drilling for?"

It was a fight to speak.

"Trisha?"

Suddenly, she snapped out of it with Adam's help. She silently blessed Yuri for his innovative brain.

"No," she said. "He did not."

Appearing to be satisfied, the professor continued on.

"Trisha, what Dr. Harlen is going for—his secret plan if you will—is to expose an ancient alien being that he believes is down below the salt."

He paused to let that sink in.

Trisha didn't blink. She just sat there and tried to be cool and collected.

"Did you hear me?" asked the professor.

Trisha looked at her nails and then at Beckham.

"Is this supposed to be a joke?"

The professor looked serious. The trick was that although Trisha knew about the Dhole, she mustn't show it, or think it. Trisha had the uncomfortable feeling that Professor Meridian could read her mind without Adam blocking him. To further the illusion, she looked at Beckham and yawned.

"He's serious, Trisha," said Beckham.

"Ancient alien?"

"I'm deadly serious," said Professor Meridian.

And he looked it, too. His single eye was fixed on her like a terrible laser. His face was hard and lined, and he looked like a an Inquisitor in the dim light.

Trisha tried to look disinterested.

"All right, say he's going for some ancient alien. So what? What's that got to do with us?" said Trisha.

"Ah," said Professor Meridian, "we would like to catch him red-handed in the act. We must know when he's going to break through the salt barrier."

"Why?"

This seemed to take Professor Meridian aback.

"What do you mean, why?" he asked.

"That's none of your business, Trisha," snapped Beckham.

"Oh, but I think it is. Why should we be concerned if Jimmy wants to go off on some half-baked idea of drilling for an ancient alien?"

"Because I—" began Beckham.

"Yes," said Trisha.

"Because we want it first," said Professor Meridian.

"Well, okay, then. Because there won't be anything down there at all, but if there is, we can shoulder Jimmy aside and just take it. End of story. Then Jimmy can get on with getting the Earth Battery to work and everyone will be happy."

This seemed to please Professor Meridian no end. But he held up a hand in caution.

"We must know in advance when he intends to break through. Do you comprehend?"

"Yes, I've got it."

"I think I like you, Trisha. I do indeed," said the professor.

Beckham relaxed at that.

"But one thing," said the professor.

"What's that?" said Trisha.

"Don't ever lie to me."

Trisha's breath hitched in her throat. She hadn't expected that.

"Is that all?" she asked.

"Of course. Why don't we tour the house. Mr. Beckham, you are dismissed."

Without a word, Beckham stiffly got up and left the room. Sanzar and Abarran were not given a second thought. And yet there was fear.

"Come, my dear. Let us take a walk, shall we? I will give you a tour of the house."

53

"Trisha. Sanzar and Abarran are right behind us."

"Now this house is ancient, Miss Daytona. It is much older than you or I, I daresay. They built it in the late 1800's, right around 1892, I think. With twenty-four rooms, it is a very modest mansion, but sufficient for my modest needs."

They passed up several Sanzar and Abarran clones along the way to their tour of Professor Meridian's house. Trisha began to grow disturbed at the similarities. Each of them looked the same as the others. It was genuinely creepy. Was it possible that they were all... clones of the same man?

"Yes, they are clones, Trisha, and none of them are human. We are in a great deal of danger here."

"I know, Adam, I feel it, too. We're trapped in this house with Meridian and all of these clones."

"What does he want? There must be something."

"You are familiar with the balcony because you came in this way. Come let us go down this way and I will finish showing you the house."

As Trisha stepped down the stairway, she was suddenly gripped from behind and found herself leaned forward to the tipping point when she would fall over. Her arms were pinned to her sides and her head was yanked back by the hair. Her scalp was on fire and try as she might, she could not get away. She was forced to look down at the dizzying drop before her of endless stairs, and she felt suddenly sick.

Professor Meridian stepped around to her front and looked at her through his one good eye.

"Are you crazy?" she yelled.

"Why no, Miss Daytona, I assure you that I am quite sane. Sanzar and Abarran are too, if only they could talk they would tell you that themselves. They are all that stands between you and certain death."

"Let me go," she demanded.

She was held so tightly she could barely breathe.

"Do you know, these stairs are unfortunately high, don't you think? Why if someone weren't careful, they could end up with a broken neck. A simple fall and voila, they could tumble down these stairs and, well, they could be quite dead. Now that would be most unfortunate, do you not agree?"

"Dammit, let me go or I'll—"

"What, Trisha? Tell me what exactly you would do by the time your body hit the bottom? Would you tell the police, perhaps? Would you run to your supervisor at the NSA? Oh, that's right. You would be quite dead and couldn't tell anyone anything at all."

"What," she gasped, "do you want?"

"Ah, now that's my girl. What do I want? Let me see—I would like the truth from you. Did Dr. Harlen tell you about the ancient alien? Yes or no. I would be very careful how you answer, Miss Trisha. Very careful indeed."

"Trisha, listen very carefully. Tell him yes, but you didn't believe him."

"Yes," she said, "but I didn't believe him and I don't believe you."

Professor Meridian considered this very carefully, and finally he nodded to Sanzar and Abarran, who lowered her almost gently to the stairs. Trisha coughed uncontrollably. She felt like throwing up.

"I told you never to lie to me, Trisha."

She coughed some more and held her head in her hands.

"I didn't think it mattered. I would just do my job and that would be it."

Trisha looked up at him. His single eye seemed to be on fire. Then, when she looked behind him, she couldn't believe her eyes. Assembled at the foot of the stairs seemed to be an army of Sanzars and Abarrans. All of them were staring up at her. They were like foot soldiers of the dead.

"Sweet Jesus," she said under her breath.

"Ah, yes. You see, each one of them is a duplicate of the others. Each one of them would unquestionably take a bullet for me. But would a bullet be enough to kill them? It's not hard to say. They are each already dead. So a single bullet would not stop them."

"You've got to be kidding."

"No, my dear, I am not. Now get up and come with me to meet the main attraction, hmm? The piece de resistance of this entire spacious house of mine."

"No thanks. I'd better be going now. I have work to do."

"Oh, but I insist. Come along. Sanzar and Abarran will escort you."

Trisha slowly, reluctantly got to her feet. Sanzar and Abarran stood to either side, but she didn't make the mistake of assuming that they were there to help her. She slowly limped down the stairs, and then walked more normally. Her neck and scalp were sore, and her back and arms from where they had bent her back.

"I'm going to be all right," she said.

"Yes, you will be fine, Trisha. I think that all of this is to impress upon you that he holds the power."

He led the way down the steps and to a back room. The army of the dead parted to let them through. Trisha felt their eyes upon her as she walked by. They are not human. Adam's words echoed through her brain. She wondered which of them was which. It didn't really matter—they were all the same. The army of the dead. Trisha shivered at the thought.

Professor Meridian stopped at the open door.

"After you," he said.

Trisha reluctantly went in to the room ahead of Professor Meridian. It was a lavishly appointed study surrounded with bookshelves. High ceilinged as were all the rooms in this old mansion. In its center was a large desk and high backed chair, covered with papers and more books. Facing the desk were two chairs. There was a barred window with thick, luxuriously tapestried accoutrements that was to the right side of the desk. Professor Meridian walked past it, and stopped at a bookshelf. He fiddled with something that Trisha could not see, and then suddenly, the bookshelf slid back as though on hinges revealing a stairway leading down into the earth.

"Come- you shall go first," said Professor Meridian.

She noticed that Sanzar and Abarran were right behind the professor.

Down the stone stairs she went. They descended in a circular fashion, with torches every twenty feet or so to light the way. Her steps were quiet, but they still echoed throughout the chamber. She went round and round so that she wondered how deep they were going. No sooner had she thought that, though, then the stairs gave way to a stone landing. The room that opened up from there was lined with doors. Thick doors, which were padlocked from the outside. More torches lined the walls and Sanzar and Abarran stood by one of the doors.

"But how did they—"

Professor Meridian was right behind her.

"I told you. There are many Sanzars and Abarrans."

"But—"

"Move along, Miss Daytona. There is something that you sincerely must see. Hurry up, you mustn't dawdle."

Trisha walked slowly toward the door that was guarded by the Sanzar and Abarran lookalikes. Along the way were doors upon doors and she looked at them each in their turn as she passed them. They all looked the same, like prison doors. No windows, except on a very few that looked to be a thick sliding door at eye level. Finally, she arrived. This was a door with just such a small sliding door built on it. The two men stood silently to one side. A sense of dread that this door was for her, that she was to be imprisoned here forever.

"Now Miss Daytona, do step aside so that Sanzar here may show you what lies within."

Without warning, one of the two men turned on her and again she found her arms pinned to her sides. The other slid the sliding door back.

"What—"

Suddenly, a roar as loud as anything she had heard echoed through the chamber. She watched in terror as the face of a wild animal appeared. It was like the head of a gigantic wolf, with yellow eyes, and slavering jaws. She screamed. The beast pawed at the door and the opening and let out a howl. Professor Meridian appeared unfazed and simply nodded at the man who had opened it, who now closed it. Immediately the sound stopped.

"Let her go," said the professor.

Trisha was hyperventilating.

"Now you see, Miss Daytona, what becomes of those that lie to me. I feed them to the beast."

"I get the point," she said between gasping for breath.

"Good. Now you may go. Sanzar and Abarran will follow you out. But Miss Daytona?"

"Yes?"

"Make sure that I know when Dr. Harlen breaks through the salt barrier. I have a sacrifice to perform then. Now good-bye."

54

"So, he's got Sasha. Sasha's alive," said Hauck.

Sveta gently squeezed Hauck's arm.

"Yes," she said. "At least there's that. Now to get him out without getting trapped inside."

"I'll kill him," said Jimmy.

"Better men than you have tried that, and ended up dead," said the Instructor.

"Will you stop bickering about it?" said Trisha.

"I've got to get Sasha out of there. Once he's safely away from Professor Meridian, we can work on a cure. He deserves that much from me. I..." said Hauck, but his voice drifted off and no one said anything for a minute.

Jimmy, Marty and Trisha sat in his special office in front of the computer screens. Adam had vacated Trisha's head and was now in resident in the big computer. Hauck. Sveta, Yuri, Charlene and the Instructor sat in front of the other computer screens in Hauck's condominium.

"Enough," said Hauck, snapping back to the moment. "Adam, what have you to report?"

Trisha and Adam had been back twenty minutes or so, but Trisha was still fuming.

"I observed that the clones, as Trisha calls them, were all of the same DNA. Not typecast, not approximate, but the same. Genetically an impossibility even for a clone. There should be some variation."

"How do you explain that?" said Hauck.

"I don't," said Adam. "As I said, it is genetically an impossibility. Professor Meridian was a different matter altogether, though. He had some modifications that I hadn't seen before. I can't identify them, though. Other than that he was human. But you must understand that the difference between a man and a chimpanzee is only 2.3%. He was bordering on 5%."

"What?" asked an incredulous Hauck. "There is that much difference? What on earth can that be caused by?"

"I don't know."

"Why, he's not human then."

"I wouldn't say that. He certainly looks human enough, but he's just genetically different," said Adam. "And the differences have no known correlation in the databases."

"Well, he's got Sasha," said Sveta.

"He's the werewolf, right?" asked Marty.

"Yes," said Hauck.

"Well, if it wasn't nightfall, and there was no full moon out, then why was he a werewolf?"

"I don't know," said Hauck. "I just don't know."

"Wait," said the Instructor, "he's right. Why would he?"

"What if it's got something to do with the planetary alignment? What if Sasha's a special kind of werewolf and he's more affected by it than others? Or what if, unknown to Sasha, Professor Meridian is secretly feeding him something that prolongs his time as a werewolf?" said Jimmy.

"Feeding him something? Like what?" demanded the Instructor.

"Maybe... maybe something he learned?" said Jimmy.

"Wait a minute," said Hauck. "When we first met Meridian, he was talking about Drogol as intimately as if he knew him. Drogol's labs and his chemicals... I wonder if he could have learned something from him?"

"Yes," said Jimmy, "that could be it. Wasn't Drogol some kind of a chemist?"

"He certainly was," said Sveta. "Self-taught to be exact, but brilliant. And with the lab in his house in Detroit and the underground lab, especially the underground lab, hell yes, he could have discovered some drink or something to eat that would make Sasha turn into a werewolf that would last longer. Hell, yes."

"Now we're talking," said the Instructor.

Hauck checked his watch.

"It's getting near dark; you better head to your cage."

"No. A little bit longer."

"We'll fill you in come morning."

"I said," roared the Instructor, "just a little longer."

If Hauck seemed taken aback by the Instructor's behavior, he didn't show it.

"Now."

His tone of voice brooked no answer other than a yes.

"Yuri," said Hauck, "escort the Instructor to his cage."

The Instructor seemed to be about to say something, but changed his mind. Instead, he knocked his chair over on the way to the door. Yuri looked at Hauck, and then followed the Instructor out the door. For a long moment, Sveta stared after the two men.

"What's on your mind, Sveta?" Hauck asked.

"Does he seem like he's getting more violent to you?"

Hauck considered the question very carefully before answering.

"No, he doesn't."

"I'm not sure that Yuri and I agree."

"Sveta, you don't know him the way that I do. He's always had these mood swings. Answer me this—how would you react under the circumstances? Bitten by a werewolf, knowing that your friends were considering killing you? Having to stay in a cage every night because you might turn at any moment in time?"

After a moment's thought, Sveta gave a long sigh.

"I guess you're right. I wouldn't be any too happy about it. But I'd watch him just the same."

"Well," said Charlene, "aren't you forgetting about the fact that it isn't a full moon and he's turning into a werewolf anyway?"

Hauck looked at Charlene with new found respect. The girl was handy to have around. Not one in a million would have figured that out.

"Who says that men only change into werewolves during the full moon anyway?" he said. "There's so much about them we don't know. It's only with the advent of books and films that the full moon part of the tales have turned into gospel. We don't know if every night they turn into werewolves or not."

"Yeah, but that's bunk and you know it," said Charlene. "There would be bodies everywhere if men turned into killing machines every night of the week, wouldn't there?"

"Smart girl," said Marty, "but no. The lock themselves away just like the Instructor does—otherwise they would be hunted down and killed. But not all werewolves are like that. Some are subject to the full moon cycle."

"Why?" asked Charlene.

Marty shrugged.

"The truth is we just don't know. I think there different types of werewolves, but opinions vary. The one that bit the Instructor must have been the type that turns every night. Or, the coming planetary alignment exhibits a stronger pull on werewolves than we thought."

"How come you know so much about werewolves?"

"I've spent a lot of my life tracking down the paranormal, believe me."

"Could we please get back to the topic," said Jimmy. "Professor Meridian threatened Trisha."

"Yes, we know, Jimmy," said Hauck.

"Is that all you can say?"

"Jimmy," said Trisha, "I'm okay now. I was just a little rattled at the time is all."

"We can't have you go back to that man's house," said Jimmy.

"We won't have to," said Hauck. "The Instructor will though. He's got an old score to settle with Meridian."

"What about Beckham?" said Sveta.

"We will have to take him first."

"Take him where?"

Hauck turned to the computer screen.

"Trisha, where is he most vulnerable?"

"At home," she said, after some thought.

"Anywhere else?"

"I don't know of anywhere else where he would be. I mean

normally, he keeps tabs on where I am, not the other way around."

"Is he married, or does he have kids stay at his house?"

"No. Kids? No? He was married once that I know of, but she got rid of him a long time ago. Good riddance."

"Adam can help," said Jimmy. "Professor Meridian may not have that house of his wired, but Beckham certainly does."

"Yes," said Trisha. "I'm going to bet he's wired to the gills."

"Where does he live?" said Hauck.

"1183 Mulberry Lane, in Grosse Pointe."

"And where do you live?"

"17435 Cherry Hill Drive, in Southfield. Why?"

"Because," said Sveta, "I'm willing to bet he's got your place already bugged."

"Adam," said Jimmy, "go check out Trisha's place."

"Yes, Dr. Harlen."

Yuri came back into the room just then. He looked haggard. The Instructor had evidently not been happy about going back into his cage for the night.

"You know," he said, "I really hate that man. It's not my fault he got bit by a werewolf."

"Don't worry," said Charlene, "he'll get over it. I think he's conflicted by this whole thing."

"What? The Instructor? Conflicted? No way."

"Hauck?" broke in Adam.

"Yes?"

"I did indeed find numerous devices intended to eavesdrop on Miss Trisha. Several recording devices, too."

"What?" said Trisha. "That son of a bitch. That dirty rotten—"

"It should be easy enough for me to break into, so that Sveta can get in after me. I reversed course for the spying mechanisms and saw that it leads to a station in his office, which was easy to get into. I have all the information regarding all of his operations, including Miss Trisha's. Would you like me to delete them from his machine?"

"You know," said Hauck, "I'm beginning to like working with you, Adam. No to deleting everything from his machine, though, until we have him."

"Shall I disable the devices in Trisha's home?"

"Yes," said Trisha.

"No," said Hauck. "We'll want them active until we have him. Understood?"

"Yes," said Adam.

"God, I hate this," said Trisha.

"It only makes good sense," said Sveta. "We can't alert him early."

Trisha chewed her lip on that one. Hauck was right. It wouldn't do to trip the wire to Beckham first.

"Yeah," she said. "I guess so. I'd just like to pay him back for getting me into this mess."

"Oh, I suspect Mr. Beckham will be paid back in full before this is through. Trust me on that," said Sveta.

What she didn't say was that they would have to kill Mr. Beckham.

"All right, if that is about it I'd like to go home and wash the Professor Meridian smell off my body," said Trisha.

"I'm afraid that won't be possible, Trisha. I think you would be better off staying right where you are, until Mr. Beckham is nailed down and Adam has disabled the devices," said Hauck. "Now when is Mr. Beckham at home?"

"I don't know exactly, about nine I think."

"I can keep an eye on him at his office," suggested Adam.

"I think not. It's more important to keep an eye on his house."

"I can do both at the same time," said Adam.

"You can?"

"I can."

"Adam, can you monitor more than two places?"

"Yes, he can," said Jimmy.

"Fascinating," said Hauck.

"Adam can monitor a virtual plethora of places, although I have no way to calculate how many," said Jimmy.

"We can use that to our advantage."

"What can he do, Jimmy?" asked Sveta.

"Well," said Yuri, "he can turn on the exercise bike by remote."

"What?" said Hauck.

"Yeah, he can turn on the exercise bike. He did it for me when you were driving with Sveta."

"It doesn't surprise me, although I didn't teach him that trick," said Jimmy. "It is only logical now that I think of it. For example, if your exercise bike is connected to the Internet, well, he should be able to port over to it. Yes, that makes sense. He can control CCTV cameras as well, since they are connected to the Internet."

"I can control most things that are connected to the Internet, doctor," said Adam.

"Yuri," said Hauck, "I believe we're back in business."

55

Alex had to leave early that day. He had a doctor's appointment, and he'd told the men to shut down at five. It got dark around seven o'clock, so that should be plenty of time to shut down the equipment.

"Hey, you know Diane, I think we can make it through tonight if we just keep drilling," said Matt Smith, dusting off some salt dust.

"We might, but Jimmy said knock it off at night time," said Diane Perino.

He shrugged.

"Why don't we ask the guys?"

"I don't know, Matt—"

"Come on, since the wife died I got nothing to do except go to an empty apartment. And speaking of empty apartments, considering that your husband took off with a younger woman what have you got to do tonight?"

"Hey, I've got men lined up, you know?"

They both had to laugh at that. It wasn't so easy to get a date when you were fifty-five years old. The boys didn't line up like they used to. When she used to be young, though...

"Hey boys," yelled Matt, "you want to stay and finish this thing up? Give Uncle Jimmy a big surprise when he gets here tomorrow morning?"

"What?" yelled one of them.

He couldn't hear Matt over the whine of the twin drills. Taking down his strap, he walked over to where Matt was standing.

"What did you say?"

"I said, how about staying until we finish this thing."

Jamal Stevens rubbed his chin.

"Come on."

"What's in it for me?"

"Time and a half."

"I don't know, man…"

"Diane?"

Jimmy had been explicit. No working at night, still they were almost through. The last fifty feet had gone easier than expected, and they could finish it up tonight. Matt was right about that. And it would be a big surprise for him in the morning.

"All right, double time," she said.

"Well, what about it? Think you can convince the other guys?" Matt asked.

"Hell yes, for double time we'll stay all night."

"That's the spirit," said Matt. "You just convince the other guys and we're on."

When Jamal had left, Matt said, "You know, we've got a good group of guys."

"Don't I know it. But look, I can only stay until eight or nine at the latest. I've got a doctor's appointment to be at in the morning. Think you can handle it?"

Matt grinned.

"It's not like you do anything except paperwork anyway. I can take care of business; go on and take care of your medical stuff."

"Thanks, Matt. Now remember, if anything breaks down —"

"Yes, mom. Don't worry, this salt seems to be easier to drill through than that last batch."

****

It was eleven thirty, and things were proceeding faster than they had on the previous nights. By Matt's calculations, the only had ten feet of salt left to burn through. The twin drills were cutting through mercilessly and things were going smoothly. In another two hours, they should be through, provided they didn't into any trouble on the last few feet. Matt crossed himself.

"Hey, Matt," said Jamal, "I think we've made it. Just seven more feet to go."

"Nah, I've got…"

He looked up at the depth meter, and saw that they had gone three feet in a little under twenty minutes. Huh, well that was something.

"How fast is it going?"

"Same as always," said Jamal.

"That seems odd. Well, maybe I screwed up. I figured we had at least two hours left. The way this is going, we should be through in a half an hour."

"Yeah, I'd say," said Jamal. "Look at the depth reading now."

He turned to look at the depth gauge, and saw that, according to the digital readout, they had only three feet to go. He couldn't believe it. He wondered if the gauge was wrong.

"It is what it is, I guess. Unless the gauge is wrong."

"I already checked that. I thought it was wrong, too."

"Then I guess we'll have to… wait a minute. We'd better get ready to stop drilling. Man I wish this had all been this easy. We've only got two feet left to go."

Matt got ready to back off on the drill, while Jamal hurried to his work station and yelled the results to the other guys. One foot left to go now —it was like the drills were punching through butter. And then, they were through. He hurried up and backed off on the master controls for the drills and shut them down and breathed a sigh of relief. They had done it. They had made it all the way through the salt, and man was he glad they had stayed late. It violated Jimmy's orders, but he would be ecstatic that they had made it through in one night.

"Hey, we made it," yelled Miguel.

With the drills turned off, Matt could actually hear across the empty expanse.

"We sure did," he yelled back. "Let's see what kind of damage we done, shall we?"

After making sure all the power to the twin drills was cut off, he left his control board and walked the long distance to the drills. It was

sure quiet without the constant drilling. Thank God for small favors.
He slapped Jamal and the back and hugged him.

"Hey, where's the other guys?" he said.

"Ah, they are probably around her somewhere."

He called out, "Hey, Miguel, Trin, Arturo. Come on, we're through.
Time to close up for the night."

But there was no answer.

"Where are those guys," asked Matt.

"Don't worry, boss, I'll find them," said Jamal.

While he was gone, Matt shut off the water jacket to the drills. He
watched the temperature go down. Flicking off a few switches, a loud
cry from Jamel suddenly startled him.

Looking up, he called, "Jamal? Are you okay?"

When there was no response, he dashed around the drill bits to
come face to face with the most hideous creature that he had ever seen.
He stopped, breathless to get a grip. It had a combination lizard's
body except that it had hair on it. It was three feet tall and had long
arms ending in sharp talons. But the most frightening part of it was
the head. It was a combination bat's head with long lupine jaws and
sharp teeth. And the tongue was forked and long and distended.
Sharp ears on tufts of hair and its eyes were a bright searing red.

Matt backed up.

The thing was horrifying, but from the shadows came two more.

"Jamal," Matt called desperately.

No answer.

Matt backed up another step. He looked around for a tool he could
wave at them to get them to back off, but he was now surrounded by
snarling faces with tongues that went in and out, in and out. They
gibbered gleefully. Matt's breath came in gasps. God, what could he
do?

He decided to break for it.

Swinging his arms frantically and flailing his fists, one of them
grabbed him from behind and bit his hamstrings, sending him
collapsing in a heap to the ground. They were on him then, biting him
savagely. He was bleeding all over as he was buried beneath a pile of
pop-up killers.

56

"Dr. Harlen?"

"Yes Brittany," said Jimmy.

"I think there's something you should see."

It was twelve o'clock midnight, and Jimmy, Marty and Trisha had been up most of the night so far talking about Jason, the Dhole and Hauck's team. The consensus was that they missed Jason, the Dhole was incomprehensible to Trisha but Jimmy and Marty seemed to understand it very well and Hauck and his team were a mystery, but dependable.

The computer screen lit up.

"Jimmy," it was Hauck.

"Yes?"

"Don't go out on the floor. Lock your door and stay inside. Where are Trisha and Marty."

"Right here, they—"

Jimmy suddenly stopped talking. Trisha and Marty were glued to the computer screen and after a few seconds, so was he. Brittany had brought up the recording of Matt, Jamal and the other three being butchered.

"Oh, God," he said. "I told them not to work at night. I told them."

"Yes, well they obviously weren't listening," Trisha said, "Marty, go lock the door."

"It locks once your inside," said Marty.

"I wish I had brought a gun," said Trisha.

"I wish you had, too," said Hauck.

"How did you know about this?" asked Marty.

"Adam showed me. I had him monitoring the cameras at your place, too."

"What can we do?" asked Jimmy.

"I'm sorry to say this, but nothing, absolutely nothing until it's safe to go in there- until the morning, I would think."

"Yes," said Sveta who joined him, "stay inside and be safe. No matter what you think your chances are or the reasons for going out there—don't, just don't."

"But—" said Jimmy.

"No buts about it," said Sveta.

And Hauck agreed.

"Look," said Jimmy, "unless they can operate an elevator, they're restricted to that floor."

"Then how did they when you were kids travel all the way to Flat Rock, hmm? They don't need an elevator to get out of their Jimmy. They've got some other way. We've been naive about this. All this time we've been concentrating on the salt mines, and they've been out there, on the streets of Detroit at night, in the suburbs, who knows where they've been? They've probably been killing and disappearing people and we didn't even know it."

"Oh shit," said Marty, "you know he's right."

"You mean, they could be everywhere and we never thought of this?" said Trisha.

"It's my fault," said Jimmy. "I thought that since before they only came out on a Red Moon night, that they were restricted somehow."

Jimmy slammed his fist into his palm.

"It's not your fault, Jimmy," said Trisha. "If it wasn't for you we would have thought that whole thing when we were kids was just a bad dream. Now at least we have a fighting chance."

"She's right," said Marty.

"Blaming is not going to get us anywhere," said Hauck. "Just stay alive until morning. Don't attempt to go out."

"But what about all the people who—"

"Forget them. What will happen, will happen."

"But—"

"No one will believe you. There's no time. You've got to stay inside where it's safe. You're the only one who can stop them. If that thing wakes up like you say it will, there will be a whole lot more people dead than you can believe now," said Hauck.

Jimmy walked around in circles. He sat down and put his face in his hands. Trisha and Marty went over to him and consoled him, Marty by patting him on the shoulder and Trisha hugging him.

"Hauck's right, you know. No one would have believed you if you had warned them," she said.

"But Matt and those others—"

"Jimmy, listen to me. No one would have believe you, and when you found out you said that they couldn't work in the evening. What were they thinking?"

"I don't know but—"

He trailed off, lost in thought. What was Matt doing there? With a full shift no less.

"Brittany, what was Matt doing there?"

"Completing drilling the holes, doctor."

"You mean he finished?"

"Yes, doctor."

"My God, that means we can electrocute the Dhole now."

"Jimmy," said Hauck, "you can save that for tomorrow. Not tonight."

"I understand. I just don't want all those people to die for nothing."

"Good. You are secure in there?"

"Yes."

"Then I'll sign off. We have preparations to attend to."

"We do, too," said Jimmy. "With that hole complete, your damned straight we do."

"What do we do, Jimmy?" asked Marty.

"Well, the first thing we'll have to do is… give everyone here the day off tomorrow, because tomorrow, we'll electrocute this thing. Brittany?"

"Yes, doctor."

"Send out an email under my name tonight to that effect."

"Yes, doctor."

"The second thing we'll do is replace the drill bit motors with the charging unit."

"Hey," said Marty, "we can't do that until tomorrow. We promised Hauck."

"Yes, it's not worth it to go out there," said Trisha. "Those things are everywhere."

"We won't have to go out there, we can control the entire operation from here."

"Well, excuse the hell out of me," said Marty, "what in the hell are we waiting for?"

For the first time in a long time, Jimmy grinned and Trisha thought it was like a ray of sunshine on this otherwise dreary world. Because outside, the pop-up killers reigned supreme.

****

Eddie turned over in his cardboard shack and sat up. It was cool outside, but not for October, he supposed. His coat had slipped off, the long gray coat that he used whenever it was cold- it wasn't quite cold enough for it, but it was getting there. He snuggled up against his make shift pillow, made of three old shirts. For a homeless man, he was living pretty good with a pillow and a blanket, and a piece of cardboard to sleep on. The library was within walking distance, so he had a place to use their rest room. Yes, as he settled down to sleep, he felt that he was safe.

He'd lost everything due to a drug problem. His wife and kids were the first to go... no he had to admit that wasn't true. His money had been the first. He' got in trouble with his work for spiking his expense account so that he'd lost his job. And when he had not been able to make his house payment and car payment month after month, when he hadn't paid the electric and water bills, that had been the breaking point. That is when the wife and kids had packed it in, and he didn't blame them. Dad hadn't hit bottom yet, that was to come .

But he was clean now. He had been for a week and a half. If he could just make it for three more weeks, then he felt it would be permanent. But he had to sleep now. He couldn't, though, and he turned over in his makeshift bed and tried to make himself comfortable. Somewhere outside of his torn and raggedy tent, there were stars twinkling and the full moon was shining down on the cold city that was Detroit. The night flowed by as a relentless, slow moving stream, ticking off the minutes of his life.

Beneath a viaduct was where he had pitched his tent, and it did a good enough job keeping the rain off him, he had to admit. He was mostly dry, and his dog, who he made sleep outside staked out, and he wished that he could sleep inside, too, but in Detroit, he needed the early warning system. You never knew when some punk kid, or other homeless person or druggie would want to score something off you, or hassle you for something you didn't have. No, better to leave the dog outside, save on those nights when it got too cold.

He sat up in bed and absently scratched his face. It had been weeks since he had a good shave. That was… how long ago was it? For some reason, the exact date eluded him. Grabbing his great coat that served as a blanket, he lay down again and settled in for a long sleep. Funny how the lack of drugs running through his veins kept him awake at night.

Suddenly, he sat bolt upright. His dog had begun barking fiercely, and then louder, frantically and then, abruptly, had cut off just as quickly as he had started. He got his knife out from his left boot, and grasped it tightly, not knowing whether to defend his dog, or to stay inside and hunker down for safety. Maybe they, whoever his mysterious attackers were, just felt like they wanted to inflict injury on his dog and that was all. Even now, they could be leaving.

But that was not to be.

Eddie held his breath, he even closed his eyes for a minute wishing that they would just go away. Why wouldn't they just leave him alone? And his dog. That silence from his dog was heartbreaking. He envisioned his dog dead, his neck broken or maybe stabbed through the heart. He was a good dog. Eddie felt tears forming in the corners of his eyes.

The flap that secured the tent opening pulled back, and a horrifying visage greeted Eddie, so that he recoiled in horror. A bat face, with long slavering jaws was staring at him. He screamed. He scooted back as to the far end of his tent to get away from the ghastly creature, but suddenly the back of his tent exploded and twin pairs of arms reached through the fabric and grabbed him with taloned hands. He screamed some more. Twisting he tried to stab the demon with his knife only to discover to his horror that he had dropped it.

While he was writhing in the grasp of the unknown assailant, his entire tent was ripped aside and thrown away like the old rags that it was. Eddie stared in horror at the small army of pop-up killers with their red eyes and slabbering mouths. He screamed as if his very life depended on it.

And it did.

****

Lincoln Park.

It was three in the morning and it was developing a slight shiver in the air.

Sue Ann had partied until two-thirty, until a boy had hit on her. She looked around for her wingman and protector, but he had taken a hit off something and was lying sprawled out in the floor. She told him no thanks, she had come with someone and better leave with him. But the boy was persistent, pushy even. She said no thanks again and went to the restroom.

She opened the door slowly, cautiously.

"My name is Sam," said a voice that scared her because he had come up behind her undetected.

"Look," she said, "it's good to meet you, Sam, but I've really got to go. My boyfriend's waiting for me."

"Aw, your boyfriend is passed out on the floor. Why don't you let me take you home?"

"I told you, thanks for the offer, but no."

He grabbed for her arm but she ducked out of the way.

"No means no, okay."

But he was determined and pressed her up against the wall. He pinned her shoulders and tried for a kiss. She dodged the kiss and panicked for a second and then had just about enough of this joker. So she kneed him in the crotch with every ounce of strength she possessed and he doubled up and let go of her. He dropped to the floor in agony, and after a quick glance around to see that everyone was too wasted to be watching her, she fled out the front door. She walked quickly down off the porch and kept right on going. She turned right, then went a few blocks and turned left and she was on her way through the back alleys of Lincoln Park hoping that pushy son of a bitch would be in pain for the rest of the night, and would not come looking for her.

What was she thinking, leaving the party without a ride? God, that was just stupid. She bundled up her blouse around her against the cool night air. Jesus on a pony it was getting cold out. Fall must be coming quicker than the weatherman said. And she had three and a half miles to go to home. Man she should have looked around for someone to go home with, or stolen her friend Larry's keys out of his right pocket, like he would know. He was so passed out that it would take a cannon firing near his ears to wake him up.

At three-twenty in the morning, the streets were empty. No friendly police cars to pick her up and take her home because she had taken the back roads so she should be safe from Mr. Grabby-Hands. So far, so good. Now she was on a stretch of road that was uninhabited, that lasted about a mile and a half. Brother, about half way down all the streetlights were out. She just couldn't grab a break could she? Looking at her watch, she saw that it was about three forty-five now and so she just had to make it past that creepy section with the streetlights off or knocked out and she would be home free.

She was in the ominous section now. It was impossible to run in the shoes that she was wearing—spike high heels with platforms to boot. She was lucky she didn't fall on her ass when she'd kicked the guy in the nuts. Her short skirt wasn't helping any at all, either.

What was that noise?

Coming to a sudden halt, she looked in front of her. She was on an overpass with guard wires that cut up and leaned over a good eight feet. There didn't seem to be anything in front of her, though. She heard the same sound, only this time it was coming from behind her. Whirling around there was nothing. Well, shit, that was creepy. She turned around again just in time to see a manhole cover explode, and when she turned again to run another exploded. And suddenly, a manhole cover in the middle of the street exploded and shot may eight feet into the air and caromed down the street.

"Well, shit," she cried turning around in circles.

And then the strangest thing happened.

From each of the exposed manholes, a gangly creature about three feet tall emerged. Horrified, she pressed back against the wire fence. She was trapped and looked desperately for a way out. They were bat like creatures with folded wings on their backs. They had taloned hands and feet, and were covered with hair except for a scaly stomach. But their faces were horrible. Those long jaws and sharp teeth and flaming red eyes were terrifying. They had sharp ears and almost wolf like features and they were coming for her.

She screamed and screamed but there was no one in that section of town to hear her.

And then, they fell on her with their sharp teeth.

****

In the soundproofed room, the werewolf raged. The Instructor rattled the bars, and screamed at the night.

The cage was placed dead center of the room. The first night, he had gone wild and torn it from it's moorings, so by the second night they had re-bolted down so that nothing could rip it from its fastenings. This just served to infuriate the beast that was the Instructor. It was driving him crazier and crazier by the minute. The cage was small to begin with and that just served to enrage to beast.

But he didn't tire; he just kept ramming and ramming the bars. Had they not been made of three inch in diameter titanium steel they would surely have broken by now.

Hauck was having two bigger cages built. They would be finished by tomorrow. One for the Instructor and the second for his son. But the Instructor didn't understand that in his current form. All he understood was the rage directed against what confined him.

Outside the soundproofed room, Hauck stood with Sveta and worried.

"I don't think he can get out of the cage. Still I should have taken the opportunity to reinforce the bars while I had the chance," said Hauck.

"Don't worry" said Sveta "even a werewolf cannot break out of three inch titanium bars. Trust me. I nearly died loading that thing into the truck. It weighs a ton, so if he can break out of that, we'll just have to shoot him."

To emphasize her point, she raised her high-powered rifle loaded with mercury and silver composite shells.

"We need him, Sveta."

She looked at him seriously.

"I know that. But I can dream, can't I?"

57

Daylight.

It was eight thirty a.m in the morning, and the day was gray as a pallid man ready to be buried. There was no sun anywhere to be seen, and dirty clouds littered the sky.

With Marty and Trisha's help, Jimmy finished retrofitting the last electrical wires to the drills.

"It's eerie working here with everyone else gone," said Trisha.

Jimmy was busy with checking the digital readouts for the connections.

"Yeah, I know what you mean," he said over one shoulder.

"Brittany says that we have to go down another seven feet," Marty said, "in order to make contact with the Dhole."

"Got it," Jimmy replied, "I've just got to make sure that everything is connected right and then we'll lower it the rest of the way."

"Jimmy?" asked Trisha.

"Yes?"

"Stop for a minute, just a second so I can tell you something, okay?"

"Sure, Trisha. What is it?"

When he turned around, she stepped in to meet him. They were only inches apart now, and Jimmy felt her heat like a blast furnace.

"I- I had to tell you I'm sorry I doubted you. I should have known better. You never lost focus on what was important and I did. You did the right thing, Jimmy, and I'm proud of you."

She leaned in and kissed him. Jimmy was flabbergasted.

"Now, get to work and kill that thing," she said.

For a moment, the world stood still for Jimmy. For just a moment, it was like the angels in heaven were cheering him on.

"Aye, aye, captain," was all he could think of to say.

She turned away, to see Marty smiling at them. Jimmy, flushed red at the incident, turned back to the control panel.

"What time is it?" she asked.

"Ten o'clock," said Marty.

"I'm going to go wash my face again. I still feel dirty. And then I'm going to shop for some clothes for us. All right?"

"Get some lunch while you're at it and bring it back, will you?" said Marty.

"Check," said Trisha, and she was gone.

Marty ambled over to where Jimmy stood, working the control panel. The last seven feet of salt was about to be drilled through. He patted Jimmy on the back.

"You are doing the right thing, Jimmy, although I won't kiss you to confirm it," Marty grinned.

"It was only a friendly kiss," protested Jimmy.

"Sure. You ready to turn this thing on yet?"

"Yes, the drills are ready to go in ten, nine, eight, seven, six, five, four, three, two, one—oh wait, I almost forgot earmuffs."

He handed a pair to Marty, and took one for himself. When he had them on, he looked at Marty inquiringly, got a nod from him and turned on the drills. In half an hour, he had gone the last seven feet so he shut the drills down, and then took his earmuffs off. Marty did the same.

"Let's go upstairs so we can get a look."

****

The Dhole had slept for hundred of millions of years between the modern city of Detroit.

He had come across time and space, looking for a world to claim as his own, and this was the planet he had chosen. But he had miscalculated because most of the planet's surface was covered with water. He had crashed on this watery world, helpless to escape to dry land and so, desperate for something to sink his tentacles into but finding nothing, instead, he sank beneath the waves. Trapped within the chilling water that had held him captive for so many eons, he had succumbed to a state of deep hibernation.

The water had begun to evaporate after millions of years, and the salt remained, piling up trillions of tons of salt. With the result that he was trapped in layers upon layers of salt. And the Dhole was buried beneath them.

All he could do was dream endless dreams that would not let him go.

His dimensions were staggering. He was three thousand feet wide of undiscovered horror and he was one thousand feet tall of towering, massive beast. But he was asleep.

Time passed and a fantastical variety of beasts appeared on the face of the earth. Amoebas, trilobites, all sorts of insects, rodents, and hopping animals, dinosaurs of all shapes and sizes, raptors and, eventually mammals.

Throughout all these changes, the Dhole slept on. Periodically, it would dream—chaotic, monstrous dreams of the pop-up killers that it commanded on its home world. This happened on a night where the moon was red and sailed high in the sky like a beacon of horror. The Dhole did not understand why it dreamed such vivid dreams on the Red Moon nights, but it did. And then it sunk back into dreaming quieter dreams, remaining dormant until a Red Moon night caused him to unleash a storm of creatures.

Men came upon the planet, and spread like the scourge from hell, but still the Dhole slept on, dreaming, always dreaming. On the Red Moon nights, the pop-up killers would come and claim the people that were around. In the early centuries of Detroit, the little creatures went by the name of Nain Rouge, and always they were associated with disaster, but no one associated them with the Red Moon nights.

But all that changed in the spring of 1895, when salt was discovered beneath Detroit. There were many challenges for them before the explorers could get at the salt, however. There was hydrogen sulfide gas and hundreds of feet of stone and glacial drift in between them and the desired salt. Putting down the first shaft was an expensive proposition, and the company that they formed to dig this went bankrupt. But after a retrofitting of the organization, they pursued it again, and this time they were successful. They penetrated the earth to an unheard of depth of one thousand feet. The Detroit salt mine was off and running.

But, on the red moon nights, the Dhole dreamed in color; the rest of the nights were spent in dreaming in dark black and white. But on those nights, when the moon was full and red, the pop-up killers appeared fully formed, as though they had sprung from the very mind of a vengeful god. And on those nights, the pop-up killers ram amok.

The coming night was different, however, in that the planets would be in alignment. On this night, Dhole would awaken, never to fall asleep again. It would still be buried beneath the salt, but the pop-up killers could roam free, free of their bonds.

On that night, Detroit would fall.

****

Jimmy and Marty were back in his office, looking at the computer screen. It was filled with a full screen image of the Dhole.

"I can't believe how big it is," said Marty.

"Yes, the best I can tell, it's three thousand feet long and weighs, I don't know, around five thousand tons."

"Whew, that's a big fella," said Marty.

"Yes, it certainly is."

"What kind of juice are you going to feed it?"

"Twelve million volts."

"Are sure that's not overkill?"

"I've got another six million in reserve, if that's not enough."

"Okay, then, you're playing for keeps."

"I certainly am," said Jimmy.

"You ready to do this?"

"Not until Trisha gets back. The drill probes are right against his flesh and I'm ready to juice this bastard back to the stone age."

"I hope it works, Jimmy."

"Why, you got some concerns?"

"No, I just… well, I wish we had a backup plan is all. This thing is so… I just never thought that it was so big."

"Don't worry—I got twelve million volts of electricity and I told you, for back up we've got another six million."

"Are you sure that's enough?"

"It better be."

"I hope so, for all our sakes."

"You've got doubts, Marty?"

Marty looked at Jimmy, and Jimmy stared back.

"I don't know, Jimmy, it's just it's so big, you know. I don't know if even eighteen million volts is enough."

Jimmy laid a hand on his friends shoulder.

"Believe me, I've calculated it out. Twelve million volts is enough, but for an added precaution, I'll give it the full eighteen for extra yardage. Is that good enough for you?"

"Deal. Sorry to worry so much, but believe me, I've seen plenty go wrong in my life at the most unexpected times."

"Well, hopefully this won't be one of them," said Jimmy. "Hey, here's Trisha. I'll buzz her in."

Trisha came in with a changes of clothes for herself and lunch for everyone. She set the bags on the conference table, and said that lunch was served. Then she disappeared into one of the rooms that Jimmy used as a guest bedroom to change. Marty dropped everything to grab a bite.

"French fries fresh from McDonald's and a big Mac, you can't ask for more than that," he said.

Jimmy grinned and checked his figures again. He plotted the weight, the estimated weight of the Dhole versus the electrical requirements. What if the Marty was right? What if he was underestimating the weight of the Dhole? What if….too many what ifs. He couldn't over think this. He had the calculations just right this time, he was sure of it. Just then Trisha came in, looking radiantly refreshed in her new clothes. They had agreed that she wouldn't be going home until this was over and Professor Meridian was dead. Jimmy and Marty were approximately the same size, so Jimmy had loaned him some clothes to see him through and they had changed while Trisha was out.

While they finished up the lunch that Trisha had brought, they discussed the plans for the evening. Jimmy would electrocute the Dhole, Sveta would capture Beckham and Yuri would dump the Instructor at Professor Meridian's mansion. It all seemed so simple to say. And, of course, there was the matter of the Earth Battery not working, which necessitated Hauck getting Jimmy out of town.

Jimmy looked over at Trisha eating the last of the fries. Suddenly, he didn't want to go. He had never had a girlfriend. Always at the back of his mind Trisha preferred Jason over him, and so he devoted his life to discovering the true origin of the pop-up killers and putting an end to it. But that goal was now at an end. He felt strange knowing that, surreal almost while looking at Trisha.

She looked up at him.

"What?" she said.

"Nothing. I mean I was just thinking that it will be the end of the Dhole, is all. Twelve million volts—excuse me—eighteen million volts" here he grinned at Marty, "and that will be the end of the Dhole. Without anyone ever knowing about it, he'll be dead. And, well, without the Earth Battery working, it will be the end of my career. I will have to disappear."

Trisha looked at him quizzically.

"What do you mean the Earth Battery won't work?"

Jimmy grinned ruefully.

"It was all a ruse so that I could get at the Dhole, Trisha. I had to have everyone believe in this dream so that I could buy the salt mine and drill into it."

"Really?"

"Really. So when this is all over, Hauck will help me disappear. Start a new life."

Trisha seemed genuinely shocked and overwhelmed by this turn of events.

"But why?"

"Think of it, Trisha. The world's biggest experiment a flop? Jimmy drills down to what? To destroy an ancient alien? I think the NSA or the DOE or the FBI or the CIA or pick your favorite government acronym would have me disappeared quicker than you could say the single word gone. It's their favorite response to ancient alien extermination. Kill the rat who dares bring something like this in the open. Never mind the fact that the Earth Battery doesn't work. They'll come after me for burning the alien. I've got to destroy the entire salt mine when I leave."

Trisha grew serious suddenly.

"You have destroy everything you built? That's crazy, Jimmy. Marty, tell him it's crazy."

"Well, Trisha, I kind of think Jimmy's right. After he destroys the Dhole, he'll have to get rid of the evidence. Yes, I think he's going to have destroy every computer here with everything associated with it. He's going to have to burn this thing down to the ground, and then disappear. It would be best for him to die—figuratively speaking, of course—in the fire that burns this place."

"But where will you go?"

"I don't know," said Jimmy. "That's up to Hauck. That's what I've got him for to disappear me. And to make sure there is no trace. Like I didn't know Edwina was spying on me and he took care of her for me. Now he's going to take care of Beckham. He's done more than I can ask him for, and now if he can just take care of Professor Meridian, well, my concerns will be over."

"I see," said Trisha. "You'll just disappear? Cut off all ties with the world?"

Jimmy seemed embarrassed by question. For so many years, he had been after the Dhole that he never thought he would actually finish the job. The act of disappearing just seemed more like a dream than not. But now the time had finally come.

"Yes, I guess so. But we'll stay in touch, if you guys still want?"

"I want," said Marty.

Trisha seemed like a lost person.

"Sure. I guess me, too," she said.

Brittany interrupted them.

"I've got Hauck and the others for you, Dr. Harlen."

"Well, showtime," said Jimmy. "Hello, Hauck. We're all here."

Hauck's face appeared on the computer screen.

"You ready to go?" Hauck asked.

"Yes."

"You stayed locked in your room all night?"

"Yes. We aligned what we could of the electrical by remote and waited to finish the rest until this morning."

"Good," said Hauck. "First thing we do is pick up Beckham. Adam will get us into his house, where Sveta will be waiting for him. Next, we electrocute the Dhole, at as close to sunset as you can get. Say a half an hour until. Got it? And the next thing we do is Yuri will drop the Instructor off at Professor Meridian's mansion. The Instructor goes inside and does what he does best."

"Finally, we get to the good part," said the Instructor.

"Wait a minute," said Jimmy, "how exactly do we get Beckham to his house?"

"A good question," said Sveta. "I was going to ask Trisha to contact him and arrange a meeting at his house. Can you do that, Trisha?"

"Sure," said Trisha with a wicked grin. "I'll be glad to. When should the meeting be for?"

"Let's make it for three o'clock. Why don't you call him now?"

"Got you covered."

Trisha got her cell phone out and went to the other side of the room. She dialed it and waited for Beckham to answer it. One ring, two rings and on the third ring he picked up. She talked to him for awhile, listened patiently to his response, stressed the urgency of the meeting and that she didn't trust her own cell phone anymore, and finally got him to agree.

Walking back over to where everyone was, she nodded his acceptance.

"Three o'clock?" asked Sveta.

"He will be there precisely at three."

"Good," said Hauck. "You sure that you have everything ready to electrocute the Dhole?"

"Yes."

"All right, then I will be over in the next hour with the charges to take the place down. Good luck everybody."

And with that Hauck was gone.

58

It was two thirty when Beckham arrived home at his house on the far end of town. He parked his car in the attached garage and got out of the car. Then he closed the garage door, and entered the code to disable his security system for the house. With the door system disabled, he entered his house, took off his shoes and slid on his slippers and set his briefcase down on the kitchen table. He yawned and went into his study to pour himself a drink. Then, settling down behind his desk, he loosened his tie.

What was this mysterious meeting that Trisha had called? Well, he would soon enough find out, he supposed. After that, though, they had to get things straight—no more meetings at his house. Just do the the job as Professor Meridian outlined and be done with it. Beckham shivered at the thought of Professor Meridian—that man gave him the creeps. He held the key to the Dhole. That was enough, but still, there was something not right about that man.

Perhaps it was the way that he was fixated on his "enemy," whoever that was. Whenever he gave himself that lecture, the one where the enemy took his eye, he would get hyperactive and slam things around the room before calming down. Perhaps it was the presence of the innumerable Sanzars and Abarrans- the fact that they never talked, that was enough to get goose pimples running up and down his arms.

But all that was secondary to the immense power he would be

given when the Dhole awakened. It would be a glorious new world where he would finally—

"Hello," said Sveta.

Beckham almost spilled his drink. He hadn't heard her come in. How had she gotten past his security system? Oh yes, he had it turned off for Trisha to get in. But who was this woman?

She had a silenced Beretta pointed right at him, and he had both hands on the desk. He slowly moved his right hand, the hand away from her, toward the edge of the desk.

"You don't want me to shoot you, do you? Then you had better quit moving that hand toward you."

He stopped moving right then.

"Good."

She walked toward him.

"Your phone please. Yes, that's it. Now slide it over to me on the desk.

"That's all you want?"

He was confused as she pocketed it.

And then, she shot him, right between the eyes.

Without another word, she left the house, walked to her car, got in and called Hauck.

"Yes?"

"It's done," she said.

"Good, come over here to the salt mines. You know the way," Hauck said. "I could use the help setting these charges. Stop and pick up Charlene on the way."

She started the car and put it in drive.

"On the way," she said.

****

Sveta and Charlene arrived at the salt mines at five after four. They parked the car and met Marty at the door.

"Hey nice to meet you in person instead over a computer screen," said Marty.

"Hey," said Charlene.

He held the door open for them and let them inside. They made their way through the lobby of the official Earth Battery and down the hallways to Jimmy's second office. Marty introduced them

"This is Jimmy, and Trisha," he said. "You already know Hauck."

"Is he—" began Trisha.

"Dead. Yes, he's no longer a problem," said Sveta. "You got the charges?"

"Yes," said Hauck.

"Come on, let's get them set. How many are there?"

"Twenty. Come on, Trisha you can help."

"What about me?" asked Charlene.

"Do you know how to set charges?" asked Hauck.

"No, but I can learn."

"You go with Sveta and help her, then. Trisha, with me. Marty, you with Jimmy for whatever he needs."

"It gets dark at around seven-thirty, so hurry."

"Got it."

They took the elevator down to the main salt mine and split up. Each team carried ten explosive devices. No one spoke on the way down. When the elevator finally came to the bottom floor, they wished each other good luck, and then took off.

Hauck and Trisha got to the first juncture and planted a charge, in a never ending wall of white. They did it by simply pounding the prongs in the wall with a hammer, but very gently. Small clouds of salt dust puffed where they hammered. Hauck then flicked the switch to "on." Trisha carried the charges.

"Nine to go," muttered Hauck.

With each planted charge, they went deeper into the mine, taking one of the elevators for each trip. But they did not go as far as Randy and Stacy had. Jimmy had warned them off of going that far down. He'd told them what had happened to them. As a result of that, they had stayed close to the elevators when planting their charges. But on the last floor, after they had gotten in to the elevator cage and were rising, Hauck and Trisha both saw a sea of red eyes lurking in the shadows.

"I thought they only come out at night," said Trisha.

Hauck brought out his Czech CZ 75 pistol.

"I thought from what you and Jimmy said that they did, too. But maybe they wait for dark to come out except on the coming planetary alignment. I don't know the reason," said Hauck as the elevator continued to rise, "but they're there all right."

Trisha threw the empty satchel that she had carried the charges in on the floor.

"I need a gun, too."

"Sorry, but I only have this one. You'll have to stay close to me," said Hauck.

"Like glue; I've fought these things before, remember? And I don't want to do it again."

"Now I'm worried about Sveta and Charlene. Why did we split up?"

"We were stupid, that's why. We thought that we would be safe but we didn't count on the planetary alignment that you and Jimmy were talking about."

Hauck glanced at her.

"Yes," he said after a moments reflection. "Can't this thing go any faster?"

The never ending walls of white were oddly disorienting. It made it seem as, no matter how fast you went up them, you hadn't gone anywhere. But finally, they made it to the main floor. The cage doors opened ever so slowly. At last, when they had opened enough for a man to squeeze through, Hauck slid out and Trisha came out after him. They ran to the main elevator where they were to meet up with Sveta and Charlene, but they were nowhere to be seen.

"Don't worry, they can't be far behind us," said Trisha.

Hauck said nothing. With the pop-up killers down there, now that they had seen the red eyes, it was a different story. He paced, waiting for Sveta to appear. But she did not, nor did Charlene.

"You stay here at the elevator to the surface," Hauck said. "I've got to the other elevator that Sveta took. You've got to be here in case I've called it wrong and she needs an escape route."

"But—"

He was already stepping away from her and on his phone.

"Yuri," he said.

"Yep. Here boss. You know the Instructor is getting on my nerves."

"Never mind that, Yuri. Load him in the car now. Come to the salt mines and bring lots of guns and ammunition. Lots."

"Now?"

"Now," said Hauck. "I think Sveta's in trouble."

"Got it. I'm on my way."

Worry took front and center as he strode fast as he could to where the other elevator was still down. Still down. Shit. That meant that Sveta was down there with the pop-up killers. Hauck knew why they had split up, it simply for expediency. It would get it done faster, and Jimmy had never before seen the pop-up killers except at night. Trisha was right. They had fooled themselves. Now with the planetary alignment all bets were off. He had seen their eyes. At first, he could admit it now, he had been playing Jimmy along to see what his game was. Gradually, he thought that four kids had just had a bad dream or something that they had come up with this pop-up killers was just a story that the kids had concocted. A story that the others had outgrown, but that Jimmy had not because of his father being put in prison and later killed. His mistake, the pop-up killers were real, and Sveta was in danger because of his mistake.

His mistake. Damn it. Now what was he supposed to do?

Nothing. Absolutely nothing. He couldn't help. There was nothing he could do except wait.

Suddenly, the elevator cable began to move.

Oh thank, God, he thought.

Now he could relax. He could go back to the main elevator and tell Trisha, but he just wanted to see that Sveta was okay.

When the elevator was finally in sight, he breathed a lot easier until he saw to his horror Sveta and Charlene.

"Run," screamed Charlene.

The elevator doors opened and Hauck saw that Charlene had Sveta over one shoulder and Sveta was bloodied on one leg, with numerous other cuts like scratch marks on her body. Charlene and Sveta hobbled out.

"What—" began Hauck.

"Get moving," shouted Charlene.

Hauck handed Charlene the Czech and traded her for Sveta, lifting her in his arms. Just then the floor of the elevator gave a mighty heave, and without looking back, the three of them ran for their lives. The sounds coming from the elevator were like it was being ripped apart.

"Get ready for company," screamed Charlene.

Trisha looked confused at first, then horrified. She bolted in the elevator and was ready to push the button. Charlene was in first, then Hauck and Sveta. Trisha didn't think twice but jammed the button. The cage door closed. Charlene fired the Czech once, twice, three times and kept firing. Hauck had Sveta down and no sooner had her feet touched the floor and she began firing.

The pop-up killers had climbed the elevator cables and were coming in droves after them.

"Creee…. Creee," they screamed as they came straight at them.

Multitudes fell under the withering fire of Charlene and Sveta, but they still kept coming.

"Save your ammunition," shouted Hauck as the elevator ascended.

When Sveta stopped firing, he gently took her gun from her hands on handed it to Trisha. He appropriated two replacement ammo clips from her belt, also and gave these to Trisha.

"I assume you know how to fire it?" he asked.

"I sure do," said Trisha.

"Charlene, are you okay with the pistol?" he said as he took two ammo clips from inside his coat.

"Hell, yes."

"Good girl. Sveta, where does it hurt the most?"

"My leg," said Sveta, gasping for breath.

"All right, I'll carry you. Don't worry. Trisha, when we've unloaded the elevator, shoot the controls."

"Why?" asked Trisha.

"Because it's bad enough they can climb. We don't want them following us."

"We got seven of the charges set," said Sveta, gritting her teeth, "the other three they attacked us and we couldn't—"

"Hush," said Hauck, "you did fine, Sveta, you did fine."

The final words, he almost whispered.

"We're here," said Trisha.

The elevator doors slid open and Hauck and Sveta went out first, Hauck carrying Sveta in his arms. Charlene was next and Trisha finally, blasting the elevator on the way out. Running ahead of the pack, not sure if the pop-up killers were behind them, Hauck ran for Sveta's life. She had lost a lot of blood, and Hauck was worried that the pop-up killers had knicked an artery.

He made it to the door to Jimmy's second office and Marty opened the door ahead of him. Hauck ran in and shouted, "Clear off that table." Jimmy and Marty shoved stuff to the floor and Hauck laid Sveta on the table. Trisha and Charlene were right behind and gathered around her.

"What happened to her," said Jimmy.

Hauck had a knife out and was cutting off Sveta's pants open so he could see the extent of her injuries.

"We were planting the charges when those things attacked us," said Charlene.

"Is she okay?" asked Jimmy.

"Get me some towels and boil some water," said Hauck.

Jimmy got some water, threw it in the microwave and gathered some towels. He took them to Hauck, who immediately began to swab down the afflicted areas. Marty brought a first aid kid.

"Wait," said Sveta "Give me one of those towels."

Charlene gave her a towel and she bit down on it hard.

Hauck looked grim, but kept on wiping the areas down where the pop-up killers had swiped her with their talons. When he had finished, he set down the towels and asked for some butterfly bandages.

"All right," he said, visibly relieved, "there doesn't seem to be any arterial blood, but those are nasty cuts, so I'm going to have bandage them up. Okay, Sveta?"

Sveta just nodded.

"Also, I think you've lost a lot of blood so we're going to have a transfusion."

Sveta took the towel out of her mouth temporarily.

"Shut up and do it," she said, and put the towel back in.

"Charlene, I'm going to need you to put the pistol down and squeeze the wound while I bandage it. Have you got that? After I finish swabbing this again. Jimmy, do you have any pain pills in that kit?"

"No, but I've got some excess Vicodin in a bottle for when I had surgery."

"Good, I'll take a handful of them for Sveta."

She emphatically shook her head from side to side "No."

"Look, take the pills, be a tough guy some other day."

Jimmy brought over three round, white pills. Hauck checked the dosage on them, nodded and said, "Now get me a glass of water for Sveta."

This time, it was Trisha who complied.

Marty all the while watched the computer screens for signs that the pop-up killers hand broken through. They hadn't yet, and Marty didn't wish to spook the others. It must be that they would stay down until nightfall came. Or maybe, that wasn't enough to hold them back with the coming planetary alignment. Marty wished that he could remember the word that stopped the pop-up killers when they were kids, but try as he might, he just couldn't remember. And, he didn't think that it work anyway. Not now. Not with the coming planetary alignment. Still, he watched.

Trisha couldn't stand to watch Hauck operate on all of Sveta's wounds, so she joined Marty at the computer.

"I just couldn't… you know," she said.

"Yeah, I know," said Marty.

"Is that why you…"

"No, I'm keeping watch on this floor for the pop-up killers."

"Wait a minute, there's Yuri," said Trisha.

"What? Oh, all right, you watch the screens and I'll go let him in."

"Marty?"

"Yes?"

"Be careful, one friend lost is one too many."

He grinned and headed for the door.

"Yuri's here," he said and headed out the door.

"Good," said Hauck, under his breath. "You're a good nurse, Charlene."

The Vicodin had taken effect, and Sveta was breathing stertorously. She seemed unaware of what they were doing, and that was good, Hauck thought. The best thing would be for her to sleep, but he'd given her two Vicodin's already. He wrapped her leg up like a mummy.

"Hauck?" said Sveta.

"He leaned in close to her.

"Yes?"

"Thank you. I love you, you know."

"Yes, I know."

The drugs must finally be taking effect. Her left leg was wrapped up tightly as well as her right arm.

"Do we have an IV?" he asked Jimmy.

"The first aid room is on the same floor as the pop-killers," said Jimmy.

"Oh no," said Charlene.

The door opened and Marty let in Yuri and the Instructor.

They were carrying a lot of firearms.

<h1 style="text-align:center">59</h1>

"Yuri, you've got to take Sveta with you to get some medical attention quickly," said Hauck. "She's delirious."

"What? Have you forgotten? I've got to take the Instructor to Professor Meridian's."

"I'll go," said Charlene.

"Do you need me here?" Hauck asked Jimmy.

Jimmy hesitated, then decided.

"No, I don't need you. In fact I don't need anyone here but me to electrocute the Dhole and blow this place."

"But Jimmy, how will you—" began Trisha.

"No," said Marty, and then to Hauck, "you go take care of Sveta. Lord knows you left us enough guns, and besides, we're in this bulletproof office of Jimmy's. Take Trisha with you."

"I'm staying."

"Trisha—"

"It's settled. Go take care of Sveta. Hurry. We'll meet up with you later. Go."

Hauck didn't need anymore prodding. He and Charlene grabbed Charlene, but the Instructor pushed her aside and got hold of her leg.

"Careful," Hauck said.

"I know, I know. Yuri or Charlene—get the door, will you?"

And so Hauck, Sveta, the Instructor and Charlene exited the office. Marty watched them go while Jimmy cleaned off the table where

Sveta had lay. Trisha picked up the bloody towels.

"Well," said Jimmy, "it's just like old times again isn't it?"

"Yeah, except for Jason," said Trisha.

"Except for Jason," agreed Marty.

Jimmy looked down at his hands. He missed Jason. He still couldn't believe that he was gone. One minute he was driving to pick up the Instructor, and the next minute he was dead. The Instructor had killed him, of course, but he had been a werewolf at the time. He hadn't meant to get bitten, of course, but... still, it was so hard to believe.

"Except for Jason," said Jimmy softly.

"Yeah, well, anyway, what do we do?" said Marty.

"At seven o'clock, we throw this switch," here he showed a computer switch, "and if all goes well, we electrocute the Dhole three days before the planetary alignment. Then, we take this switch," and here he pointed to a device that Hauck had given him, "this remote detonator, and we arm it. It's set for a half an hour, so we've got to be careful when we set it. But it should blow the whole place sky high. We'll be well away by then."

Trisha looked thoughtful.

"Hey, Jimmy, don't you think that you should let the security guards know? I mean shouldn't you tell them to take the night off?"

"That's a good idea, but no. They just sit in the shed far enough away from the blast epicenter that they will be okay. But Adam?"

"Yes, Dr. Harlen?"

"You'll have to wipe all computers clean when I tell you. Including the security guards. I forgot about them, thanks for reminding me, Trisha. We can't have any loose ends to where you and Marty are identified."

"Of course, Dr. Harlen."

"Don't they have records, manual records, of which license plates come and go?" asked Marty.

"No, I set that up so that security took snapshots of the cars that enter the buildings, and uploaded it to my personal computer. So, they don't have any manual records."

"You certainly covered all the angles, Jimmy," said Trisha. "Are you sure you have to do this?"

He hesitated before answering. His father and mother would be proud of him, he was sure of that. He was doing the right thing. But destroying the Dhole meant destroying the salt mines. Bringing down the whole thing to protect his secret. That he was destroying an alien being that no one believed in save for a close circle of friends?

He smiled, tight grim smile.

"Yeah, I'm sure. There will be too many questions if I don't disappear. I've just got to get used to being the invisible man for awhile."

"If that's the worse that happens, consider you've got off free and clear, Jimmy," said Marty.

****

Charlene drove while Hauck sat in the back seat with Sveta resting on his lap. He gave directions to Charlene as he stroked her hair. Not for the first time, Hauck contemplated what life would be like without her. But she wasn't going to die. No, she was definitely not going to die, was she?

"Here, turn here," said Hauck suddenly. "Park in the back."

They got out of the car, with Hauck picking Sveta up and carrying her. Being careful not to bump Sveta, they navigated the steps. Charlene pressed the buzzer. There was no answer.

"Open up, Gennady, I know you're in there. It's me, the Magician."

Charlene glanced upward at Hauck curiously.

"God dammit, open up. It's an emergency," Hauck shouted.

He kicked the door in frustration.

Slowly the door opened with a chain holding it in place. Seeing that it was indeed Hauck, Gennady unhooked the chain and swung the door open wide enough for Hauck, Sveta and Charlene to come in. He hurriedly closed the door shut after them.

"Put her on the table," said Gennady roughly.

Hauck maneuvered through the tiny kitchen, down the hallway and into what served as a dining room/operating room. It was a nightmare of bottles, syringes, operating table, lights and medical paraphernalia. With Charlene's help, Hauck set her down as gently as possible.

"What happened to her?" asked Gennady.

"You wouldn't believe me if I told you. Multiple wounds from a wild beast to her leg and arm. She's lost a lot of blood. I bandaged it up as best I could, but it isn't enough."

Gennady was a doctor once, but he had crossed someone in Russian, someone high up, and now he just did 'favors' for the underworld. As Hauck talked, he flicked on a light and took out a pair of surgical scissors from a tray and began to cut away Sveta's bandages.

"I gave her two Vicodins to calm her down and reduce the pain," said Hauck.

"Yes, you did good, but I am afraid she will need more than that," he said, surveying the damage.

He called to his wife, who came slowly into the room. Motioning for a salt solution and a stand, he got a needle and fixed it to the bag. A pinprick later by his wife and the fluid was running into her body.

"Look, you will not want to see this—" he began.

"I'm not leaving her."

Gennady shook his head.

"I don't want you to see this. Why don't you and the young lady go sit in the parlor, yes?"

Eventually, Gennady got Hauck to go sit in the living room, and Charlene along with her and he got to work, drawing a curtain to separate off the area.

Hauck was absolutely miserable for the next two hours and a half. He couldn't keep his mind on the mission at hand, and it was an unfamiliar feeling to him. Sveta had always been strong and independent. He thought of the time she had escaped him, the time she had withstood being captured by the Mafiya and the time she had been with Drogol, the king werewolf and survived. Now, she was vulnerable and there was nothing he could to help.

"Hey," said Charlene, "you did real good bringing her here. Not many men would have done that."

"What?"

"You listening to me now? I said, you should be proud of yourself that you brought her here."

"I don't know if it's enough."

"Trust me. It was enough. Look, the doctor is coming out."

Hauck shot to his feet.

"How is she?" he asked Gennady.

"I will not lie to you, Hauck, she was pretty torn up. That must have been some wild animal."

He waited for a response from Hauck, but didn't get one. He sighed and continued on.

"Anyway, like I said she was pretty torn up. But with all that damage, her arteries escaped damage. I don't know how they did, but they did. She lost a lot of blood, Hauck. I assume you don't know her blood type."

Hauck flushed.

"It never came up in conversation."

"I see. Well, it's 'O' in case it ever does. I put one hundred and four stitches in her."

"Wow," said Charlene. "That's a lot, isn't it?"

"Yes it is, young lady."

"Could I see her?" said Hauck.

"No. She's resting. Besides, what could you do?"

"It would mean a lot to him, doc. We would be really quiet, please?"

"No."

"Please?"

The doctor threw up his hands.

"What do I know? I'm just her—well, anyway, you'll have to find some chairs to drag in to sit down. But you have to be quiet, she's sleeping. Promise?"

"King's X," said Charlene.

"All right, get some chairs."

"Thanks, Doc. We'll be quiet as mice," said Charlene.

When Gennady had left the room and they were scrounging for chairs, Hauck told Charlene, "I've been meaning to say—"

"No, problem," she said, and carried a chair before her.

Hauck decided then and there that he would make the girl an offer to stay, despite the multiple earrings, chin stud and black outfit. He carried a chair into the room where Charlene was at the foot of the table, while he, without giving it a second thought, was near Sveta's head. Sveta's hair was normally rich and full, but now it was a greasy, tangled mess. Gennady had thoroughly bandaged her legs and her one arm and he left shoulder. She didn't look good.

He studied her for a minute, and began to stroke her hair. She would be all right. She would recover. Now if only the Instructor's plan worked and Sasha could come home.

****

Yuri was nervous. The Instructor was like a powder keg waiting to go off at the best of times, but since he was a werewolf, he seemed even more aggressive, if that was possible. As he drove the car towards Professor Meridian's house, he couldn't get comfortable. What if the Instructor turned into a werewolf before the moon was full? What if he had car trouble- what would he do then?

"Relax, Yuri. I'm not going to bite."

Oh God, that sounded ominous.

"I was just a little... I was thinking of Professor Meridian. What if he expects me to stay?"

"Let me off outside the fence. You can take off from there."

"Really?"

"Nah."

Yuri's shoulders slumped.

"Come on, I'm only kidding. Hey, did I ever tell you how I got involved with Meridian?"

They were at a stoplight now, and Yuri nervously checked the time.

"Uh—no."

"So, this Professor Meridian. My uncle killed his father, you got that?"

"Yes."

"Aren't you going to ask me how?"

Yuri swallowed hard. Normally, he would just play along with these games. But now with the Instructor being a werewolf, it was a different matter. He never knew when he would go off. And he wasn't so sure about that full moon thing.

"How?" he finally asked.

"He caught him one night without Sanzar and Abarran around, see? And as luck would have it, he did the one unexpected thing- he cut off his head."

"What?"

"You heard me—he cut off his head."

The Instructor laughed uproariously at that. He slapped his thighs, and then punched Yuri in the shoulder to emphasize how funny it was.

"Anyway, my uncle cut out his sternum."

Yuri felt like he was going to be ill.

"He made me a knife out of it. It was tradition, like the one who wins, gets to cut out the other's sternum, make a knife out it and then give it to the successor. I was the successor, the one that got all the bone knives, you see. Man, I miss my uncle. He was one mean son of a bitch, I tell you what. It was like a tradition among warring tribes, right? They had so many, and we had so many. I think that the old man put us over the top, though. We had more of theirs than they had of ours. It meant something to them, I don't what, but it was some kind of religious significance, you know?"

Yuri was really getting nervous now. Would the Instructor wake up one morning and decide to kill him just because he had some secret knowledge about him? In other words, was he telling him way too much?

"Anyway, unbeknown to my uncle, the guy was a father. He had a kid. Now the kid was the one who found the father. He went berserk when he did, like berserk with grief, which turned into an obsession with revenge. Well, when he got old enough, my uncle was an old man and sick at the time. I was away at the time on a mission, so I couldn't help him. So Meridian sneaked up on him, and cut his head off, too. The old man didn't deserve to die like that."

The Instructor was quiet so long after that Yuri thought at first that he had fallen asleep. A few minutes passed with the Instructor lost in reverie. Then, as abruptly as he had stopped, he continued.

"So anyway, I was pretty torn up about it, but little did I know that the kid was gunning for me, too. But I was a cautious guy. I stayed away from him laying low, you know. One night, though, he caught up with me. Damn if I wasn't stupid that night. He swung that sword to separate my head from my neck and I don't know why, I just ducked instinctively. Saved my life it did. He came at me again, but this time I was ready. I took out his eye, but he got away. He cut me bad, though he didn't stay around to find out. He was good, but I got his eye. He's hated me ever since."

"Uh, this is as far as I go."

The Instructor looked up from his retelling of the story.

"Yeah, I guess it is."

They were outside the Meridian mansion. The sun was going down fast. Yuri worried about that.

He opened the car door.

"Oh Yuri?"

"Yes."

"I wouldn't be going outside tonight. I'd stay locked inside, nice and comfy."

"But, Hauck might need me to—"

The Instructor stopped him.

"I know where you live."

"Yes, but-"

"Maybe the werewolf does, too."

Yuri gulped.

60

The Instructor walked nonchalantly across the vast expanse that was the lawn of Professor Meridian's mansion. He didn't worry about getting caught, after all, that was the point of the whole exercise, wasn't it? Eyes were upon him, he knew that. It was getting darker now. He could feel the pull of the moon that was coming out like a magnet.

Coming closer to the main door, he could definitely feel eyes on him. Now if only they didn't just shoot him before he made it to the front door. He made it to the steps to the front porch. A light rain started to fall on him. He could feel the sting of raindrops pelting him. He looked up at the night sky, and it was threatening a worse downpour. Great, just great. He looked around at the mansion, tried to picture it from Adam's description of the place. No use putting it off anymore, he rang the doorbell.

Two men answered the door. That would be Sanzar and Abarran, according to Adam. They said nothing, just moved aside to let him in. They were powerfully built, squat men, much like the Instructor himself.

"Hi, how you doing?" asked the Instructor. "Is the professor in? Does he have time to talk?"

The two men looked at each other, and then, like robots, looked back. They didn't move.

"What's the matter? You don't talk? Cat got your tongues?"

Still they stood there. Impassive. Like rocks.

"Okay, so I guess you guys just want me to step inside? Cause I'm willing. You know, it's starting to rain outside."

The Instructor looked up again, and saw the dark storm clouds gathering to really have a torrential rainstorm. He looked at the sun, saw that it was three quarters of the way sunken below the horizon, and smiled. He thought briefly of Hauck's son Sasha. The kid was probably too far gone to save. He thought of his uncle, his head cleaved off, his sternum cut open to make a bone knife. The thought angered him more than he thought possible. Tonight was going be a night for revenge. Tonight there would be no holding back and no limits. Tonight, he felt sure, was going to be payback.

"Okey, dokey then, I'll just come right on in."

So the Instructor stepped inside and one of the two closed the door behind him. The other held out a hand and then walked away. After a few steps, he stopped and waited for the Instructor to follow him.

"Oh, you want me to follow you? Well, why didn't you just say so?"

The man turned back, and began walking toward the stairs. He walked with a rolling gait, as though he were a sailor on a ship. But the Instructor was on the alert. Everything around him was cataloged precisely because it was a danger. Every doorway he passed had a carbon copy of Sanzar and Abarran staring at him. He counted ten of them, each one, as Adam had said, was an exact clone of the one before. It would bother him if he took too much time on it. Now, right now, he had to concentrate on staying alive.

As the man led them up the winding staircase, the Instructor saw two more of the clones on either side of the stairs. The Instructor rolled his shoulders and added them to the list. That made twelve. Twelve physically fit men to take out. The Instructor didn't like his odds one bit. At the top of the stairs, the two men separated to let him and his chaperon through, and the Instructor looked back to see that the remaining ten were lined up, looking after him. The single man still followed behind him. They were non-threatening yet threatening by their very presence. God, they were creepy. There were five or six more—no wait. There were like ten of them. Did that make twenty-two or twenty or twenty-four? Enough, anyway. All well-muscled, all in shape, from what he could tell. Could he take them, that was the question.

The lead man escorted him to the study door, where he stood to one side. Two clones waited inside. The Instructor wondered which were the original Sanzar and Abarran.

Professor Meridian sat inside at his well polished desk. He was a sleek man in his sixties. Sleek, salt and pepper glossy hair combed straight back; his eye patch and mustache were both gray and his one eye stared curiously at the Instructor. He was a trim and athletic looking man, and he gave off a dangerous vibe. His smile, thought the Instructor, that was what was dangerous about him

"Won't you come inside?" asked Professor Meridian.

"Don't mind if I do," said the Instructor. "I was in the neighborhood and thought I'd drop by."

As the Instructor stepped in the room, both men grabbed his arms. He didn't resist, not yet.

"Search him," instructed Professor Meridian.

Two more men came in the room, and they conducted the thorough search.

"So you come weaponless, do you?"

The Instructor shrugged.

"I thought we could talk first. See if we could work this out. I'm an old man you know."

Professor Meridian waived the men away two steps away. The Instructor walked over and pulled out a chair and sat down. He could feel the men behind him with their stares locked on him. But he couldn't show it, not with this crowd.

"You know, I've waited all these years to have you at my mercy. All these years of hunting, waiting patiently and you just stroll up to my front door and pay me a visit. How very... quaint. Are you, perhaps, a distraction to the main event? An all out frontal assault, perhaps, on my domain, hmm? Or were you planning something a little more elegant? I think, that is a bit too fortuitous to have you show up unexpectedly. No, you must have something much more sinister in mind. Let me guess—Hauck is planning a sneak attack while you keep me distracted, is that it? An attempt to save Sasha?"

"No, just to talk."

Professor Meridian drew a sword he had been holding beneath

the desk out in the open and set it on his desk. It was still in its scabbard, and just lay there. The Instructor was sure that it was the very sword that Meridian had cut off his uncle's head, and that he had used to cut out his sternum on that fateful day.

At that moment, the Instructor felt a familiar tug on his insides. The moon was coming out or the darkness had enveloped Professor Meridian's mansion. He wasn't sure which it was, but it flooded his body with the strangest, sweetest agony. He broke out in a sweat.

"I don't think you have much of value to tell me," said the professor, drawing his sword out of the case.

"Oh, I think you'd be surprised."

His tongue felt thick. It would be hard to talk.

"Really, surprise me then. Tell me something I already don't know."

The Instructor's forearm and leg hair started to grow. His leg bones started to reverse. He gasped and doubled over.

"What's that?" said Professor Meridian. "You're sick now? Perhaps dying?"

"No," gasped the Instructor.

"Well, what is it then?"

"I-I"

"Sanzar, Abarran—hold him up please. Get him over closer to me so that I can cut his head out and force him to his knees."

"I... said... no," said the Instructor, only his voice came out thick and garbled.

As Sanzar and Abarran grabbed him, he threw them off. The change was full on him, and he was rippling with power. Professor Meridian jumped to his feet and stepped backwards, knocking over his chair.

The Instructor howled in pain as his bones snapped into place and his face began to extend. His jaws began to distend and his teeth came out and were replaced with those of a monster. White hair began to sprout all over him. Professor Meridian edged around the desk, and slipped by the Instructor who was now in full out change mode. The professor made a move to cut of his head with his sword, but the Instructor had sharp claws now and he swiped at the professor first. The professor leaped back and ran for the door, leaving Sanzar and

Abarran to guard.   The door was filled by competing Sanzars and Abarrans, but the werewolf attacked before they could even reposition themselves.   His terrible jaws opened and shut on a neck and literally ripped it from its shoulders.   Blood geysered from the stump.   Another one was trying to defend itself against the monster's horrifying claws, but couldn't.   The blood spray was all over the room, fountain up from the body.   He howled a hideous howl of triumph.

The Sanzars and Abarrans were scattering far and wide outside the door as the werewolf burst through.   Professor Meridian was already down the stairs and headed for his secret door to the underground lair.   Sanzars and Abarran's laid down a withering fire in the meantime, but the werewolf ran to the balcony knocking over two of them and eviscerating them with his claws.   He leaped over the railing, landing all the way down at the bottom of the stairs.   Two more men appeared in the hallway, but before they could draw their guns, one man was cut in half with a vicious swipe and the other was backhanded with such a rage that his head cracked open.   He saw Professor Meridian disappear around the corner and into a room and let out an awful howl.

The professor scrambled across the room and entered the security code for the secret door.   The panel slid inward.   He fairly dashed down the stairs.   Before the door could close all the way though, a huge clawed hand inserted itself.   Immense shoulders forced their way through the doorway, breaking the door in the process.

From somewhere behind, the fire of automatic weapons slammed into the werewolf's back and he howled in rage.   But he kept bounding down the stairs.   He saw Meridian inserting his key nervously into a lock and open it.   Then, he ran to another door next to it with the werewolf coming ever closer.   He opened the door and reached for the key, but seeing that the werewolf was right behind him, he ducked in the room and slammed the door shut behind him.   The key was left inserted in the lock.   The werewolf slammed into the door.   The key snapped off at the base like a twig.   Meridian cowered in the room.

The werewolf howled in frustration at seeing his prey escape.   He crashed the door repeatedly, but he couldn't get passed the wooden, steel lined door.   Suddenly, more bullets slammed into his side, and the werewolf leaned back his head and roared.   Just as quickly, he jumped back and saw that the men firing their machine pistols were glancing around the corner and firing. There were three of them. He charged the stairs, and ran through a hail of bullets to get to the top. The men scattered and ran, but the werewolf leapt at one and tore out his back, blood was everywhere. There werewolf tore at the soft meat of his back, but then he remembered the other and bounded after them.

The first he caught up with in the main atrium and ripped his arm off, leaving the man screaming. The second he seized in his massive jaws and ate his face. More automatic weapons fire from the balcony just as the werewolf was howling his triumph, and he screamed in pain. But just then, a noise caught his attention. It was a howling from the door behind him. He whirled and came face to face with another werewolf. Meridian in his last act, had set the other werewolf free to save himself.

Frantic machine pistols began firing at both of the animals. Both werewolves turned at the same time, looked back at one another and bounded off after the shooters. They were at the top of the stairs firing down, but when they saw the two werewolves tearing up after them, they ran.

But they didn't make it very far.

****

Professor Krikor Meridian breathed a sigh of relief. At least in this room, which was designed to be Sasha's "free room," there was no danger of the werewolf getting in. And, he had, let Sasha the werewolf loose to counteract the first werewolf. Now all he had to do was wait until the fighting was through to have one of the Sanzars or Abarrans to set him free. That was a close call, though. Too close for comfort.

He could hear the automatic weapons fire and the roars and the howling. The werewolves must be putting up one hell of a fight. The professor paced back and forth, listening, hoping against hope that the firing would end, but it didn't. Finally, he gave up and sat down on the same couch that Sasha had sat down before him. Well, the Sanzars and Abarrans would come for him soon enough. And they would bring Sasha's body with them and his enemy.

Had he been foolish to let him into his house? Just stroll up to his front door and invite him in? He thought about that. Of course, how was he to know that his enemy was a werewolf? How indeed. Still, the automatic weapons fire continued. Professor Meridian waited patiently for it to end. What was taking them so long?

****

Sasha held the man's head in his claws and chomped down. The man's skull was crunchy and oh so satisfying. Blood spurted out of his head but not so much as brains. Another man tried to attack him with a gun, but Sasha dropped the man he was chewing on, and turned a rammed his clawed hand through his stomach. He pulled and twisted on the man's spine, but it broke before he ripped it out of his body. Tossing the man's body aside, he ran after the next man who was firing at him. He felt invincible. He felt god-like. Nothing could get between himself and his victims. Nothing could stop him.

The man who was firing at him, could fire all his bullets but it did not matter. He was unable to be stopped. He leapt on the man, tearing at his neck, whipping it from side to side until finally the neck broke free from his body.

Another man shot him and it enraged him. He turned his head and there he was. Unfortunately for the man, his gun chose that exactly moment to jam. The werewolf snarled and dropped the man he had been chewing on and ran on all fours over to the man and bit him horribly on the leg. The man screamed and screamed. He flung the injured man to the ground and saw that he was missing one half of a leg and bleeding what would soon be to death.

He howled and shook the mansions walls. From somewhere in the mansion, where the other werewolf hunted humans, he heard an answering howl.

He stalked his prey deliberately now. He came to a closed door and tried to open it but could not get his clawed fingers around it, so he rammed into it, shoulder first, once, twice and it splintered open. Three men were huddled in a corner of the library, with nowhere to hide. He advanced steadily toward them. They were weaponless, and terrified. He snarled and one of them broke for the door, but the werewolf was quicker and a quick slash to his throat led to his hands grasping his neck while blood burbled out past his helpless fingers.

He roared and advanced on the other two men.

61

Jimmy was watching the computer screen timer. Forty-five minutes to go until dark. On another screen, the pop-killers were amassing on the main floor, but they hadn't attempted to scale the elevator cable that led up to the main floor.

"What are they waiting for?" he muttered.

"Full dark," said Marty. "That's when everything bad happens."

"Well, aren't you a cheerful ray of sunshine," said Trisha.

Marty grinned nervously. They'd all been nervous. Marty with his nervous laugh, Trisha with her equally nervous laugh and Jimmy with his lame attempts at humor. They just didn't know what to do with themselves.

"Well, this is it then, right Adam?" said Jimmy.

"Yes, Dr. Harlen."

"And Brittany? You remember what to do?"

"Yes, Dr. Harlen."

"Good. You want me to go over it one more time?"

"No, Dr. Harlen."

"Wait," said Trisha, "what exactly is she supposed to do?"

"Get rid of all the computer evidence we have. Just on the off chance that something won't blow up when we push the button. I gave the security guards the go ahead to clear the premises two hours ago—just in case. I thought about what you said earlier, Trisha, and decided not to take a chance on anyone getting hurt. So there's just us

three here on the entire premises. Us and the pop-up killers, that is.
They just sit there like they're waiting for something, I don't know
what. The planetary alignment isn't for two days, so I can't figure
them out."

Marty considered the matter. What were they doing?

"I think Marty was right. They're waiting for full dark," said
Trisha.

"Well," said Jimmy, "let's get a jump on them. Let's electrocute the
big guy now. Okay?"

"Yeah," said Trisha, "I'm for that plan."

"Suits me," said Marty.

"All right, Adam, throw the switch."

"Yes, Dr. Harlen."

A sudden hum filled the air as the electricity began to flow.
Jimmy, Trisha and Marty held their breath. The drill bits that were
now electrodes began to glow. Sparks jumped and grew.

"I just wish Jason was here to see this," said Jimmy.

Trisha put her hand in his and clasped it tight.

"He's watching from the other side, Jimmy," she said.

"I hope there is another side," said Jimmy.

"Oh there is, count on it," said Marty.

"Whoa, look at the screen with the Dhole on it."

On the computer screen with the Dhole, the giant Dhole began to
move.

"Oh my God, it's working; the god of Chaos is coming alive," said
Marty.

And it was true. The Dhole was moving. It was fluid and
changing direction with every motion. It was like it was trapped and
trying to get away from the death dealing electricity. It was
shimmering and glittery and almost beautiful in its movement. And
yet, it seemed to thrive on the power.

"Dial it up to twelve million volts," said Jimmy.

"It seems to be almost enjoying it," said Marty.

"Wait until it receives the entire voltage."

"Yes," said a visibly nervous Trisha.

"Twelve million volts, doctor," said Adam.

On the screen, the Dhole seemed to ululate with the increased voltage. It was an amorphous blob gyrating at fourteen hundred feet down in the earth. Jimmy, Trisha and Marty held their breath. But the Dhole didn't die.

"Adam," said a by now nervous Jimmy, "raise the voltage to eighteen million volts."

"Yes, doctor."

Adam did raise the voltage to eighteen million volts. The Dhole rippled with the energy flowing through it. It seemed to Jimmy that it glowed iridescent blue under the influence of the electricity. Still, the Dhole didn't die.

"Oh my God," said Jimmy, "its eating the electricity. Shut it down, Adam, shut it down."

The lights went dim and then brightened and then dimmed again and then brightened.

"I can't shut it down, doctor, the Dhole is now self-sustaining."

"What?" screamed a frantic Jimmy. "That's impossible."

"Nonetheless, doctor, it is true."

"What does that mean, Jimmy?" asked a suddenly desperate Trisha.

"Twenty-five minutes until full dark, doctor," said Brittany.

Jimmy looked hopelessly at her and was about to say something but he bit his lip instead. What was happening? This was impossible. Jimmy racked his brain for a solution. But none would come. On the screen, the Dhole was actually getting bigger. The salt around him was cracking, and there was nothing he could do. The number of pop-killers was increasing. Oh God, what would happen to Detroit if they got out? Murder and mayhem on an incalculable scale.

He looked at the clock and it said twenty-three minutes until the pop-up killers had full reign.

"Jimmy? What do we do man?" asked Marty.

He looked from Marty to Trisha and had no answer for either of them. They were running out of time and solutions. He didn't have a solution, this was not supposed to happen.

"Cut the power cables to the Dhole," he exclaimed.

He grabbed a screwdriver and began unscrewing the screws beneath a table.

"Get me something to cut the cable with," he called to Trisha and

Marty.

Frantically, he kept unscrewing the seemingly endless screws.

"How big is the cable?" Marty asked.

"Big. It runs through here. It must be three feet thick."

"What?" said Marty. "God, we don't have anything that big."

Jimmy stopped unscrewing. Marty was right. They simply didn't have any tool that would cut through three feet of cable. All the tools were on the floor at the end of the elevator where the pop-up killers were. And besides, there wasn't enough time. Wait, there was a fuse box that might do the trick, and it was right in Jimmy's office. He ran over to the wall and was mystified where it was. There were just paintings and that was it. Finally, he had it, and swung a painting that was blocking in the fuse box.

"Fuse box," he shouted triumphantly.

He opened it up, and saw to his delight eighteen breakers. Trisha and Marty were at his side now, desperate to do something, anything.

"What can we do?" asked Trisha.

"We've got to find the one marked 'Power.' It should be somewhere around here."

"What if we open the other paintings?" asked Marty.

"Good idea," said Jimmy.

They immediately scrambled for the other paintings and found one that was on hinges, the one that Marty tried. He opened it and Trisha came over to help.

"Jimmy, that's not one marked 'Power' on this entire panel," called Marty.

"Never mind," he cried, exultant that he had found it.

It was at the top of the panel, and looked different from the others.

"Get ready to go to back up power, Brittany and Adam," he called out.

"Yes, doctor," they said at the same time.

"Get a flashlight. Okay, ready? In five... four... three... two... one," and he threw the manual switch.

The power immediately went out. Emergency lights flooded the area with red. The computers stayed on with their back up power, though, and the office was lit with their screens. Jimmy ran to a computer screen followed by Marty and Trisha. He checked the status of the Dhole, and found that electricity was still flowing to it.

"That's…" began Jimmy.

"Surreal," said Trisha.

Jimmy ran through the calculations in his head again. There was simply no way that this was happening. Twelve million volts should have been enough to fry the Dhole. Eighteen million volts was enough to turn him into a crispy critter.

"Fifteen minutes until full dark," said Brittany.

"I know, I know…" said Jimmy.

How could this be happening?

"He's fed off the electricity," said Marty.

"But how can he still? The power is off," said Trisha.

"He's the god of Chaos," said Jimmy. "That's how. He's generating the electricity himself. He would have woken up fine three days from now, all by himself. We just jump-started him with the eighteen million volts."

Jimmy felt despair wash over him like a tide. For the first time, he felt helpless to do anything, and it was not a good feeling. By feeding him eighteen million volts of electricity, the Dhole was powering up three days early.

"What does this mean, Jimmy?" said Trisha. "And I'm not just saying that to hear myself think, either. What does it really mean?"

"It means, Trisha, that we're royally screwed," said Marty. "Just look at them, will you. There's thousands of the pop-killers just waiting for full dark. Think what the people of Detroit will experience."

"Why can't we just set off the explosives."

"I don't think it will do any good. The Dhole is fourteen hundred feet underground. The explosion won't touch him."

"Yes, but it will take care of the killers beneath us. It will at least kill those little bastards."

Here she pointed to the computer screen that showed thousands of the pop-up killers massed, ready and eager to the Dhole's work. They were fighting among each other, they were squabbling among themselves. It was like watching wild animals caged and impatient to be set free.

"He'll just make new ones," said Marty. "Whose to say he hasn't been doing that all alone."

"What?" said a genuinely shocked Jimmy. "What do you mean?"

"He might have been making them all over the world, for all we know. London, Paris, Berlin, Moscow you name it."

"That's horrible," said Trisha.

"But probably true," said Marty. "I guess we were stupid to think we had evolved to the point where we could take on a creature who has been alive for hundreds of millions of years."

"Five minutes until full dark," said Brittany.

Jimmy was desperate. He had to think but he had not time to think. Damn, there wasn't anything at all to do about it. Except...

"Adam?"

"Yes, Dr. Harlen."

"Does the electrical wire to the Dhole, all fourteen hundred feet of it, provide you with a direct pathway to the Dhole's brain?"

"Yes, Dr. Harlen, it should. Of course, I can't promise anything. What were you thinking, Dr. Harlen?"

"I want you to go down that electrical conduit and enter the Dhole's brain and control it. I want you to vanish all the pop-up killers around the world. I want them stopped."

"Yes, but Dr. Harlen, that would mean I would have to stay in the Dhole's brain forever."

"Adam, I'm sorry about this, but yes. Can you do it?"

"I will try, Dr. Harlen."

"Please hurry, Adam. I hate to say good-bye."

"Good bye, Trisha and Marty. Good-bye, Dr. Harlen. Good-bye, Brittany."

Jimmy looked at the computer countdown. There was two minutes left.

"Adam, now!"

For the first minute, Jimmy couldn't tell anything. The pop-up killers stood frozen where they were. Good, thought Jimmy, so far so good. For the final minute, he held his breath. Trisha put her hand in his and squeezed. He desperately did not want this good woman exposed to the pop-up killers en masse. But then his thoughts turned to all the residents that were in the city of Detroit, and for that matter, the citizens of the world. He counted off the seconds. Ten, nine, eight… come on Adam, do your job… seven, six, five, four… take over the Dhole's consciousness… three, two, one.

The pop-up killers came alive. The started to climb up the main elevator cable. They started appearing in the building's lobby. They started appearing in the parking lot.

"Oh, no," said Trisha, "oh God, please no."

Marty turned to Jimmy.

"I'm sorry it didn't work, Jimmy."

Jimmy ran over to where the switch was that started the power back on and threw it. But instead of power flowing into the Dhole, it was flowing out to power the circuit. He hurried back to the computer screens and saw the pop-up killers assembling to rip down the fence and going pouring out to the city. It was hopeless. Just then, the power blew out the circuit. Jimmy didn't have time to figure that out. He had bigger problems now, and the Dhole was creating more pop-up killers. This was going downhill fast. Juicing the Dhole with eighteen million volts hadn't worked. Sending Adam down to establish a connection and dominate the Dhole's mind hadn't worked. And now, the pop-up killers had torn down the section of fencing and were pouring through.

Jimmy was out of ideas.

"Jimmy, what do we do now?" asked Trisha.

"I don't know," said Jimmy. "I really don't know what to do."

That admission cost him more than he would like to say. All these years to stop the Dhole… and what had happened? He hadn't slowed the creature more than a microsecond. Of all the things to happen, Jimmy hadn't even considered failure as an option He walked away from Trisha to stand by himself. He was a beaten man.

"Jimmy, look at this," said Marty.

"What is it," he said without moving.

"Quick, goddammit."

It was the urgency in Marty's voice that snapped him out of it. He hurried over to the screen.

"What? I don't seen anything."

He seemed bewildered.

"Shouldn't you be seeing something."

Marty seemed to be trying to tell him. But for the life of him,

Jimmy couldn't tell what.

"There are no pop-up killers to be seen anywhere," said Trisha. "Not one. Nada."

Jimmy examined the screen more carefully now. No pop-up killers, anywhere to be seen. Well I'll be darned. There weren't any. He did a reverse zoom on the camera lens and tried to find evidence of the pop-up killers, but as Marty had said, there simply wasn't any to be found.

"Well, all right," he said, all smiles, "I guess Adam worked."

"I guess so," admitted Marty.

Trisha just hugged and kissed Jimmy.

"Whoa," he said, "what was that for?"

She kissed him again.

"For being the biggest, baddest genius that that there is," and she smiled.

Marty only got a hug and a pat on the back, though, but he accepted it gratefully.

"Man, I am happy for you... for us... for the whole world, buddy," said Marty.

Brittany said, "Is Adam coming back to us?"

"No, I'm afraid not, Brittany. Adam has to stay merged consciousness for us to stay safe. He made a brave choice Brittany, and look at how many lives he saved. Thousands, maybe millions of lives. Is it possible that he will attempt communication with us? Possible, but not too likely. I think he's gone for good. But he saved us —no question about that."

In the silence that followed, they were all thinking about the remarkable life-form called Adam. He was an artificial intelligence, but oh so much more than that. It affected Jimmy the most, because where the others had only known Adam for days, Jimmy had know him for a whole year.

"Hey Jimmy?" said Marty.

"Yes?"

"What's with the power blowing a fuse the second time? I mean, shouldn't the power be going to the Dhole rather than the other way around?"

Come to think about, it should. That was certainly odd. Jimmy walked back over to the popped circuit breaker and tried to figure it out, but it didn't make any sense. Why on earth would that be? He threw the switch one more time and the circuit breaker popped again.

"Wait a minute," he said. "What if Adam is using the Dhole to produce the electric current?"

Was that possible?

Trisha and Marty gathered around the circuit breaker.

"That means that, even though my plan to fake it was real enough —I fooled them into believing it was possible—that Adam has given me a way to still power the city of Detroit."

"I don't understand," said Trisha.

"Well it's simplicity itself. Adam used the Dhole for power. A creature three thousand feet long and one thousand feet wide and God know how dense, and he used him for power. Don't you see, I don't have to go into hiding anymore. Earth Battery does work. I've got the proof right in my hands. I don't care how it works, but it works."

"That's genius, Jimmy. Now if we can get the government to buy into it..."

"It won't matter if they believe that its working, because it is working," said Jimmy.

"That's awesome, Jimmy," said Trisha.

"Yep, and I owe it all to Adam. Now if Hauck and the Instructor's plan worked and we're rid of Professor Meridian for good, I can die happy.

62

Hauck and Charlene took Sveta home with an ample supply of pain pills the next morning. She was sleeping- she slept a lot. When they got to the building that Hauck owned, they pulled the SUV into a parking space inside, and Hauck gently led Sveta to a wheelchair and from there took her home. Hauck and Charlene carefully put her into bed so that the process of healing could begin. As Hauck tidied her up, and got her ready to sleep some more, she grabbed his wrist. Hauck looked at her curiously for a moment before lowering his head down enough to hear her speak.

"Thank you," she said.

The pain pills made it difficult to understand her, but Hauck got the gist and smiled. He reached over with his free hand and cupped her face in it. Hard to believe that such a tough woman had a vulnerable side, but he went with it. It was one of the reasons that he —

"Hauck?"

"Yes, Charlene?"

He didn't take his eyes off of Sveta's face when he said it.

"You've got company. Yuri and the Instructor are back, and it seems they have brought someone with them."

"What? They have?"

Now Hauck was all attention. He turned to Sveta and was about to say something when she said, "Go."

It was all the absolution that he needed. Hauck left the room in a hurry.

"Sorry, Sveta," she said. "It seemed important."

Sveta waived her off as she fell back to sleep. Charlene grabbed a chair near enough the door that she could hear the ensuing conversation.

Yuri came in first and held the door for the Instructor and his charge, who was blindfolded, a gag around his mouth and tied up. He could use his legs, but not much else. The Instructor was batting him in the head to get him to move.

"Come on," he said. "What are you, brain dead or something? Oh yeah, I forgot you can't talk. But you can listen, can't you? Get a move on."

The Instructor slapped him in the head again to keep him moving.

"Where do you want him?" asked the Instructor.

"Take him to the study," said Hauck.

"Gladly," said the Instructor. "He's getting on my nerves."

The Instructor frog marched Sasha into the study behind Hauck and forcibly sat him down. Yuri waited by the door. The Instructor remained standing and Hauck walked around the desk and sat down.

"How did you acquire him? I assume all went successful?"

"Oh yeah, everything went smoothly. We—I do mean we because Meridian did let Sasha out in his wolf state and then locked himself into a cage."

"Could you explain that a little more?" said Hauck.

Sasha sat gagged and his head covered and tied, but he tried constantly to get out. The Instructor slapped him again in the head just for good measure.

"Quit wriggling around. You ain't going nowhere. Anyways, after we killed every living person in the house, we slept as is normal coming out of the trance, you see? And I woke up first, so I tied him up good before he could escape—lucky for us that I woke up first, right? I hooded him and gagged him and called Yuri. I asked him to bring along some extra clothes for me and yo-yo here, didn't I yo-yo? Oh, I forgot you can't talk. Anyways, about Meridian."

"Yes," said Hauck, "what about Meridian?"

"Well, the place he locked himself into, he can't get out. Seems I broke the key off at the stem, you know. So, I couldn't get him out, but he can't get out neither. You see, from inside the cell, he can't reach. And even if he could, the way the keys broke up and jammed in there, he can't pry of connive his way out. You can go back and retrieve him in the morning. He ain't going anywhere."

Hauck considered Sasha for a moment. There was no easy polite way to this. Might as well tell him and get it over with.

"Take off the hood," he said.

"Gladly," said the Instructor and proceeded to take it off.

Sasha blinked furiously against the sudden light. It took a few minutes to adjust, but eventually when his eyes had settled down, he stared at Hauck.

The Instructor said, "Remember me junior?"

If looks could kill, this would be the moment. Sasha tried to stare down the Instructor and got slapped in the head again for his trouble.

"I am Hauck," Hauck said.

Sasha's eyes widened and he leaned back in the chair as far as he could go with his hands tied behind his back.

"You have heard of me?"

Sasha nodded his head vigorously. It was clear he ways desperately afraid of this man.

"I am your father, Sasha. I paid Dr. Pazyryk to switch the test results that were yours. You weren't Drogol's son, you were mine."

A look of confusion stole across Sasha's face. He blanched visibly. He looked to the Instructor for confirmation, who nodded and went back to cleaning his nails.

"You've been bitten by a werewolf, therefore you have got the disease. The Instructor," here he pointed at the Instructor, who when Sasha looked at him, merely shrugged, "has been bitten by one, too."

"You know," said the Instructor, "I was out looking for you when I got bit, too. I'll never forgive you for that. Now I've got spend my nights in a titanium cage like you will, too. We can either kill you now, or you can agree to our terms of nightly lock up with me."

The Instructor, thought Hauck, has such a way with words.

"What the Instructor just said, is true. It makes me sad to have to say it Sasha, but it's true. I've spent a long time searching for you, Sasha. I didn't even know that Anna Kazakova had a child. When I found out too late to do anything, I gave up. But I shouldn't have Sasha. I would like to make that up to—at least as much as is possible. But I have to have your word to be imprisoned at night. I won't have you killing people, Sasha. That would be too much to bear. Will you agree to be imprisoned each and every night? Because it not, then we will have to kill you. I'm sorry. But wait, before you answer, let the Instructor remove the gag. You can scream as much as you want, but I guarantee you that no one will hear you."

"You go screaming you fool head off, and you'll get slapped by me, you dig?"

The Instructor took the gag off and sat down again.

'You're my father? Ha."

"It's true, Sasha, it's true."

"Bullshit."

"We can argue about that later."

"You're full of it."

"Will you go in the cage at night or not?"

"I will not."

Hauck studied him carefully before he spoke.

"Okay, Instructor, you may take him out back and shoot him."

"Now that's more like it," said the Instructor. "Come on junior, let's get it over with."

Hauck kept staring at him as though interested, but not vested in the outcome one way or the other.

"Wait—"

The Instructor whacked him in the head.

"Look, I'm not going to keep getting up and sitting down," said the Instructor. "Make up your mind your going to play nice or get shot. And, look, if you try to get away, we'll find you. Trust me. We found you at the professor's house, we can find you anywhere."

"Okay, I'll do it. You can lock me up at night, even if you're not my father."

"Instructor, take off his arm restraints."

"You sure?" said the Instructor.

"I think he would be unwise to be playing with us. We will work very hard to find a cure, believe me."

"Sure," said Sasha.

"What do you say I hit him in the head again before I untie him?"
said the Instructor.

"No, just untie him. And Yuri, get him something to eat."

"Yes, boss," said Yuri from the doorway.

Sasha rubbed his wrists together. They were sore from the car
ride with his wrists tied behind his back. The Instructor watched him
very closely for signs he would bolt and run, but he didn't. He seemed
like he was trying to process all that Hauck had told him.

"Sasha, I understand how confusing this must be to you, but
everything your mother told you about me is a lie. I am not who you
think I am."

"Fah," said Sasha.

"Trust will take time to develop, I understand that, and I only ask
that you reserve you judgment until later. Deal?"

Before Sasha could answer, Hauck's computer chimed. It was
Jimmy on the line for a video conference call.

"You want I should take Bozo out of the room?" said the
Instructor.

"No, we should all hear what he has to say."

Sasha seemed worn out, but intrigued. Wary, but interested
enough. Hauck was a dangerous man, this much he knew from what
his mother had told him. It would pay him to learn everything he
could.

"Hello, Hauck," said Jimmy.

"Hello, Jimmy."

"I have good news. The Dhole is dead, and the pop-up killers are
no longer with us. How did you do?"

"Beckham has been disposed of, Meridian and his men have been
neutralized."

"Man, I can't thank you enough for your hard work. Oh, and
Adam was the final key to the Dhole, and he even got the Dhole to
produce electricity for us. So, I won't have to run from the
government. But Adam sacrificed himself in the process."

"Wait a minute. With Adam gone, who is going to help my son
and the Instructor beat the curse of the werewolf?"

"Not to worry about that—I have Brittany to help with that. If
there's a way to cure your son, we'll find it."

Hauck let go of his breath and his temper. He didn't know who Brittany was, but he felt confident he could count on Jimmy. Suddenly, the screen was split between the face of a beautiful young woman.

"Hello, Hauck. I am Brittany. I understand we will be working together."

Surprised, Hauck studied the face. She looked way too young for the job, but on the other hand, she was just a computer rendition of the face.

"Hello, Brittany, it's a pleasure to meet you. Jimmy, I'm genuinely pleased that things went so well on your half of the assignment. Now, I have something that I want you to see."

Puzzled, Jimmy asked, "What?"

"It's Drogol's hidden laboratory."

"Seriously?"

"Oh, I'm quite serious about this. It is a complex that I have no idea what it means, but I've purchased every property for two acres around it. So maybe you could tell me what it means and if it can be applied to the problem of solving my son's and the Instructor's lycanthropy."

"When do I see it?" asked Jimmy.

"How about the day after tomorrow. You can call me with a convenient time."

"You've really got me intrigued, Hauck."

"Good-bye, Jimmy."

"Good-bye, Hauck."

****

Jimmy looked particularly thoughtful after his teleconference with Hauck, and Trisha could see why. She had listened in on the call. Marty was back in his room taking a shower. Brittany had wiped clean the surveillance gear at her house and she had gone home and cleaned up before coming back to the salt mines for Jimmy.

"Hey, Jimmy," she said.

"Yes?" he said without taking his eyes off the screen

"Let's go out tonight and celebrate."

"What?"

He looked up, confused.

"I said, let's go out and celebrate. Yes?"

"Umm—"

"You know, you may be the smartest boy in Flat Rock, but you sure are dumb when it comes to girls."